KT-437-921

LIFE

Great short stories
by women chosen by
Victoria Hislop

HEAD
of
ZEUS

The paperback collection *Life* was first published within *The Story* as 'The Lives of Women', a hardback published in the UK in 2013 by Head of Zeus Ltd. This paperback edition published in the UK in 2014 by Head of Zeus Ltd.

Introduction Copyright © Victoria Hislop, 2013

The moral right of Victoria Hislop to be identified as the editor of this work has been asserted in accordance with the Copyright, Designs and Patents Act of 1988.

The moral right of the contributing authors of this anthology to be identified as such is asserted in accordance with the Copyright, Designs and Patents Act of 1988.

Th[...] [...]ve copyrights to
be found [...] [...]ssion of this copyright page.

A[...] [...]served. No part of this publication may be
reprodu[...] [...]ed in a retrieval system, or transmitted in any form
or by an[...] means, electronic, mechanical, photocopying, recording
or othe[...] [...]or permission of both the copyright
owner and the above publisher of this book.

This is an a[...]nthology of fiction. All characters, organizations, and events
portrayed in this work are either produ[...] [...] author's imagination
or are used fictitiously.

South Lanarkshire
Library Service

HW

C70160310U

Askews & Holts

G £8.99

4313496

A CIP catalogue record for this book is available from the British Library.

Paperback ISBN: 9781781856666
Ebook ISBN: 9781781857311

Printed and bound by CPI Group (UK) Ltd., Croydon, CR0 4YY.

Typeset by Ellipsis Digital Limited, Glasgow

Head of Zeus Ltd
Clerkenwell House
45–47, Clerkenwell Green
London EC1R 0HT

www.headofzeus.com

C70160310U

SOUTH LANARKSHIRE
Leisure & Culture
www.library.southlanarkshire.gov.uk

South Lanarkshire Libraries

This book is to be returned on or before
the last date stamped below or may be
renewed by telephone or online.

Delivering services for South Lanarkshire

2 5 SEP 2014   0 9 JAN 2017   2 9 JUL 2019

16. 05. 16.   13/3/17   1 8 DEC 2020

13. 06. 16.   3/7/17

23. 08. 16.   2 3 DEC 2017

    4/1

27. 09. 16.   2 8 FEB 2019

13. 10. 16.

GENERAL
HISLOP, VICTORIA
LIFE

BLANTYRE LIBRARY
1a CLYDEVIEW
SHOPPING CENTRE
BLANTYRE
G72 0QD
01698 823808

THE
STORY

· ·

LOVE · LOSS · LIFE

THE STORY is an anthology in three parts: LOVE, LOSS and LIFE. It comprises one hundred pieces celebrating women writers working in the short story form.

The selection ranges from Willa Cather's story *Consequences*, to the inaugural winner of the Costa Short Story Award, Avril Joy's story, *Millie and Bird*. One hundred stories for the last hundred years.

Each story and themed volume is a personal selection by the bestselling author and champion of the short story, Victoria Hislop.

CONTENTS

....

Introduction

THE
STORY

······································

A GENERAL INTRODUCTION
TO LOVE, LIFE AND LOSS
BY VICTORIA HISLOP

······································

While gathering the short stories for the anthology in which this volume *Life* originally appeared, I read some of the most brilliant and profound pieces of writing that I have ever come across.

The authors in the anthology range from a Nobel Prize winner, Doris Lessing, to the acknowledged queen of short stories, Alice Munro. There are Man Booker winners, Costa winners and Pulitzer winners. A few were born in the 19th century but the majority are more modern. Several of them are as yet unknown, others are household names, like Virginia Woolf. Many of the most vivid and passionate storytellers are young. And without doubt many of the most powerfully original are contemporary writers.

Apart from the writers all being female, the other guiding factor in the selection is that the stories have been written in English. The stories are varied and I am sure that no single reader will like them all. Perhaps I enjoyed certain stories because they meant something very personal to me. Others I think would be admired by any reader.

I discovered that it is possible for a short story (unlike a novel) to attain something close to perfection. Its brevity can mean that an author has the chance to produce a series of almost perfectly formed sentences, where every carefully chosen word contributes to its meaning. Occasionally the result is flawless, something a novel can never be.

Readers are allowed to be impatient with short stories. My own patience limit for a novel which I am not hugely enjoying may be three or four chapters. If it has not engaged me by then, it has lost me and is returned to the library or taken to a charity shop. With a short story, three or four pages are the maximum I allow (sometimes they are only five or six pages long in any case). A short story can entice us in without preamble or background information, and for that reason it has no excuse. It must not bore us even for a second.

If a short story has no excuse for being dull, it has even less reason to be bland. As I selected the stories for this anthology, I found myself reading stories that made me laugh out loud, gasp and often weep. If a story did not arouse a strong response in me, then I did not select it. Even if it is elegaic or whimsical, it must still stir something deep in the pit of the stomach or make the heart race.

Some stories had such a strong effect on me that I had to put a collection down and do something different with the rest of my day. I could read nothing else. I needed to ponder it, or possibly read it for a second time. Muriel Spark's 'The First Year of My Life' (*Loss*) dazzled me with its brilliance. That was a day when I didn't need to do anything other than reflect on her wisdom. For different reasons, Alice Munro's 'Miles City, Montana' (*Loss*) rendered me incapable of continuing to read. She moves seamlessly from a description of a drowned boy's funeral to an incident on a family outing where we believe that one of the children will drown. Even the relief I felt at the story's relatively happy conclusion was not enough to lift my mood.

Quite often an anthology is named after the author's favourite short story, and if that were the case I would read the eponymous story first. More often, there is no particular entry point into an anthology (unless you are happy to read them in the order they appear, something I usually resisted) and in that case, there was no better guide than simply whether the title intrigued me. Who, for example, would not go straight to a story entitled 'How I Finally Lost My Heart' (Doris Lessing, *Love*), 'A Weight Problem' (Elspeth Davie, *Life*), 'How Did I Get Away with Killing One of the Biggest Lawyers in the State? It Was Easy.' (Alice Walker, *Life*) or even the intriguingly named: 'The Life You Save May Be Your Own' (Flannery O'Connor, *Loss*)?

A short story can be more surreal than many readers might tolerate with a novel and, perhaps, less grounded in reality. Succinctness sometimes allows a writer to explore ideas that may not sustain over a greater length. An example of this is Nicola Barker's 'Inside Information' (*Loss*), a shiningly original story told through the voice of an unborn child who is considering the suitability of its soon-to-be mother. Personally, I love the slightly quirky in a short story, but I would probably not be so patient if I had to listen to the voice of a foetus over three hundred pages.

I think the short story can give a writer the opportunity to experiment and to try a style or a voice that they would not use in the novel form, so there is often an element of freshness and surprise for the reader – and perhaps for the writer too.

For me, the stories that make the greatest impact are those that are the most emotional. On a few occasions, when I was reading in the library, I noted curious glances from my neighbours. They gave me sympathetic looks, but tactfully chose to ignore my tears, the context probably reassuring them that I was weeping over the fate of a fictional character rather than some personal catastrophe. Perhaps a few hours later, I would be shaking with suppressed laughter. I think I must have been a very annoying person with whom to share a desk.

I have divided the stories into three categories – *Love, Loss* and *Life* – but these titles are loose.

Love is, of course, a central preoccupation of literature, but a love story is so often a story of loss, or indeed a story of life. Many of these stories take an amusing and sardonic look at love, so the division, though slightly artificial, is designed to give a reader the chance to read according to her or his mood. Many of them could appear under more than one heading and, I will admit, some stories could probably fit happily into all three categories.

LIFE

Life provides infinite shades of light and dark and in this section there are many curious tales and unusual settings. There is a handful of stories that made me ask: What on earth gave her this idea? Where did this come from? One example is 'The Axe' by Penelope Fitzgerald. It is a chilling horror story that takes place in the deceptively banal environment of an office and describes what happens when a man finds his job has been 'axed'. The narrator leaves us, as she should in such a story, with our hairs standing on end.

There is plenty of humour in this section and this is often provided by an unexpected or rather marvellous twist. 'How Did I Get Away with Killing One of the Biggest Lawyers in the State? It Was Easy.' by Alice Walker is flawless. And Penelope Lively's 'Corruption' is too, with the most brilliant visual image perhaps of any story – where a judge, involved in a pornography trial, takes some of his 'research papers' on holiday. A gust of wind sends copies of the offending magazines flying around the beach to be gathered by innocent children and even a woman who, until this moment, has been flirting with the judge. It is brilliantly comic. I felt I was watching the action unfold scene by scene, just as if I was watching a film.

There is a mildly pornographic element too in A. M. Homes' darkly comic 'A Real Doll'. It's almost about love, but more to do with sex. A boy uses his sister's Barbie as a sex toy and all sorts of jealousies ensue (Ken has an opinion, naturally). It's funny, outrageous and totally original.

Alison Lurie's 'Fat People' is once again funny, dark and unique. One could say it is about dieting, but that would only be one per cent of it. But, for me, Nicola Barker is the wittiest and often the most original. I chose three of her stories for the anthology but had to restrain myself from selecting so many more. In 'G-String', her powers of description had me laughing out loud: 'It felt like her G-string was making headway from between her buttocks up into her throat... now she knew how a horse felt when offered a new bit and bridle for the first time.' Most women will know how accurate this is. Needless to say, this is a hilarious tale right to the very end, where the woman ends up 'knickerless... a truly modern female'.

Ali Smith's 'The Child' is also comic and surreal. A baby with the voice of an adult is placed in a woman's supermarket trolley. It's the reverse of a baby-snatching drama, and is both farcical and strangely daring. It was one of my favourites, and visits to the supermarket have not been the same since...

Elspeth Davie's 'Change of Face' about a street artist is haunting as is her story 'A Weight Problem'. The situations she describes seem to have been magicked from thin air.

Other stories are slightly more shocking: a death may take place, but the loss is not, in itself, a focal point. It is perhaps more to do with learning. Margaret Atwood's very clever story, 'Betty', is about this. Over a small number of pages, one gets a strong sense of the narrator's identity, her stages of growing up and how she reinterprets the past in the light of her age and experience. It is full of wisdom.

Helen Simpson's story 'Ahead of the Pack' is brief but brilliant. The central notion is that we should have a quota of carbon points each day (in the same way that people on diets allow themselves a certain number of calories). It is such a clever idea that I wondered if it should not become a reality. What better way to ensure that we do not get 'in terms of [our] planetary profile... an absolutely vast arse'.

I happily included the slightly self-referential 'A Society' by Virginia Woolf, where the character of Poll is left a fortune by her father on condition that she reads all the books in the London Library. She declares them 'for the most part unutterably bad!' Having done most of my research for this anthology there, I can confirm that Poll is wrong.

LOVE

In the volume entitled *Love*, love appears in all its guises and disguises. As Yiyun Li describes in 'Love in the Marketplace': 'A romance is more than a love story with a man.'

Perhaps maternal love is the most visceral of all loves. At least it felt so the first time I read the phenomenal 'My Son the Hero' by Clare Boylan. 'Reach' by Rachel Seiffert and 'The Turtle' by Roshi Fernando also powerfully evoke the strength of a mother's love, and 'Even Pretty Eyes Commit Crimes' by M. J. Hyland touches beautifully on the love between father and son.

In this section there is the painful poignancy of romantic love in Margaret Drabble's 'Faithful Lovers', love that is more like madness in 'Master' by Angela Carter and love that is unrecognised until it is too late in 'The Man from Mars' by Margaret Atwood. There is love that for some reason is not meant to be. Chimamanda Ngozi Adichie writes about this in 'The Thing Around your Neck'. There is love as infatuation, short-lived and potentially destructive, in Jennifer Egan's 'The

Watch Trick', and the making of love, sometimes kinkily, as in Anne Enright's 'Revenge'.

Many readers will know the experience of being haunted by an ex, and Alison Lurie writes vividly about the effect of lost or past loves in her characters' lives ('In the Shadow' and also the even more extraordinary 'Ilse's House').

LOSS

Many of the stories in the *Loss* volume are tragic, some are shocking. All of them are emotional.

From Katherine Mansfield's almost unbearably poignant 'The Canary', which is written with a feather-light touch, to Alice Munro's 'Gravel', which is blunt to the point of brutality, I think few of these stories will leave readers cold.

There are lost lives, lost loves, lost innocence, a lost mother (Colette Paul's 'Renaissance'), lost breasts (Ellen Gilchrist's 'Indignities'), loss of hearing (Helen Simpson's 'Sorry?') and even a lost leopard (Anna Kavan's extraordinary 'A Visit').

'The First Year of My Life' by Muriel Spark takes the idea that babies are born omniscient and gradually lose their power and their knowledge. In this story, a baby is born in 1913, 'in the very worst year that the world had ever seen so far', and watches, dismayed, unsmiling, sardonic: 'My teeth were coming through very nicely in my opinion, and well worth all the trouble I was put to in bringing them forth. I weighed twenty pounds. On all the world's fighting fronts the men killed in action or dead of wounds numbered 8,538,315 and the warriors wounded and maimed were 21,219,452. With these figures in mind I sat up in my high chair and banged my spoon on the table.'

It is a profound story – a curious companion piece to others in the anthology in which the story is also told by a wise, all-knowing baby: Nicola Barker's masterful 'Inside Information' and Ali Smith's 'The Child' (*Life*) are especially engaging and fresh.

Carol Shields' 'Fragility', with its hinterland story of a disabled child and a couple's lost happiness, shares much of the pathos of Yiyun Li's 'After a Life', in which a dying child lies incarcerated in a small apartment. Both stories are agonising to read. Lorrie Moore's 'Agnes of Iowa' is similarly tragic but even more open-ended, with a couple doomed to live in perpetuity with their woes.

Susan Hill's 'Father, Father', a story of two daughters 'losing' their father to a second wife, their step-mother, is insightful and real, a common situation faultlessly described.

I have had interesting discussions about whether there is a female 'voice' and whether women write differently from men. I believe there are some quintessentially feminine writers – and some whose writing provides no clues as to their identity. Angela Carter's 'The Bloody Chamber' (*Love*), for example, is neither masculine nor feminine. It is simply one of the most powerful, imaginative and sensual pieces of writing that I have ever come across. If I did not have the knowledge, I would certainly not be able to identify that A. M. Homes' stories are from a woman's pen. Her male protagonists are totally convincing and their 'voices' provocative and disturbing.

Some stories are so vivid that it is hard to imagine them as anything other than autobiography – even when the writer is female and the narrator is male. 'Before He Left the Family' by Carrie Tiffany (*Loss*) is a very matter-of-fact, no-blame narration of parental separation, but in subtle ways leaves the reader with little doubt over the effect this had on the sons. It is masterful storytelling. The male voice is very real.

I believe that many of the writers in this volume have the ability to leave their gender behind in their writing, whether through deliberately disguising themselves behind a male narrator, or adopting a masculine sensibility. Once again, this is something that would be more difficult to sustain over the duration of an entire novel.

Short stories seem ideally suited to how many of us are reading now. They are perfect to read on an iPad, even on a phone. They can last as long as a short bus or train journey. They are complete in themselves – though from time to time they leave us hanging in mid-air with some kind of twist or ambiguity, as if this story we have in our hands is merely a beginning.

This is a very personal selection of my favourite stories. There will definitely be omissions (some of them accidental, some of them deliberate). Many of these writers were suggested by friends and colleagues. It seems that everyone has a favourite writer of short stories – and whenever I mentioned to people what I was doing they all insisted that I must read one author or another. I always followed up on recommendations, but I did not always find that I shared their taste.

It's been a glorious adventure putting this book together. I hope readers will share some of my excitement and enthusiasm and use it as a starting point for their own explorations into this extraordinary genre.

Victoria Hislop
June 2014

Adapted from the introduction to *The Story: Love Loss and The Lives of Women* (Head of Zeus, 2013)

CONSEQUENCES

Willa Cather

Willa Cather (1873–1947) was an American author who wrote highly praised novels depicting frontier life on the Great Plains. She was awarded the Pulitzer Prize in 1923 for her novel *One of Ours*. Cather received the Gold Medal for Fiction from the National Institute of Arts and Letters in 1944, an award given once a decade for an author's complete body of work.

Henry Eastman, a lawyer, aged forty, was standing beside the Flatiron Building in a driving November rainstorm, signaling frantically for a taxi. It was six-thirty, and everything on wheels was engaged. The streets were in confusion about him, the sky was in turmoil above him, and the Flatiron Building, which seemed about to blow down, threw water like a mill-shoot. Suddenly, out of the brutal struggle of men and cars and machines and people tilting at each other with umbrellas, a quiet, well-mannered limousine paused before him, at the curb, and an agreeable, ruddy countenance confronted him through the open window of the car.

"Don't you want me to pick you up, Mr. Eastman? I'm running directly home now."

Eastman recognized Kier Cavenaugh, a young man of pleasure, who lived in the house on Central Park South, where he himself had an apartment.

"Don't I?" he exclaimed, bolting into the car. "I'll risk getting your cushions wet without compunction. I came up in a taxi, but I didn't hold it. Bad economy. I thought I saw your car down on Fourteenth Street about half an hour ago."

The owner of the car smiled. He had a pleasant, round face and round eyes, and a fringe of smooth, yellow hair showed under the brim of his soft felt hat. "With a lot of little broilers fluttering into it? You did. I know some girls who work in the cheap shops down there. I happened to be downtown and I stopped and took a load of them home. I do sometimes. Saves their poor little clothes, you know. Their shoes are never any good."

Eastman looked at his rescuer. "Aren't they notoriously afraid of cars and smooth young men?" he inquired.

Cavenaugh shook his head. "They know which cars are safe and which are chancy. They put each other wise. You have to take a bunch at a time, of course. The Italian girls can never come along; their men shoot. The girls understand, all right; but their fathers don't. One gets to see queer places, sometimes, taking them home."

Eastman laughed drily. "Every time I touch the circle of your acquaintance, Cavenaugh, it's a little wider. You must know New York pretty well by this time."

"Yes, but I'm on my good behavior below Twenty-third Street," the young man replied with simplicity. "My little friends down there would give me a good character. They're wise little girls. They have grand ways with each other, a romantic code of loyalty. You can find a good many of the lost virtues among them."

The car was standing still in a traffic block at Fortieth Street, when Cavenaugh suddenly drew his face away from the window and touched Eastman's arm. "Look, please. You see that hansom with the bony gray horse – driver has a broken hat and red flannel around his throat. Can you see who is inside?"

Eastman peered out. The hansom was just cutting across the line, and the driver was making a great fuss about it, bobbing his head and waving his whip. He jerked his dripping old horse into Fortieth Street and clattered off past the Public Library grounds toward Sixth Avenue. "No, I couldn't see the passenger. Someone you know?"

"Could you see whether there was a passenger?" Cavenaugh asked.

"Why, yes. A man, I think. I saw his elbow on the apron. No driver ever behaves like that unless he has a passenger."

"Yes, I may have been mistaken," Cavenaugh murmured absent-mindedly.

Ten minutes or so later, after Cavenaugh's car had turned off Fifth Avenue into Fifty-eighth Street, Eastman exclaimed, "There's your same cabby, and his cart's empty. He's headed for a drink now, I suppose." The driver in the broken hat and the red flannel neck cloth was still brandishing the whip over his old gray. He was coming from the west now, and turned down Sixth Avenue, under the elevated.

Cavenaugh's car stopped at the bachelor apartment house between Sixth and Seventh Avenues where he and Eastman lived, and they went up in the elevator together. They were still talking when the lift stopped at Cavenaugh's floor, and Eastman stepped out with him and walked down the hall, finishing his sentence while Cavenaugh found his latch-key. When he opened the door, a wave of fresh cigarette smoke greeted them. Cavenaugh stopped short and stared into his hallway. "Now how in the devil – !" he exclaimed angrily.

"Someone waiting for you? Oh, no, thanks. I wasn't coming in. I have to work tonight. Thank you, but I couldn't." Eastman nodded and went up the two flights to his own rooms.

Though Eastman did not customarily keep a servant he had this winter a man who had been lent to him by a friend who was abroad. Rollins met him at the door and took his coat and hat.

"Put out my dinner clothes, Rollins, and then get out of here until ten o'clock. I've promised to go to a supper tonight. I shan't be dining. I've had a late tea and I'm going to work until ten. You may put out some kumiss and biscuit for me."

Rollins took himself off, and Eastman settled down at the big table in his sitting-room. He had to read a lot of letters submitted as evidence in a breach of contract case, and before he got very far he found that long paragraphs in some of the letters were written in German. He had a German dictionary at his office, but none here. Rollins had gone, and anyhow, the bookstores would be closed. He remembered having seen a row of dictionaries on the lower shelf of one of Cavenaugh's bookcases. Cavenaugh had a lot of books, though he never read anything but new stuff. Eastman prudently turned down his student's lamp very low – the thing had an evil habit of smoking – and went down two flights to Cavenaugh's door.

The young man himself answered Eastman's ring. He was freshly dressed for the evening, except for a brown smoking jacket, and his yellow hair had been brushed until it shone. He hesitated as he confronted his caller, still holding the door knob, and his round eyes and smooth forehead made their best imitation of a frown. When Eastman began to apologize, Cavenaugh's manner suddenly changed. He caught his arm and jerked him into the narrow hall. "Come in, come in. Right along!" he said excitedly. "Right along," he repeated as he pushed Eastman before him into his sitting-room. "Well I'll—" He stopped short at the door and looked about his own room with an air of complete mystification. The back window was wide open and a strong wind was blowing in. Cavenaugh walked over to the window and stuck out his head, looking up and down the fire escape. When he pulled his head in, he drew down the sash.

"I had a visitor I wanted you to see," he explained with a nervous smile. "At least I thought I had. He must have gone out that way," nodding toward the window.

"Call him back. I only came to borrow a German dictionary, if you have one. Can't stay. Call him back."

Cavenaugh shook his head despondently. "No use. He's beat it. Nowhere in sight."

"He must be active. Has he left something?" Eastman pointed to a very dirty white glove that lay on the floor under the window.

"Yes, that's his."

Cavenaugh reached for his tongs, picked up the glove, and tossed it into the grate, where it quickly shriveled on the coals. Eastman felt that he had happened in upon something disagreeable, possibly something shady, and he wanted to get away at once. Cavenaugh stood staring at the fire and seemed stupid and dazed; so he repeated his request rather sternly, "I think I've seen a German dictionary down there among your books. May I have it?"

Cavenaugh blinked at him. "A German dictionary? Oh, possibly! Those were my father's. I scarcely know what there is." He put down the tongs and began to wipe his hands nervously with his handkerchief.

Eastman went over to the bookcase behind the Chesterfield, opened the door, swooped upon the book he wanted and stuck it under his arm. He felt perfectly certain now that something shady had been going on in Cavenaugh's rooms, and he saw no reason why he should come in for any hang-over. "Thanks. I'll send it back tomorrow," he said curtly as he made for the door.

Cavenaugh followed him. "Wait a moment. I wanted you to see him. You did see his glove," glancing at the grate.

Eastman laughed disagreeably. "I saw a glove. That's not evidence. Do your friends often use that means of exit? Somewhat inconvenient."

Cavenaugh gave him a startled glance. "Wouldn't you think so? For an old man, a very rickety old party? The ladders are steep, you know, and rusty." He approached the window again and put it up softly. In a moment he drew his head back with a jerk. He caught Eastman's arm and shoved him toward the window. "Hurry, please. Look! Down there." He pointed to the little patch of paved court four flights down.

The square of pavement was so small and the walls about it were so high, that it was a good deal like looking down a well. Four tall buildings backed upon the same court and made a kind of shaft, with flagstones at the bottom, and at the top a square of dark blue with some stars in it. At the bottom of the shaft Eastman saw a black figure, a man in a caped coat and a tall hat stealing cautiously around, not across the square of pavement, keeping close to the dark wall and avoiding the streak of light that fell on the flagstones from a window in the opposite house. Seen from that height he was of course fore-shortened and probably looked more shambling and decrepit than he was. He picked his way along with exaggerated care and looked like a silly old cat crossing a wet street. When he reached the gate that led into an alley way between two buildings, he felt about for the latch, opened the door a mere crack, and then shot out under the feeble lamp that burned in the brick arch over the gateway. The door closed after him.

"He'll get run in," Eastman remarked curtly, turning away from the window. "That door shouldn't be left unlocked. Any crook could come in. I'll speak to the janitor about it, if you don't mind," he added sarcastically.

"Wish you would." Cavenaugh stood brushing down the front of his jacket, first with his right hand and then with his left. "You saw him, didn't you?"

"Enough of him. Seems eccentric. I have to see a lot of buggy people. They don't take me in any more. But I'm keeping you and I'm in a hurry myself. Good night."

Cavenaugh put out his hand detainingly and started to say something; but Eastman rudely turned his back and went down the hall and out of the door. He had never felt anything shady about Cavenaugh before, and he was sorry he had gone down for the dictionary. In five minutes he was deep in his papers; but in the half hour when he was loafing before he dressed to go out, the young man's curious behavior came into his mind again.

Eastman had merely a neighborly acquaintance with Cavenaugh. He had been to a supper at the young man's rooms once, but he didn't particularly like Cavenaugh's friends; so the next time he was asked, he had another engagement. He liked Cavenaugh himself, if for nothing else than because he was so cheerful and trim and ruddy. A good complexion is always at a premium in New York, especially when it shines reassuringly on a man who does everything in the world to lose it. It encourages fellow mortals as to the inherent vigor of the human organism and the amount of bad treatment it will stand for. "Footprints that perhaps another," etc.

Cavenaugh, he knew, had plenty of money. He was the son of a Pennsylvania preacher, who died soon after he discovered that his ancestral acres were full of petroleum, and Kier had come to New York to burn some of the oil. He was thirty-two and was still at it; spent his life, literally, among the breakers. His motor hit the Park every morning as if it were the first time ever. He took people out to supper every night. He went from restaurant to restaurant, sometimes to half-a-dozen in an evening. The head waiters were his hosts and their cordiality made him happy. They made a life-line for him up Broadway and down Fifth Avenue. Cavenaugh was still fresh and smooth, round and plump, with a lustre to his hair and white teeth and a clear look in his round eyes. He seemed absolutely unwearied and unimpaired; never bored and never carried away.

Eastman always smiled when he met Cavenaugh in the entrance hall, serenely going forth to or returning from gladiatorial combats with joy, or when he saw him rolling smoothly up to the door in his car in the morning after a restful night in one of the remarkable new roadhouses he was always finding. Eastman had seen a good many young men disappear on Cavenaugh's route, and he admired this young man's endurance.

Tonight, for the first time, he had got a whiff of something unwholesome about the fellow – bad nerves, bad company, something on hand that he was ashamed of, a visitor old and vicious, who must have had a key to Cavenaugh's apartment, for he was evidently there when Cavenaugh returned at seven o'clock. Probably it was the same man Cavenaugh had seen in the hansom. He must have been able to let himself in, for Cavenaugh kept no man but his chauffeur; or perhaps the janitor had been instructed to let him in. In either case, and whoever he was, it was clear enough that Cavenaugh was ashamed of him and was mixing up in questionable business of some kind.

Eastman sent Cavenaugh's book back by Rollins, and for the next few weeks he had no word with him beyond a casual greeting when they happened to meet in the hall or the elevator. One Sunday morning Cavenaugh telephoned up to him to ask if he could motor out to a road-house in Connecticut that afternoon and have supper; but when Eastman found there were to be other guests he declined.

On New Year's eve Eastman dined at the University Club at six o'clock and hurried home before the usual manifestations of insanity had begun in the streets. When Rollins brought his smoking coat, he asked him whether he wouldn't like to get off early.

"Yes, sir. But won't you be dressing, Mr. Eastman?" he inquired.

"Not tonight." Eastman handed him a bill. "Bring some change in the morning. There'll be fees."

Rollins lost no time in putting everything to rights for the night, and Eastman couldn't help wishing that he were in such a hurry to be off somewhere himself. When he heard the hall door close softly, he wondered if there were any place, after all, that he wanted to go. From his window he looked down at the long lines of motors and taxis waiting for a signal to cross Broadway. He thought of some of their probable destinations and decided that none of those places pulled him very hard. The night was warm and wet, the air was drizzly. Vapor hung in clouds about the *Times* Building, half hid the top of it, and made a luminous haze along Broadway. While he was looking down at the army of wet, black carriage-tops and their reflected headlights and tail-lights, Eastman heard a ring at his door. He deliberated. If it were a caller, the hall porter would have telephoned up. It must be the janitor. When he opened the door, there stood a rosy young man in a tuxedo, without a coat or hat.

"Pardon. Should I have telephoned? I half thought you wouldn't be in."

Eastman laughed. "Come in, Cavenaugh. You weren't sure whether you wanted company or not, eh, and you were trying to let chance decide it? That was exactly my state of mind. Let's accept the verdict." When they emerged from the narrow hall into his sitting-room, he pointed out a seat by the fire to his guest. He brought a tray of decanters and soda bottles and placed it on his writing table.

Cavenaugh hesitated, standing by the fire. "Sure you weren't starting for somewhere?"

"Do I look it? No, I was just making up my mind to stick it out alone when you rang. Have one?" He picked up a tall tumbler.

"Yes, thank you. I always do."

Eastman chuckled. "Lucky boy! So will I. I had a very early dinner. New York is the most arid place on holidays," he continued as he rattled the ice in the glasses. "When one gets too old to hit the rapids down there, and tired of gobbling food to heathenish dance music, there is absolutely no place where you can get a chop and some milk toast in peace, unless you have strong ties of blood brotherhood on upper Fifth Avenue. But you, why aren't you starting for somewhere?"

The young man sipped his soda and shook his head as he replied:

"Oh, I couldn't get a chop, either. I know only flashy people, of course." He looked up at his host with such a grave and candid expression that Eastman decided there couldn't be anything very crooked about the fellow. His smooth cheecks were positively cherubic.

"Well, what's the matter with them? Aren't they flashing tonight?"

"Only the very new ones seem to flash on New Year's eve. The older ones fade away. Maybe they are hunting a chop, too."

"Well" – Eastman sat down – "holidays do dash one. I was just about to write a letter to a pair of maiden aunts in my old home town, up-state; old coasting hill, snow-covered pines, lights in the church windows. That's what you've saved me from."

Cavenaugh shook himself. "Oh, I'm sure that wouldn't have been good for you. Pardon me," he rose and took a photograph from the bookcase, a handsome man in shooting clothes. "Dudley, isn't it? Did you know him well?"

"Yes. An old friend. Terrible thing, wasn't it? I haven't got over the jolt yet."

"His suicide? Yes, terrible! Did you know his wife?"

"Slightly. Well enough to admire her very much. She must be terribly broken up. I wonder Dudley didn't think of that."

Cavenaugh replaced the photograph carefully, lit a cigarette, and standing before the fire began to smoke. "Would you mind telling me about him? I never met him, but of course I'd read a lot about him, and I can't help feeling interested. It was a queer thing."

Eastman took out his cigar case and leaned back in his deep chair. "In the days when I knew him best he hadn't any story, like the happy nations. Everything was properly arranged for him before he was born. He came into the world happy, healthy, clever, straight, with the right sort of connections and the right kind of fortune, neither too large nor too small. He helped to make the world an agreeable place to live in until he was twenty-six. Then he married as he should have married. His wife was a Californian, educated abroad. Beautiful. You have seen her picture?"

Cavenaugh nodded. "Oh, many of them."

"She was interesting, too. Though she was distinctly a person of the world, she had retained something, just enough of the large Western manner. She had the habit of authority, of calling out a special train if she needed it, of using all our ingenious mechanical contrivances lightly and easily, without over-rating them. She and Dudley knew how to live better than most people. Their house was the most charming one I have ever known in New York. You felt freedom there, and a zest of life, and safety – absolute sanctuary – from everything sordid or petty. A whole society like that would justify the creation of man and would make our planet shine with a soft, peculiar radiance among the constellations. You think I'm putting it on thick?"

The young man sighed gently. "Oh, no! One has always felt there must be people like that. I've never known any."

"They had two children, beautiful ones. After they had been married for eight years, Rosina met this Spaniard. He must have amounted to something. She wasn't a flighty woman. She came home and told Dudley how matters stood. He persuaded her to stay at home for six months and try to pull up. They were both fair-minded people, and I'm as sure as if I were the Almighty, that she did try. But at the end of the time, Rosina went quietly off to Spain, and Dudley went to hunt in the Canadian Rockies. I met his party out there. I didn't know his wife had left him and talked about her a good deal. I noticed that he never drank anything, and his light used to shine through the log chinks of his room until all hours, even after a hard day's hunting. When I got back to New York, rumors were creeping about. Dudley did not come back. He bought a ranch in Wyoming, built a big log house and kept splendid dogs and horses. One of his sisters went out to keep house for him, and the children were there when they were not in school. He had a great many visitors, and everyone who came back talked about how well Dudley kept things going.

"He put in two years out there. Then, last month, he had to come back on business. A trust fund had to be settled up, and he was administrator. I saw him at the club; same light, quick step, same gracious handshake. He was getting gray, and there was something softer in his manner; but he had a fine red tan on his face and said he found it delightful to be here in the season when everything is going hard. The Madison Avenue house had been closed since Rosina left it. He went there to get some things his sister wanted. That, of course, was the mistake. He went alone, in the afternoon, and didn't go out for dinner – found some sherry and tins of biscuit in the sideboard. He shot himself sometime that night. There were pistols in his smoking-room. They found burnt-out candles beside him in the morning. The gas and electricity were shut off. I suppose there, in his own house, among his own things, it was too much for him. He left no letters."

Cavenaugh blinked and brushed the lapel of his coat. "I suppose," he said slowly, "that every suicide is logical and reasonable, if one knew all the facts."

Eastman roused himself. "No, I don't think so. I've known too many fellows who went off like that – more than I deserve, I think – and some of them were absolutely inexplicable. I can understand Dudley; but I can't see why healthy bachelors, with money enough, like ourselves, need such a device. It reminds me of what Dr. Johnson said, that the most discouraging thing about life is the number of fads and hobbies and fake religions it takes to put people through a few years of it."

"Dr. Johnson? The specialist? Oh, the old fellow!" said Cavenaugh imperturbably. "Yes, that's interesting. Still I fancy if one knew the facts – Did you know about Wyatt?"

"I don't think so."

"You wouldn't, probably. He was just a fellow about town who spent money. He wasn't one of the *forestieri*, though. Had connections here and owned a fine old place over on Staten Island. He went in for botany, and had been all over, hunting things; rusts, I believe. He had a yacht and used to take a gay crowd down about the South Seas, botanizing. He really did botanize, I believe. I never knew such a spender – only not flashy. He helped a lot of fellows and he was awfully good to girls, the kind who come down here to get a little fun, who don't like to work and still aren't really tough, the kind you see talking hard for their dinner. Nobody knows what becomes of them, or what they get out of it, and there are hundreds of new ones every year. He helped dozens of 'em; it was he who got me curious about the little shop girls.

"Well, one afternoon when his tea was brought, he took prussic acid instead. He didn't leave any letters, either; people of any taste don't. They wouldn't leave any material reminder if they could help it. His lawyers found that he had just $314.72 above his debts when he died. He had planned to spend all his money, and then take his tea; he had worked it out carefully."

Eastman reached for his pipe and pushed his chair away from the fire. "That looks like a considered case, but I don't think philosophical suicides like that are common. I think they usually come from stress of feeling and are really, as the newspapers call them, desperate acts; done without a motive. You remember when Anna Karenina was under the wheels, she kept saying, 'Why am I here?'"

Cavenaugh rubbed his upper lip with his pink finger and made an effort to wrinkle his brows. "May I, please?" reaching for the whiskey. "But have you," he asked, blinking as the soda flew at him, "have you ever known, yourself, cases that were really inexplicable?"

"A few too many. I was in Washington just before Captain Jack Purden was married and I saw a good deal of him. Popular army man, fine record in the Philippines, married a charming girl with lots of money; mutual devotion. It was the gayest wedding of the winter, and they started for Japan. They stopped in San Francisco for a week and missed their boat because, as the bride wrote back to Washington, they were too happy to move. They took the next boat, were both good sailors, had exceptional weather. After they had been out for two weeks, Jack got up from his deck chair one afternoon, yawned, put down his book, and stood before his wife. 'Stop reading for a moment and look at me.' She laughed and asked him why. 'Because you happen to be good to look at.' He nodded to her, went back to the stern and was never seen again. Must have gone down to the lower deck and slipped overboard, behind the machinery. It was the luncheon hour, not many people about; steamer cutting through a soft green sea. That's one of the most baffling cases I know. His friends raked up his past, and it was as trim as a cottage garden. If he'd so much as dropped an ink spot on his fatigue uniform, they'd have found it. He wasn't emotional or moody; wasn't, indeed, very interesting; simply a good soldier, fond of all the pompous little formalities that make up a military man's life. What do you make of that, my boy?"

Cavenaugh stroked his chin. "It's very puzzling, I admit. Still, if one knew everything –"

"But we do know everything. His friends wanted to find something to help them out, to help the girl out, to help the case of the human creature."

"Oh, I don't mean things that people could unearth," said Cavenaugh uneasily. "But possibly there were things that couldn't be found out."

Eastman shrugged his shoulders. "It's my experience that when there are 'things' as you call them, they're very apt to be found. There is no such thing as a secret. To make any move at all one has to employ human agencies, employ at least one human agent. Even when the pirates killed the men who buried their gold for them, the bones told the story."

Cavenaugh rubbed his hands together and smiled his sunny smile.

"I like that idea. It's reassuring. If we can have no secrets, it means that we can't, after all, go so far afield as we might," he hesitated, "yes, as we might."

Eastman looked at him sourly. "Cavenaugh, when you've practised law in New York for twelve years, you find that people can't go far in any direction, except –" He thrust his forefinger sharply at the floor. "Even in that direction, few people can do anything out of the ordinary. Our range is limited. Skip a few baths, and we become personally objectionable. The slightest carelessness can rot a man's integrity or give him ptomaine poisoning. We keep up only by incessant cleansing operations, of mind and body. What we call character is held together by all sorts of tacks and strings and glue."

Cavenaugh looked startled. "Come now, it's not so bad as that, is it? I've always thought that a serious man, like you, must know a lot of Launcelots." When Eastman only laughed, the younger man squirmed about in his chair. He spoke again hastily, as if he were embarrassed. "Your military friend may have had personal experiences, however, that his friends couldn't possibly get a line on. He may accidentally have come to a place where he saw himself in too unpleasant a light. I believe people can be chilled by a draft from outside, somewhere."

"Outside?" Eastman echoed. "Ah, you mean the far outside! Ghosts, delusions, eh?"

Cavenaugh winced. "That's putting it strong. Why not say tips from the outside? Delusions belong to a diseased mind, don't they? There are some of us who have no minds to speak of, who yet have had experiences. I've had a little something in that line myself and I don't look it, do I?"

Eastman looked at the bland countenance turned toward him. "Not exactly. What's your delusion?"

"It's not a delusion. It's a haunt."

The lawyer chuckled. "Soul of a lost Casino girl?"

"No; an old gentleman. A most unattractive old gentleman, who follows me about."

"Does he want money?"

Cavenaugh sat up straight. "No. I wish to God he wanted anything – but the pleasure of my society! I'd let him clean me out to be rid of him. He's a real article. You saw him yourself that night when you came to my rooms to borrow a dictionary, and he went down the fire escape. You saw him down in the court."

"Well, I saw somebody down in the court, but I'm too cautious to take it for granted that I saw what you saw. Why, anyhow, should I see your haunt? If it was your friend I saw, he impressed me disagreeably. How did you pick him up?"

Cavenaugh looked gloomy. "That was queer, too. Charley Burke and I had motored out to Long Beach, about a year ago, sometime in October, I think. We had supper and stayed until late. When we were coming home, my car broke down. We had a lot of girls along who had to get back for morning rehearsals and things; so I sent them all into town in Charley's car, and he was to send a man back to tow me home. I was driving myself, and didn't want to leave my machine. We had not taken a direct road back; so I was stuck in a lonesome, woody place, no houses about. I got chilly and made a fire, and was putting in the time comfortably enough, when this old party steps up. He was in shabby evening clothes and a top hat, and had on his usual white gloves. How he got there, at three o'clock in the morning, miles from any town or railway, I'll leave it to you to figure out. *He* surely had no car. When I saw him coming up to the fire, I disliked him. He had a silly, apologetic walk. His teeth were chattering and I asked him to sit down. He got down like a clothes-horse folding up. I offered him a cigarette, and when he took off his gloves I couldn't help noticing how knotted and spotty his hands were. He was asthmatic, and took his breath with a wheeze. 'Haven't you got anything – refreshing in there?' he asked, nodding at the car. When I told him I hadn't, he sighed. 'Ah, you young fellows arc greedy. You drink it all up. You drink it all up, all up – up!' he kept chewing it over."

Cavenaugh paused and looked embarrassed again. "The thing that was most unpleasant is difficult to explain. The old man sat there by the fire and leered at me with a silly sort of admiration that was – well, more than humiliating. 'Gay boy, gay dog!' he would mutter, and when he grinned he showed his teeth, worn and yellow – shells. I remembered that it was better to talk casually to insane people; so I remarked carelessly that I had been out with a party and got stuck.

"'Oh yes, I remember,' he said, 'Flora and Lottie and Maybelle and Marcelline, and poor Kate.'

"He had named them correctly; so I began to think I had been hitting the bright waters too hard.

"Things I drank never had seemed to make me woody; but you can never tell when trouble is going to hit you. I pulled my hat down and tried to look as uncommunicative as possible; but he kept croaking on from time to time, like this: 'Poor Katie! Splendid arms, but dope got her. She took up with Eastern religions after she had her hair dyed. Got to going to a Swami's joint, and smoking opium. Temple of the Lotus, it was called, and the police raided it.'

"This was nonsense, of course; the young woman was in the pink of condition. I let him rave, but I decided that if something didn't come out for me pretty soon, I'd foot it across Long Island. There wasn't room enough for the two of us. I got up and took another try at my car. He hopped right after me.

"'Good car,' he wheezed, 'better than the little Ford.'

"I'd had a Ford before, but so has everybody; that was a safe guess.

"'Still,' he went on, 'that run in from Huntington Bay in the rain wasn't bad. Arrested for speeding, he-he.'

"It was true I had made such a run, under rather unusual circumstances, and had been arrested. When at last I heard my life-boat snorting up the road, my visitor got up, sighed, and stepped back into the shadow of the trees. I didn't wait to see what became of him, you may believe. That was visitation number one. What do you think of it?"

Cavenaugh looked at his host defiantly. Eastman smiled.

"I think you'd better change your mode of life, Cavenaugh. Had many returns?" he inquired.

"Too many, by far." The young man took a turn about the room and came back to the fire. Standing by the mantel he lit another cigarette before going on with his story.

"The second visitation happened in the street, early in the evening, about eight o'clock. I was held up in a traffic block before the Plaza. My chauffeur was driving. Old Nibbs steps up out of the crowd, opens the door of my car, gets in and sits down beside me. He had on wilted evening clothes, same as before, and there was some sort of heavy scent about him. Such an unpleasant old party! A thorough-going rotter; you knew it at once. This time he wasn't talkative, as he had been when I first saw him. He leaned back in the car as if he owned it, crossed his hands on his stick and looked out at the crowd – sort of hungrily.

"I own I really felt a loathing compassion for him.

"We got down the avenue slowly. I kept looking out at the mounted police. But what could I do? Have him pulled? I was afraid to. I was awfully afraid of getting him into the papers.

"'I'm going to the New Astor,' I said at last. 'Can I take you anywhere?'

"'No, thank you,' says he. 'I get out when you do. I'm due on West Forty-fourth. I'm dining tonight with Marcelline – all that is left of her!'

"He put his hand to his hat brim with a gruesome salute. Such a scandalous, foolish old face as he had! When we pulled up at the Astor, I stuck my hand in my pocket and asked him if he'd like a little loan.

"'No, thank you, but' – he leaned over and whispered, ugh! – 'but save a little, save a little. Forty years from now – a little – comes in handy. Save a little.'

"His eyes fairly glittered as he made his remark. I jumped out. I'd have jumped into the North River. When he tripped off, I asked my chauffeur if he'd noticed the man who got into the car with me. He said he knew someone was with me, but he hadn't noticed just when he got in. Want to hear any more?"

Cavenaugh dropped into his chair again. His plump cheeks were a trifle more flushed than usual, but he was perfectly calm. Eastman felt that the young man believed what he was telling him.

"Of course I do. It's very interesting. I don't see quite where you are coming out though."

Cavenaugh sniffed. "No more do I. I really feel that I've been put upon. I haven't deserved it any more than any other fellow of my kind. Doesn't it impress you disagreeably?"

"Well, rather so. Has anyone else seen your friend?"

"You saw him."

"We won't count that. As I said, there's no certainty that you and I saw the same person in the court that night. Has anyone else had a look in?"

"People sense him rather than see him. He usually crops up when

I'm alone or in a crowd on the street. He never approaches me when I'm with people I know, though I've seen him hanging about the doors of theatres when I come out with a party; loafing around the stage exit, under a wall; or across on the street, in a doorway. To be frank, I'm not anxious to introduce him. The third time, it was I who came upon him. In November my driver, Harry, had a sudden attack of appendicitis. I took him to the Presbyterian Hospital in the car, early in the evening. When I came home, I found the old villain in my rooms. I offered him a drink, and he sat down. It was the first time I had seen him in a steady light, with his hat off.

"His face is lined like a railway map, and as to color – Lord, what a liver! His scalp grows tight to his skull, and his hair is dyed until it's perfectly dead, like a piece of black cloth."

Cavenaugh ran his fingers through his own neatly trimmed thatch, and seemed to forget where he was for a moment.

"I had a twin brother, Brian, who died when we were sixteen. I have a photograph of him on my wall, an enlargement from a kodak of him, doing a high jump, rather good thing, full of action. It seemed to annoy the old gentleman. He kept looking at it and lifting his eyebrows, and finally he got up, tip-toed across the room, and turned the picture to the wall.

"'Poor Brian! Fine fellow, but died young,' says he.

"Next morning, there was the picture, still reversed."

"Did he stay long?" Eastman asked interestedly.

"Half an hour, by the clock."

"Did he talk?"

"Well, he rambled."

"What about?"

Cavenaugh rubbed his pale eyebrows before answering.

"About things that an old man ought to want to forget. His conversation is highly objectionable. Of course he knows me like a book; everything I've ever done or thought. But when he recalls them, he throws a bad light on them, somehow. Things that weren't much off color, look rotten. He doesn't leave one a shred of self-respect, he really doesn't. That's the amount of it." The young man whipped out his handkerchief and wiped his face.

"You mean he really talks about things that none of your friends know?"

"Oh, dear, yes! Recalls things that happened in school. Anything disagreeable. Funny thing, he always turns Brian's picture to the wall."

"Does he come often?"

"Yes, oftener, now. Of course I don't know how he gets in downstairs. The hall boys never see him. But he has a key to my door. I don't know how he got it, but I can hear him turn it in the lock."

"Why don't you keep your driver with you, or telephone for me to come down?"

"He'd only grin and go down the fire escape as he did before. He's often done it when Harry's come in suddenly. Everybody has to be alone sometimes, you know. Besides, I don't want anybody to see him. He has me there."

"But why not? Why do you feel responsible for him?"

Cavenaugh smiled wearily. "That's rather the point, isn't it? Why do I? But I absolutely do. That identifies him, more than his knowing all about my life and my affairs."

Eastman looked at Cavenaugh thoughtfully. "Well, I should advise you to go in for something altogether different and new, and go in for it hard; business, engineering, metallurgy, something this old fellow wouldn't be interested in. See if you can make him remember logarithms."

Cavenaugh sighed. "No, he has me there, too. People never really change; they go on being themselves. But I would never make much trouble. Why can't they let me alone, damn it! I'd never hurt anybody, except, perhaps –"

"Except your old gentleman, eh?" Eastman laughed. "Seriously, Cavenaugh, if you want to shake him, I think a year on a ranch would do it. He would never be coaxed far from his favorite haunts. He would dread Montana."

Cavenaugh pursed up his lips. "So do I!"

"Oh, you think you do. Try it, and you'll find out. A gun and a horse beats all this sort of thing. Besides losing your haunt, you'd be putting ten years in the bank for yourself. I know a good ranch where they take people, if you want to try it."

"Thank you. I'll consider. Do you think I'm batty?"

"No, but I think you've been doing one sort of thing too long. You need big horizons. Get out of this."

Cavenaugh smiled meekly. He rose lazily and yawned behind his hand. "It's late, and I've taken your whole evening." He strolled over to the window and looked out. "Queer place, New York; rough on the little fellows. Don't you feel sorry for them, the girls especially? I do. What a fight they put up for a little fun! Why, even that old goat is sorry for them, the only decent thing he kept."

Eastman followed him to the door and stood in the hall, while Cavenaugh waited for the elevator. When the car came up Cavenaugh extended his pink, warm hand. "Good night."

The cage sank and his rosy countenance disappeared, his round-eyed smile being the last thing to go.

Weeks passed before Eastman saw Cavenaugh again. One morning, just as he was starting for Washington to argue a case before the Supreme Court, Cavenaugh telephoned him at his office to ask him about the Montana ranch he had recommended; said he meant to take his advice and go out there for the spring and summer.

When Eastman got back from Washington, he saw dusty trunks, just up from the trunk room, before Cavenaugh's door. Next morning, when he stopped to see what the young man was about, he found Cavenaugh in his shirt sleeves, packing.

"I'm really going; off tomorrow night. You didn't think it of me, did you?" he asked gaily.

"Oh, I've always had hopes of you!" Eastman declared. "But you are in a hurry, it seems to me."

"Yes, I am in a hurry." Cavenaugh shot a pair of leggings into one of the open trunks. "I telegraphed your ranch people, used your name, and they said it would be all right. By the way, some of my crowd are giving a little dinner for me at Rector's tonight. Couldn't you be persuaded, as it's a farewell occasion?" Cavenaugh looked at him. Hopefully.

Eastman laughed and shook his head. "Sorry, Cavenaugh, but that's too gay a world for me. I've got too much work lined up before me. I wish I had time to stop and look at your guns, though. You seem to know something about guns. You've more than you'll need, but nobody can have too many good ones." He put down one of the revolvers regretfully. "I'll drop in to see you in the morning, if you're up."

"I shall be up, all right. I've warned my crowd that I'll cut away before midnight."

"You won't, though," Eastman called back over his shoulder as he hurried downstairs.

The next morning, while Eastman was dressing, Rollins came in greatly excited.

"I'm a little late, sir. I was stopped by Harry, Mr. Cavenaugh's driver. Mr. Cavenaugh shot himself last night, sir."

Eastman dropped his vest and sat down on his shoe-box. "You're drunk, Rollins," he shouted. "He's going away today!"

"Yes, sir. Harry found him this morning. Ah, he's quite dead, sir. Harry's telephoned for the coroner. Harry don't know what to do with the ticket."

Eastman pulled on his coat and ran down the stairway. Cavenaugh's trunks were stripped and piled before the door. Harry was walking up and down the hall with a long green railroad ticket in his hand and a look of complete stupidity on his face.

"What shall I do about this ticket, Mr. Eastman?" he whispered. "And what about his trunks? He had me tell the transfer people to come early. They may be here any minute. Yes, sir. I brought him home in the car last night, before twelve, as cheerful as could be."

"Be quiet, Harry. Where is he?"

"In his bed, sir."

Eastman went into Cavenaugh's sleeping-room. When he came back to the sitting-room, he looked over the writing table; railway folders, time-tables, receipted bills, nothing else. He looked up for the photograph of Cavenaugh's twin brother. There it was, turned to the wall. Eastman took it down and looked at it; a boy in track clothes, half lying in the air, going over the string shoulders first, above the heads of a crowd of lads who were running and cheering. The face was somewhat blurred by the motion and the bright sunlight. Eastman put the picture back, as he found it. Had Cavenaugh entertained his visitor last night, and had the old man been more convincing than usual?

"Well, at any rate, he's seen to it that the old man can't establish identity. What a soft lot they are, fellows like poor Cavenaugh!" Eastman thought of his office as a delightful place.

A SOCIETY

Virginia Woolf

Virginia Woolf (1882–1941) was a British writer and one of the foremost modernists of the 20th-century. She was a significant figure in London literary society and a central figure in the influential Bloomsbury Group. Her most famous works include the novels *Mrs Dalloway*, *To the Lighthouse* and *Orlando* and the long essay *A Room of One's Own*.

This is how it all came about. Six or seven of us were sitting one day after tea. Some were gazing across the street into the windows of a milliner's shop where the light still shone brightly upon scarlet feathers and golden slippers. Others were idly occupied in building little towers of sugar upon the edge of the tea tray. After a time, so far as I can remember, we drew round the fire and began as usual to praise men – how strong, how noble, how brilliant, how courageous, how beautiful they were – how we envied those who by hook or by crook managed to get attached to one for life – when Poll, who had said nothing, burst into tears. Poll, I must tell you, has always been queer. For one thing her father was a strange man. He left her a fortune in his will, but on condition that she read all the books in the London Library. We comforted her as best we could; but we knew in our hearts how vain it was. For though we like her, Poll is no beauty; leaves her shoe laces untied; and must have been thinking, while we praised men, that not one of them would ever wish to marry her. At last she dried her tears. For some time we could make nothing of what she said. Strange enough it was in all conscience. She told us that, as we knew, she spent most of her time in the London Library, reading. She had begun, she said, with English literature on the top floor; and was steadily working her way down to *The Times* on the bottom. And now half, or perhaps only a quarter, way through a terrible thing had happened. She could read no more. Books were not what we thought them. 'Books,' she cried, rising to her feet and speaking with an intensity of desolation which I shall never forget, 'are for the most part unutterably bad!'

Of course we cried out that Shakespeare wrote books, and Milton and Shelley.

'Oh, yes,' she interrupted us. 'You've been well taught, I can see. But you are not members of the London Library.' Here her sobs broke forth anew. At length, recovering a little, she opened one of the pile of books which she always carried about with her – 'From a Window' or 'In a Garden' or some such name as that it was called, and it was written by a man called Benton or Henson or something of that kind. She read the first few pages. We listened in silence. 'But that's not a book,' someone said. So she chose another. This time it was a history, but I have forgotten the writer's name. Our trepidation increased as she went on. Not a word of it seemed to be true, and the style in which it was written was execrable.

'Poetry! Poetry!' we cried, impatiently. 'Read us poetry!' I cannot describe the desolation which fell upon us as she opened a little volume and mouthed out the verbose, sentimental foolery which it contained.

'It must have been written by a woman,' one of us urged. But no. She told us that it was written by a young man, one of the most famous poets of the day. I leave you to imagine what the shock of the discovery was. Though we all cried and begged her to read no more she persisted and read us extracts from the Lives of the Lord Chancellors. When she had finished, Jane, the eldest and wisest of us, rose to her feet and said that she for one was not convinced.

'Why,' she asked, 'if men write such rubbish as this, should our mothers have wasted their youth in bringing them into the world?'

We were all silent; and, in the silence, poor Poll could be heard sobbing out, 'Why, why did my father teach me to read?'

Clorinda was the first to come to her senses. 'It's all our fault,' she said. 'Every one of us knows how to read. But no one, save Poll, has ever taken the trouble to do it. I, for one, have taken it for granted that it was a woman's duty to spend her youth in bearing children. I venerated my mother for bearing ten; still more my grandmother for bearing fifteen; it was, I confess, my own ambition to bear twenty. We have gone on all these ages supposing that men were equally industrious, and that their works were of equal merit. While we have borne the children, they, we supposed, have borne the books and the pictures. We have populated the world. They have civilised it. But now that we can read, what prevents us from judging the results? Before we bring another child into the world we must swear that we will find out what the world is like.'

So we made ourselves into a society for asking questions. One of us was to visit a man-of-war; another was to hide herself in a scholar's study; another was to attend a meeting of business men; while all were to read books, look at pictures, go to concerts, keep our eyes open in the streets, and ask questions perpetually. We were very young. You can judge of our simplicity when I tell you that before parting that night we agreed that the objects of life were to produce good people and good books. Our questions were to be directed to find out how far these objects were now attained by men. We vowed solemnly that we would not bear a single child until we were satisfied.

Off we went then, some to the British Museum; others to the King's Navy; some to Oxford; others to Cambridge; we visited the Royal Academy and the Tate; heard modern music in concert rooms, went to the Law Courts, and saw new plays. No one dined out without asking her parents certain questions and carefully noting his replies. At intervals we met together and compared our observations. Oh, those were merry meetings! Never have I laughed so much as I did when Rose read her notes upon 'Honour' and described how she had dressed herself as an Aethiopian Prince and gone aboard one of His Majesty's ships. Discovering the hoax, the Captain visited her (now disguised as a private gentleman) and demanded that honour should be satisfied. 'But how?' she asked. 'How?' he bellowed. 'With the cane of course!' Seeing that he was beside himself with rage and expecting that her last moment had come, she bent over and received, to her amazement, six light taps upon the behind. 'The honour of the British Navy is avenged!' he cried, and, raising herself, she saw him with the sweat pouring down his face holding out a trembling right hand. 'Away!' she exclaimed, striking an attitude and imitating the ferocity of his own expression. 'My honour has still to be satisfied!' 'Spoken like a gentleman!' he returned, and fell into profound thought. 'If six

strokes avenge the honour of the King's Navy,' he mused, 'how
many avenge the honour of a private gentleman?' He said he
would prefer to lay the case before his brother officers. She replied
haughtily that she could not wait. He praised her sensibility. 'Let
me see,' he cried suddenly, 'did your father keep a carriage?' 'No,'
she said. 'Or a riding horse?' 'We had a donkey,' she bethought her,
'which drew the mowing machine.' At this his face lightened. 'My
mother's name–' she added. 'For God's sake, man, don't mention
your mother's name!' he shrieked, trembling like an aspen and
flushing to the roots of his hair, and it was ten minutes at least
before she could induce him to proceed. At length he decreed
that if she gave him four strokes and a half in the small of the
back at a spot indicated by himself (the half conceded, he said,
in recognition of the fact that her great-grandmother's uncle was
killed at Trafalgar) it was his opinion that her honour would be
as good as new. This was done; they retired to a restaurant; drank
two bottles of wine for which he insisted upon paying; and parted
with protestations of eternal friendship.

Then we had Fanny's account of her visit to the Law Courts.
At her first visit she had come to the conclusion that the Judges
were either made of wood or were impersonated by large animals
resembling man who had been trained to move with extreme
dignity, mumble and nod their heads. To test her theory she had
liberated a handkerchief of bluebottles at the critical moment of a
trial, but was unable to judge whether the creatures gave signs of
humanity for the buzzing of the files induced so sound a sleep that
she only woke in time to see the prisoners led into the cells below.
But from the evidence she brought we voted that it is unfair to
suppose that the Judges are men.

Helen went to the Royal Academy, but when asked to deliver
her report upon the pictures she began to recite from a pale blue
volume, 'O! for the touch of a vanished hand and the sound of a
voice that is still. Home is the hunter, home from the hill. He gave
his bridle reins a shake. Love is sweet, love is brief. Spring, the fair
spring, is the year's pleasant King. O! to be in England now that
April's there. Men must work and women must weep. The path
of duty is the way to glory –' We could listen to no more of this
gibberish.

'We want no more poetry!' we cried.

'Daughters of England!' she began, but here we pulled her down, a vase of water getting spilt over her in the scuffle.

'Thank God!' she exclaimed, shaking herself like a dog. 'Now I'll roll on the carpet and see if I can't brush off what remains of the Union Jack. Then perhaps –' here she rolled energetically. Getting up she began to explain to us what modern pictures are like when Castalia stopped her.

'What is the average size of a picture?' she asked. 'Perhaps two feet by two and a half,' she said. Castalia made notes while Helen spoke, and when she had done, and we were trying not to meet each other's eyes, rose and said, 'At your wish I spent last week at Oxbridge, disguised as a charwoman. I thus had access to the rooms of several Professors and will now attempt to give you some idea – only,' she broke off, 'I can't think how to do it. It's all so queer. These Professors,' she went on, 'live in large houses built round grass plots each in a kind of cell by himself. Yet they have every convenience and comfort. You have only to press a button or light a little lamp. Their papers are beautifully filed. Books abound. There are no children or animals, save half a dozen stray cats and one aged bullfinch – a cock. I remember,' she broke off, 'an Aunt of mine who lived at Dulwich and kept cactuses. You reached the conservatory through the double drawing-room, and there, on the hot pipes, were dozens of them, ugly, squat, bristly little plants each in a separate pot. Once in a hundred years the Aloe flowered, so my Aunt said. But she died before that happened –' We told her to keep to the point. 'Well,' she resumed, 'when Professor Hobkin was out I examined his life work, an edition of Sappho. It's a queer looking book, six or seven inches thick, not all by Sappho. Oh, no. Most of it is a defence of Sappho's chastity, which some German had denied, and I can assure you the passion with which these two gentlemen argued, the learning they displayed, the prodigious ingenuity with which they disputed the use of some implement which looked to me for all the world like a hairpin astounded me; especially when the door opened and Professor Hobkin himself appeared. A very nice, mild, old gentleman, but what could *he* know about chastity?' We misunderstood her.

'No, no,' she protested, 'he's the soul of honour I'm sure – not that he resembles Rose's sea captain in the least. I was thinking rather of my Aunt's cactuses. What could they know about chastity?'

Again we told her not to wander from the point, – did the Oxbridge professors help to produce good people and good books? – the objects of life.

'There!' she exclaimed. 'It never struck me to ask. It never occurred to me that they could possibly produce anything.'

'I believe,' said Sue, 'that you made some mistake. Probably Professor Hobkin was a gynaecologist. A scholar is a very different sort of man. A scholar is overflowing with humour and invention – perhaps addicted to wine, but what of that? – a delightful companion, generous, subtle, imaginative – as stands to reason. For he spends his life in company with the finest human beings that have ever existed.'

'Hum,' said Castalia. 'Perhaps I'd better go back and try again.'

Some three months later it happened that I was sitting alone when Castalia entered. I don't know what it was in the look of her that so moved me; but I could not restrain myself, and dashing across the room, I clasped her in my arms. Not only was she very beautiful; she seemed also in the highest spirits. 'How happy you look!' I exclaimed, as she sat down.

'I've been at Oxbridge,' she said.

'Asking questions?'

'Answering them,' she replied.

'You have not broken our vow?' I said anxiously, noticing something about her figure.

'Oh, the vow,' she said casually. 'I'm going to have a baby if that's what you mean. You can't imagine,' she burst out, 'how exciting, how beautiful, how satisfying –'

'What is?' I asked.

'To – to – answer questions,' she replied in some confusion. Whereupon she told me the whole of her story. But in the middle of an account which interested and excited me more than anything I had ever heard, she gave the strangest cry, half whoop, half holloa –

'Chastity! Chastity! Where's my chastity!' she cried. 'Help ho! The scent bottle!'

There was nothing in the room but a cruet containing mustard, which I was about to administer when she recovered her composure.

'You should have thought of that three months ago,' I said severely.

'True,' she replied. 'There's not much good in thinking of it now. It was unfortunate, by the way, that my mother had me called Castalia.'

'Oh, Castalia, your mother –' I was beginning when she reached for the mustard pot.

'No, no, no,' she said shaking her head. 'If you'd been a chaste woman yourself you would have screamed at the sight of me – instead of which you rushed across the room and took me in your arms. No, Cassandra. We are neither of us chaste.' So we went on talking.

Meanwhile the room was filling up, for it was the day appointed to discuss the results of our observations. Everyone, I thought, felt as I did about Castalia. They kissed her and said how glad they were to see her again. At length, when we were all assembled, Jane rose and said that it was time to begin. She began by saying that we had now asked questions for over five years, and that though the results were bound to be inconclusive – here Castalia nudged me and whispered that she was not so sure about that. Then she got up, and, interrupting Jane in the middle of a sentence, said:

'Before you say any more, I want to know – am I to stay in the room? Because,' she added, 'I have to confess that I am an impure woman.'

Everyone looked at her in astonishment.

'You are going to have a baby?' asked Jane.

She nodded her head.

It was extraordinary to see the different expressions on their faces. A sort of hum went through the room, in which I could catch the words 'impure', 'baby', 'Castalia', and so on. Jane, who was herself considerably moved, put it to us:

'Shall she go? Is she impure?'

Such a roar filled the room as might have been heard in the street outside.

'No! No! No! Let her stay! Impure? Fiddlesticks!' Yet I fancied that some of the youngest, girls of nineteen or twenty, held back as if overcome with shyness. Then we all came about her and began asking questions, and at last I saw one of the youngest, who had kept in the background, approach shyly and say to her:

'What is chastity then? I mean is it good, or is it bad, or is it nothing at all?' She replied so low that I could not catch what she said.

'You know I was shocked,' said another, 'for at least ten minutes.'

'In my opinion,' said Poll, who was growing crusty from always reading in the London Library, 'chastity is nothing but ignorance – a most discreditable state of mind. We should admit only the unchaste to our society. I vote that Castalia shall be our President.'

This was violently disputed.

'It is as unfair to brand women with chastity as with unchastity,' said Poll. 'Some of us haven't the opportunity either. Moreover, I don't believe Cassy herself maintains that she acted as she did from a pure love of knowledge.'

'He is only twenty-one and divinely beautiful,' said Cassy, with a ravishing gesture.

'I move,' said Helen, 'that no one be allowed to talk of chastity or unchastity save those who are in love.'

'Oh, bother,' said Judith, who had been enquiring into scientific matters, 'I'm not in love and I'm longing to explain my measures for dispensing with prostitutes and fertilising virgins by Act of Parliament.'

She went on to tell us of an invention of hers to be erected at Tube stations and other public resorts, which, upon payment of a small fee, would safeguard the nation's health, accommodate its sons, and relieve its daughters. Then she had contrived a method of preserving in sealed tubes the germs of future Lord Chancellors 'or poets or painters or musicians,' she went on, 'supposing, that is to say, that these breeds are not extinct, and that women still wish to bear children –'

'Of course we wish to bear children!' cried Castalia impatiently. Jane rapped the table.

'That is the very point we are met to consider,' she said. 'For five years we have been trying to find out whether we are justified in continuing the human race. Castalia has anticipated our decision. But it remains for the rest of us to make up our minds.'

Here one after another of our messengers rose and delivered their reports. The marvels of civilisation far exceeded our expectations, and as we learnt for the first time how man flies in the air, talks across space, penetrates to the heart of an atom, and embraces the universe in his speculations a murmur of admiration burst from our lips.

'We are proud,' we cried, 'that our mothers sacrificed their youth in such a cause as this!' Castalia, who had been listening intently, looked prouder than all the rest. Then Jane reminded us that we had still much to learn, and Castalia begged us to make haste. On we went through a vast tangle of statistics. We learnt that England has a population of so many millions, and that such and such a proportion of them is constantly hungry and in prison; that the average size of a working man's family is such, and that so great a percentage of women die from maladies incident to childbirth. Reports were read of visits to factories, shops, slums, and dockyards. Descriptions were given of the Stock Exchange, of a gigantic house of business in the City, and of a Government Office. The British Colonies were now discussed, and some account was given of our rule in India, Africa and Ireland. I was sitting by Castalia and I noticed her uneasiness.

'We shall never come to any conclusion at all at this rate,' she said. 'As it appears that civilisation is so much more complex than we had any notion, would it not be better to confine ourselves to our original enquiry? We agreed that it was the object of life to produce good people and good books. All this time we have been talking of aeroplanes, factories, and money. Let us talk about men themselves and their arts, for that is the heart of the matter.'

So the diners out stepped forward with long slips of paper containing answers to their questions. These had been framed after much consideration. A good man, we had agreed, must at any rate be honest, passionate, and unworldly. But whether or not a particular man possessed those qualities could only be discovered by asking questions, often beginning at a remote distance from the centre. Is Kensington a nice place to live in? Where is your son being educated – and your daughter? Now please tell me, what do you pay for your cigars? By the way, is Sir Joseph a baronet or only a knight? Often it seemed that we learnt more from trivial questions of this kind than from more direct ones. 'I accepted my peerage,' said Lord Bunkum, 'because my wife wished it.' I forget how many titles were accepted for the same reason. 'Working fifteen hours out of the twenty-four, as I do –' ten thousand professional men began.

'No, no, of course you can neither read nor write. But why do you work so hard?' 'My dear lady, with a growing family –' 'But *why* does your family grow?' Their wives wished that too, or perhaps it was the British Empire. But more significant than the answers were the refusals to answer. Very few would reply at all to questions about morality and religion, and such answers as were given were not serious. Questions as to the value of money and power were almost invariably brushed aside, or pressed at extreme risk to the asker. 'I'm sure,' said Jill, 'that if Sir Harley Tightboots hadn't been carving the mutton when I asked him about the capitalist system he would have cut my throat. The only reason why we escaped with our lives over and over again is that men are at once so hungry and so chivalrous. They despise us too much to mind what we say.'

'Of course they despise us,' said Eleanor. 'At the same time how do you account for this – I made enquiries among the artists. Now no woman has ever been an artist, has she, Poll?'

'Jane–Austen–Charlotte–Bronte–George–Eliot,' cried Poll, like a man crying muffins in a back street.

'Damn the woman!' someone exclaimed. 'What a bore she is!'

'Since Sappho there has been no female of first rate –' Eleanor began, quoting from a weekly newspaper.

'It's now well known that Sappho was the somewhat lewd invention of Professor Hobkin,' Ruth interrupted.

'Anyhow, there is no reason to suppose that any woman ever has been able to write or ever will be able to write,' Eleanor continued. 'And yet, whenever I go among authors they never cease to talk to me about their books. Masterly! I say, or Shakespeare himself! (for one must say something) and I assure you, they believe me.'

'That proves nothing,' said Jane. They all do it. 'Only,' she sighed, 'it doesn't seem to help *us* much. Perhaps we had better examine modern literature next. Liz, it's your turn.'

Elizabeth rose and said that in order to prosecute her enquiry she had dressed as a man and been taken for a reviewer.

'I have read new books pretty steadily for the past five years,' said she. 'Mr Wells is the most popular living writer; then comes

Mr Arnold Bennett; then Mr Compton Mackenzie; Mr McKenna and Mr Walpole may be bracketed together.' She sat down.

'But you've told us nothing!' we expostulated. 'Or do you mean that these gentlemen have greatly surpassed Jane–Eliot and that English fiction is – where's that review of yours? Oh, yes, "safe in their hands."'

'Safe, quite safe,' she said, shifting uneasily from foot to foot. 'And I'm sure that they give away even more than they receive.'

We were all sure of that. 'But,' we pressed her, 'do they write good books?'

'Good books?' she said, looking at the ceiling. 'You must remember,' she began, speaking with extreme rapidity, 'that fiction is the mirror of life. And you can't deny that education is of the highest importance, and that it would be extremely annoying, if you found yourself alone at Brighton late at night, not to know which was the best boarding house to stay at, and suppose it was a dripping Sunday evening – wouldn't it be nice to go to the Movies?'

'But what has that got to do with it?' we asked.

'Nothing – nothing – nothing whatever,' she replied.

'Well, tell us the truth,' we bade her.

'The truth? But isn't it wonderful,' she broke off – 'Mr Chitter has written a weekly article for the past thirty years, upon love or hot buttered toast and has sent all his sons to Eton –'

'The truth!' we demanded.

'Oh, the truth,' she stammered, 'the truth has nothing to do with literature,' and sitting down she refused to say another word.

It all seemed to us very inconclusive.

'Ladies, we must try to sum up the results,' Jane was beginning when a hum, which had been heard for some time through the open window, drowned her voice.

'War! War! War! Declaration of War!' men were shouting in the stteet below.

We looked at each other in horror.

'What war?' we cried. 'What war?' We remembered, too late, that we had never thought of sending anyone to the House of Commons. We had forgotten all about it. We turned to Poll, who had reached the history shelves in the London Library, and asked her to enlighten us.

'Why,' we cried, 'do men go to war?'

'Sometimes for one reason, sometimes for another,' she replied calmly. 'In 1760, for example –' The shouts outside drowned her words. 'Again in 1797 – in 1804 – It was the Austrians in 1866 – 1870 was the Franco-Prussian – In 1900 on the other hand –'

'But it's now 1914!' we cut her short.

'Ah, I don't know what they're going to war for now,' she admitted.

The war was over and peace was in process of being signed, when I once more found myself with Castalia in the room where our meetings used to be held. We began idly turning over the pages of our old minute books. 'Queer,' I mused, 'to see what we were thinking five years ago.' 'We are agreed,' Castalia quoted, reading over my shoulder, 'that it is the object of life to produce good people and good books.' We made no comment upon *that*. 'A good man is at any rate honest, passionate and unworldly.' 'What a woman's language!' I observed. 'Oh, dear,' cried Castalia, pushing the book away from her, 'what fools we were! It was all Poll's father's fault,' she went on. 'I believe he did it on purpose – that ridiculous will, I mean, forcing Poll to read all the books in the London Library. If we hadn't learnt to read,' she said bitterly, 'we might still have been bearing children in ignorance and that, I believe, was the happiest life after all. I know what you're going to say about war,' she checked me, 'and the horror of bearing children to see them killed, but our mothers did it, and their mothers, and their mothers before them. And *they* didn't complain. They couldn't read. I've done my best,' she sighed, 'to prevent my little girl from learning to read, but what's the use? I caught Ann only yesterday with a newspaper in her hand and she was beginning to ask me if it was "true". Next she'll ask me whether Mr Lloyd George is a good man, then whether Mr Arnold Bennett is a good novelist, and finally whether I believe in God. How can I bring my daughter up to believe in nothing?' she demanded.

'Surely you could teach her to believe that a man's intellect is, and always will be, fundamentally superior to a woman's?' I suggested. She brightened at this and began to turn over our old minutes again. 'Yes,' she said, 'think of their discoveries, their mathematics, their science, their philosophy, their scholarship –' and then she began to laugh, 'I shall never forget old Hobkin and the hairpin,' she said, and went on reading and laughing and I thought she was quite happy, when suddenly she threw the book from her and burst out, 'Oh, Cassandra, why do you torment me? Don't you know that our belief in man's intellect is the greatest fallacy of them all?' 'What?' I exclaimed. 'Ask any journalist, schoolmaster, politician or public house keeper in the land and they will all tell you that men are much cleverer than women.' 'As if I doubted it,' she said scornfully. 'How could they help it? Haven't we bred them and fed and kept them in comfort since the beginning of time so that they may be clever even if they're nothing else? It's all our doing!' she cried. 'We insisted upon having intellect and now we've got it. And it's intellect,' she continued, 'that's at the bottom of it. What could be more charming than a boy before he has begun to cultivate his intellect? He is beautiful to look at; he gives himself no airs; he understands the meaning of art and literature instinctively; he goes about enjoying his life and making other people enjoy theirs. Then they teach him to cultivate his intellect. He becomes a barrister, a civil servant, a general, an author, a professor. Every day he goes to an office. Every year he produces a book. He maintains a whole family by the products of his brain – poor devil! Soon he cannot come into a room without making us all feel uncomfortable; he condescends to every woman he meets, and dares not tell the truth even to his own wife; instead of rejoicing our eyes we have to shut them if we are to take him in our arms. True, they console themselves with stars of all shapes, ribbons of all shades, and incomes of all sizes – but what is to console us? That we shall be able in ten years' time to spend a weekend at Lahore? Or that the least insect in Japan has a name twice the length of its body? Oh, Cassandra, for Heaven's sake let us devise a method by which men may bear children! It is our only chance. For unless we provide them with some innocent occupation we shall get neither good people nor good books; we shall perish beneath the fruits of their unbridled activity; and not a human being will survive to know that there once was Shakespeare!'

'It is too late,' I replied. 'We cannot provide even for the children that we have.'

'And then you ask me to believe in intellect,' she said.

While we spoke, men were crying hoarsely and wearily in the street, and, listening, we heard that the Treaty of Peace had just been signed. The voices died away. The rain was falling and interfered no doubt with the proper explosion of the fireworks.

'My cook will have bought the *Evening News*,' said Castalia, 'and Ann will be spelling it out over her tea. I must go home.'

'It's no good – not a bit of good,' I said. 'Once she knows how to read there's only one thing you can teach her to believe in – and that is herself.'

'Well, that would be a change,' said Castalia.

So we swept up the papers of our Society, and though Ann was playing with her doll very happily, we solemnly made her a present of the lot and told her we had chosen her to be President of the Society of the future – upon which she burst into tears, poor little girl.

GENEROUS PIECES

Ellen Gilchrist

> Ellen Gilchrist (b. 1935) is an American author and poet who studied creative writing under Eudora Welty. Her 1981 collection of stories, *In the Land of Dreamy Dreams*, received immense critical acclaim and, in 1984, she won the National Book Award for her collection of stories, *Victory Over Japan*.

I am poking around the house looking for change to spend at the Sweet Shoppe. It is afternoon, November. The light coming through the windows of my parents' room is flat and gray and casts thick shadows on the rug my father brought home from China after the war.

I am going through the pockets of his gabardine topcoat. The pockets are deep and cool. The rubbers are in the right-hand pocket. I pull them out, look at them for a moment, then stick my hand back in the pocket and leave it there. I stand like that for a long time, halfway into the closet with my hand deep in the pocket, listening to the blood run through my body, to the sound of my own breathing.

I smell the cold safety of his suits and shirts. I stare down at the comforting order of his shoes and boots. I hold one of the little packets between my fingers, feeling the hard rim, the soft yielding center. It gives way, like the hide of a mouse.

Behind me is the walnut bed in which he was born far away in Georgia. Beside it, the old-fashioned dresser with a silver tray onto which he empties his pockets in the evenings. While he dreams the tray holds his daytime life, his plumb bob, his pocketknife, his pens and pencils, his onyx Kappa Sigma ring, his loose change, his money clip.

How do I know what the rubbers are? How do I know with such absolute certainty that they are connected with Christina Carver's mother and the pall that has fallen over our house on Calvin Boulevard?

I stand in the closet door for a long time. I want to take out the little package and inspect it more closely, but I cannot bring myself to withdraw it from the pocket, as if to pull it out into the light would make it real. After a while I become afraid my mother will come home and find me in her room so I take my hand from the pocket and leave.

I wander into the kitchen and make a sugar sandwich and talk for a while to the elderly German housekeeper. She is a kindly woman with a thick accent who smiles all the time. She has a small grandson who is deaf, and occasionally she brings him to work and talks with him in the language deaf people make with their hands. I feel sorry for her because of the deaf child and try to remember to pick up my clothes so she won't have to bend over to reach them. When I am good about this she bakes me gingerbread men with buttons and smiles made out of raisins.

I leave the house and begin walking aimlessly across the small Indiana town. Usually I go by Christina's after school. We are best friends. We spend the night together on weekends. We stand by each other in lines. I work hard to make Christina my friend. I need her for an ally as we have only lived in this town six months and she is the most popular girl in the class.

We have lived in five towns in three years. Every time we move my father makes more money. Every place we live we have a nicer house. This time we are not going to move anymore he promises. This time we are going to stay put.

I want to stay put. When the junior-high cheerleader elections are held in the spring the girls will try out in pairs. If I try out with Christina I know I will win.

My mother was a cheerleader at the University of Georgia. Her senior year in college she was voted Most Popular Girl. There is a full-page photograph of her in the 1929 University of Georgia yearbook. She is wearing a handmade lace dress the color of snow, the color of marble. Her face is small and sweet and full of sadness. Underneath her feet in black letters it says, *Most Popular Girl.*

I will never be popular. But at least I can get elected cheerleader. I do Christina's homework. I write her book reports. I carry messages to her secret boyfriend. He is a college boy named Dawson who plays the saxophone and is dying of cancer in an apartment behind his Jewish grandmothers mansion. I carry their messages. I stand guard when she goes to visit him. I listen to her love stories. They lie down together on a bed with their clothes on and strange things happen. One thing they do is called dryfucking. I don't really understand what it is but I feel funny and excited when she talks about it.

Once I went with her to Dawson's apartment, some rooms above a brick garage of the only mansion in Seymour, Indiana. There were phonograph albums and cartoons nailed to the walls. Dawson was very nice to me. He kept making me listen to something called *Jazz at the Philharmonic*. I pretended to like it. I pretended to like the worst part of all when someone named Jojo plays the drums for about fifteen minutes.

I pass the grade school and turn onto Duncan Street where Christina has lived every day of her life. Next door to her house is a vacant lot. A bicycle I used to own is rusting in a corner of the lot. It has a flat tire but I have never bothered walking it to the service station to get it fixed. I have a new bicycle with shiny fenders. Christina's mother always teases me about the old bike. "It must be nice to be rich," she says, laughing.

She thinks it is funny that no one makes me do anything about it. Christina has to do all kinds of things my mother would never dream of making me do. She has to help with the dishes and iron her own clothes and practice the piano for an hour every day and go horseback riding on Saturday.

When I get to Christina's house she is in the dining room with her mother looking at the fabrics they have spread out all over the dining room table. They have been to a sale and the dining room table is covered with bright plaid wools and gold and blue corduroy and a heavy quilted cotton with little flowers on a green background.

"Here's Margaret now," her mother says, smiling at me, moving closer, her small, brisk body making me feel heavy and awkward and surprised. "Margaret, look at these bargains we got at Hazard's. We're going to make skirts and weskits. Look, we bought something for you. So you and Christina can have twin outfits." She holds up the quilted fabric. "Isn't it darling? Isn't it the darlingest thing you've ever seen?"

She is always so gay, so full of plans. I think of her getting into the Packard with my father the night they went off to Benton to the ballgame, the night my mother wouldn't go. Christina's father was out of town and I stood on the porch watching my father put her into his big car. My mother stood in the dark doorway not saying a word and later she went into the bedroom and locked the door. My mother has not been well lately. She is worn out. She has hot flashes. She takes hormones and writes long letters to Mississippi and is always mad at me.

"Do you like it?" Christina's mother says, holding the fabric against her body as if she were a model.

"Oh, my," I say, taking the material. "I love it. It's darling. Is it really for me?"

"Look," Christina says, "the one with the green background is for you, to go with your red hair. We got the same print with a blue background for me. Won't we look great together? You aren't supposed to mix blue and green together but who cares. We can wear them to the Christmas Follies if we get them made in time."

"You're going to *make* it tor me?" I say.

"Of course we are," her mother says. "I'll get started on it tomorrow morning. I can't wait to see how cute you'll look together. Besides I need to do something to pay your father back for all the help he's been to us with our taxes. I'll have to measure you first, though. Can I do it now?"

"I can't stay that long today," I say quickly, not wanting her to know how big my waist is. It is twenty-six. I will never be a belle. "I'll come back tomorrow and let you do it, if that's O.K."

"Whenever you have time," she says. "I can go on and start on Christina's."

Christina walks me out into the yard. "She's going to a horse show on Saturday," she says. "Do you want to go with me to see Dawson?"

"Sure," I say.

"I don't know what I'd do without you," Christina says. "I don't know what I did before you moved here. Dawson says you're darling. He thinks you're smart as a whip. He wants you to come back over. He wants you to meet a friend of his from college."

"I'll see you tomorrow then," I say. "I'll come by in the morning. And thanks a lot about the skirt. That's really nice of your mother."

I walk off down Duncan Street for a few blocks, then change my mind about going home. I decide to walk out toward the railroad tracks and get some exercise to make myself smaller before I get measured.

It will be light for another hour. I think about going by Janet Ingram's house to see what she is doing. Janet lives on the edge of town in a house that is very different from the ones Christina and I live in. There are stained red carpets on the floors and over the mantel is a collection of china bulls her father wins at carnivals. I know I am not supposed to go there although my mother has never actually told me so.

Janet's father sleeps in the daytime and works at night in a factory. Once I was there in the afternoon and he was just getting up, walking around the house in a sleeveless T-shirt. I walk along, thinking about the way Janet's house smells, warm and close and foreign, as though the air were full of germs.

I try not to think about Christina's mother. If I think of her I remember how she leans over my father's chair handing him things when they have dinner at our house. I think of him putting her into his car. Then I think of the beautiful quilted material. I think of Christina and me walking into the junior high together, wearing our matching outfits.

I am walking along a new street where houses are under construction. Two men are still hammering on the high beams of one. They are standing on the slanting half-finished roof. I am afraid they will fall while I am watching them and I turn my face away. It is terrible for people to have dangerous jobs like that. I'm glad my father doesn't have a dangerous job. People who are poor have to have jobs like that. Perhaps it doesn't matter as much what happens to them.

Janet comes to the door. Her father is in the living room putting on his shoes. "I can't ask you to stay," she says. "My dad's getting ready to leave for work and I have to help with dinner."

"That's all right," I say. "I was just walking around. I just came by to see what you were doing."

I am staring at Janet's breasts, which are even larger than mine. I wonder if it is true that Janet lets boys touch her breasts.

I begin walking home. Dark is falling faster than I expected. The days grow shorter. It is almost Thanksgiving.

A group of children playing in a yard begins following me. One of them recognizes me from school. He picks up a dirt clod and throws it at me. It hits my coat. I don't know what to do. No one has ever thrown anything at me before. I look up. Another dirt clod hits me on the shoulder. I begin to run, trying to figure out what is going on. I run through the darkening streets as fast as I can. Streetlights flicker and come on. Here and there a yellow porch light shines brightly. I run and run, afraid of falling down, afraid of every shadow, afraid to look up, afraid of the trees, afraid of the moon.

Now it is full dark. How did it get dark so quickly? I fear the dark. I never sleep without a light in my room. If I wake in the night in the dark I am terrified and jump out of bed and run down to my parents' room and tremble between them until morning.

The night is so still I can hear the branches of the trees reaching out their arms for me. A huge moon has appeared in the eastern sky. I run past the construction site. The exposed beams stand out against the dark blue sky. I think if I looked inside I would find the bodies of the carpenters broken and bleeding on the floor.

I run past an alley where I found an automatic card shuffler in a trashcan once when my grandmother was visiting us. When I brought it home she flew into hysterics and bathed me with lye soap, lecturing me about diseases I could catch from strangers.

Now I am on my own street. I run past the Dustins' house. I run into my house and down the hall and turn around and around and run into the kitchen and find my father sitting at the table with my brother. They are laughing and cutting fat green olives into generous pieces.

I throw myself upon him screaming, "Look what they did to me! Look what they did to me! Look what they did!"

He takes me into the bedroom and sits on the bed with me. He holds me in his arms. My face is against his shirt. I burrow into the strength of his body. Once I look up and there are tears running down his cheeks.

My mother is touching my hair. "It's from living like this," she says. "This insane life in this hick Yankee town. I don't know who she's with half the time. God knows who she plays with. God knows what she's doing."

"What do you want me to do?" he says. "Go home and starve in Waycross? Run a hardware store the rest of my life?"

"I don't know," she says. "I don't know what I want you to do."

After a while my mother undresses me and puts me in bed in her soft flowered nightgown. She brings me a hot toddy and feeds it to me with a spoon. The hot liquor runs down my throat and soothes me. My mother promises to stay with me till I sleep. She turns off the lamp. She sits touching my arm with her soft hands. And the terror draws in its white arms and is still, watching me with cold eyes from the mirror on my father's dresser.

THE WALTZ

Dorothy Parker

Dorothy Parker (1893–1967) was an American critic, satirical poet, and short story writer. Best known for her wit and eye for 20th-century foibles, Parker wrote book reviews, poetry and short fiction for the fledgling magazine the *New Yorker*. She wrote the screenplay for the Hitchcock film *Saboteur*, but her involvement with Communism led to her being blacklisted in Hollywood.

Why, *thank you so much. I'd adore to.*

I don't want to dance with him. I don't want to dance with anybody. And even if I did, it wouldn't be him. He'd be well down among the last ten. I've seen the way he dances; it looks like something you do on Saint Walpurgis Night. Just think, not a quarter of an hour ago, here I was sitting, feeling so sorry for the poor girl he was dancing with. And now *I'm* going to be the poor girl. Well, well. Isn't it a small world?

And a peach of a world, too. A true little corker. Its events are so fascinatingly unpredictable, are not they? Here I was, minding my own business, not doing a stitch of harm to any living soul. And then he comes into my life, all smiles and city manners, to sue me for the favor of one memorable mazurka. Why, he scarcely knows my name, let alone what it stands for. It stands for Despair, Bewilderment, Futility, Degradation, and Premeditated Murder, but little does he wot. I don't wot his name, either; I haven't any idea what it is. Jukes, would be my guess from the look in his eyes. How do you do, Mr. Jukes? And how is that dear little brother of yours, with the two heads?

Ah, now why did he have to come around me, with his low requests? Why can't he let me lead my own life? I ask so little – just to be left alone in my quiet corner of the table, to do my evening brooding over all my sorrows. And he must come, with his bows and his scrapes and his may-I-have-this-ones. And I had to go and tell him that I'd adore to dance with him. I cannot understand why I wasn't struck right down dead. Yes, and being struck dead would look like a day in the country, compared to struggling out a dance with this boy. But what could I do? Everyone else at the table had got up to dance, except him and me. There was I, trapped. Trapped like a trap in a trap.

What can you say, when a man asks you to dance with him? I most certainly will *not* dance with you, I'll see you in hell first. Why, thank you, I'd like to awfully, but I'm having labor pains. Oh, yes, *do* let's dance together – it's so nice to meet a man who isn't a scaredy-cat about catching my beri-beri. No. There was nothing for me to do, but say I'd adore to. Well, we might as well get it over with. All right, Cannonball, let's run out on the field. You won the toss; you can lead.

Why, I think it's more of a waltz, really. Isn't it? We might just listen to the music a second. Shall we? Oh, yes, it's a waltz. Mind? Why, I'm simply thrilled. I'd love to waltz with you.

I'd love to waltz with you. I'd love to waltz with you, I'd love to have my tonsils out, I'd love to be in a midnight fire at sea. Well, it's too late now. We're getting under way. *Oh.* Oh, dear. Oh, dear, dear, dear. Oh, this is even worse than I thought it would be. I suppose that's the one dependable law of life – everything is always worse than you thought it was going to be. Oh, if I had any real grasp of what this dance would be like, I'd have held out for sitting it out. Well, it will probably amount to the same thing in the end. We'll be sitting it out on the floor in a minute, if he keeps this up.

I'm so glad I brought it to his attention that this is a waltz they're playing. Heaven knows what might have happened, if he had thought it was something fast; we'd have blown the sides right out of the building. Why does he always want to be somewhere that he isn't? Why can't we stay in one place just long enough to get acclimated? It's this constant rush, rush, rush, that's the curse of American life. That's the reason that we're all of us so – *Ow!* For God's sake, don't *kick*, you idiot; this is only second down. Oh, my shin. My poor, poor shin, that I've had ever since I was a little girl!

Oh, no, no, no. Goodness, no. It didn't hurt the least little bit. And anyway it was my fault. Really it was. Truly. Well, you're just being sweet, to say that. It really was all my fault.

I wonder what I'd better do – kill him this instant with my naked hands, or wait and let him drop in his traces. Maybe it's best not to make a scene. I guess I'll just lie low, and watch the pace get him. He can't keep this up indefinitely – he's only flesh and blood. Die he must, and die he shall, for what he did to me. I don't want to be of the over-sensitive type, but you can't tell me that kick was unpremeditated. Freud says there are no accidents. I've led no cloistered life, I've known dancing partners who have spoiled my slippers and torn my dress; but when it comes to kicking, I am Outraged Womanhood. When you kick me in the shin, *smile*.

Maybe he didn't do it maliciously. Maybe it's just his way of showing his high spirits. I suppose I ought to be glad that one of us is having such a good time. I suppose I ought to think myself lucky if he brings me back alive. Maybe it's captious to demand of a practically strange man that he leave your shins as he found them. After all, the poor boy's doing the best he can. Probably he grew up in the hill country, and never had no larnin'. I bet they had to throw him on his back to get shoes on him.

Yes it's lovely, isn't it? It's simply lovely. It's the loveliest waltz. Isn't it? Oh, I think it's lovely too.

Why, I'm getting positively drawn to the Triple Threat here. He's my hero. He has the heart of a lion, and the sinews of a buffalo. Look at him – never a thought of the consequences, never afraid of his face, hurling himself into every scrimmage, eyes shining, cheeks ablaze. And shall it be said that I hung back? No, a thousand times no. What's it to me if I have to spend the next couple of years in a plaster cast? Come on, Butch, right through them! Who wants to live forever?

Oh. Oh, dear. Oh, he's all right, thank goodness. For a while I thought they'd have to carry him off the field. Ah, I couldn't bear to have anything happen to him. I love him. I love him better than anybody in the world. Look at the spirit he gets into a dreary, commonplace waltz; how effete the other dancers seem, beside him. He is youth and vigor and courage, he is strength and gaiety and – *Ow!* Get off my instep, you hulking peasant! What do you think I am, anyway – a gangplank? *Ow!*

No, of course it didn't hurt. Why, it didn't a bit. Honestly. And it was all my fault. You see, that little step of yours – well, it's perfectly lovely, but it's just a tiny bit tricky to follow at first. Oh, did you work it up yourself? You really did? Well, aren't you amazing! Oh, now I think I've got it. Oh, I think it's lovely. I was watching you do it when you were dancing before. It's awfully effective when you look at it.

It's awfully effective when you look at it. I bet I'm awfully effective when you look at me. My hair is hanging along my cheeks, my skirt is swaddling about me. I can feel the cold damp of my brow. I must look like something out of "The Fall of the House of Usher." This sort of thing takes a fearful toll of a woman my age. And he worked up his little step himself, he with his degenerate cunning. And it was just a tiny bit tricky at first, but now I think I've got it. Two stumbles, slip, and a twenty-yard dash; yes. I've got it. I've got several other things, too, including a split shin and a bitter heart. I hate this creature I'm chained to. I hated him the moment I saw his leering, bestial face. And here I've been locked in his noxious embrace for the thirty-five years this waltz has lasted. Is that orchestra never going to stop playing? Or must this obscene travesty of a dance go on until hell burns out?

Oh, they're going to play another encore. Oh, goody. Oh, that's lovely. Tired? I should say I'm not tired. I'd like to go on like this forever.

I should say I'm not tired. I'm dead, that's all I am. Dead, and in what a cause! And the music is never going to stop playing, and we're going on like this, Double Time Charlie and I, throughout eternity. I suppose I won't care any more, after the first hundred thousand years. I suppose nothing will matter then, not heat nor pain nor broken heart nor cruel, aching weariness. Well. It can't come too soon for me.

I wonder why I didn't tell him I was tired. I wonder why I didn't suggest going back to the table. I could have said let's just listen to the music. Yes, and if he would, that would be the first bit of attention he has given it all evening. George Jean Nathan said that the lovely rhythms of the waltz should be listened to in stillness and not be accompanied by strange gyrations of the human bo￼ I think that's what he said. I think it was George Jean N￼ Anyhow, whatever he said and whoever he was and whate￼ doing now, he's better off than I am. That's safe. Anyb￼

isn't waltzing with this Mrs. O'Leary's cow I've got here is having a good time.

Still if we were back at the table, I'd probably have to talk to him. Look at him – what could you say to a thing like that! Did you go to the circus this year, what's your favorite kind of ice cream, how do you spell cat? I guess I'm as well off here. As well off as if I were in a cement mixer in full action.

I'm past all feeling now. The only way I can tell when he steps on me is that I can hear the splintering of bones. And all the events of my life are passing before my eyes. There was the time I was in a hurricane in the West Indies, there was the day I got my head cut open in the taxi smash, there was the night the drunken lady threw a bronze ash-tray at her own true love and got me instead, there was that summer that the sailboat kept capsizing. Ah, what an easy, peaceful time was mine, until I fell in with Swifty, here. I didn't know what trouble was, before I got drawn into this *danse macabre*. I think my mind is beginning to wander. It almost seems to me as if the orchestra were stopping. It couldn't be, of course; it could never, never be. And yet in my ears there is a silence like the sound of angel voices …

Oh they've stopped, the mean things. They're not going to play any more. Oh, darn. Oh, do you think they would? Do you really think so, if you gave them twenty dollars? Oh, that would be lovely. And look, do tell them to play this same thing. I'd simply adore to go on waltzing.

THROUGH THE TUNNEL

Doris Lessing

Doris Lessing (b. 1919) is a British novelist, poet, playwright, biographer and short story writer. In 2001, Lessing was awarded the David Cohen Prize for a lifetime's achievement in British Literature and she was ranked fifth on *The Times* list of the '50 Greatest British Writers Since 1945'. Lessing was awarded the 2007 Nobel Prize in Literature.

Going to the shore on the first morning of the vacation, the young English boy stopped at a turning of the path and looked down at a wild and rocky bay, and then over to the crowded beach he knew so well from other years. His mother walked on in front of him, carrying a bright striped bag in one hand. Her other arm, swinging loose, was very white in the sun. The boy watched that white naked arm, and turned his eyes, which had a frown behind them, towards the bay and back again to his mother. When she felt he was not with her, she swung around. "Oh, there you are, Jerry!" she said. She looked impatient, then smiled. "Why, darling, would you rather not come with me? Would you rather—" She frowned, conscientiously worrying over what amusements he might secretly be longing for, which she had been too busy or too careless to imagine. He was very familiar with that anxious, apologetic smile. Contrition sent him running after her. And yet, as he ran, he looked back over his shoulder at the wild bay; and all morning, as he played on the safe beach, he was thinking of it.

Next morning, when it was time for the routine of swimming and sunbathing, his mother said, "Are you tired of the usual beach, Jerry? Would you like to go somewhere else?"

"Oh, no!" he said quickly, smiling at her out of that unfailing impulse of contrition – a sort of chivalry. Yet, walking down the path with her, he blurted out, "I'd like to go and have a look at those rocks down there."

She gave the idea her attention. It was a wild-looking place, and there was no one there; but she said, "Of course, Jerry, When you've had enough, come to the big beach. Or just go straight back to the villa, if you like." She walked away, that bare arm, now slightly reddened from yesterday's sun, swinging. And he almost ran after her again, feeling it unbearable that she should go by herself, but he did not.

She was thinking, Of course he's old enough to be safe without me. Have I been keeping him too close? He mustn't feel he ought to be with me. I must be careful.

He was an only child, eleven years old. She was a widow. She was determined to be neither possessive nor lacking in devotion. She went worrying off to her beach.

As for Jerry, once he saw that his mother had gained her beach, he began the steep descent to the bay. From where he was, high up among red-brown rocks, it was a scoop of moving blueish green fringed with white. As he went lower, he saw that it spread among small promontories and inlets of rough, sharp rock, and the crisping, lapping surface showed stains of purple and darker blue. Finally, as he ran sliding and scraping down the last few yards, he saw an edge of white surf and the shallow, luminous movement of water over white sand, and, beyond that, a solid, heavy blue.

He ran straight into the water and began swimming. He was a good swimmer. He went out fast over the gleaming sand, over a middle region where rocks lay like discoloured monsters under the surface, and then he was in the real sea – a warm sea where irregular cold currents from the deep water shocked his limbs.

When he was so far out that he could look back not only on the little bay but past the promontory that was between it and the big beach, he floated on the buoyant surface and looked for his mother. There she was, a speck of yellow under an umbrella that looked like a slice of orange peel. He swam back to shore, relieved at being sure she was there, but all at once very lonely.

On the edge of a small cape that marked the side of the bay away from the promontory was a loose scatter of rocks. Above them, some boys were stripping off their clothes. They came running, naked, down to the rocks. The English boy swam towards them, but kept his distance at a stone's throw. They were of that coast; all of them were burned smooth dark brown and speaking a language he did not understand. To be with them, of them, was a craving that filled his whole body. He swam a little closer; they turned and watched him with narrowed, alert dark eyes. Then one smiled and waved. It was enough. In a minute, he had swum in and was on the rocks beside them, smiling with a desperate, nervous supplication. They shouted cheerful greetings at him; and then, as he preserved his nervous, uncomprehending smile, they understood that he was a foreigner strayed from his own beach, and they proceeded to forget him. But he was happy. He was with them.

They began diving again and again from a high point into a well of blue sea between rough, pointed rocks. After they had dived and come up, they swam around, hauled themselves up, and waited their turn to dive again. They were big boys – men, to Jerry. He dived, and they watched him; and when he swam around to take his place, they made way for him. He felt he was accepted and he dived again, carefully, proud of himself.

Soon the biggest of the boys poised himself, shot down into the water, and did not come up. The others stood about, watching. Jerry, after waiting for the sleek brown head to appear, let out a yell of warning; they looked at him idly and turned their eyes back towards the water. After a long time, the boy came up on the other side of a big dark rock, letting the air out of his lungs in a sputtering gasp and a shout of triumph. Immediately the rest of them dived in. One moment, the morning seemed full of chattering boys; the next, the air and the surface of the water were empty. But through the heavy blue, dark shapes could be seen moving and groping.

Jerry dived, shot past the school of underwater swimmers, saw a black wall of rock looming at him, touched it, and bobbed up at once to the surface, where the wall was a low barrier he could see across. There was no one visible; under him, in the water, the dim shapes of the swimmers had disappeared. Then one, and then another of the boys came up on the far side of the barrier of rock, and he understood that they had swum through some gap or hole in it. He plunged down again. He could see nothing through the stinging salt water but the blank rock. When he came up the boys were all on the diving rock, preparing to attempt the feat again. And now, in a panic of failure, he yelled up, in English, "Look at me! Look!" and he began splashing and kicking in the water like a foolish dog.

They looked down gravely, frowning. He knew the frown. At moments of failure, when he clowned to claim his mother's attention, it was with just this grave, embarrassed inspection that she rewarded him. Through his hot shame, feeling the pleading grin on his face like a scar that he could never remove, he looked up at the group of big brown boys on the rock and shouted, *"Bonjour! Merci! Au revoir! Monsieur, monsieur!"* while he hooked his fingers round his ears and waggled them.

Water surged into his mouth; he choked, sank, came up. The rock, lately weighted with boys, seemed to rear up out of the water as their weight was removed. They were flying down past him now, into the water; the air was full of falling bodies. Then the rock was empty in the hot sunlight. He counted one, two, three ...

At fifty, he was terrified. They must all be drowning beneath him, in the watery caves of the rock! At a hundred, he stared around him at the empty hillside, wondering if he should yell for help. He counted faster, faster, to hurry them up, to bring them to the surface quickly, to drown them quickly – anything rather than the terror of counting on and on into the blue emptiness of the morning. And then, at a hundred and sixty, the water beyond the rock was full of boys blowing like brown whales. They swam back to the shore without a look at him.

He climbed back to the diving rock and sat down, feeling the hot roughness of it under his thighs. The boys were gathering up their bits of clothing and running off along the shore to another promontory. They were leaving to get away from him. He cried openly, fists in his eyes. There was no one to see him, and he cried himself out.

It seemed to him that a long time had passed, and he swam out to where he could see his mother. Yes, she was still there, a yellow spot under an orange umbrella. He swam back to the big rock, climbed up, and dived into the blue pool among the fanged and angry boulders. Down he went, until he touched the wall of rock again. But the salt was so painful in his eyes that he could not see.

He came to the surface, swam to shore and went back to the villa to wait for his mother. Soon she walked slowly up the path, swinging her striped bag, the flushed, naked arm dangling beside her. "I want some swimming goggles," he panted, defiant and beseeching.

She gave him a patient, inquisitive look as she said casually, "Well, of course, darling."

But now, now, now! He must have them this minute, and no other time. He nagged and pestered until she went with him to a shop. As soon as she had bought the goggles, he grabbed them from her hand as if she were going to claim them for herself, and was off, running down the steep path to the bay.

Jerry swam out to the big barrier rock, adjusted the goggles, and dived. The impact of the water broke the rubber-enclosed vacuum, and the goggles came loose. He understood that he must swim down to the base of the rock from the surface of the water. He fixed the goggles tight and firm, filled his lungs, and floated, face down, on the water. Now he could see. It was as if he had eyes of a different kind – fish eyes that showed everything clear and delicate and wavering in the bright water.

Under him, six or seven feet down, was a floor of perfectly clean, shining white sand, rippled firm and hard by the tides. Two greyish shapes steered there, like long, rounded pieces of wood or slate. They were fish. He saw them nose towards each other, poise motionless, make a dart forward, swerve off, and come around again. It was like a water dance. A few inches above them the water sparkled as if sequins were dropping through it. Fish again – myriads of minute fish, the length of his fingernail – were drifting through the water, and in a moment he could feel the innumerable tiny touches of them against his limbs. It was like swimming in flaked silver. The great rock the big boys had swum through rose sheer out of the white sand – black, tufted lightly with greenish weed. He could see no gap in it. He swam down to its base.

Again and again he rose, took a big chestful of air, and went down. Again and again he groped over the surface of the rock, feeling it, almost hugging it in the desperate need to find the entrance. And then, once, while he was clinging to the black wall, his knees came up and he shot his feet out forward and they met no obstacle. He had found the hole.

He gained the surface, clambered about the stones that littered the barrier rock until he found a big one, and, with this in his arms, let himself down over the side of the rock. He dropped, with the weight, straight to the sandy floor. Clinging tight to the anchor of stone, he lay on his side and looked in under the dark shelf at the place where his feet had gone. He could see the hole. It was an irregular, dark gap; but he could not see deep into it. He let go of his anchor, clung with his hands to the edges of the hole, and tried to push himself in.

He got his head in, found his shoulders jammed, moved them in sidewise, and was inside as far as his waist. He could see nothing ahead. Something soft and clammy touched his mouth; he saw a dark frond moving against the greyish rock, and panic filled him. He thought of octopuses, of clinging weed. He pushed himself out backward and caught a glimpse, as he retreated, of a harmless tentacle of seaweed drifting in the mouth of the tunnel. But it was enough. He reached the sunlight, swam to shore, and lay on the diving rock. He looked down into the blue well of water. He knew he must find his way through that cave, or hole, or tunnel, and out the other side.

First, he thought, he must learn to control his breathing. He let himself down into the water with another big stone in his arms, so that he could lie effortlessly on the bottom of the sea. He counted. One, two, three. He counted steadily. He could hear the movement of blood in his chest. Fifty-one, fifty-two … His chest was hurting. He let go of the rock and went up into the air. He saw that the sun was low. He rushed to the villa and found his mother at her supper. She said only "Did you enjoy yourself?" and he said "Yes."

All night the boy dreamed of the water-filled cave in the rock, and as soon as breakfast was over he went to the bay.

That night, his nose bled badly. For hours he had been underwater, learning to hold his breath, and now he felt weak and dizzy. His mother said, "I shouldn't overdo things, darling, if I were you."

That day and the next, Jerry exercised his lungs as if everything, the whole of his life, all that he would become, depended upon it. Again his nose bled at night, and his mother insisted on his coming with her the next day. It was a torment to him to waste a day of his careful self-training, but he stayed with her on that other beach, which now seemed a place for small children, a place where his mother might lie safe in the sun. It was not his beach.

He did not ask for permission, on the following day, to go to his beach. He went, before his mother could consider the complicated rights and wrongs of the matter. A day's rest, he discovered, had improved his count by ten. The big boys had made the passage while he counted a hundred and sixty. He had been counting fast, in his fright. Probably now, if he tried, he could get through that long tunnel, but he was not going to try yet. A curious, most unchildlike persistence, a controlled impatience, made him wait. In the meantime, he lay underwater on the white sand, littered now by stones he had brought down from the upper air, and studied the entrance to the tunnel. He knew every jut and corner of it, as far as it was possible to see. It was as if he already felt its sharpness about his shoulders.

He sat by the clock in the villa, when his mother was not near, and checked his time. He was incredulous and then proud to find he could hold his breath without strain for two minutes. The words "two minutes," authorised by the clock, brought close the adventure that was so necessary to him.

In another four days, his mother said casually one morning, they must go home. On the day before they left, he would do it. He would do it if it killed him, he said defiantly to himself. But two days before they were to leave – a day of triumph when he increased his count by fifteen – his nose bled so badly that he turned dizzy and had to lie limply over the big rock like a bit of seaweed, watching the thick red blood flow on to the rock and trickle slowly down to the sea. He was frightened. Supposing he turned dizzy in the tunnel? Supposing he died there, trapped? Supposing – his head went around, in the hot sun, and he almost gave up. He thought he would return to the house and lie down, and next summer, perhaps, when he had another year's growth in him – *then* he would go through the hole.

But even after he had made the decision, or thought he had, he found himself sitting up on the rock and looking down into the water; and he knew that now, this moment, when his nose had only just stopped bleeding, when his head was still sore and throbbing – this was the moment when he would try. If he did not do it now, he never would. He was trembling with fear that he would not go; and he was trembling with horror at the long, long tunnel under the rock, under the sea. Even in the open sunlight, the barrier rock seemed very wide and very heavy; tons of rock pressed down on where he would go. If he died there, he would lie until one day – perhaps not before next year – those big boys would swim into it and find it blocked.

He put on his goggles, fitted them tight, tested the vacuum. His hands were shaking. Then he chose the biggest stone he could carry and slipped over the edge of the rock until half of him was in the cool enclosing water and half in the hot sun. He looked up once at the empty sky, filled his lungs once, twice, and then sank fast to the bottom with the stone. He let it go and began to count. He took the edges of the hole in his hands and drew himself into it; wriggling his shoulders in sidewise as he remembered he must, kicking himself along with his feet.

Soon he was clear inside. He was in a small rock-bound hole filled with yellowish-grey water. The water was pushing him up against the roof. The roof was sharp and pained his back. He pulled himself along with his hands – fast, fast – and used his legs as levers. His head knocked against something; a sharp pain dizzied him. Fifty, fifty-one, fifty-two ... He was without light, and the water seemed to press upon him with the weight of rock. Seventy-one, seventy-two ... There was no strain on his lungs. He felt like an inflated balloon, his lungs were so light and easy, but his head was pulsing.

He was being continually pressed against the sharp roof, which felt slimy as well as sharp. Again he thought of octopuses, and wondered if the tunnel might be filled with weed that could tangle him. He gave himself a panicky, convulsive kick forward, ducked his head, and swam. His feet and hands moved freely, as if in open water. The hole must have widened out. He thought he must be swimming fast, and he was frightened of banging his head if the tunnel narrowed.

A hundred, a hundred and one ... The water paled. Victory filled him. His lungs were beginning to hurt. A few more strokes and he would be out. He was counting wildly; he said a hundred and fifteen, and then, a long time later, a hundred and fifteen again. The water was a clear jewel-green all around him. Then he saw, above his head, a crack running up through the rock. Sunlight was falling through it, showing the clean, dark rock of the tunnel, a single mussel shell, and darkness ahead.

He was at the end of what he could do. He looked up at the crack as if it were filled with air and not water, as if he could put his mouth to it to draw in air. A hundred and fifteen, he heard himself say inside his head – but he had said that long ago. He must go on into the blackness ahead, or he would drown. His head was swelling, his lungs cracking. A hundred and fifteen, a hundred and fifteen pounded through his head, and he feebly clutched at rocks in the dark, pulling himself forward, leaving the brief space of sunlit water behind. He felt he was dying. He was no longer quite conscious. He struggled on in the darkness between lapses into unconsciousness. An immense, swelling pain filled his head, and then the darkness cracked with an explosion of green light. His hands, groping forward, met nothing; and his feet, kicking back, propelled him out into the open sea.

He drifted to the surface, his face turned up to the air. He was gasping like a fish. He felt he would sink now and drown; he could not swim the few feet back to the rock. Then he was clutching it and pulling himself up onto it. He lay face down, gasping. He could see nothing but a red-veined, clotted dark. His eyes must have burst, he thought; they were full of blood. He tore off his goggles and a gout of blood went into the sea. His nose was bleeding, and the blood had filled the goggles.

He scooped up handfuls of water from the cool, salty sea, to splash on his face, and did not know whether it was blood or salt water he tasted. After a time, his heart quieted, his eyes cleared, and he sat up. He could see the local boys diving and playing half a mile away. He did not want them. He wanted nothing but to get back home and lie down.

In a short while, Jerry swam to shore and climbed slowly up the path to the villa. He flung himself on his bed and slept, waking at the sound of feet on the path outside. His mother was coming back. He rushed to the bathroom, thinking she must not see his face with bloodstains, or tearstains, on it. He came out of the bathroom and met her as she walked into the villa, smiling, her eyes lighting up.

"Have a nice morning?" she asked, laying her hand on his warm brown shoulder a moment.

"Oh, yes, thank you," he said.

"You look a bit pale." And then, sharp and anxious, "How did you bang your head?"

"Oh, just banged it," he told her.

She looked at him closely. He was strained; his eyes were glazed-looking. She was worried. And then she said to herself, Oh, don't fuss! Nothing can happen. He can swim like a fish.

They sat down to lunch together.

"Mummy," he said, "I can stay underwater for two minutes – three minutes, at least." It came bursting out of him.

"Can you, darling?" she said. "Well, I shouldn't overdo it. I don't think you ought to swim any more today."

She was ready for a battle of wills, but he gave in at once. It was no longer of the least importance to go to the bay.

THE AXE

Penelope Fitzgerald

Penelope Fitzgerald (1916–2000) was a Man Booker Prize-winning British novelist, poet, essayist and biographer. In 2008, *The Times* included her in a list of the '50 Greatest British Writers Since 1945' and, in 2012, the *Observer* named her final novel, *The Blue Flower*, as one of 'The 10 Best Historical Novels'. A collection of Fitzgerald's short stories, *The Means of Escape*, and a volume of her non-fiction writings, *A House of Air*, were published posthumously.

You will recall that when the planned redundancies became necessary as the result of the discouraging trading figures shown by this small firm – in contrast, so I gather from the Company reports, with several of your other enterprises – you personally deputed to me the task of 'speaking' to those who were to be asked to leave. It was suggested to me that if they were asked to resign in order to avoid the unpleasantness of being given their cards, it might be unnecessary for the firm to offer any compensation. Having glanced personally through my staff sheets, you underlined the names of four people, the first being that of my clerical assistant, W. S. Singlebury. Your actual words to me were that he seemed fairly old and could probably be frightened into taking a powder. You were speaking to me in your 'democratic' style.

From this point on I feel able to write more freely, it being well understood, at office-managerial level, that you do not read more than the first two sentences of any given report. You believe that anything which cannot be put into two sentences is not worth attending to, a piece of wisdom which you usually attribute to the late Lord Beaverbrook.

As I question whether you have ever seen Singlebury, with whom this report is mainly concerned, it may be helpful to describe him. He worked for the Company for many more years than myself, and his attendance record was excellent. On Mondays, Wednesdays and Fridays, he wore a blue suit and a green knitted garment with a front zip. On Tuesdays and Thursdays he wore a pair of grey trousers of man-made material which he called 'my flannels', and a fawn cardigan. The cardigan was omitted in summer. He had, however, one distinguishing feature, very light blue eyes, with a defensive expression, as though apologizing for something which he felt guilty about, but could not put right. The fact is that he was getting old. Getting old is, of course, a crime of which we grow more guilty every day.

Singlebury had no wife or dependants, and was by no means a communicative man. His room is, or was, a kind of cubby-hole adjoining mine – you have to go through it to get into my room – and it was always kept very neat. About his 'things' he did show some mild emotion. They had to be ranged in a certain pattern in respect to his in and out trays, and Singlebury stayed behind for two or three minutes every evening to do this. He also managed to retain every year the complimentary desk calendar sent to us by Dino's, the Italian cafe on the corner. Singlebury was in fact the only one of my personnel who was always quite certain of the date. To this too his attitude was apologetic. His phrase was, 'I'm afraid it's Tuesday.'

His work, as was freely admitted, was his life, but the nature of his duties – though they included the post-book and the addressograph – was rather hard to define, having grown round him with the years. I can only say that after he left, I was surprised myself to discover how much he had had to do.

Oddly connected in my mind with the matter of the redundancies is the irritation of the damp in the office this summer and the peculiar smell (not the ordinary smell of damp), emphasized by the sudden appearance of representatives of a firm of damp eliminators who had not been sent for by me, nor is there any record of my having done so. These people simply vanished at the end of the day and have not returned. Another firm, to whom I applied as a result of frequent complaints by the female staff, have answered my letters but have so far failed to call.

Singlebury remained unaffected by the smell. Joining, very much against his usual habit, in one of the too frequent discussions of the subject, he said that he knew what it was; it was the smell of disappointment. For an awkward moment I thought he must have found out by some means that he was going to be asked to go, but he went on to explain that in 1942 the whole building had been requisitioned by the Admiralty and that relatives had been allowed to wait or queue there in the hope of getting news of those missing at sea. The repeated disappointment of these women, Singlebury said, must have permeated the building like a corrosive gas. All this was very unlike him. I made it a point not to encourage anything morbid. Singlebury was quite insistent, and added, as though by way of proof, that the lino in the corridors was Admiralty issue and had not been renewed since 1942 either. I was astonished to realize that he had been working in the building for so many years before the present tenancy. I realized that he must be considerably older than he had given us to understand. This, of course, will mean that there are wrong entries on his cards.

The actual notification to the redundant staff passed off rather better, in a way, than I had anticipated. By that time everyone in the office seemed inexplicably conversant with the details, and several of them in fact had gone far beyond their terms of reference, young Patel, for instance, who openly admits that he will be leaving us as soon as he can get a better job, taking me aside and telling me that to such a man as Singlebury dismissal would be like death. Dismissal is not the right word, I said. But death is, Patel replied. Singlebury himself, however, took it very quietly. Even when I raised the question of the Company's Early Retirement pension scheme, which I could not pretend was over-generous, he said very little. He was generally felt to be in a state of shock. The two girls whom you asked me to speak to were quite unaffected, having already found themselves employments as hostesses at the Dolphinarium near here. Mrs Horrocks, of Filing, on the other hand, *did* protest, and was so offensive on the question of severance pay that I was obliged to agree to refer it to a higher level. I consider this as one of the hardest day's work that I have ever done for the Company.

Just before his month's notice (if we are to call it that) was up, Singlebury, to my great surprise, asked me to come home with him one evening for a meal. In all the past years the idea of his having a home, still less asking anyone back to it, had never arisen, and I did not at all want to go there now. I felt sure, too, that he would want to reopen the matter of compensation, and only a quite unjustified feeling of guilt made me accept. We took an Underground together after work, travelling in the late rush-hour to Clapham North, and walked some distance in the rain. His place, when we eventually got to it, seemed particularly inconvenient, the entrance being through a small cleaner's shop. It consisted of one room and a shared toilet on the half-landing. The room itself was tidy, arranged, so it struck me, much on the lines of his cubby-hole, but the window was shut and it was oppressively stuffy. This is where I bury myself, said Singlebury.

There were no cooking arrangements and he left me there while he went down to fetch us something ready to eat from the Steakorama next to the cleaner's. In his absence I took the opportunity to examine his room, though of course not in an inquisitive or prying manner. I was struck by the fact that none of his small store of stationery had been brought home from the office. He returned with two steaks wrapped in aluminium foil, evidently a special treat in my honour, and afterwards he went out on to the landing and made cocoa, a drink which I had not tasted for more than thirty years. The evening dragged rather. In the course of conversation it turned out that Singlebury was fond of reading. There were in fact several issues of a colour-printed encyclopaedia which he had been collecting as it came out, but unfortunately it had ceased publication after the seventh part. Reading is my hobby, he said. I pointed out that a hobby was rather something that one did with one's hands or in the open air – a relief from the work of the brain. Oh, I don't accept that distinction, Singlebury said. The mind and the body are the same. Well, one cannot deny the connection, I replied. Fear, for example, releases adrenalin, which directly affects the nerves. I don't mean connection, I mean identity, Singlebury said, the mind is the blood. Nonsense, I said, you might just as well tell me that the blood is the mind. It stands to reason that the blood can't think.

I was right, after all, in thinking that he would refer to the matter of the redundancy. This was not till he was seeing me off at the bus-stop, when for a moment he turned his grey, exposed-looking face away from me and said that he did not see how he could manage if he really had to go. He stood there like someone who has 'tried to give satisfaction' – he even used this phrase, saying that if the expression were not redolent of a bygone age, he would like to feel he had given satisfaction. Fortunately we had not long to wait for the 45 bus.

At the expiry of the month the staff gave a small tea-party for those who were leaving. I cannot describe this occasion as a success.

The following Monday I missed Singlebury as a familiar presence and also, as mentioned above, because I had never quite realized how much work he had been taking upon himself. As a direct consequence of losing him I found myself having to stay late – not altogether unwillingly, since although following general instructions I have discouraged overtime, the extra pay in my own case would be instrumental in making ends meet. Meanwhile Singlebury's desk had not been cleared – that is, of the trays, pencil-sharpener and complimentary calendar which were, of course, office property. The feeling that he would come back – not like Mrs Horrocks, who has rung up and called round incessantly – but simply come back to work out of habit and through not knowing what else to do, was very strong, without being openly mentioned. I myself half expected and dreaded it, and I had mentally prepared two or three lines of argument in order to persuade him, if he *did* come, not to try it again. Nothing happened, however, and on the Thursday I personally removed the 'things' from the cubby-hole into my own room.

Meanwhile in order to dispel certain quite unfounded rumours I thought it best to issue a notice for general circulation, pointing out that if Mr Singlebury should turn out to have taken any unwise step, and if in consequence any inquiry should be necessary, we should be the first to hear about it from the police. I dictated this to our only permanent typist, who immediately said, oh, he would never do that. He would never cause any unpleasantness like bringing police into the place, he'd do all he could to avoid that. I did not encourage any further discussion, but I asked my wife, who is very used to social work, to call round at Singlebury's place in Clapham North and find out how he was. She did not have very much luck. The people in the cleaner's shop knew, or thought they knew, that he was away, but they had not been sufficiently interested to ask where he was going.

On Friday young Patel said he would be leaving, as the damp and the smell were affecting his health. The damp is certainly not drying out in this seasonably warm weather.

I also, as you know, received another invitation on the Friday, at very short notice, in fact no notice at all; I was told to come to your house in Suffolk Park Gardens that evening for drinks. I was not unduly elated, having been asked once before after I had done rather an awkward small job for you. In our Company, justice has not only not to be done, but it must be seen not to be done. The food was quite nice; it came from your Caterers Grade 3. I spent most of the evening talking to Ted Hollow, one of the area sales-managers. I did not expect to be introduced to your wife, nor was I. Towards the end of the evening you spoke to me for three minutes in the small room with a green marble floor and matching wallpaper leading to the ground-floor toilets. You asked me if everything was all right, to which I replied, all right for whom? You said that nobody's fault was nobody's funeral. I said that I had tried to give satisfaction. Passing on towards the washbasins, you told me with seeming cordiality to be careful and watch it when I had had mixed drinks.

I would describe my feeling at this point as resentment, and I cannot identify exactly the moment when it passed into unease. I do know that I was acutely uneasy as I crossed the hall and saw two of your domestic staff, a man and a woman, holding my coat, which I had left in the lobby, and apparently trying to brush it. Your domestic staff all appear to be of foreign extraction and I personally feel sorry for them and do not grudge them a smile at the oddly assorted guests. Then I saw they were not smiling at my coat but that they seemed to be examining their fingers and looking at me earnestly and silently, and the collar or shoulders of my coat was covered with blood. As I came up to them, although they were still both absolutely silent, the illusion or impression passed, and I put on my coat and left the house in what I hope was a normal manner.

I now come to the present time. The feeling of uneasiness which I have described as making itself felt in your house has not diminished during this past weekend, and partly to take my mind off it and partly for the reasons I have given, I decided to work over-time again tonight, Monday the twenty-third. This was in spite of the fact that the damp smell had become almost a stench, as of something putrid, which must have affected my nerves to some extent, because when I went out to get something to eat at Dino's I left the lights on, both in my own office and in the entrance hall. I mean that for the first time since I began to work for the Company I left them on deliberately. As I walked to the corner I looked back and saw the two solitary lights looking somewhat forlorn in contrast to the glitter of the Arab-American Mutual Loan Corporation opposite. After my meal I felt absolutely reluctant to go back to the building, and wished then that I had not given way to the impulse to leave the lights on, but since I had done so and they must be turned off, I had no choice.

As I stood in the empty hallway I could hear the numerous creakings, settlings and faint tickings of an old building, possibly associated with the plumbing system. The lifts for reasons of economy do not operate after 6.30 p.m., so I began to walk up the stairs. After one flight I felt a strong creeping tension in the nerves of the back such as any of us feel when there is danger from behind; one might say that the body was thinking for itself on these occasions. I did not look round, but simply continued upwards as rapidly as I could. At the third floor I paused, and could hear footsteps coming patiently up behind me. This was not a surprise; I had been expecting them all evening.

Just at the door of my own office, or rather of the cubby-hole, for I have to pass through that, I turned, and saw at the end of the dim corridor what I had also expected, Singlebury, advancing towards me with his unmistakable shuffling step. My first reaction was a kind of bewilderment as to why he, who had been such an excellent timekeeper, so regular day by day, should become a creature of the night. He was wearing the blue suit. This I could make out by its familiar outline, but it was not till he came halfway down the corridor towards me, and reached the patch of light falling through the window from the street, that I saw that he was not himself – I mean that his head was nodding or rather swivelling irregularly from side to side. It crossed my mind that Singlebury was drunk. I had never known him drunk or indeed seen him take anything to drink, even at the office Christmas party, but one cannot estimate the effect that trouble will have upon a man. I began to think what steps I should take in this situation. I turned on the light in his cubby-hole as I went through and waited at the entrance of my own office. As he appeared in the outer doorway I saw that I had not been correct about the reason for the odd movement of the head. The throat was cut from ear to ear so that the head was nearly severed from the shoulders. It was this which had given the impression of nodding, or rather, lolling. As he walked into his cubby-hole Singlebury raised both hands and tried to steady the head as though conscious that something was wrong. The eyes were thickly filmed over, as one sees in the carcasses in a butcher's shop.

I shut and locked my door, and not wishing to give way to nausea, or to lose all control of myself, I sat down at my desk. My work was waiting for me as I had left it – it was the file on the matter of the damp elimination – and, there not being anything else to do, I tried to look through it. On the other side of the door I could hear Singlebury sit down also, and then try the drawers of the table, evidently looking for the 'things' without which he could not start work. After the drawers had been tried, one after another, several times, there was almost total silence.

The present position is that I am locked in my own office and would not, no matter what you offered me, indeed I could not, go out through the cubby-hole and pass what is sitting at the desk. The early cleaners will not be here for seven hours and forty-five minutes. I have passed the time so far as best I could in writing this report. One consideration strikes me. If what I have next door is a visitant which should not be walking but buried in the earth, then its wound cannot bleed, and there will be no stream of blood moving slowly under the whole width of the communicating door. However, I am sitting at the moment with my back to the door, so that, without turning round, I have no means of telling whether it has done so or not.

BETTY

Margaret Atwood

Margaret Atwood (b. 1939) is a Canadian writer and environmental activist. She is amongst the most honoured authors of fiction in recent history. She is a winner of the Arthur C. Clarke Award and has been shortlisted for the Man Booker Prize five times, winning in 2000 for her novel *The Blind Assassin*. She is the author of more than fifty volumes of poetry, children's literature, fiction and non-fiction.

When I was seven we moved again, to a tiny wooden cottage on the Saint Marys River, upstream from Sault Sainte Marie. We were only renting the cottage for the summer, but for the time being it was our house, since we had no other. It was dim and mousy-smelling and very cramped, stuffed with all the things from the place before that were not in storage. My sister and I preferred to spend most of our time outside it.

There was a short beach, behind which the cottages, with their contrasting trim – green against white, maroon against robin's-egg blue, brown against yellow – were lined up like little shoeboxes, each with its matching outhouse at an unsanitary distance behind. But we were forbidden to swim in the water, because of the strong current. There were stories of children who had been swept away, down toward the rapids and the locks and the Algoma Steel fires of the Soo which we could sometimes see from our bedroom window on overcast nights, glowing dull red against the clouds. We were allowed to wade though, no further than the knee, and we would stand in the water, strands of loose weed tangling against our ankles, and wave at the lake freighters as they slid past, so close we could see not only the flags and sea gulls at their stems but the hands of the sailors and the ovals of their faces as they waved back to us. Then the waves would come, washing over our thighs up to the waists of our bloomered and skirted seersucker bathing suits, and we would scream with delight.

Our mother, who was usually on the shore, reading or talking to someone but not quite watching us, would sometimes mistake the screams for drowning. Or she would say later, "You've been in over your knees," but my sister would explain that it was only the boat waves. My mother would look at me to see if this was the truth. Unlike my sister, I was a clumsy liar.

The freighters were huge, cumbersome, with rust staining the holes for their anchor chains and enormous chimneys from which the smoke spurted in grey burps. When they blew their horns, as they always did when approaching the locks, the windows in our cottage rattled. For us, they were magical. Sometimes things would drop or be thrown from them, and we would watch these floating objects eagerly, running along the beach to be there when they landed, wading out to fish them in. Usually these treasures turned out to be only empty cardboard boxes or punctured oil cans, oozing dark brown grease and good for nothing. Several times we got orange crates, which we used as cupboards or stools in our hideouts.

We liked the cottage partly because we had places to make these hideouts. There had never been room before, since we had always lived in cities. Just before this it was Ottawa, the ground floor of an old three-tiered red-brick apartment building. On the floor above us lived a newly married couple, the wife English and Protestant, the husband French and Catholic. He was in the Air Force, and was away a lot, but when he came back on leave he used to beat up his wife. It was always about eleven o'clock at night. She would flee downstairs to my mother for protection, and they would sit in the kitchen with cups of tea. The wife would cry, though quietly, so as not to wake us – my mother insisted on that, being a believer in twelve hours of sleep for children – display her bruised eye or cheek, and whisper about his drinking. After an hour or so there would be a discreet knock on the door, and the airman, in full uniform, would ask my mother politely if he could have his wife back upstairs where she belonged. It was a religious dispute, he would say. Besides, he'd given her fifteen dollars to spend on food and she had served him fried Kam. After being away a month, a man expected a good roast, pork or beef, didn't my mother agree? "I kept my mouth shut and my eyes open," my mother would say. He never seemed that drunk to her, but with the polite kind you couldn't tell what they would do.

I wasn't supposed to know about any of this. I was considered either too young or too good; but my sister, who was four years older, was given hints, which she passed along to me with whatever she thought fit to add. I saw the wife a number of times, going up or down the stairs outside our door, and once she did have a black eye. I never saw the man, but by the time we left Ottawa I was convinced he was a murderer.

This might have explained my father's warning when my mother told him she had met the young couple who lived in the right-hand cottage. "Don't get too involved," he said. "I don't want her running over here at all hours of the night." He had little patience with my mother's talents as a sympathetic listener, even when she teased him by saying, "But I listen to you, dear." She attracted people he called sponges.

He didn't seem to have anything to worry about. This couple was very different from the other one. Fred and Betty insisted on being called Fred and Betty, right away. My sister and I, who had been drilled to call people Mr. and Mrs., had to call them Fred and Betty also, and we could go over to their house whenever we wanted to. "I don't want you to take that at face value," our mother said. Times were hard but our mother had been properly brought up, and we were going to be, too. Nevertheless, at first we went to Fred and Betty's as often as we could.

Their cottage was exactly the same size as ours, but since there was less furniture in it it seemed bigger. Ours had Ten-Test walls between the rooms, painted lime green, with lighter squares on the paint where other people had once hung pictures. Betty had replaced her walls with real plywood and painted the inside bright yellow, and she'd made yellow and white curtains for the kitchen, a print of chickens coming out of eggshells. She'd sewed herself a matching apron from the leftover material. They owned their cottage rather than renting it; as my mother said, you didn't mind doing the work then. Betty called the tiny kitchen a kitchenette. There was a round ironwork table tucked into one corner, with two scrolled ironwork chairs, painted white, one for Betty and one for Fred. Betty called this corner the breakfast nook.

There was more to do at Fred and Betty's than at our house. They had a bird made of hollow coloured glass that perched on the edge of a tumbler of water, teetering back and forth until it would finally dip its head into the water and take a drink. They had a front door knocker in the shape of a woodpecker, you pulled a string, and the woodpecker pecked at the door. They also had a whistle in the shape of a bird that you could fill with water and blow into and it would warble, "like a canary," Betty said. And they took the Saturday coloured funnies. Our parents didn't, and they didn't like us reading trash, as they called it. But Fred and Betty were so friendly and kind to us, what, as my mother said, could they do?

Beyond all these attractions there was Fred. We both fell in love with Fred. My sister would climb into his lap and announce that he was her boyfriend and she was going to marry him when she grew up. She would then make him read the funnies to her and tease him by trying to take the pipe out of his mouth or by tying his shoelaces together. I felt the same way, but I knew it was no good saying so. My sister had staked her claim, when she said she was going to do a thing she usually did it. And she hated my being what she called a copycat. So I would sit in the breakfast nook on one of the scrolled ironwork chairs while Betty made coffee, watching my sister and Fred on the living-room couch.

There was something about Fred that attracted people. My mother, who was not a flirtatious woman – she went in for wisdom, instead – was livelier when he was around. Even my father liked him, and would sometimes have a beer with him when he got back from the city. They would sit on the porch of Fred's cottage in Betty's yellow wicker chairs, swatting at the sand flies and discussing baseball scores. They seldom mentioned their jobs. I'm not sure what Fred did, but it was in an office. My father was "in wallpaper," my mother said, but I was never very clear about what that meant. It was more exciting when they talked about the war. My father's bad back had kept him out of it, much to his disgust, but Fred had been in the Navy. He never said too much about it, though my father was always prompting him; but we knew from

Betty that they were engaged just before Fred left and married right after he came back. Betty had written letters to him every single night and mailed them once a week. She did not say how often Fred had written to her. My father didn't like many people, but he said that Fred wasn't a fool.

Fred didn't seem to make any efforts to be nice to people. I don't think he was even especially handsome. The difficulty is that though I can remember Betty down to the last hair and freckle, I can't remember what Fred looked like. He had dark hair and a pipe, and he used to sing to us if we pestered him enough. "Sioux City Sue," he would sing, "Your hair is red, your eyes are blue, I'd swap my horse and dog for you … " Or he would sing "Beautiful Brown Eyes" to my sister, whose eyes were brown as compared with my own watery blue. This hurt my feelings, as the song contained the line, "I'll never love blue eyes again." It seemed so final, a whole lifetime of being unloved by Fred. Once I cried, which was made worse by the fact that I couldn't explain to anyone what was wrong; and I had to undergo the humiliation of Fred's jocular concern and my sister's scorn, and the worse humiliation of being comforted by Betty in the kitchenette. It was a humiliation because it was obvious even to me that Betty didn't grasp things very well. "Don't pay any attention to *him*," she said, having guessed that my tears had something to do with Fred. But that was the one piece of advice I couldn't take.

Fred, like a cat, wouldn't go two steps out of his way for you really, as my mother said later. So it was unfair that everyone was in love with Fred, but no one, despite her kindness, was in love with Betty. It was Betty who always greeted us at the door, asked us in, and talked to us while Fred slouched on the couch reading the paper. She fed us cookies and milk shakes and let us lick out the bowls when she was baking. Betty was such a nice person; everyone said so, but no one would have called Fred exactly that. Fred, for instance, did not laugh much, and he only smiled when he was making rude remarks, mostly to my sister. "Stuffing your face again?" he would say. "Hey, baggy pants." Whereas Betty never said things like that, and she was always either smiling or laughing.

She laughed a lot when Fred called her Betty Grable, which he did at least once a day. I couldn't see why she laughed. It was supposed to be a compliment, I thought. Betty Grable was a famous movie star; there was a picture of her thumb-tacked to the wall in Fred and Betty's outhouse. Both my sister and I preferred Fred and Betty's outhouse to our own. Theirs had curtains on the window, unlike ours, and it had a little wooden box and a matching wooden scoop for the lye. We only had a cardboard box and an old trowel.

Betty didn't really look like Betty Grable, who was blonde and not as plump as our Betty. Still, they were both beautiful, I thought. I didn't realize until much later that the remark was cruel; for Betty Grable was renowned for her legs, whereas our Betty had legs that started at her waist and continued downwards without a curve or a pause until they reached her feet. At the time they seemed like ordinary legs. Sitting in the kitchenette, I saw a lot of Betty's legs, for she wore halter tops and shorts, with her yellow apron over them. Somehow Betty could never get her legs to tan, despite the hours she spent crocheting in her wicker chair, the top part of her in the shade of the porch but her legs sticking out into the sun.

My father said that Betty had no sense of humour. I couldn't understand this at all. If you told her a joke she would always laugh, even if you got it mixed up, and she told jokes of her own, too. She would print the word "BED," making the E smaller and thicker than the B and the D. "What's this?" she would say. "It's the little dark E in BED." I didn't get this joke the first time she told it and she had to explain it to me. "Little darkie," she said, her slightly protruding teeth shining with good humour. We had never been to the United States, even though we could see it across the river, a strip of green trees that faded west into the blue of Lake Superior, and the only black people I had seen were the characters in the comics. There was L'il 8-Ball, and the Africans in Tarzan, and Lothar in Mandrake the Magician, who wore a lion skin. I couldn't see what any of them had to do with the word "bed."

My father also said that Betty had no sex appeal. This didn't seem to bother my mother in the least. "She's a very nice girl," she would answer complacently, or, "She has very nice colouring." My mother and Betty were soon collaborating on a scheme for making the preserving easier. Most people still had Victory gardens, though the war was over, and the months of July and August were supposed to be spent putting up as many jars of fruit and vegetables as you could. My mother's garden was half-hearted, like most of her housekeeping efforts. It was a small patch beside the outhouse where squash vines rambled over a thicket of overgrown tomato plants and a few uneven lines of dwarfed carrots and beets. My mother's talent, we had heard her say, was for people. Betty and Fred didn't have a garden at all. Fred wouldn't have worked in it, and when I think of Betty now I realize that a garden would have been too uncontained for her. But she had Fred buy dozens of six-quart baskets of strawberries, peaches, beans, tomatoes and Concord grapes, on his trips into the city; and she persuaded my mother to give up on her own garden and join her in her mammoth canning sessions.

My mother's wood stove was unbearably hot for such an operation, and Betty's little electric range was too small; so Betty got "the boys," as she called Fred and my father, to set up the derelict wood stove that until then had been rusting behind Betty's outhouse. They put it in our backyard, and my mother and Betty would sit at our kitchen table, which had been carried outside, peeling, slicing and talking, Betty with her round pincushion cheeks flushed redder than usual by the heat and my mother with an old bandanna wrapped around her head, making her look like a gypsy. Behind them the canning kettles bubbled and steamed, and on one side of the table the growing ranks of Crown jars, inverted on layers of newspapers, cooled and sometimes leaked or cracked. My sister and I hung around the edges, not wanting to be obvious enough to be put to work, but coveting the empty six-quart baskets. We could use them in our hideout, we felt; we were never sure what for, but they fitted neatly into the orange crates.

I learned a lot about Fred during Betty's canning sessions: how he liked his eggs, what size socks he took (Betty was a knitter), how well he was doing at the office, what he refused to eat for dinner. Fred was a picky eater, Betty said joyfully. Betty had almost nothing else to talk about, and even my mother, veteran of many confidences, began to talk less and smoke more than usual when Betty was around. It was easier to listen to disasters than to Betty's inexhaustible and trivial cheer. I began to think that I might not want to be married to Fred after all. He unrolled from Betty's mouth like a long ribbon of soggy newspaper printed from end to end with nothing but the weather. Neither my sister nor I was interested in sock sizes, and Betty's random, unexciting details diminished Fred in our eyes. We began to spend less of our playtime at Fred and Betty's and more in our hideout; which was in a patch of scrubby oak on a vacant lot along the shore. There we played complicated games of Mandrake the Magician and his faithful servant Lothar, with our dolls as easily hypnotized villains. My sister was always Mandrake. When we tired of this we would put on our bathing suits and go wading along the shore, watching for freighters and throwing acorns into the river to see how quickly they would be carried away by the current.

It was on one of these wading expeditions that we met Nan. She lived ten lots down, in a white cottage with red trim. Unlike many of the other cottages, Nan's had a real dock, built out into the river and anchored around the posts with piles of rocks. She was sitting on this dock when we first saw her, chewing gum and flipping through a stack of airplane cards from Wings cigarettes. Everyone knew that only boys collected these. Her hair and her face were light brown, and she had a sleek plump sheen, like caramel pudding.

"What're you doing with *those*?" were my sister's first words. Nan only smiled.

That same afternoon Nan was allowed into our hideout, and after a cursory game of Mandrake, during which I was demoted to the lowly position of Narda, the two of them sat on our orange crates and exchanged what seemed to me to be languid and pointless comments.

"You ever go to the store?" Nan asked. We never did. Nan smiled some more. She was twelve, my sister was only eleven and three-quarters.

"There's cute boys at the store," Nan said. She was wearing a peasant blouse with a frill and an elastic top that she could slide down over her shoulders if she wanted to. She stuck her airplane cards into her shorts pocket and we went to ask my mother if we could walk to the store. After that, my sister and Nan went there almost every afternoon.

The store was a mile and a half from our cottage, a hot walk along the shore past the fronts of other cottages where fat mothers basked in the sun and other, possibly hostile children paddled in the water; past rowboats hauled up on the sand, along cement breakwaters, through patches of beach grass that cut your ankles if you ran through it and beach peas that were hard and bitter-tasting. In some places we could smell the outhouses. Just before the store, there was an open space with poison ivy, which we had to wade around.

The store had no name. It was just "the store," the only store for the cottagers since it was the only one they could walk to. I was allowed to go with my sister and Nan, or rather, my mother insisted that I go. Although I hadn't said anything to her about it, she could sense my misery. It wasn't so much my sister's desertion that hurt, but her blithe unconsciousness of it. She was quite willing to play with me when Nan wasn't around.

Sometimes, when the sight of my sister and Nan conspiring twenty paces ahead of me made me too unhappy, I would double back and go to Fred and Betty's. There I would sit facing backwards on one of Betty's kitchen chairs, my two hands rigid in the air, holding a skein of sky blue wool while Betty wound it into balls. Or, under Betty's direction, I crocheted sweaty, uneven little pink and yellow dolls' dresses for the dolls my sister was, suddenly, too old to play with.

On better days I would make it as far as the store. It was not beautiful or even clean, but we were so used to wartime drabness and grime that we didn't notice. It was a two-storey building of unpainted wood which had weathered grey. Parts of it were patched with tar paper, and it had coloured metal signs nailed around the front screen door and windows: Coca-Cola, 7-Up, Salada Tea. Inside, it had the sugary, mournful smell of old general stores, a mixture of the cones for the icecream cones, the packages of Oreo cookies, the open boxes of jawbreakers and licorice whips that lined the counter, and that other smell, musky and sharp, part dry-rot and part sweat. The bottles of pop were kept in a metal cooler with a heavy lid, filled with cold water and chunks of ice melted to the smoothness of the sand-scoured pieces of glass we sometimes found on the beach.

The owner of the store and his wife lived on the second floor, but we almost never saw them. The store was run by their two daughters, who took turns behind the counter. They were both dark and they both wore shorts and polka-dot halter tops, but one was friendly and the other one, the thinner, younger one, was not. She would take our pennies and ring them into the cash register without saying a word, staring over our heads out the front window with its dangling raisin-covered fly-papers as if she was completely detached from the activity her hands were performing. She didn't dislike us; she just didn't see us. She wore her hair long and done in a sort of roll at the front, and her lipstick was purplish.

The first time we went to the store we found out why Nan collected airplane cards. There were two boys there, sitting on the grey, splintery front steps, their arms crossed over their knees. I had been told by my sister that the right thing to do with boys was to ignore them, otherwise they would pester you. But these boys knew Nan, and they spoke to her, not with the usual taunts, but with respect.

"You got anything new?" one of them said.

Nan smiled, brushed back her hair and wiggled her shoulders a little inside her peasant blouse. Then she slid her airplane cards slowly out of her shorts pocket and began riffling through them.

"You got any?" the other boy said to my sister. For once she was humbled. After that, she got my mother to switch brands and built up her own pack. I saw her in front of the mirror about a week later, practising that tantalizing slide, the cards coming out of her pocket like a magician's snake.

When I went to the store I always had to bring back a loaf of wax-papered bread for my mother, and sometimes a package of "Jiffy" Pie Crust, if they had any. My sister never had to: she had already discovered the advantages of being unreliable. As payment, and, I'm sure, as compensation for my unhappiness, my mother gave me a penny a trip, and when I had saved five of these pennies I bought my first Popsicle. Our mother had always refused to buy them for us, although she permitted ice-cream cones. She said there was something in Popsicles that was bad for you, and as I sat on the front steps of the store, licking down to the wooden stick, I kept looking for this thing. I visualized it as a sort of core, like the white fingernail-shaped part in a kernel of corn, but I couldn't find anything.

My sister and Nan were sitting beside me on the front steps. There were no boys at the store that day, so they had nothing else to do. It was even hotter than usual, and airless; there was a shimmer over the river, and the freighters wavered as they passed through it. My Popsicle was melting almost before I could eat it. I had given my sister half of it; which she had taken without the gratitude I had hoped for. She was sharing it with Nan.

Fred came around the corner of the building and headed towards the front door. This was no surprise, as we had seen him at the store several times before.

"Hi, beautiful," he said to my sister. We moved our rumps along the step to let him in the door.

After quite a long time he came out, carrying a loaf of bread. He asked us if we wanted a lift with him in his car: he was just coming back from the city, he said. Of course we said yes. There was nothing unusual about any of this, except that the daughter, the thinner, purple one, stepped outside the door and stood on the steps as we were driving off. She folded her arms across her chest in that slump-shouldered pose of women idling in doorways. She wasn't smiling. I thought she had come out to watch the Canada Steamship lines freighter that was going past, but then I saw that she was staring at Fred. She looked as if she wanted to kill him.

Fred didn't seem to notice. He sang all the way home. "Katy, oh beautiful Katy," he sang, winking at my sister, whom he sometimes called Katy since her name was Catherine. He had the windows open, and dust from the rutted gravel road poured over us, whitening our eyebrows and turning Fred's hair grey. At every jolt my sister and Nan screamed gleefully, and after a while I forgot my feelings of exclusion and screamed too.

It seemed as if we had lived in the cottage for a long time, though it was only one summer. By August I could hardly remember the apartment in Ottawa and the man who used to beat up his wife. That had happened in a remote life; and, despite the sunshine, the water, the open space, a happier one. Before, our frequent moves and the insecurities of new schools had forced my sister to value me: I was four years younger, but I was loyal and always there. Now those years were a canyon between us, an empty stretch like a beach along which I could see her disappearing ahead of me. I longed to be just like her, but I could no longer tell what she was like.

In the third week of August the leaves started to turn, not all at once, just a single red one here and there, like a warning. That meant it would soon be time for school and another move. We didn't even know where we would be moving to this time, and when Nan asked us what school we went to, we were evasive.

"I've been to eight different schools," my sister said proudly. Because I was so much younger, I had only been to two. Nan, who had been to the same one all her life, slipped the edge of her peasant blouse over her shoulders and down to her elbows to show us that her breasts were growing. The rings around her nipples had softened and started to puff out; otherwise she was as flat as my sister.

"So what," said my sister, rolling up her jersey. This was a competition I couldn't be part of. It was about change, and, increasingly, change frightened me. I walked back along the beach to Betty's house, where my latest piece of grubby crocheting was waiting for me and where everything was always the same.

I knocked on the screen door and opened it. I meant to say, "Can I come in?" the way we always did, but I didn't say it. Betty was sitting by herself at the iron table of the breakfast nook. She had on her shorts and a striped sailor top, navy blue and white with a little anchor pin, and the apron with the yellow chickens coming out of their eggs. For once she wasn't doing anything, and there was no cup of coffee in front of her. Her face was white and uncomprehending, as if someone had just hit her for no reason.

She saw me, but she didn't smile or ask me in. "What am I going to do?" she said.

I looked around the kitchen. Everything was in its place: the percolator gleamed from the stove, the glass bird was teetering slowly down, there were no broken dishes, no water on the floor. What had happened?

"Are you sick?" I said.

"There's nothing I can do," Betty said.

She looked so strange that I was frightened. I ran out of the kitchen and across the hillocky grass to get to my mother, who always knew what should be done.

"There's something wrong with Betty," I said.

My mother was mixing something in a bowl. She rubbed her hands together to get the dough off, then wiped them on her apron. She didn't look surprised or ask me what it was. "You stay here," she said. She picked up her package of cigarettes and went out the door.

That evening we had to go to bed early because my mother wanted to talk to my father. We listened, of course; it was easy through the Ten-Test walls.

"I saw it coming," my mother said. "A mile away."

"Who is it?" my father said.

"She doesn't know," said my mother. "Some girl from town."

"Betty's a fool," my father said. "She always was." Later, when husbands and wives leaving each other became more common, he often said this, but no matter which one had left it was always the woman he called the fool. His highest compliment to my mother was that she was no fool.

"That may be," said my mother. "But you'd never want to meet a nicer girl. He was her whole life,"

My sister and I whispered together. My sister's theory was that Fred had run away from Betty with another woman. I couldn't believe this: I had never heard of such a thing happening. I was so upset I couldn't sleep, and for a long time after that I was anxious whenever my father was away overnight, as he frequently was. What if he never came back?

We didn't see Betty after that. We knew she was in her cottage, because every day my mother carried over samples of her tough and lumpy baking, almost as if someone had died. But we were given strict orders to stay away, and not to go peering in the windows as our mother must have known we longed to do. "She's having a nervous breakdown," our mother said, which for me called up an image of Betty lying disjointed on the floor like a car at the garage.

We didn't even see her on the day we got into my father's second-hand Studebaker, the back seat packed to the window-tops with only a little oblong space for me to crouch in, and drove out to the main highway to begin the six hundred-mile journey south to Toronto. My father had changed jobs again; he was now in building materials, and he was sure, since the country was having a boom, that this was finally the right change. We spent September and part of October in a motel while my father looked for a house. I had my eighth birthday and my sister turned twelve. Then there was another new school, and I almost forgot about Betty.

But a month after I had turned twelve myself Betty was suddenly there one night for dinner. We had people for dinner a lot more than we used to, and sometimes the dinners were so important that my sister and I ate first. My sister didn't care, as she had boyfriends by that time. I was still in public school and had to wear lisle stockings instead of the seamed nylons my sister was permitted. Also, I had braces. My sister had had braces at that age too, but she had somehow managed to make them seem rakish and daring, so that I had longed for a mouthful of flashing silver teeth like hers. But she no longer had them, and my own mouth in its shackles felt clumsy and muffled.

"You remember Betty," my mother said.

"Elizabeth," Betty said.

"Oh yes, of course," said my mother.

Betty had changed a lot. Before, she had been a little plump; now she was buxom. Her cheeks were as round and florid as two tomatoes, and I thought she was using too much rouge until I saw that the red was caused by masses of tiny veins under her skin. She was wearing a long black pleated skirt, a white short-sleeved angora sweater with a string of black beads, and open-toed black velvet pumps with high heels. She smelled strong of Lily of the Valley. She had a job, my mother told my father later; a very good job. She was an executive secretary, and now called herself Miss instead of Mrs.

"She's doing very well," my mother said, "considering what happened. She's pulled herself together."

"I hope you don't start inviting her to dinner all the time," said my father, who still found Betty irritating in spite of her new look. She laughed more than ever now, and crossed her legs frequently.

"I feel I'm the only real friend she has," said my mother. She didn't say Betty was the only real friend she had, though when my father said "your friend" everyone knew who he meant My mother had a lot of friends, and her talent for wise listening was now a business asset for my father.

"She says she'll never marry again," said my mother.

"She's a fool," my father said.

"If I ever saw anyone cut out for marriage, it was her," said my mother. This remark increased my anxiety about any own future. If all Betty's accomplishments had not been enough for Fred, what hope was there for me? I did not have my sister's natural flair, but I had thought there would be some tricks I could learn, dutifully, painstakingly. We were taking Home Economics at school and the teacher kept saying that the way to a man's heart was through his stomach. I knew this wasn't true – my mother was still a slapdash cook, and when she gave the best dinners she had a woman in to help – but I laboured over my blancmange and Harvard beets as if I believed it.

My mother started inviting Betty to dinner with men who were not married. Betty smiled and laughed and several of the men seemed interested, but nothing came of it.

"After the way she was hurt, I'm not surprised," my mother said. I was now old enough to be told things, and besides, my sister was never around. "I heard it was a secretary at his company he ran off with. They even got married, after the divorce." There was something else about Betty, she told me, although I must never mention it as Betty found it very distressing. Fred's brother, who was a dentist, had killed his wife because he got involved – my mother said "involved" richly, as if it was a kind of dessert – with his dental technician. He had put his wife into the car and run a tube in from the exhaust pipe, and then tried to pretend it was suicide. The police had found out though, and he was in jail.

This made Betty much more interesting in my eyes. It was in Fred's blood, then, the tendency towards involvement. In fact it could just as easily have been Betty herself who had been murdered. I now came to see Betty's laugh as the mask of a stricken and martyred woman. She was not just a wife who had been deserted. Even I could see that this was not a tragic position, it was a ridiculous and humiliating one. She was much more than that: she was a woman who had narrowly escaped death. That Betty herself saw it this way I soon had no doubt. There was something smug and even pious about the way she kept Mother's single men at a polite distance, something faintly nunlike. A lurid aura of sacrificial blood surrounded her. Betty had been there, she had passed through it, she had come out alive, and now she was dedicating herself to, well, to something else.

But it was hard for me to sustain this version of Betty for long. My mother soon ran out of single men and Betty, when she came to dinner, came alone. She talked as incessantly about the details surrounding the other women at her office as she had about Fred. We soon knew how they all took their coffee, which ones lived with their mothers, where they had their hair done, and what their apartments looked like. Betty herself had a darling apartment on Avenue Road, and she had redone it all herself and even made the slipcovers. Betty was as devoted to her boss as she had once been to Fred. She did all his Christmas shopping, and each year we heard what he had given to his employees, what to his wife and children, and what each item had cost. Betty seemed, in a way, quite happy.

We saw a lot of Betty around Christmas; my mother said she felt sorry for her because she had no family. Betty was in the habit of giving us Christmas presents that made it obvious she thought we were younger than we were. She favoured Parcheesi sets and angora mittens a size too small. I lost interest in her. Even her unending cheerfulness came to seem like a perversion, or a defect almost like idiocy. I was fifteen now and in the throes of adolescent depression. My sister was away at Queen's; sometimes she gave me clothes she no longer wanted. She was not exactly beautiful – both her eyes and her mouth were too large – but everyone called her vivacious. They called me nice. My braces had come off, but it didn't seem to make any difference. What right had Betty to be cheerful? When she came to dinner, I excused myself early and went to my room.

One afternoon, in the spring of Grade Eleven, I came home from school to find my mother sitting at the dining-room table. She was crying, which was so rare that my immediate fear was that something had happened to my father. I didn't think he had left her, that particular anxiety was past. But perhaps he had been killed in a car crash.

"Mum, what is it?" I said.

"Bring me a glass of water," she said. She drank some of it and pushed back her hair. "I'm all right now," she said. "I just had a call from Betty. It was very upsetting; she said horrible things to me."

"Why?" I said. "What did you do?"

"She accused me of ... horrible things." My mother swabbed at her eyes. "She was screaming. I've never heard Betty scream in my life before. After all that time I spent with her. She said she never wanted to speak to me again. Where would she get such an idea?"

"What idea?" I said. I was just as mystified as my mother was. My mother was a bad cook, but she was a good woman. I could not imagine her doing anything that would make anyone want to scream at her.

My mother held back slightly. "Things about Fred," she said. "She must be crazy. I hadn't seen her for a couple of months, and then suddenly, just like that."

"There must be something wrong with her," my father said at dinner that night. Of course he was right. Betty had an undetected brain tumour, which was discovered when her strange behaviour was noticed at the office. She died in the hospital two months later, but my mother didn't hear about it till afterwards. She was contrite; she felt she should have visited her friend in the hospital, despite the abusive phone call.

"I ought to have known it was something like that," she said. "Personality change, that's one of the clues." In the course of her listening, my mother had picked up a great deal of information about terminal illnesses.

But for me, this explanation wasn't good enough. For years after that, Betty followed me around, waiting for me to finish her off in some way more satisfactory to both of us. When I first heard about her death I felt doomed. This, then, was the punishment for being devoted and obliging, this was what happened to girls such as (I felt) myself. When I opened the high-school yearbook and my own face, in pageboy haircut and tentative, appeasing smile, stared back at me, it was Betty's eyes I superimposed on mine. She had been kind to me when I was a child, and with the callousness of children towards those who are kind but not enchanting, I had preferred Fred. In my future I saw myself being abandoned by a succession of Freds who were running down the beach after a crowd of vivacious girls, all of whom looked remarkably like my sister. As for Betty's final screams of hatred and rage, they were screams of protest against the unfairness of life. That anger, I knew, was my own, the dark side of that terrible and deforming niceness that had marked Betty like the aftermath of some crippling disease.

People change, though, especially after they are dead. As I passed beyond the age of melodrama I came to see that if I did not want to be Betty, I would have to be someone else. Furthermore, I was already quite different from Betty. In a way, she had absolved me from making the demanded choices by having made them so thoroughly herself. People stopped calling me a nice girl and started calling me a clever one, and after a while I enjoyed this. Betty herself, baking oatmeal cookies in the ephemeral sunlight of fifteen years before, slid back into three dimensions. She was an ordinary woman who had died too young of an incurable disease. Was that it, was that all?

From time to time I would like to have Betty back, if only for an hour's conversation. I would like her to forgive me for my rejection of her angora mittens, for my secret betrayals of her, for my adolescent contempt. I would like to show her this story I have told about her and ask her if any of it is true. But I can think of nothing I want to ask her that I could phrase in a way that she would care to understand. She would only laugh in her accepting, uncomprehending way and offer me something, a chocolate brownie, a ball of wool.

Fred, on the other hand, no longer intrigues me. The Freds of this world make themselves explicit by what they do and choose. It is the Bettys who are mysterious.

A WORLD OF HER OWN

Penelope Lively

Penelope Lively (b. 1933) is a critically acclaimed British
author of fiction for both children and adults. She won the
Carnegie Medal for children's fiction in 1973, for *The
Ghost of Thomas Kempe*, and also the Man Booker Prize
for her 1987 novel, *Moon Tiger*. Lively was made Dame
Commander of the Order of the British Empire in the 2012
New Year Honours list.

My sister Lisa is an artist: she is not like other people.

Lisa is two years younger than I am, and we knew quite early on
that she was artistic, partly because she could always draw so
nicely, but also because of the way she behaved. She lives in a world
of her own, our mother used to say. She was always the difficult
one, always having tempers and tantrums and getting upset about
one thing and another, but once mother realised about her being
artistic she made allowances. We all did. She's got real talent, the
art master at school said, you'll have to take care of that, Mrs
Harris, she's going to need all the help she can get. And mother was
thrilled to bits, she's always admired creative people, she'd have
loved to be able to write or paint herself but having Lisa turn out
that way was the next best thing, or better, even, perhaps. When
Lisa was fifteen mother went to work at Luigi's, behind the counter,
to save up so there'd be a bit extra in hand for Lisa, when she went
to art school. Father had died three years before. It worried me
rather, mother going out to work like that; she's had asthma on and
off for years now, and besides she felt awkward, serving in a shop.
But the trouble is, she's not qualified at anything, and in any case,
as she said, a delicatessen isn't quite like an ordinary grocer or a
supermarket.

I was at college, by then, doing my teaching diploma. Lisa went
to one of the London art schools, and came back at the end of her
first term looking as weird as anything, you'd hardly have known

her, her hair dyed red and wearing black clothes with pop art cut-outs stuck on and I don't know what. It was just as well mother *had* saved up, because it all turned out much more expensive than we'd thought, even with Lisa's grant. There was so much she had to do, like going to plays and things, and of course she needed smarter clothes, down there, and more of them, and then the next year she had to travel on the continent all the summer, to see great paintings and architecture. She was away for months, we hardly saw anything of her, and when she came back she'd changed completely all over again – her hair was blonde and frizzed out, and she was wearing a lot of leather things, very expensive, boots up to her thighs and long suede coats. She came home for Christmas and sometimes she was gay and chatty and made everybody laugh and other times she was bad-tempered and moody, but as mother said, she'd always been like that, from a little girl, and of course you had to expect it, with her temperament.

Mother had left Luigi's by then, some time before, because of her leg (she got this trouble with her veins, which meant she mustn't stand much) but she started doing a bit of work at home, for pin-money, making cushions and curtains for people: she's always been good at needlework, she sometimes says she wonders if possibly that's where Lisa's creativity came from, if maybe there's something in the family ...

It missed me out, if there is. Still, I got my diploma (I did rather well, as it happens, one of the best in my year) and started teaching and not long after that I married Jim, whom I'd known at college, and we had the children quite soon, because I thought I'd go back to work later, when they were at school.

Lisa finished at her art college, and got whatever it is they get, and then she couldn't find a job. At least she didn't want any of the jobs she could have got, like window-dressing or jobs on magazines or for publishers or that kind of thing. And can you blame her, said mother, I mean, what a waste of her talents, it's ridiculous, all that time she's spent developing herself, and then they expect her to be tied down to some nine-to-five job like anyone else!

Lisa was fed up. She had to come and live at home. Mother turned out of her bedroom and had the builders put a skylight in and made it into a studio for Lisa, really very nice, with a bare polished floor and a big new easel mother got by selling that silver tea-set that was a wedding present (she says she never really liked it anyway). But then it turned out Lisa didn't do that kind of painting, but funny things to do with bits of material all sort of glued together, and coloured paper cut out and stuck on to other sheets of paper. And when she did paint or draw it would be squatting on the floor, or lying on her stomach on the sofa.

I can't make head nor tail of the kind of art Lisa does. I mean, I just don't *know* if it's any good or not. But then, I wouldn't, would I? Nor Jim, nor mother, nor any of us. We're not experienced in things like that; it's not up to us to say.

Lisa mooched about at home for months. She said she wouldn't have minded a job designing materials for some good firm – Liberty's or something like that – provided there was just her doing it because she's got this very individual style and it wouldn't mix with other people's, or may be she might arrange the exhibitions at the Victoria and Albert or the Tate or somewhere. She never seemed to get jobs like that, though, and anyway mother felt it would be unwise for her to commit herself because what she really ought to be doing was her own work, that's all any artist should do, it's as simple as that.

Actually Lisa did less and less painting, which mother said was tragic, her getting so disillusioned and discouraged, such a waste of talent. Mother would explain to people who asked what Lisa was doing nowadays about how disgraceful it was that the government didn't see that people like her were given the opportunities and encouragement they need. Goodness knows, she'd say with a sigh, it's rare enough – creative ability – and Mrs Watkins next door, or the vicar, or whoever it was, would nod doubtfully and say yes, they supposed so.

And then Bella Sims arrived and opened up this new gallery in the town. The Art Centre. Before, there'd only been the Craft Shop, which does have some quite odd-looking pictures but goes in for glass animals and corn dollies and all that too; Lisa was vicious about the Craft Shop. But Bella Sims's place was real art, you could see that at once – lots of bare floor and pictures hung very far apart and pottery vases and bowls so expensive they didn't even have a price on them. And Lisa took along some of her things one day and believe it or not Bella Sims said she liked them, and she'd put three of them in her next exhibition which was specially for local artists. Mother was so thrilled she cried when Lisa first told her.

Lisa was a bit off-hand about it all; she seemed to take the attitude that it was only to be expected. She got very thick with Bella Sims.

Bella Sims was fiftyish, one of those people with a loud, posh voice and hair that's just been done at the hairdresser and lots of clunky expensive-looking jewellery. She scared the wits out of me, and mother too, actually, though mother kept saying what a marvellous person she was, and what an asset for the town. I didn't enjoy the preview party for the exhibition, and nor did Jim; I was expecting Judy then, and Clive was eighteen months, so I was a bit done in and nobody talked to us much. But Lisa was having a good time, you could see; she was wearing all peasanty things then, and had her hair very long and shiny, she did look really very attractive. She met Melvyn at that party.

Melvyn was Bella's son. He taught design at the Poly. That meant he was sort of creative too, though of course not a real artist like Lisa. He fell for her, heavily, and who could blame him I suppose, and they started going round together, and then quite soon they said they were getting married. We were all pleased, because Melvyn's nice – you'd never know he was Bella's son – and we didn't realise till later that it was because of Francesca being on the way. Mother was rather upset about that, and felt she might have been a bit to blame, maybe she should have talked to Lisa about things more, but frankly I don't think that would have made any difference. Actually she worried more about Lisa not being able to paint once the baby was born. She was pleased, of course, about Francesca, but she did feel it might be a pity for Lisa to tie herself down so soon.

Actually it didn't work out that way. Lisa got into a habit almost at once of leaving Francesca with mother or with me whenever she wanted some time to herself – she was having to go up and down to London quite a lot by then to keep in touch with her old friends from college, and to try to find openings for her work. I had my two, of course, so, as she said, an extra one didn't make much difference. It did get a bit more of a strain, though, the next year, after she'd had Jason and there was him too. Four children is quite a lot to keep an eye on, but of course mother helped out a lot, whenever her leg wasn't too bad. Bella Sims, I need hardly say, didn't go much for the granny bit.

Lisa had Alex the year after that. I've never understood, I must say, why Lisa has babies so much; I mean, she must *know*. Of course, she is vague and casual, but all the same ... I've had my two, and that's that, barring accidents, and I'm planning to go back to work when I can, eventually. I daresay Lisa would think that all very cold and calculating, but that's the way I am. Lisa says she doesn't believe in planning life, you just let things happen to you, you see what comes next.

Alex had this funny Chinese look from a tiny baby and it took us ages to cotton on, in fact I suppose he was eleven months or so before the penny finally dropped and we realised that, to put it frankly, Melvyn wasn't the father.

It came as a bit of a blow, especially to poor mother. She went all quiet for days, and I must admit she's never really liked Alex ever since, not like she dotes on the others.

The father was someone Lisa knew in London. He was from Thailand, not Chinese, actually. But in fact it was all over apparently sometime before Alex was born and she didn't see him again.

Melvyn took it very well. I suppose he must have known before we did. In fact, Melvyn has been very good to Lisa from the start, nothing of what's happened has been his fault in any way. Not many men would have coped with the children like he has, right from the beginning, which he had to because of Lisa being away quite a bit, or involved in her own things. Truth to tell, he was better with them, too. It's not that Lisa's a bad mother – I mean she doesn't get cross or impatient, specially, she just doesn't bother about them much. She says the worst thing you can do is to be over-protective; she says mother was a bit over-protective with her.

Bella Sims had some fairly nasty things to say; but then soon after that she sold the gallery and moved back to London and we never saw any more of her. This was the wrong kind of provincial town, apparently; art was never going to be a viable proposition.

Things got worse after Alex was born. Lisa went off more and more. Sometimes I'd find we had the children for days on end, or Melvyn would come round, pretty well at the end of his tether, saying could we lend a hand, Lisa was down in London seeing about some gallery which might show her stuff, or she'd gone off to Wales to see a woman who was doing the most fantastic ceramics.

It was after the time Francesca wandered off and got lost for a whole day, and the police found her in the end and then it turned out Lisa had been somewhere with Ravi, this Indian friend of hers, that things rather came to a head. Lisa and Melvyn had a row and Lisa brought all the children round to me, late one night, in their pyjamas, and said she was so upset about everything she'd have to go off on her own for a few days to try to think things over. Jim had flu and I'd just got over it myself so I was a bit sharp with her: I said couldn't Melvyn have them, and she said no, Melvyn had to teach all next day, which was probably true enough. And anyway, she said, they're my children, I'm responsible for them, I've got to work out what to do. She was wearing a long red and blue thing of some hand-blocked stuff, and lots of silver bracelets, and she looked exhausted and very dashing both at the same time, somehow; the children were all crying.

So I took them, of course, and she was gone for a week or so. We talked things over while she was gone. Jim and I talked, and Jim said (which he never had before) that he thought Lisa ought to pull herself together a bit, and I had to agree. It was easier with her not being there; somehow when Lisa's with you, you always end up feeling that she really can't be expected to do what other people do, I actually feel bad if I see Lisa washing a floor or doing nappies or any of the things I do myself every day. It does seem different for her, somehow.

And mother talked to Melvyn, who'd been round to find out where the children were. Mother was very sympathetic; she knows what living with Lisa is like; we all do. She said to Melvyn that of course Lisa had been silly and irresponsible, nobody could deny that. She told Melvyn, with a little laugh to try to cheer things up a bit, that there'd been occasions when Lisa was a small girl and was being particularly wilful and tiresome that she'd been on the verge of giving her a good smack. And then, she said, one used to remember just in time that there is a point beyond which she – people like her – simply cannot help themselves. One just can't expect the same things you can from other people.

I don't know what Melvyn thought about that; he didn't say. After the divorce came through he married Sylvie Fletcher who works in the library; I was at school with her and she's very nice but quite ordinary. Mother always says it must seem such a come down after Lisa. They've got a little boy now, and Melvyn takes a lot of trouble to see Francesca and Jason (and Alex too, in fact) as much as he can – and it *is* trouble because he has to trail down to London and try to find where Lisa's moved to now, unless it's one of the times Jim and I are having the children, or mother.

Mother and I had to talk, too. I'd gone round there and found her up in Lisa's old studio, just standing looking at a great thing Lisa had done that was partly oil paint slapped on very thick and partly bits of material stuck on and then painted over; in the top corner there was a picture of the Duke of Edinburgh from a magazine, sideways on and varnished over. I think it must have been meant to be funny, or sarcastic or something. We both stood in front of it for a bit and mother said, 'Of course, it is very good, isn't it?'

I said I honestly didn't know.

We both felt a bit awkward in there; Lisa has always been very fussy about her privacy. She says the one thing people absolutely have no right to do is push themselves into other people's lives; she is very strong for people being independent and having individual rights. So mother and I just had a quick tidy because the dust was bothering mother, and then we went downstairs and drank a cup of tea and chatted. Mother talked about this book she'd been reading about Augustus John; she's very interested in biographies of famous poets and artists and people like that. She was saying what a fascinating person he must have been but of course he did behave very badly to people, his wife and all those other women, but all the same it must have been terribly exhilarating, life with someone like that. You could see she was half thinking of Lisa. I was feeling snappish, the children were getting me down rather, and I said Lisa wasn't Augustus John, was she? We don't really know, do we – if she's any good or not.

There was a silence. We looked at each other. And then mother looked away and said, 'No. I know we don't. But she just might be, mightn't she? And it would be so awful if she was and nobody had been understanding and helpful.'

Lisa came back for the children once she'd found a flat. She'd had her hair cut off and what was left was like a little boy's, all smoothed into the back of her neck; it made her look about sixteen. Lisa is very small and thin, I should say; people always offer to carry suitcases for her, if you see her doing anything involving effort you automatically find yourself offering to do it for her because you feel she won't be able to manage and anyway it makes you feel guilty watching her.

She said the hair was symbolic; she was making a fresh start and getting rid of the atmosphere that had been holding her back (I suppose she meant poor Melvyn) and actually everything was going to be good because Ravi's father who was an Indian businessman and quite rich was going to buy a little gallery in Islington that Ravi was going to run and she was frantically busy getting enough stuff together for an exhibition.

The gallery didn't last long because it kept losing money and after a bit Ravi's father, who turned out to be quite an ordinary businessman after all and not as sensitive and interested in art as Lisa had thought, said he was cutting his losses and selling up. In fact Ravi and Lisa weren't living together by then anyway because Lisa had realised that the reason her work wasn't really right was that she'd always been in cities and in fact what she needed to fulfil herself properly was to get away somewhere remote and live a very simple, hard-working life. Actually, she thought, pottery was the right medium for her, once she could scrape up enough for a wheel and everything.

Mother helped out with that, financially, and Lisa took the children down to this place in Somerset where a man she knew, someone quite rich, had this big old house that was a sort of commune for artists, and for parties of young people to come and study nature and the environment. We went down there, once when Lisa wanted us to take Alex for a bit, because he'd not been well and she was finding it a bit of a strain coping with him. There was certainly a lot of environment there, it was miles from anywhere, except the village, and there wasn't much of that, so that there seemed to be more artists than ordinary village people. It was a hot summer and Lisa and the rest were going round with just about no clothes on, more like the south of France than west Somerset and I rather got the impression that some of the older village people didn't like it all that much, and there was an outdoor pop festival one weekend that went on to all hours, and this man who owned the place had made the church into an exhibition room for the artists. It was one of those little grey stone churches with old carvings and so on and it looked queer, all done out inside with huge violent-coloured paintings and peculiar sculptures. Lisa said actually it was frightfully good for these people, to be exposed to a today kind of life, they were so cut off down there, and to be given the sort of visual shock that might get them really looking and thinking.

Eventually Lisa began to feel a bit cut off herself, and there'd been some trouble with the county child care people which Lisa said was a lot of ridiculous fuss, it was just that Francesca had got this funny habit of wandering off sometimes and actually it was good that she felt so free and uninhibited, most people *stifle* their children so. Francesca was six by then, and Jason five. Jason had this bad stammer; he still has, sometimes he can't seem to get a word out for hours.

Lisa came home to mother's for a bit then, because rents in London were sky-high and it would have meant her getting a job, which of course was out of the question, if she was going to keep up her potting, and the weaving she had got very keen on now. And at mother's she had the studio, so it might work out quite well, she thought, provided she kept in touch with people and didn't feel too much out on a limb.

Jim and I had Alex more or less permanently by then; we are very fond of him, he seems almost like ours now which is just as well, I suppose. It is just as well too that Jim is the kind of person he is; Lisa thinks he is dull, I know, but that is just her opinion, and as I have got older I have got less and less certain that she gets things right. In fact, around this time I did have a kind of outburst, with mother, which I suppose was about Lisa, indirectly. She had gone down to London to keep in touch with people, and there had been a business with Francesca at school (sometimes she steals things, it is very awkward, they are going to have the educational psychologist people look at her) and I had had to see to it all. I was feeling a bit fed up too because what with Alex, and having so much to do, I'd realised it wasn't going to be any good trying to go back to work at the end of the year as I'd planned. Maybe you should be like Lisa, and not plan. Anyway, mother was telling me about this biography of Dylan Thomas she'd been reading, and what an extraordinary eccentric person he was and how fascinating to know. Actually I'd read the book too and personally I don't see why you shouldn't write just as good poetry without borrowing money off people all the time and telling lies.

Once, when I was at college, one of the tutors got this well-known poet to come and give a talk to the second-year English. He had glasses with thick rims and a rather old-fashioned-looking suit and frankly he might have been somebody's father, or your bank manager. He was very friendly and he talked to us in the common-room afterwards and he wasn't rude to anyone. I told mother about it, later, and she said she wondered if he was all that good – as a poet, that is.

And I suddenly blew up when she was going on like this about Dylan Thomas. I said – shouted – 'T. S. Eliot worked in an office. Gustav Holst was a bloody schoolteacher.'

Mother looked startled. She said, 'Who?' She's less interested in musicians.

I said crossly, 'Oh, never mind. Just there's more than one way of going about things.' And then the children started squabbling and we were distracted and the subject never came up again, not quite like that.

Lisa got a part-share of a flat in London with a friend; she had to be down there because there was this person who was talking of setting up a craft workshop for potters and weavers and that, a fantastic new scheme, and she needed to be on the spot for when it came off. It was difficult for her to have the children there, so Francesca stayed with mother and the two little ones with us. Francesca settled down well at school and began to behave a lot better, and Jason's stammer was improving, and then all of a sudden Lisa turned up, as brown as a conker, with her hair long again, and henna-dyed now, and said she'd met these incredible Americans in Morocco, who had this atelier, and she was going to work there and learn this amazing new enamelling technique. That was what she ought to have been doing all along, she said, if only she'd realised, not messing about with pots and fabrics. She was taking the children with her, she said, because growing up in an English provincial town was so stultifying for them, and it was nice and cheap out there.

She took Alex too, but after six months she suddenly sent him back again with a peculiar German friend of hers; we had to collect him at Heathrow. He kept wetting the bed apparently and although Lisa isn't particularly fussy about that kind of thing she said she had the feeling he wasn't very adaptable.

And so it goes on. She came back from Morocco after a couple of years, and there was a spell in London when a rather well-off Dutch person that we thought she was going to marry bought her a house in Fulham. For six months Francesca went to a very expensive school where all the teaching was done in French, and then the Dutch person went off and Lisa found the house was rented, not paid for like she'd thought, so she came home again for a bit to sort things out, and Francesca went to the comprehensive.

And then there was Wales with the Polish sculptor, and then the Dordogne with the tapestry people, and London again, and back here for a bit, and the cottage in Sussex that someone lent her ...

The last time she was here she had a curious creased look about her, like a dress that had been put away in a drawer and not properly hung out, and I suddenly realised that she is nearly forty now, Lisa. It doesn't seem right; she is a person that things have always been in front of, somehow, not behind.

Mother and I cleaned out her old studio, the other day. Mother has this feeling that Francesca may be talented, in which case she will need to use it. We dusted and polished and sorted out the cupboard with Lisa's old paintings and collages and whatnot. They all looked rather shabby, and somehow withered – not quite as large or bright as one had remembered. Mother said doubtfully, 'I wonder if she would like any of these sent down to London?' And then, 'Of course it is a pity she has had such an unsettled sort of life.'

That 'had' did not strike either of us for a moment or two. After a bit mother began to put the things away in the cupboard again, very carefully; mother is past seventy now and the stooping was awkward for her. I persuaded her to sit down and I finished off.

There was one portfolio of things Lisa did at school, really nice drawings of flowers and leaves and a pencil portrait of another girl whose name neither mother nor I could remember. Mother put these aside; she thought she might have them framed and hang them in the hall. Holding them, she said, 'Though with her temperament I suppose you could not expect that she would settle and at least she has always been free to express herself, which is the important thing.' When I did not answer she said, 'Isn't it, dear?' and I said, 'Yes. Yes, I think so, mother.'

SALE

Anita Desai

Anita Desai (b. 1937) is an Indian writer whose published
works include novels, children's books and short stories.
She is a member of the Advisory Board for English of the
National Academy of Letters in Delhi and a Fellow of the
Royal Society of Literature in London. She has been
shortlisted for the Man Booker Prize three times.

There they are, at the door now, banging. They had met him, written
a note and made an appointment – and here they are, as a direct result
of it all, rattling. He stands on the other side of the door, in the dusk-
mottled room, fingering an unshaven chin and dropping cigarette
butts on the floor which is already littered with them. There is a
pause in the knocking. He hears their voices – querulous, impatient.
He turns and silently goes towards the inner door that opens onto
a passage. He pushes it ajar, quietly, holding his breath. At the end
of the passage another door stands open: it is like a window or an
alcove illuminated by the deep glow of the fire. There his wife sits,
kneading dough in a brass bowl, with her head bowed so that her
long hair broods down to her shoulders on either side of her heavy,
troubled face. The red border of her sari cuts a bright gash through
the still tableau. The child sits on the mat beside her, silent, absorbed
in the mysteries of a long-handled spoon which he turns over with
soft, wavering fingers that are unaccustomed to the unsympathetic
steel. His head, too, is bowed so that his father, behind him, can see
the small wisps of hair on the back of his neck. He looks at them,
holding his breath till it begins to hurt his chest. Then the knocking
is resumed and his wife, hearing it, raises her head. She sees him
then, at the door, like a dog hanging about, wanting something, and
immediately her nostrils flare. 'Can't you answer the door?' she cries.
'What's the matter with you? It must be them – this is your chance.'
Startled, the child drops the spoon with a clatter. Quickly he shuts
the door. Then he goes and opens the front door and lets them in.

'We were about to give up,' one man cries, laughing, and brings in his friend and also a woman, seeing whom the artist, who is not expecting her, finds himself dismayed and confused. A woman – therefore someone in league with his wife, he thinks, and stares at her lush, unreluctant face and the bright enamelled ear-rings that frame it. He is silent. The two men stare at him.

'You *were* expecting us, weren't you?' enquires the jovial man whom he had liked, once. 'We wrote—'

'Yes,' he murmurs. 'Oh yes, yes,' and stands there, on the threshold, with an empty match box in his hand, his face looking like a house from which ghosts had driven away all inhabitants.

Then the man introduces his wife. 'She also paints,' he says, 'and was so interested in seeing your pictures, I brought her along. You don't mind, do you?'

'No,' he says, gathering himself together with a laboured effort, and steps aside to let them in. Then it is they who are silent, staring in dismay at the shambles about them. There are pictures to look at, yes, but one lies on the floor with a bundle of rags and some cigarette stubs on it, another is propped up on a shelf with bottles of hair oil, clay toys and calendars before it, and others have drifted off the wooden divan into corners of the room, peering out from under old newspapers and dirty clothes. The artist watches them, wondering at the imbecility of their appearance as they huddle together and gape. 'Oh,' he says, recovering, 'the light,' and switches it on. It is unshaded and hangs low over the flat table at which he paints so that they are illuminated weirdly from the waist downwards, leaving their faces more confused with shadows than before. The woman is quickest to relax, to make herself known, to become acquainted. 'Ah,' she cries, hurrying to the shelf to pull out a picture. 'What are they?' she asks him, gazing first at the flowers that blaze across the dirty paper, then at him, coaxing him for their secret with an avidly enquiring look. 'Not cannas, not lotuses – what can they be?'

He smiles at her curiosity. 'Nothing,' he says. 'Not real flowers – just anything at all.'

'Really!' she exclaims, shaking her enamelled ear-rings. 'How wonderful to be able to imagine such forms, such colours. Look, Ram, aren't they pretty?' The two men become infected by her exaggerated attitude of relaxation. They begin to prowl about the room, now showing amusement at the litter which is, after all, only to be expected in an artist's studio, then crinkling their noses for, one has to admit, it *does* smell, and then showing surprised interest in the pictures of which they have come to select one for their home which is newly built and now to be furnished. What with the enthusiasm and thoroughness they bring to their task, the rags and grime of the studio are soon almost obliterated by the fanfare of colour that spills forth, a crazy whorl of them, unknown colours that cannot be named, spilling out of forms that cannot be identified. One cannot pinpoint any school, any technique, any style – one can only admit oneself in the presence of a continuous and inspired act of creation: so they tell themselves. The woman gives cry upon cry of excitement and turns again and again to the artist who stands watching them thoughtfully. 'But how did you get this colour? You must tell me because I paint – and I could never get anything like this. What is it?'

'Ahh, Naples Yellow,' he says, as if making a guess.

'No, but there is some orange in it too.'

'Ah yes, a little orange also.'

'And green?'

'Yes, a little perhaps.'

'No, but that special tinge – how did you get it? A little bit of white – or flesh pink? What is it? Ram, Ram, just look, isn't it pretty – this weird bird? I don't suppose it has a name?'

'No, no, it is not real. I am a city man, I know nothing about birds.'

'But you know everything about birds! And flowers. I suppose they *are* birds and flowers, all these marvellous things. And your paintings are full of them. How can it possibly be that you have never seen them?'

He has to laugh then – she is so artless, so completely without any vestige of imagination, and so completely unlike his wife. 'Look,' he says, suddenly buoyant, and points to the window. She has to stand on her toes to look out of the small aperture, through the bars, and then she gazes out with all the intentness she feels he expects of her, at the deep, smoke-ridden twilight wound around the ill-lit slum, the smoking heaps of dung-fires and the dark figures that sit and stand in it hopelessly. Like fog-horns, conch shells begin to blow as tired housewives summon up their flagging spirits for the always lovely, always comforting ritual of evening prayers. She tries to pierce the scene with her sharp eyes, trying to see what he sees in it, till she hears him laughing behind her with a cracked kind of hilarity. 'There you see – my birds and my flowers,' he tells her, clapping his hands as though enjoying a practical joke he has played on her. 'I see a tram – and that is my mountain. I see a letter-box – and that is my tree. Listen! Do you hear my birds?' He raises his hand and, with its gesture, ushers in the evening voices of children uttering those cries and calls peculiar to the time of parting, the time of relinquishing their games, before they enter their homes and disappear into sleep – voices filled with an ecstasy of knowledge, of sensation drawn to an apex, brought on by the realization of imminent departure and farewell: voices panicky with love, with lament, with fear and sacrifice.

The artist watches the three visitors and finds them attentive, puzzled. 'There,' he says, dropping his hand. 'There are my birds. I don't see them – but I hear them and imagine how they look. It is easy, no, when you can hear them so clearly?'

'You are a magician,' says the quiet man, shaking his head and turning to a crayon drawing of pale birds delicately stalking the shallows of a brooding sea. 'Look at these – I can't believe you haven't actually painted them on the spot.'

'No, I have not, but I do know the sea. You know, I am a fisherman! I should have been – my people are. How do you like this one of fishing boats? I used to see them coming in like this, in the evening, with the catch. And then my mother would cook one large one for dinner – oh, it was good, good!'

They all stand around him, smiling at this unexpected burst of childish exuberance. 'You paint from memory then?' enquires one, but the woman cries, 'You like fish? You must come and eat it at our house one day – I cook fish very well.'

'I will, I will,' he cries, scurrying about as though he were looking for something he had suddenly remembered he needed, hunting out seascapes for them to see, and more of the successful flowers. 'Oh, I will love that – to see this new house of yours and eat a meal cooked by you. Yes, I will come. Here, look, another one – a canal scene. Do you like it? That is paddy growing there – it is so green …' Now he wants to turn out the entire studio for them, bring out his best. He chatters, they laugh. Pictures fall to the floor. Crayons are smeared, oils are smudged – but he does not mind. He does not even sign his pictures. When the woman pauses over a pastel that is blurred by some stroke of carelessness, he says, 'Oh that is nothing, I can touch it up. Do you see the blue? Do you like it? Yes, I will see your paintings and I will tell you plainly what I like and what I don't like, and you will appreciate anyway. Oh, I love fish …' Only now and then he grows aware of his wife, breathing heavily because of the weight of the child asleep on her arm, straining to hear at the door, frowning because she cannot understand, is not certain, is worried, worried to death … and then he draws down the corners of his mouth and is silent. But when a picture of curled flowers is brought to him, he stares at it till it comes into proper focus and explains it to them. 'Ah,' he says, 'I painted that long ago – for my son, when he was born. I wanted him to have flowers, flowers all about his bed, under his head, at his feet, everywhere. And I did not have any. I did not know of a garden from where I could get some. So I painted them. That is one of them. Ah yes, yes,' he smiles, and the three who watch him grow tender, sympathetic. The woman says, '*This* one? It is your son's? How lovely – how lucky.'

'No,' he cries loudly. 'I mean, you can have it. Do you like it? It is what you want for your new house?'

'Oh no,' she says softly and puts it away. 'You painted it for your child. I can't take it from him.'

The artist finds himself sweating and exhausted – he had not realized how he was straining himself. He has had nothing but tea and cigarettes since early that morning and there is no breath of air coming through the barred window. He wipes his face with his hand and blotches another crayon with his wet fingers as he picks it up and flings it away. 'Then what do you want?' he asks in a flat voice. 'What do you like? What do you want to have – a flower picture or a landscape?'

'Perhaps figures – people always make a room seem bright.'

'I don't paint figures,' he says shortly. 'You told me you wanted a landscape. Here they are – all sizes, big, small, medium; hills, seas, rivers; green, blue, yellow. Is there nothing you like?'

'Yes, yes,' they all assure him together, upset by his change of tone, and one holds up a picture at arm's length to admire it lavishly, another bends to shuffle through the pile on the table. But there are so many, they say, it is hard to choose. That is nothing, he says, *he* will choose for them. Oh no, they laugh, glancing to see if he is serious, for they have something very special in mind – something that will light up their whole house, become its focal point, radiate and give their home a tone, an atmosphere. No, not this one, not *quite* – it is lovely, but … Before he knows it, they are at the door, descending the stairs with one backward look at all the heroic mass of colour inside, saying goodbye. He rushes down the stairs after them, spreading out his arms. Their car stands under the lamp-post. He flings himself at the door, hangs on to it.

'There is not one you liked? I thought you had come to buy – you said – '

'Yes, we wanted to,' says the man whom he had liked, once. 'But not one of these. You see, we have something very special in mind, something quite extraordinary – '

'But – not one of those I showed you? I thought you liked them – you said – '

'I did, I did,' chirps the woman from the soft recesses of the back seat. 'Oh and those lovely flowers you painted for your son – *lucky* child!'

'You liked them? I will paint you another like it, just like it – '

'But we wanted a landscape really,' says the man. 'Something in those cool greys and whites. Perhaps a snow scene – now *that* would be something different.'

'Snow?' shouts the artist. 'I will paint snow. I will paint the Himalayas for you. How big do you want it? So big? So?'

'No, no,' they laugh. 'Not so big. That would be too expensive.'

'All right, smaller. I will paint it. By the end of the week you will have it.'

They laugh at his haste, his trembling, shrill excitement. 'But, my friend, have you ever seen snow?' enquires the jovial one, patting his arm.

'Ah!' he gives such a cry that it halts them in their movements of departure, to turn and see him spread out his arms till his fingers reach out of the smoke of the dung fires and the dust of the unlit lanes, to reach out to the balm of ice and snow and isolation. 'I will paint such snow for you as you have never seen, as no one has ever painted. I can see it all, here,' and he taps his forehead with such emphasis that they smile – he is quite a comic. Or even a bit crazy. Drunk?

'Now, now, my friend,' says the man, patting his arm again. 'Don't be in a hurry about it. You paint it when you are in the mood. Then it will be good.'

'I am in the mood now,' he cries. 'I am always in the mood, don't you see? Tomorrow, tomorrow I will have it ready. I will bring it to your house. Give me the address!'

They laugh. The engine stutters to life and there is a metallic finality in the sound of the doors being shut. But he clings to the handle, thrusts his head in, his eyes blazing. 'And will you give me an advance?' he asks tensely. 'I need money, my friend. Can you give me an advance?'

The woman creeps away into a corner, wrapping herself closely in a white shawl. One man, in embarrassment, falls silent. The other laughs and puts his hands in his pockets, then draws them out to show they are empty. 'Brother, if I had some with me, I would give it to you – all of it – but since we only came to see, I didn't bring any. I'm sorry.'

'I need it.'

'Listen, when you bring the picture, I will give you something, even if I don't want it, I will give you something – in advance, for the one we will buy. But today, just now, I have nothing.'

The artist steps back to let them go. As they drive out of the lane and the smoke smudges and obscures the tail-lights, he hears his wife come out on the stairs behind him.

MISCHIEF

Alice Munro

Alice Munro (b. 1931) is a Canadian short story writer and winner of the 2009 Man Booker International Prize, which honours her complete body of work. She has been awarded Canada's Governor General's Award for fiction three times, the Giller Prize twice and is a perennial contender for the Nobel Prize for Fiction. She was awarded the National Book Critics Circle Award in 1998 for her collection, *The Love of a Good Woman*.

Rose fell in love with Clifford at a party which Clifford and Jocelyn gave and Patrick and Rose attended. They had been married about three years at this time, Clifford and Jocelyn a year or so longer.

Clifford and Jocelyn lived out past West Vancouver, in one of those summer cottages, haphazardly winterized, that used to line the short curving streets between the lower highway and the sea. The party was in March, on a rainy night. Rose was nervous about going to it. She felt almost sick as they drove through West Vancouver, watched the neon lights weeping in the puddles on the road, listened to the condemning tick of the windshield wipers. She would often afterwards look back and see herself sitting beside Patrick, in her low-cut black blouse and black velvet skirt which she hoped would turn out to be the right thing to wear; she was wishing they were just going to the movies. She had no idea that her life was going to be altered.

Patrick was nervous too, although he would not have admitted it. Social life was a puzzling, often disagreeable business for them both. They had arrived in Vancouver knowing nobody. They followed leads. Rose was not sure whether they really longed for friends, or simply believed they ought to have them. They dressed up and went out to visit people, or tidied up the living room and waited for the people who had been invited to visit them. In some cases they established steady visiting patterns. They had some drinks, during those evenings, and around eleven or eleven-thirty – which hardly ever came soon enough – Rose went out to the kitchen and made coffee and something to eat. The things she made to eat were usually squares of toast, with a slice of tomato on top, then a square of cheese, then a bit of bacon, the whole thing broiled and held together with a toothpick. She could not manage to think of anything else.

It was easier for them to become friends with people Patrick liked than with people Rose liked because Rose was very adaptable, in fact deceitful, and Patrick was hardly adaptable at all. But in this case, the case of Jocelyn and Clifford, the friends were Rose's. Or Jocelyn was. Jocelyn and Rose had known enough not to try to establish couple-visiting. Patrick disliked Clifford without knowing him because Clifford was a violinist; no doubt Clifford disliked Patrick because Patrick worked in a branch of his family's department store. In those days the barriers between people were still strong and reliable; between arty people and business people; between men and women.

Rose did not know any of Jocelyn's friends, but understood they were musicians and journalists and lecturers at the University and even a woman writer who had had a play performed on the radio. She expected them to be intelligent, witty, and easily contemptuous. It seemed to her that all the time she and Patrick were sitting in the living rooms, visiting or being visited, really clever and funny people, who had a right to despise them, were conducting irregular lives and parties elsewhere. Now came the chance to be with those people, but her stomach rejected it, her hands were sweating.

Jocelyn and Rose had met in the maternity ward of the North Vancouver General Hospital. The first thing Rose saw, on being taken back to the ward after having Anna, was Jocelyn sitting up in bed reading the Journals of André Gide. Rose knew the book by its colors, having noticed it on the drugstore stands. Gide was on the list of writers she meant to work through. At that time she read only great writers.

The immediately startling and comforting thing to Rose, about Jocelyn, was how much Jocelyn looked like a student, how little she had let herself be affected by the maternity ward. Jocelyn had long black braids, a heavy pale face, thick glasses, no trace of prettiness, and an air of comfortable concentration.

A woman in the bed beside Jocelyn was describing the arrangement of her kitchen cupboards. She would forget to tell where she kept something – rice, say, or brown sugar – and then she would have to start all over again, making sure her audience was with her by saying "Remember on the right hand highest shelf next the stove, that's where I keep the packages of soup but not the canned soup, I keep the canned soup underneath the counter in with the canned goods, well, right next to that—"

Other women tried to interrupt, to tell how they kept things, but they were not successful, or not for long. Jocelyn sat reading, and twiddling the end of a braid between her fingers, as if she was in a library, at college, as if she was researching for a paper, and this world of other women had never closed down on her at all. Rose wished she could manage as well.

She was still dazed from the birth. Whenever she closed her eyes she saw an eclipse, a big black ball with a ring of fire. That was the baby's head, ringed with pain, the instant before she pushed it out. Across this image, in disturbing waves, went the talking woman's kitchen shelves, dipping under their glaring weight of cans and packages. But she could open her eyes and see Jocelyn, black and white, braids falling over her hospital nightgown. Jocelyn was the only person she saw who looked calm and serious enough to match the occasion.

Soon Jocelyn got out of bed, showing long white unshaved legs and a stomach still stretched by pregnancy. She put on a striped bathrobe. Instead of a cord, she tied a man's necktie around her waist. She slapped across the hospital linoleum in her bare feet. A nurse came running, warned her to put on slippers.

"I don't own any slippers."

"Do you own shoes?" said the nurse rather nastily.

"Oh, yes. I own shoes."

Jocelyn went back to the little metal cabinet beside her bed and took out a pair of large, dirty, run-over moccasins. She went off making as sloppy and insolent a noise as before.

Rose was longing to know her.

The next day Rose had her own book out to read. It was *The*

Last Puritan, by George Santayana, but unfortunately it was a library copy; the title on the cover was rubbed and dim, so it was impossible that Jocelyn should admire Rose's reading material as Rose had admired hers. Rose didn't know how she could get to talk to her.

The woman who had explained about her cupboards was talking about how she used her vacuum cleaner. She said it was very important to use all the attachments because they each had a purpose and after all you had paid for them. Many people didn't use them. She described how she vacuumed her living-room drapes. Another woman said she had tried to do that but the material kept getting bunched up. The authoritative woman said that was because she hadn't been doing it properly.

Rose caught Jocelyn's eye around the corner of her book.

"I hope you polish your stove knobs," she said quietly.

"I certainly do," said Jocelyn.

"Do you polish them every day?"

"I used to polish them twice a day but now that I have the new baby I just don't know if I'll get around to it."

"Do you use that special stove-knob polish?"

"I certainly do. And I use the special stove-knob cloths that come in that special package."

"That's good. Some people don't."

"Some people will use anything."

"Old dishrags."

"Old snotrags."

"Old snot."

After this their friendship bloomed in a hurry. It was one of those luxuriant intimacies that spring up in institutions; in schools, at camp, in prison. They walked in the halls, disobeying the nurses. They annoyed and mystified the other women. They became hysterical as schoolgirls, from the things they read aloud to each other. They did not read Gide or Santayana but the copies of *True Love* and *Personal Romances* which they had found in the waiting room.

"It says here you can buy false calves," Rose read. "I don't see how you'd hide them, though. I guess you strap them on your legs. Or maybe they just sit here inside your stockings but wouldn't you think they'd show?"

"On your legs?" said Jocelyn. "You strap them on your legs? Oh, false calves! False calves! I thought you were talking about false *calves*! False baby cows!"

Anything like that could set them off.

"False baby cows!"

"False tits, false bums, false baby cows!"

"What will they think of next!"

The vacuum-cleaning woman said they were always butting in and spoiling other people's conversations and she didn't see what was so funny about dirty language. She said if they didn't stop the way they carried on they would sour their milk.

"I've been wondering if maybe mine is sour," Jocelyn said. "It's an awfully disgusting color."

"What color?" Rose asked.

"Well. Sort of blue."

"Good God, maybe it's ink!"

The vacuum-cleaning woman said she was going to tell the nurse they were swearing. She said she was no prude, but. She asked if they were fit to be mothers. How was Jocelyn going to manage to wash diapers, when anybody could see she never washed her dressing gown?

Jocelyn said she planned to use moss, she was an Indian.

"I can believe it," the woman said.

After this Jocelyn and Rose prefaced many remarks with: *I'm no prude, but.*

"I'm no prude but would you look at this pudding!"

"I'm no prude but it feels like this kid has a full set of teeth."

The nurse said, wasn't it time for them to grow up?

Walking in the halls, Jocelyn told Rose that she was twenty-five, that her baby was to be called Adam, that she had a two-year-old boy at home, named Jerome, that her husband's name was Clifford and that he played the violin for a living. He played in the Vancouver Symphony. They were poor. Jocelyn came from Massachusetts and had gone to Wellesley College. Her father was a psychiatrist and her mother was a pediatrician. Rose told Jocelyn that she came from a small town in Ontario and that Patrick came from Vancouver Island and that his parents did not approve of the marriage.

"In the town I come from," Rose said, exaggerating, "everybody says yez. What'll yez have? How're yez doin."

"Yez?"

"Youse. It's the plural of you."

"Oh. Like Brooklyn. And James Joyce. Who does Patrick work for?"

"His family's store. His family has a department store."

"So aren't you rich now? Aren't you too rich to be in the ward?"

"We just spent all our money on a house Patrick wanted."

"Didn't you want it?"

"Not so much as he did."

That was something Rose had never said before.

They plunged into more random revelations.

Jocelyn hated her mother. Her mother had made her sleep in a room with white organdy curtains and had encouraged her to collect ducks. By the time she was thirteen Jocelyn had probably the largest collection in the world of rubber ducks, ceramic ducks, wooden ducks, pictures of ducks, embroidered ducks. She had also written what she described as a hideously precocious story called "The Marvelous Great Adventures of Oliver the Grand Duck," which her mother actually got printed, and distributed to friends and relatives at Christmas time.

"She is the sort of person who just covers everything with a kind of rotten smarminess. She sort of oozes over everything. She never talks in a normal voice, never. She's coy. She's just so filthy coy. Naturally she's a great success as a pediatrician. She has these rotten coy little names for all the parts of your body."

Rose, who would have been delighted with organdy curtains, perceived the fine lines, the ways of giving offence, that existed in Jocelyn's world. It seemed a much less crude and provisional world than her own. She doubted if she could tell Jocelyn about Hanratty but she began to try. She delivered Flo and the store in broad strokes. She played up the poverty. She didn't really have to. The true facts of her childhood were exotic enough to Jocelyn, and of all things, enviable.

"It seems more real," Jocelyn said. "I know that's a romantic notion."

They talked of their youthful ambitions. (They really believed their youth to be past.) Rose said she had wanted to be an actress though she was too much of a coward ever to walk on a stage. Jocelyn had wanted to be a writer but was shamed out of it by memories of the Grand Duck.

"Then I met Clifford," she said. "When I saw what real talent was, I knew that I would probably just be fooling around, trying to write, and I'd be better off nurturing him, or whatever the hell it is I do for him. He is really gifted. Sometimes he's a squalid sort of person. He gets away with it because he is really gifted."

"I think *that* is a romantic notion," Rose said firmly and jealously. "That gifted people ought to get away with things."

"Do you? But great artists always have."

"Not women."

"But women usually aren't great artists, not in the same way."

These were the ideas of most well-educated, thoughtful, even unconventional or politically radical young women of the time. One of the reasons Rose did not share them was that she had not been well educated. Jocelyn said to her, much later in their friendship, that one of the reasons she found it so interesting to talk to Rose, from the start, was that Rose had ideas but was uneducated. Rose was surprised at this, and mentioned the college she had attended in Western Ontario. Then she saw by an embarrassed withdrawal or regret, a sudden lack of frankness in Jocelyn's face – very unusual with her – that that was exactly what Jocelyn had meant.

After the difference of opinion about artists, and about men and women artists, Rose took a good look at Clifford when he came visiting in the evening. She thought him wan, self-indulgent, and neurotic-looking. Further discoveries concerning the tact, the effort, the sheer physical energy Jocelyn expended on this marriage (it was she who fixed the leaky taps and dug up the clogged drains) made Rose certain that Jocelyn was wasting herself, she was mistaken. She had a feeling that Jocelyn did not see much point in marriage with Patrick, either.

At first the party was easier than Rose had expected. She had been afraid that she would be too dressed-up; she would have liked to wear her toreador pants but Patrick would never have stood for it. But only a few of the girls were in slacks. The rest wore stockings, earrings, outfits much like her own. As at any gathering of young women at that time, three or four were noticeably pregnant. And most of the men were in suits and shirts and ties, like Patrick. Rose was relieved. Not only did she want Patrick to fit into the party; she wanted him to accept the people there, to be convinced they were not all freaks. When Patrick was a student he had taken her to concerts and plays and did not seem overly suspicious of the people who participated in them; indeed he rather favored these things, because they were detested by his family, and at that time – the time he chose Rose – he was having a brief rebellion against his family. Once he and Rose had gone to Toronto and sat in the Chinese temple room at the Museum, looking at the frescoes. Patrick told her how they were brought in small pieces from Shansi province; he seemed quite proud of his knowledge, and at the same time disarmingly, uncharacteristically humble, admitting he had got it all on a tour. It was since he had gone to work that he had developed harsh opinions and delivered wholesale condemnations. Modern Art was a Hoax. Avant-garde plays were filthy. Patrick had a special, mincing, spitting way of saying avant-garde, making the words seem disgustingly pretentious. And so they were, Rose thought. In a way, she could see what he meant. She could see too many sides of things; Patrick had not that problem.

Except for some great periodic fights she was very docile with Patrick, she tried to keep in favor. It was not easy to do so. Even before they were married he had a habit of delivering reproving lectures, in response to a simple question or observation. Sometimes in those days she would ask him a question in the hope that he would show off some superior knowledge that she could admire him for, but she was usually sorry she had asked, the answer was so long and had such a scolding tone, and the knowledge wouldn't be so superior, either. She did want to admire him, and respect him; it seemed that was a leap she was always on the edge of taking.

Later she thought that she did respect Patrick, but not in the way he wanted to be respected, and she did love him, not in the way he wanted to be loved. She didn't know it then. She thought she knew something about him, she thought she knew that he didn't really want to be whatever he was zealously making himself into. That arrogance might be called respect; that highhandedness, love. It didn't do anything to make him happy.

A few men wore jeans and turtlenecks or sweatshirts. Clifford was one of them, all in black. It was the time of the beatniks in San Francisco. Jocelyn had called Rose up on the phone and read her *Howl*. Clifford's skin looked very tanned, against the black, his hair was long for the time and almost as light a color as unbleached cotton; his eyes too were very light in color, a bright gray-blue. He looked small and cat-like to Rose, rather effeminate; she hoped Patrick wouldn't be too put off by him.

There was beer to drink, and a wine punch. Jocelyn, who was a splendid cook, was stirring a pot of jambalaya. Rose made a trip to the bathroom to remove herself from Patrick, who seemed to want to stick close to her (she thought he was being a watchdog; she forgot that he might be shy). When she came out he had moved on. She drank three cups of punch in quick succession and was introduced to the woman who had written the play. To Rose's surprise this woman was one of the drabbest, least confident-looking people in the room.

"I liked your play," Rose told her. As a matter of fact she had found if mystifying, and Patrick had thought it was revolting. It seemed to be about a woman who ate her own children. Rose knew that was symbolic, but couldn't quite figure out what it was symbolic of.

"Oh, but the production was terrible!" the woman said. In her embarrassment, her excitement and eagerness to talk about her play, she sprayed Rose with punch. "They made it so literal. I was afraid it would just come across as gruesome and I meant it to be quite delicate, I meant it to be so different from the way they made it." She started telling Rose everything that had gone wrong, the miscasting, the chopping of the most important – the *crucial* – lines. Rose felt flattered, listening to these details, and tried inconspicuously to wipe away the spray.

"But you did see what I meant?" the woman said.

"Oh, yes!"

Clifford poured Rose another cup of punch and smiled at her.

"Rose, you look delicious."

Delicious seemed an odd word for Clifford to use. Perhaps he was drunk. Or perhaps, hating parties altogether as Jocelyn said he did, he had taken on a role; he was the sort of man who told a girl she looked delicious. He might be adept at disguises, as Rose thought she herself was getting to be. She went on talking to the writer and a man who taught English Literature of the Seventeenth Century. She too might have been poor and clever, radical and irreverent for all anybody could tell.

A man and a girl were embracing passionately in the narrow hall. Whenever anybody wanted to get through, this couple had to separate but they continued looking at each other, and did not even close their mouths. The sight of those wet open mouths made Rose shiver. She had never been embraced like that in her life, never had her mouth opened like that. Patrick thought French-kissing was disgusting.

A little bald man named Cyril had stationed himself outside the bathroom door, and was kissing any girl who came out, saying, "Welcome, sweetheart, so glad you could come, so glad you went."

"Cyril is awful," the woman writer said. "Cyril thinks he has to try to act like a poet. He can't think of anything to do but hang around the john and upset people. He thinks he's outrageous."

"Is he a poet?" Rose said.

The lecturer in English Literature said, "He told me he had burned all his poems."

"How flamboyant of him," Rose said. She was delighted with herself for saying this, and with them for laughing.

The lecturer began to think of Tom Swifties.

"I can never think of any of those things," said the writer mournfully, "I care too much about language."

Loud voices were coming from the living room. Rose recognized Patrick's voice, soaring over and subduing everyone else's. She opened her mouth to say something, anything, to cover him up – she knew some disaster was on the way – but just then a tall, curly-haired, elated-looking man came through the hall, pushing the passionate couple unceremoniously apart, holding up his hands for attention.

"Listen to this," he said to the whole kitchen. "There's this guy in the living room you wouldn't believe him. Listen."

There must have been a conversation about Indians going on in the living room. Now Patrick had taken it over.

"Take them away," said Patrick. "Take them away from their parents as soon as they're born and put them in a civilized environment and educate them and they will turn out just as good as whites any day." No doubt he thought he was expressing liberal views. If they thought this was amazing, they should have got him on the execution of the Rosenbergs or the trial of Alger Hiss or the necessity for nuclear testing.

Some girl said mildly, "Well, you know, there is their own culture."

"Their culture is done for," said Patrick. "Kaput." This was a word he was using a good deal right now. He could use some words, clichés, editorial phrases – *massive reappraisal* was one of them – with such relish and numbing authority that you would think he was their originator, or at least that the very fact of his using them gave them weight and luster.

"They want to be civilized," he said. "The smarter ones do."

"Well, perhaps they don't consider they're exactly uncivilized," said the girl with an icy demureness that was lost on Patrick.

"Some people need a push."

The self-congratulatory tones, the ripe admonishment, caused the man in the kitchen to throw up his hands, and wag his head in delight and disbelief. "This has got to be a Socred politician."

As a matter of fact Patrick did vote Social Credit.

"Yes, well, like it or not," he was saying, "they have to be dragged kicking and screaming into the twentieth century."

"Kicking and steaming?" someone repeated.

"Kicking and screaming into the twentieth century," said Patrick, who never minded saying anything again.

"What an interesting expression. So humane as well."

Wouldn't he understand now, that he was being cornered, being baited and laughed at? But Patrick, being cornered, could only grow more thunderous. Rose could not listen any longer. She headed for the back passage, which was full of all the boots, coats, bottles, tubs, toys, that Jocelyn and Clifford had pitched out of the way for the party. Thank God it was empty of people. She went out of the back door and stood burning and shivering in the cool wet night. Her feelings were as confused as anybody's can get. She was humiliated, she was ashamed of Patrick. But she knew that it was his style that most humiliated her, and that made her suspect something corrupt and frivolous in herself. She was angry at those other people who were cleverer, or at least far quicker, than he was. She wanted to think badly of them. What did they care about Indians, really? Given a chance to behave decently to an Indian, Patrick might just come out ahead of them. This was a long shot, but she had to believe it. Patrick was a good person. His opinions were not good, but he was. The core of Patrick, Rose believed, was simple, pure and trustworthy. But how was she to get at it, to reassure herself, much less reveal it to others?

She heard the back door close and was afraid that Jocelyn had come out looking for her. Jocelyn was not someone who could believe in Patrick's core. She thought him stiff-necked, thick-skulled, and essentially silly.

It was not Jocelyn. It was Clifford. Rose didn't want to have to say anything to him. Slightly drunk as she was, woebegone, wet-faced from the rain, she looked at him without welcome. But he put his arms around her and rocked her.

"Oh Rose. Rose baby. Never mind. Rose."

So this was Clifford.

For five minutes or so they were kissing, murmuring, shivering, pressing, touching. They returned to the party by the front door. Cyril was there. He said, "Hey, wow, where have you two been?"

"Walking in the rain," said Clifford coolly. The same light possibly hostile voice in which he had told Rose she looked delicious. The Patrick-baiting had stopped. Conversation had become looser, drunker, more irresponsible. Jocelyn was serving jambalaya. She went to the bathroom to dry her hair and put lipstick on her rubbed-bare mouth. She was transformed, invulnerable. The first person she met coming out was Patrick. She had a wish to make him happy. She didn't care now what he had said, or would say.

"I don't think we've met, sir," she said, in a tiny flirtatious voice she used with him sometimes, when they were feeling easy together. "But you may kiss my hand."

"For crying out loud," said Patrick heartily, and he did squeeze her and kiss her, with a loud smacking noise, on the cheek. He always smacked when he kissed. And his elbows always managed to dig in somewhere and hurt her.

"Enjoying yourself?" Rose said.

"Not bad, not bad."

During the rest of the evening, of course, she was playing the game of watching Clifford while pretending not to watch him, and it seemed to her he was doing the same, and their eyes met, a few times, without expression, sending a perfectly clear message that rocked her on her feet. She saw him quite differently now. His body that had seemed small and tame now appeared to her light and slippery and full of energy; he was like a lynx or a bobcat. He had his tan from skiing. He went up Seymour Mountain and skied. An expensive hobby, but one which Jocelyn felt could not be denied him, because of the problems he had with his image. His masculine image, as a violinist, in this society. So Jocelyn said. Jocelyn had told Rose all about Clifford's background: the arthritic father, the small grocery store in a town in upstate New York, the poor tough neighborhood. She had talked about his problems as a child; the inappropriate talent, the grudging parents, the jeering schoolmates. His childhood left him bitter, Jocelyn said. But Rose no longer believed that Jocelyn had the last word on Clifford.

The party was on a Friday night. The phone rang the next morning, when Patrick and Anna were at the table eating eggs.

"How are you?" said Clifford.

"Fine."

"I wanted to phone you. I thought you might think I was just drunk or something. I wasn't."

"Oh, no."

"I've thought about you all night. I thought about you before, too."

"Yes." The kitchen was dazzling. The whole scene in front of her, of Patrick: and Anna at the table, the coffee pot with dribbles down the side, the jar of marmalade, was exploding with joy and possibility and danger. Rose's mouth was so dry she could hardly talk.

"It's a lovely day," she said. "Patrick and Anna and I might go up the mountain."

"Patrick's home?"

"Yes."

"Oh God. That was dumb of me. I forgot nobody else works Saturdays. I'm over here at a rehearsal."

"Yes."

"Can you pretend it's somebody else? Pretend it's Jocelyn."

"Sure."

"I love you, Rose," said Clifford, and hung up.

"Who was that?" said Patrick.

"Jocelyn."

"Does she have to call when I'm home?"

"She forgot. Clifford's at a rehearsal so she forgot other people aren't working." Rose delighted in saying Clifford's name. Deceitfulness, concealment, seemed to come marvelously easy to her; that might almost be a pleasure in itself.

"I didn't realize they'd have to work Saturdays," she said, to keep on the subject. "They must work terribly long hours."

"They don't work any longer hours than normal people, it's just strung out differently. He doesn't look capable of much work."

"He's supposed to be quite good. As a violinist."

"He looks like a jerk."

"Do you think so?"

"Don't you?"

"I guess I never considered him, really."

Jocelyn phoned on Monday and said she didn't know why she gave parties, she was still wading through the mess.

"Didn't Clifford help clean it up?"

"You are joking. I hardly saw him all weekend. He rehearsed Saturday and played yesterday. He says parties are my idea, I can deal with the aftermath. It's true. I get these fits of gregariousness, a party is the only cure. Patrick was interesting."

"Very."

"He's quite a stunning type, really, isn't he?"

"There are lots and lots like him. You just don't get to meet them."

"Woe is me."

This was just like any other conversation with Jocelyn. Their conversations, their friendship, could go on in the same way.

Rose did not feel bound by any loyalty to Jocelyn because she had divided Clifford. There was the Clifford Jocelyn knew, the same one she had always presented to Rose; there was also the Clifford Rose knew, now. She thought Jocelyn could be mistaken about him. For instance, when she said his childhood had left him bitter. What Jocelyn called bitterness seemed to Rose something more complex and more ordinary; just the weariness, suppleness, deviousness, meanness, common to a class. Common to Clifford's class, and Rose's. Jocelyn had been insulated in some ways, left stern and innocent. In some ways she was like Patrick.

From now on Rose did see Clifford and herself as being one sort of people, and Jocelyn and Patrick, though they seemed so different, and so disliked each other, as being another sort. They were whole and predictable. They took the lives they were leading absolutely seriously. Compared to them, both Clifford and Rose were shifty pieces of business.

If Jocelyn fell in love with a married man, what would she do? Before she even touched his hand, she would probably call a conference. Clifford would be invited, and the man himself, and the man's wife, and very likely Jocelyn's psychiatrist. (In spite of her rejection of her family Jocelyn believed that going to a psychiatrist was something everybody should do at developing or adjusting stages of life and she went herself, once a week.) Jocelyn would consider the implications; she would look things in the face. Never try to sneak her pleasure. She had never learned to sneak things. That was why it was unlikely that she would ever fall in love with another man. She was not greedy. And Patrick was not greedy either now, at least not for love.

If loving Patrick was recognizing something good, and guileless, at the bottom of him, being in love with Clifford was something else altogether. Rose did not have to believe that Clifford was good, and certainly she knew he was not guileless. No revelation of his duplicity or heartlessness, towards people other than herself, could have mattered to her. What was she in love with, then, what did she want of him? She wanted tricks, a glittering secret, tender celebrations of lust, a regular conflagration of adultery. All this after five minutes in the rain.

*

Six months or so after that party Rose lay awake all night. Patrick slept beside her in their stone and cedar house in a suburb called Capilano Heights, on the side of Grouse Mountain. The next night it was arranged that Clifford would sleep beside her, in Powell River, where he was playing with the touring orchestra. She could not believe that this would really happen. That is, she placed all her faith in the event, but could not fit it into the order of things that she knew.

During all these months Clifford and Rose had never gone to bed together. They had not made love anywhere else, either. This was the situation: Jocelyn and Clifford did not own a car. Patrick and Rose owned a car, but Rose did not drive it. Clifford's work did have the advantage of irregular hours, but how was he to get to see Rose? Could he ride the bus across the Lions Gate Bridge, then walk up her suburban street in broad daylight, past the neighbors' picture windows? Could Rose hire a baby sitter, pretend she was going to see the dentist, take the bus over to town, meet Clifford in a restaurant, go with him to a hotel room? But they didn't know which hotel to go to; they were afraid that without luggage they would be turned out on the street, or reported to the Vice Squad, made to sit in the Police Station while Jocelyn and Patrick were summoned to come and get them. Also, they didn't have enough money.

Rose had gone over to Vancouver, though, using the dentist excuse, and they had sat in a café, side by side in a black booth, kissing and fondling, right out in public in a place frequented by Clifford's students and fellow musicians; what a risk to take. On the bus going home Rose looked down her dress at the sweat blooming between her breasts and could have fainted at the splendor of herself, as well as at the thought of the risk undertaken. Another time, a very hot August afternoon, she waited in an alley behind the theater where Clifford was rehearsing, lurked in the shadows then grappled with him deliriously, unsatisfactorily. They saw a door open, and slipped inside. There were boxes stacked all around. They were looking for some nesting spot when a man spoke to them.

"Can I do anything for you?"

They had entered the back storeroom of a shoe store. The man's voice was icy, terrifying. The Vice Squad. The Police Station. Rose's dress was undone to the waist.

Once they met in a park, where Rose often took Anna, and pushed her on the swings. They held hands on a bench, under cover of Rose's wide cotton skirt. They laced their fingers together and squeezed painfully. Then Anna surprised them, coming up behind the bench and shouting, "Boo! I caught you!" Clifford turned disastrously pale. On the way home Rose said to Anna, "That was funny when you jumped out behind the bench. I thought you were still on the swing."

"I know," said Anna.

"What did you mean, you'd caught us?"

"I *caught* you," said Anna, and giggled, in what seemed to Rose a disturbingly pert and knowledgeable way.

"Would you like a fudgsicle? I would!" Rose said gaily, with thoughts of blackmail and bargains, Anna dredging this up for *her* psychiatrist in twenty years' time. The episode made her feel shaky and sick and she wondered if it had given Clifford a distaste for her. It had, but only temporarily.

As soon as it was light she got out of bed and went to look at the day, to see if it would be good for flying. The sky was clear; no sign of the fog that often grounded planes at this time of year. Nobody but Clifford knew she was going to Powell River. They had been planning this for six weeks, ever since they knew he was going on tour. Patrick thought she was going to Victoria, where she had a friend whom she had known at college. She had pretended, during the past few weeks, to have been in touch with this friend again. She had said she would be back tomorrow night. Today was Saturday. Patrick was at home to look after Anna.

She went into the dining room to check the money she had saved from Family Allowance checks. It was in the bottom of the silver muffin dish. Thirteen dollars. She meant to add that to what Patrick gave her to get to Victoria. Patrick always gave her money when she asked, but he wanted to know how much and what for. Once when they were out walking she wanted to go into a drugstore; she asked him for money and he said, with no more than customary sternness, "What for?" and Rose began to cry, because she had been going to buy vaginal jelly. She might just as well have laughed, and would have, now. Since she had fallen in love with Clifford, she never quarreled with Patrick.

She figured out again the money she would need. The plane ticket, the money for the airport bus, from Vancouver, and for the bus or maybe it would have to be a taxi into Powell River, something left over for food and coffee. Clifford would pay for the hotel. The thought filled her with sexual comfort, submissiveness, though she knew Jerome needed new glasses, Adam needed rubber boots. She thought of that neutral, smooth, generous bed, which already existed, was waiting for them. Long ago when she was a young girl (she was now twenty-three) she had often thought of bland rented beds and locked doors, with such luxuriant hopes, and now she did again, though for a time in between, before and after she was married, the thought of anything connected with sex irritated her, rather in the way Modern Art irritated Patrick.

She walked around the house softly, planning her day as a series of actions. Take a bath, oil and powder herself, put her diaphragm and jelly in her purse. Remember the money. Mascara, face cream, lipstick. She stood at the top of the two steps leading down into the living room. The walls of the living room were moss green, the fireplace was white, the curtains and slipcovers had a silky pattern of gray and green and yellow leaves on a white background. On the mantel were two Wedgwood vases, white with a circlet of green leaves. Patrick was very fond of these vases. Sometimes when he came home from work he went straight into the living room and shifted them around a bit on the mantel, thinking their symmetrical position had been disturbed.

"Has anybody been fooling around with these vases?"

"Well of course. As soon as you leave for work I rush in and juggle them around."

"I meant Anna. You don't let her touch them, do you?"

Patrick didn't like to hear her refer to the vases in any joking way. He thought she didn't appreciate the house. He didn't know, but maybe could guess what she had said to Jocelyn, the first time Jocelyn came here, and they were standing where Rose stood now, looking down at the living room.

"The department store heir's dream of elegance."

At this treachery even Jocelyn looked abashed. It was not exactly true. Patrick dreamed of getting much more elegant. And it was not true in the implication that it had all been Patrick's choice, and that Rose had always held aloof from it. It had been Patrick's choice, but there were a lot of things she had liked at one time. She used to climb up and polish the glass drops of the dining-room chandelier, using a cloth dipped in water and baking soda. She liked the chandelier; its drops had a blue or lilac cast. But people she admired would not have chandeliers in their dining rooms. It was unlikely that they would have dining rooms. If they did, they would have thin white candles stuck into the branches of a black metal candle-holder, made in Scandinavia. Or else they would have heavy candles in wine bottles, loaded with drippings of colored wax. The people she admired were inevitably poorer than she was. It seemed a bad joke on her, after being poor all her life in a place where poverty was never anything to be proud of, that now she had to feel apologetic and embarrassed about the opposite condition – with someone like Jocelyn, for instance, who could say *middle-class prosperity* so viciously and despisingly.

But if she hadn't been exposed to other people, if she hadn't learned from Jocelyn, would she still have liked the house? No. She must have been souring on it, anyway. When people came to visit for the first time Patrick always took them on a tour, pointing out the chandelier, the powder room with concealed lighting, by the front door, the walk-in closets and the louvered doors opening on to the patio. He was as proud of this house, as eager to call attention to its small distinctions, as if he, not Rose, had grown up poor. Rose had been uneasy about these tours from the start, and tagged along in silence, or made deprecating remarks which Patrick did not like. After a while she stayed in the kitchen, but she could still hear Patrick's voice and she knew beforehand everything he would say. She knew that he would pull the dining-room curtains and point to the small illuminated fountain – Neptune with a fig-leaf – he had put in the garden, and then he would say, "Now there is our answer to the suburban swimming-pool mania!"

After she bathed she reached for a bottle of what she thought was baby oil, to pour over her body. The clear liquid ran down over her breasts and belly, stinging and burning. She looked at the label and saw that this was not baby oil at all, it was nail polish remover. She scrubbed it off, splashed herself with cold water, towelled desperately, thinking of ruined skin, the hospital; grafts, scars, punishment.

Anna was scratching sleepily but urgently at the bathroom door. Rose had locked it, for this preparation, though she didn't usually lock it when she took a bath. She let Anna in.

"Your front is all red," Anna said, as she hoisted herself on to the toilet. Rose found the baby oil and tried to cool herself with it. She used too much, and got oily spots on her new brassiere.

She had thought Clifford might write to her while he was touring, but he did not. He called her from Prince George, and was business-like.

"When do you get into Powell River?"

"Four o'clock."

"Okay, take the bus or whatever they have into town. Have you ever been there?"

"No."

"Neither have I. I only know the name of our hotel. You can't wait there."

"How about the bus depot? Every town has a bus depot."

"Okay, the bus depot. I'll pick you up there probably about five o'clock, and we can get you into some other hotel. I hope to God there's more than one. Okay then."

He was pretending to the other members of the orchestra that he was spending the night with friends in Powell River.

"I could go and hear you play," Rose said. "Couldn't I?"

"Well. Sure."

"I'd be very inconspicuous. I'd sit at the back. I'll disguise myself as an old lady. I love to hear you play."

"Okay."

"You don't mind?"

"No."

"Clifford?"

"Yes?"

"You still want me to come?"

"Oh, Rose."

"I know. It's just the way you sound."

"I'm in the hotel lobby. They're waiting for me. I'm supposed to be talking to Jocelyn."

"Okay I know. I'll come."

"Powell River. The bus depot. Five o'clock."

This was different from their usual telephone conversations. Usually they were plaintive and silly; or else they worked each other up so that they could not talk at all.

"Heavy breathing there."

"I know."

"We'll have to talk about something else."

"What else is there?"

"Is it foggy where you are?"

"Yes. Is it foggy where you are too?"

"Yes. Can you hear the foghorn?"

"Yes."

"Isn't it a horrible sound?"

"I don't mind it, really I sort of like it."

"Jocelyn doesn't. You know how she describes it? She says it's the sound of a cosmic boredom."

They had at first avoided speaking of Jocelyn and Patrick at all. Then they spoke of them in a crisp practical way, as if they were adults, parents, to be outwitted. Now they could mention them almost tenderly, admiringly, as if they were their children.

There was no bus depot in Powell River. Rose got into the airport limousine with four other passengers, all men, and told the driver she wanted to go to the bus depot.

"You know where that is?"

"No," she said. Already she felt them all watching her.

"Did you want to catch a bus?"

"No."

"Just wanted to go to the bus depot?"

"I planned to meet somebody there."

"I didn't even know there was a bus depot here," said one of the passengers.

"There isn't, that I know of," said the driver. "Now there is a bus, it goes down to Vancouver in the morning and it comes back at night, and it stops at the old men's home. The old loggers' home. That's where it stops. All I can do is take you there. Is that all right?"

Rose said it would be fine. Then she felt she had to go on explaining.

"My friend and I just arranged to meet there because we couldn't think where else. We don't know Powell River at all and we just thought, every town has a bus depot!"

She was thinking that she shouldn't have said *my friend*, she should have said *my husband*. They were going to ask her what she and her friend were doing here if neither of them knew the town.

"My friend is playing in the orchestra that's giving a concert here tonight. She plays the violin."

All looked away from her, as if that was what a lie deserved. She was trying to remember if there was a female violinist. What if they should ask her name?

The driver let her off in front of a long two-story wooden building with peeling paint.

"I guess you could go in the sunporch, there at the end. That's where the bus picks them up, anyway."

In the sunporch there was a pool table. Nobody was playing. Some old men were playing checkers; others watched. Rose thought of explaining herself to them but decided not to; they seemed mercifully uninterested. She was worn out by her explanations in the limousine.

It was ten past four by the sunporch clock. She thought she could put in the time till five by walking around the town.

As soon as she went outside she noticed a bad smell, and became worried, thinking it might come from herself. She got out the stick cologne she had bought in the Vancouver airport – spending money she could not afford – and rubbed it on her wrists and neck. The smell persisted, and at last she realized it came from the pulp mills. The town was difficult to walk around in because the streets were so steep, and in many places there was no sidewalk. There was no place to loiter. She thought people stared at her, recognizing a stranger. Some men in a car yelled at her. She saw her own reflection in store windows and understood that she looked as if she wanted to be stared at and yelled at. She was wearing black velvet toreador pants, a tight-fitting highnecked black sweater and a beige jacket which she slung over her shoulder, though there was a chilly wind. She who had once chosen full skirts and soft colors, babyish angora sweaters, scalloped necklines, had now taken to wearing dramatic sexually advertising clothes. The new underwear she had on at this moment was black lace and pink nylon. In the waiting room at the Vancouver airport she had done her eyes with heavy mascara, black eyeliner, and silver eyeshadow; her lipstick was almost white. All this was a fashion of those years and so looked less ghastly than it would seem later, but it was alarming enough. The assurance with which she carried such a disguise fluctuated considerably. She would not have dared parade it in front of Patrick or Jocelyn. When she went to see Jocelyn she always wore her baggiest slacks and sweaters. Nevertheless when she opened the door Jocelyn would say, "Hello, Sexy," in a tone of friendly scorn. Jocelyn herself had become spectacularly unkempt. She dressed exclusively in old clothes of Clifford's. Old pants that didn't quite zip up on her because her stomach had never flattened out after Adam, and frayed white shirts Clifford had once worn for performances. Apparently Jocelyn thought the whole business of keeping your figure and wearing makeup and trying to look in any way seductive was sourly amusing, beneath contempt; it was like vacuuming the curtains. She said that Clifford felt the same way. Clifford, reported Jocelyn, was attracted by the very absence of female artifice and trappings; he liked unshaved legs and hairy armpits and natural smells. Rose wondered if Clifford had really said this, and why. Out of pity, or comradeliness; or as a joke?

Rose found a public library and went in and looked at the titles of the books, but she could not pay attention. There was a fairly incapacitating though not unpleasant buzzing throughout her head and body. At twenty to five she was back in the sunporch, waiting.

She was still waiting at ten past six. She had counted the money in her purse. A dollar and sixty-three cents. She could not go to a hotel. She did not think they would let her stay in the sunporch all night. There was nothing at all that she could do except pray that Clifford might still arrive. She did not believe he would. The schedule had been changed; he had been summoned home because one of the children was sick; he had broken his wrist and couldn't play the violin; Powell River was not a real place at all but a bad-smelling mirage where guilty travelers were trapped for punishment. She wasn't really surprised. She had made the jump that wasn't to be made, and this was how she had landed.

Before the old men went in to supper she asked them if they knew of a concert being given that night in the high school auditorium. They answered grudgingly, no.

"Never heard of them giving no concerts here."

She said that her husband was playing in the orchestra, it was on tour from Vancouver, she had flown up to meet him; she was supposed to meet him here.

Here?

"Maybe got lost," said one of the old men in what seemed to her a spiteful, knowing way. "Maybe your husband got lost, heh? Husbands always getting lost!"

It was nearly dark out. This was October, and further north than Vancouver. She tried to think what to do. The only thing that occurred to her was to pretend to pass out, then claim loss of memory. Would Patrick ever believe that? She would have to say she had no idea what she was doing in Powell River. She would have to say she didn't remember anything she had said in the limousine, didn't know anything about the orchestra. She would have to convince policemen and doctors, be written about in the newspapers. Oh, where was Clifford, why had he abandoned her, could there have been an accident on the road? She thought she should destroy the piece of paper in her purse, on which she had written his instructions. She thought that she had better get rid of her diaphragm as well.

She was going through her purse when a van parked outside. She thought it must be a police van; she thought the old men must have phoned up and reported her as a suspicious character.

Clifford got out and came running up the sunporch steps. It took her a moment to recognize him.

They had beer and hamburgers in one of the hotels, a different hotel from the one where the orchestra was staying. Rose's hands were shaking so that she slopped the beer. There had been a rehearsal he hadn't counted on, Clifford said. Then he had been about half an hour looking for the bus depot.

"I guess it wasn't such a bright idea, the bus depot."

Her hand was lying on the table. He wiped the beer off with a napkin, then put his own hand over hers. She thought of this often, afterwards.

"We better get you checked in here."

"Don't we check in together?"

"Better if it's just you."

"Ever since I got here," Rose said, "it has been so peculiar. It has been so sinister. I felt everybody knew." She started telling him, in what she hoped was an entertaining way, about the limousine driver, the other passengers, the old men in the Loggers' Home. "It was such a relief when you showed up, such a terrible relief. That's why I'm shaking." She told him about her plan to fake amnesia and the realization that she had better throw her diaphragm away. He laughed, but without delight, she thought. It seemed to her that when she spoke of the diaphragm his lips tightened, in reproof or distaste.

"But it's lovely now," she said hastily. This was the longest conversation they had ever had, face to face.

"It was just your guilt-feelings," he said. "Which are natural."

He stroked her hand. She tried to rub her finger on his pulse, as they used to do. He let go. Half an hour later, she was saying, "Is it all right if I still go to the concert?"

"Do you still want to?"

"What else is there to do?"

She shrugged as she said this. Her eyelids were lowered, her lips full and brooding. She was doing some sort of imitation, of Barbara Stanwyck perhaps, in similar circumstances. She didn't intend to do an imitation, of course. She was trying to find some way to be so enticing, so aloof and enticing, that she would make him change his mind.

"The thing is, I have to get the van back. I have to pick up the other guys."

"I can walk. Tell me where it is."

"Uphill from here, I'm afraid."

"That won't hurt me."

"Rose. It's much better this way, Rose. It really is."

"If you say so." She couldn't manage another shrug. She still thought there must be some way to turn things around and start again. Start again; set right whatever she had said or done wrong; make none of this true. She had already made the mistake of asking what she had said or done wrong and he had said, nothing. Nothing. She had nothing to do with it, he said. It was being away from home for a month that had made him see everything differently. Jocelyn. The children. The damage.

"It's only mischief," he said.

He had got his hair cut shorter than she had ever seen it. His tan had faded. Indeed, indeed, he looked as if he had shed a skin, and it was the skin that had hankered after hers. He was again the pale, and rather irritable, but dutiful, young husband she had observed paying visits to Jocelyn in the maternity ward.

"What is?"

"What we're doing. It's not some big necessary thing. It's ordinary mischief."

"You called me from Prince George." Barbara Stanwyck had vanished, Rose heard herself begin to whine.

"I know I did." He spoke like a nagged husband.

"Did you feel like this then?"

"Yes and no. We'd made all the plans. Wouldn't it have been worse if I'd told you on the phone?"

"What do you mean, mischief?"

"Oh, Rose."

"What do you mean?"

"You know what I mean. If we went ahead with this, what good do you think it would do anybody? Rose? Really?"

"Us," Rose said. "It would do us good."

"No it wouldn't. It would end up in one big mess."

"Just once."

"No."

"You said just once. You said we would have a memory instead of a dream."

"Jesus. I said a lot of puke."

He had said her tongue was like a little warmblooded snake, a pretty snake, and her nipples like berries. He would not care to be reminded.

Overture to Ruslan and Ludmilla: Glinka
Serenade for Strings: Tchaikovsky
Beethoven's Sixth Symphony, the Pastoral:
First Movement
The Moldau: Smetana
William Tell Overture: Rossini

She could not hear any of this music for a long time without a specific attack of shame, that was like a whole wall crumbling in on her, rubble choking her.

Just before Clifford left on tour, Jocelyn had phoned Rose and said that her baby sitter could not come. It was the day she went to see her psychiatrist. Rose offered to come and look after Adam and Jerome. She had done this before. She made the long trip on three buses, taking Anna with her.

Jocelyn's house was heated by an oil stove in the kitchen, and an enormous stone fireplace in the small living room. The oil stove was covered with spill-marks; orange peel and coffee grounds and charred wood and ashes tumbled out of the fireplace. There was no basement and no clothes dryer. The weather was rainy, and the ceiling-racks and stand-up racks were draped with damp graying sheets and diapers, hardening towels. There was no washing machine either. Jocelyn had washed those sheets in the bathtub.

"No washer or dryer but she's going to a psychiatrist," said Patrick, to whom Rose sometimes disloyally reported what she knew he would like to hear.

"She must be crazy," Rose said. She made him laugh.

But Patrick didn't like her going to baby-sit.

"You're certainly at her beck and call," he said. "It's a wonder you don't go and scrub her floors for her."

As a matter of fact, Rose did.

When Jocelyn was there, the disorder of the house had a certain willed and impressive quality. When she was gone, it became unbearable. Rose would go to work with a knife, scraping at ancient crusts of Pablum on the kitchen chairs, scouring the coffee pot, wiping the floor. She did spare some time for investigation.

She went into the bedroom – she had to watch out for Jerome, a precocious and irritating child – and looked at Clifford's socks and underwear, all crumpled in with Jocelyn's old nursing brassieres and torn garter belts. She looked to see if he had a record on the turntable, wondering if it would be something that would make him think of her.

Telemann. Not likely. But she played it, to hear what he had been hearing. She drank coffee from what she believed to be his dirty breakfast cup. She covered the casserole of Spanish rice from which he had taken his supper the night before. She sought out traces of his presence (he didn't use an electric razor, he used old-fashioned shaving soap in a wooden bowl), but she believed that his life in that house, Jocelyn's house, was all pretense, and waiting, like her own life in Patrick's house.

When Jocelyn came home Rose felt she ought to apologize for the cleaning she had done, and Jocelyn, really wanting to talk about her fight with the psychiatrist who reminded her of her mother, agreed that it certainly was a cowardly mania, this thing Rose had about housecleaning, and she had better go to a psych herself, if she ever wanted to get rid of it. She was joking; but going home on the bus, with Anna cranky and no preparations made for Patrick's supper, Rose did wonder why she always seemed to be on the wrong end of things, disapproved of by her own neighbors because she didn't pay enough attention to housework, and reproved by Jocelyn for being insufficiently tolerant of the natural chaos and refuse of life. She thought of love, to reconcile herself. She was loved, not in a dutiful, husbandly way but crazily, adulterously, as Jocelyn and her neighbors were not. She used that to reconcile herself to all sorts of things: to Patrick, for instance, turning over in bed with an indulgent little clucking noise that meant she was absolved of all her failings for the moment, they were to make love.

The sane and decent things Clifford had said cut no ice with Rose at all. She saw that he had betrayed her. Sanity and decency were never what she had asked of him. She watched him, in the auditorium of the Powell River High School. She watched him playing his violin, with a somber and attentive expression she had once seen directed towards herself. She did not see how she could do without.

In the middle of the night she phoned him, from her hotel to his.

"Please talk to me."

"That's okay," said Clifford, after a moment's silence. "That's okay, Joss."

He must have a roommate, whom the phone might have wakened. He was pretending to talk to Jocelyn. Or else he was so sleepy he really thought she was Jocelyn.

"Clifford, it's me'."

"That's okay," Clifford said. "Take it easy. Go to sleep."

He hung up the phone.

Jocelyn and Clifford are living in Toronto. They are not poor anymore. Clifford is successful. His name is seen on record jackets, heard on the radio. His face and more frequently his hands have appeared on television as he labors at his violin. Jocelyn has dieted and become slender, has had her hair cut and styled; it is parted in the middle and curves away from her face, with a wing of pure white rising from each temple.

They live in a large brick house on the edge of a ravine. There are bird-feeders in the back yard. They have installed a sauna. Clifford spends a good deal of time sitting there. He thinks that will keep him from becoming arthritic, like his father. Arthritis is his greatest fear.

Rose used to go to see them sometimes. She was living in the country, by herself. She taught at a community college and liked to have a place to stay overnight when she came in to Toronto. They seemed glad to have her. They said she was their oldest friend.

One time when Rose was visiting them Jocelyn told a story about Adam. Adam had an apartment in the basement of the house. Jerome lived downtown, with his girlfriend. Adam brought his girls here.

"I was reading in the den," said Jocelyn, "when Clifford was out. I heard this girl, down in Adam's apartment, saying *no, no!* The noise from his apartment comes straight up into the den. We warned him about that, we thought he'd be embarrassed—"

"I didn't think he'd be embarrassed," said Clifford.

"But he just said, we should put on the record player. So, I kept hearing the poor unknown girl bleating and protesting, and I didn't know what to do. I thought these situations are really new, there are no precedents, are you supposed to stop your son from raping some girl if that's what he's doing, right under your nose or at least under your feet? I went downstairs eventually and I started getting all the family skis out of the closet that backs on his bedroom, I stayed there slamming those skis around, thinking I'd say I was going to polish them. It was July. Adam never said anything to me. I wish he'd move out."

Rose told about how much money Patrick had and how he had married a sensible woman even richer than he was, who had made a dazzling living room with mirrors and pale velvet and a wire sculpture like blasted bird cages. Patrick did not mind Modern Art any more.

"Of course it isn't the same," said Rose to Jocelyn, "it isn't the same house. I wonder what she has done with the Wedgwood vases."

"Maybe she has a campy laundry room. She keeps the bleach in one and the detergent in the other."

"They sit perfectly symmetrically on the shelf."

But Rose had her old, old, twinge of guilt.

"Just the same, I like Patrick."

Jocelyn said, "Why?"

"He's nicer than most people."

"Silly rot," said Jocelyn. "And I bet he doesn't like you."

"That's right," Rose said. She started to tell them about her trip down on the bus. It was one of the times when she was not driving her car, because too many things were wrong with it and she could not afford to get it fixed.

"The man in the seat across from me was telling me about how he used to drive big trucks. He said we never seen trucks in this country like they got in the States." She put on her country accent. "In the Yewnited States they got these special roads what they call turnpikes, and only trucks is allowed to go on them. They get serviced on these roads from one end of the country to the other and so most people never sees them at all. They're so big the cab is half the size of a bus and they got a driver in there and an assistant driver and another driver and another assistant driver havin a sleep. Toilet and kitchen and beds and all. They go eighty, ninety miles an hour, because there is never no speed limit on them turnpikes."

"You are getting very weird," said Clifford. "Living up there."

"Never mind the trucks," Jocelyn said. "Never mind the old mythology. Clifford wants to leave me again."

They settled down to drinking and talking about what Clifford and Jocelyn should do. This was not an unfamiliar conversation. What does Clifford really want? Does he really want not to be married to Jocelyn or does he want something unattainable? Is he going through a middle-age crisis?

"Don't be so banal," Clifford said to Rose. She was the one who said middle-age crisis. "I've been going through this ever since I was twenty-five. I've wanted out ever since I got in."

"That is new, for Clifford to say that," said Jocelyn. She went out to the kitchen to get some cheese and grapes. "For him to actually come out and say that," she yelled from the kitchen. Rose avoided looking at Clifford, not because they had any secrets but because it seemed a courtesy to Jocelyn not to look at each other while she was out of the room.

"What is happening now," said Jocelyn, coming back with a platter of cheese and grapes in one hand and a bottle of gin in the other, "is that Clifford is wide open. He used to bitch and stew and some other bilge would come out that had nothing to do with the real problem. Now he just comes out with it. The great blazing truth. It's a total illumination."

Rose had a bit of difficulty catching the tone. She felt as if living in the country had made her slow. Was Jocelyn's talk a parody, was she being sarcastic? No. She was not.

"But then I go and deflate the truth for you," said Clifford, grinning. He was drinking beer from the bottle. He thought beer was better for him than gin. "It's absolutely true I've wanted out ever since I got in. And it's also true that I wanted in, and I wanted to stay in. I wanted to be married to you and I want to be married to you and I couldn't stand being married to you and I can't stand being married to you. It's a static contradiction."

"It sounds like hell," Rose said.

"I didn't say that. I am just making the point that it is no middle-age crisis."

"Well, maybe that was oversimplifying," said Rose. Nevertheless, she said firmly, in the sensible, down-to-earth, countrified style she was adopting for the moment, all they were hearing about was Clifford. What did Clifford really want, what did Clifford need? Did he need a studio, did he need a holiday, did he need to go to Europe by himself? What made him think, she said, that Jocelyn could be endlessly concerned about his welfare? Jocelyn was not his mother.

"And it's your fault," she said to Jocelyn, "for not telling him to put up or shut up. Never mind what he really wants. Get out or shut up. That's all you need to say to him. Shut up or get out," she said to Clifford with mock gruffness. "Excuse me for being so unsubtle. Or frankly hostile."

She didn't run any risk at all by sounding hostile, and she knew it. She would run a risk by being genteel and indifferent. The way she was talking now was a proof that she was their true friend and took them seriously. And so she did, up to a point.

"She's right, you fucking son-of-a-bitch," said Jocelyn experimentally. "Shut up or get out."

When Jocelyn called Rose on the phone, years ago, to read her the poem *Howl*, she was not able, in spite of her usual boldness of speech, to say the word *fuck*. She tried to force herself, then she said, "Oh, it's stupid, but I can't say it. I'm going to have to say eff. You'll know what I mean when I say eff?"

"But she said it's your fault," said Clifford. "You want to be the mother. You want to be the grownup. You want to be long-suffering."

"Balls," said Jocelyn. "Oh, maybe. Maybe, yes. Maybe I do."

"I bet at school you were always latching on to those kids with the problems," said Clifford with his tender grin. "Those poor kids, the ones with acne or awful clothes or speech impediments. I bet you just persecuted those poor kids with friendliness."

Jocelyn picked up the cheese knife and waved it at him.

"You be careful. You haven't got acne or a speech impediment. You are sickeningly good-looking. And talented. And lucky."

"I have nearly insuperable problems coming to terms with the adult male role," said Clifford priggishly. "The psych says so."

"I don't believe you. Psychs never say anything like nearly

insuperable. And they don't use that jargon. And they don't make those judgments. I don't believe you, Clifford."

"Well, I don't really go to the psych at all. I go to the dirty movies down on Yonge."

Clifford went off to sit in the sauna.

Rose watched him leave the room. He was wearing jeans, and a T-shirt that said *Just passin thru*. His waist and hips were narrow as a twelve-year-old's. His gray hair was cut in a very short brush cut, showing his skull. Was this the way musicians wore their hair nowadays, when politicians and accountants were bushy and bearded, or was it Clifford's own perversity? His tan looked like pancake makeup, though it was probably all real. There was something theatrical about him altogether, tight and glittery and taunting. Something obscene about his skinniness and sweet, hard smile.

"Is he well?" she said to Jocelyn. "He's terribly thin."

"He wants to look like that. He eats yogurt and black bread."

"You can never split up," Rose said, "because your house is too beautiful." She stretched out on the hooked rug. The living room had white walls, thick white curtains, old pine furniture, large bright paintings, hooked rugs. On a low round table at her elbow was a bowl of polished stones for people to pick up and hold and run through their fingers. The stones came from Vancouver beaches, from Sandy Cove and English Bay and Kitsilano and Ambleside and Dundarave. Jerome and Adam had collected them a long time ago.

Jocelyn and Clifford left British Columbia soon after Clifford returned from his provincial tour. They went to Montreal, then to Halifax, then to Toronto. They seemed hardly to remember Vancouver. Once they tried to think of the name of the street where they had lived and it was Rose who had to supply it for them. When Rose lived in Capilano Heights she used to spend a lot of time remembering the parts of Ontario where she had lived, being faithful, in a way, to that earlier landscape. Now that she was living in Ontario she put the same sort of effort into remembering things about Vancouver, puzzling to get details straight, that were in themselves quite ordinary. For instance, she tried to remember just where you waited for the Pacific Stage bus, when you were going from North Vancouver to West Vancouver. She pictured herself getting on that old green bus around one o'clock, say, on a spring day. Going to baby-sit for Jocelyn. Anna with her, in her yellow slicker and rainhat. Cold rain. The long, swampy stretch of land as you went into West Vancouver. Where the shopping-centers and highrises are now. She could see the streets, the houses, the old Safeway, St. Mawes Hotel, the thick closing-in of the woods, the place where you got off the bus at the little store. Black Cat cigarettes sign. Cedar dampness as you walked in through the woods to Jocelyn's house. Deadness of early afternoon. Nap time. Young women drinking coffee looking out of rainy windows. Retired couples walking dogs. Pad of feet on the thick mold. Crocuses, early daffodils, the cold bulbs blooming. That profound difference of the air close to the sea, the inescapable dripping vegetation, the stillness. Anna pulling on her hand, Jocelyn's brown wooden cottage ahead. Such a rich weight of apprehension, complications descending as she neared that house.

Other things she was not so keen on remembering.

She had wept on the plane, behind her sunglasses, all the way from Powell River. She wept, sitting in the waiting room at the Vancouver airport. She was not able to stop weeping and go home to Patrick. A plainclothes policeman sat down beside her, opened his jacket to show her his badge, asked if there was anything he could do for her. Someone must have summoned him. Terrified at being so conspicuous, she fled to the Ladies'. She didn't think to comfort herself with a drink, didn't think of looking for the bar. She never went to bars then. She didn't take a tranquilizer, didn't have any, didn't know about them. Maybe there weren't such things.

The suffering. What was it? It was all a waste, it reflected no credit. An entirely dishonorable grief. All mashed pride and ridiculed fantasy. It was as if she had taken a hammer and deliberately smashed her big toe. That's what she thinks sometimes. At other times she thinks it was necessary, it was the start of wrecks and changes, the start of being where she is now instead of in Patrick's house. Life making a gigantic fuss, as usual, for a small effect.

Patrick could not speak when she told him. He had no lecture prepared. He didn't speak for a long time but followed her around the house while she kept justifying herself, complaining. It was as if he wanted her to go on talking, though he couldn't credit what she was saying, because it would be much worse if she stopped.

She didn't tell him the whole truth. She said that she had "had an affair" with Clifford, and by the telling gave herself a dim secondhand sort of comfort, which was pierced, presently, but not really destroyed, by Patrick's look and silence. It seemed ill-timed, unfair of him, to show such a bare face, such an inappropriate undigestible chunk of grief.

Then the phone rang, and she thought it would be Clifford, experiencing a change of heart. It was not Clifford, it was a man she had met at Jocelyn's party. He said he was directing a radio play, and he needed a country girl. He remembered her accent.

Not Clifford.

She would rather not think of any of this. She prefers to see through metal window-frames of dripping cedars and salmonberry bushes and the proliferating mortal greenery of the rain forest some small views of lost daily life. Anna's yellow slicker. The smoke from Jocelyn's foul fire.

"Do you want to see the junk I've been buying?" said Jocelyn, and took Rose upstairs. She showed her an embroidered skirt and a deep-red satin blouse. A daffodil-colored silk pajama suit. A long shapeless rough-woven dress from Ireland.

"I'm spending a fortune. What I would once have thought was a fortune. It took me so long. It took us both so long, just to be able to spend money. We could not bring ourselves to do it. We despised people who had color television. And you know something – color television is great! We sit around now and say, what would we like? Maybe one of those little toaster-ovens for the cottage? Maybe I'd like a hair blower? All those things everybody else has known about for years but we thought we were too good for. You know what we are, we say to each other? We're Consumers! And it's Okay!"

"And not just paintings and records and books. We always knew they were okay. Color T.V.! Hair dryers! Waffle irons!"

"Remote-control birdcages!" Rose cried cheerfully.

"That's the idea."

"Heated towels."

"Heated towel racks, dummy! They're lovely."

"Electric carving knives, electric toothbrushes, electric toothpicks."

"Some of those things are not as bad as they sound. Really they're not."

Another time when Rose came down Jocelyn and Clifford had a party. When everyone had gone home the three of them, Jocelyn and Clifford and Rose, sat around on the living-room floor, all fairly drunk, and very comfortable. The party had gone well. Rose was feeling a remote and wistful lust; a memory of lust, maybe. Jocelyn said she didn't want to go to bed.

"What can we do?" said Rose. "We shouldn't drink any more."

"We could make love," Clifford said.

Jocelyn and Rose said, "Really?" at exactly the same time. Then they linked their little fingers and said, "Smoke goes up the chimney."

Following which, Clifford removed their clothes. They didn't shiver, it was warm in front of the fire. Clifford kept switching his attention nicely from one to the other. He got out of his own clothes as well. Rose felt curious, disbelieving, hardly willing, slightly aroused and, at some level she was too sluggish to reach for, appalled and sad. Though Clifford paid preliminary homage to them both, she was the one he finally made love to, rather quickly on the nubbly hooked rug. Jocelyn seemed to hover above them making comforting noises of assent.

The next morning Rose had to go out before Jocelyn and Clifford were awake. She had to go downtown on the subway. She found she was looking at men with that speculative hunger, that cold and hurtful need, which for a while she had been free of. She began to get very angry. She was angry at Clifford and Jocelyn. She felt that they had made a fool of her, cheated her, shown her a glaring lack, that otherwise she would not have been aware of. She resolved never to see them again and to write them a letter in which she would comment on their selfishness, obtuseness, and moral degeneracy. By the time she had the letter written to her own satisfaction, in her head, she was back in the country again and had calmed down. She decided not to write it. Sometime later she decided to go on being friends with Clifford and Jocelyn, because she needed such friends occasionally, at that stage of her life.

CHANGE OF FACE

Elspeth Davie

Elspeth Davie (1918–1995) was a Scottish author. Although
she wrote novels, she is best known for her short stories.
Davie won the Katherine Mansfield Prize in 1978.

It was a mistake to imagine that only the vain or the good-looking
offered themselves to the man on the street corner. On Fridays he
drew passers-by at a pound a face, and more often than not, those
who were particularly pleased with their looks walked on with
only a passing glance at his work, for it was not work of high
quality. He used crayon – not a lasting medium at the best of times
– and he was a poor hand at it. The colours tended to be crude and
the results smudgy. Yet even if he could have managed it, he was
not after the subtleties of the human face. Always, his aim was to
make his pound quickly and sometimes, if it was possible, to please.
At any rate, he got all kinds of persons willing to pay for things
other than likenesses, even if it was only a chair to rest on. Here,
too, the natural clowns of the community enjoyed themselves, for
by mixing pantomime with the solemn sitting they could hope to
attract a crowd. They were less interested in seeing their own heads
on paper.

A few outstanding faces came his way. He almost dreaded their
coming and would occasionally ask: 'Do you really want me to
draw your face?' If they were already sitting in the chair he'd set
out, they would look up, surprised. 'Well, of course. Can't you see
– I'm all ready.'

'It takes a long time. You are going to find that chair very hard.'
But there was a cushion on it, and he was perfectly capable of
throwing off his mediocre sketches in a matter of minutes – fifteen
at the very most.

'The thing is,' he would say, 'I'm an amateur at the job, and
as a matter of fact, you have an interesting but rather a difficult
face.' He would have been incapable of uttering anything more

complimentary even if he and his sitter had been in the most private place. Certain encounters during his life had been chilled and checked by this inhibition, but there were some things he could not do or say. That was how he was made. And such sitters did not take the word 'difficult' too badly, though they were puzzled when he suggested they try a more skilled person for the job. 'Someone,' he'd say, 'who could give you a really excellent likeness. Naturally it might take longer. It would certainly be dearer – but at the end of the day worth every bit of time and money!' Usually, however, they sat on calmly, and calmly carried away his botched effort with a good grace.

His difficulties were not all with the handling of crayons. He was susceptible to certain kinds of beauty in human beings. This made him uneasy, for to fall in love in the space of a few minutes at the corner of a city street with no possibility of continuing the relationship was a serious business. Yet at the same time, he felt that so private a human state could scarcely be taken seriously, surrounded as he was by hordes of fast cars, and with the grind of heavy lorries always in his ears. Busy offices clattering with typewriters leaned above him and lines of smiling placards advertising joy. He was simply aware of the occasional wildness, the piercing sorrow within his chest as some person carrying a scrawl, an unpleasing smear of crayon lines, disappeared forever from his eyes.

Other unexpected difficulties turned up in regard to his sitters. Amongst them were a few persons, men and women who had a desire, not only to discover what they looked like in the flesh, but also to know who or what they were deep in the very core of their being. They had turned to him – he with his cheap crayons, his crumbling pinks and blues and greens, had placed themselves trustfully in a pair of clumsy, inept hands. As well hold out their delicate skulls for dissection to a blunt butcher's knife!

The young man had rigged up a kind of shelter for wet and windy days, hardly more than a covering of canvas supported by sticks and with a scrap of curtaining in front. This also provided some privacy for those persons who wanted it, and amongst them were those who so passionately wished to know what might be seen under the skull or behind the black centre of the eye. This was an awkward problem, for these were people who talked while they sat, and however quietly they talked, they managed somehow to make themselves heard above the strident traffic in the street or the constant sound of voices and footsteps on the pavement outside. They made themselves heard even on the wildest days, as though their private storms were more important than those outside and must be listened to at all costs.

He did listen. He listened to many strange things as he rubbed in the smooth pink cheeks, the red lips and brilliant eyes that were so much a part of his trade. It was evident that long ago they had decided that what they had to say could best be said to a stranger. And where was this stranger who had time to stop and talk in the street? This rigged-up shelter, then, came as an unexpected blessing. Yet they had to be quick about it. For the crayoner himself attempted to point out that his temporary shelter was neither a confessional, nor a fortune-teller's booth – tried to make clear the fact that he himself was not a medium, had no psychic power or talent for divination, that his knowledge of the world was limited, that his experiences in love could never be considered either wise or comforting, that he had no advice to give, for he himself had never taken any, that patience was not his strong suit, and, finally, that pounds were important to him and therefore time was of the essence.

Most of all he made it plain that whatever else he was, he was not a talker. On Fridays at this corner, his words had been limited to certain phrases that cropped up over and over again: 'Please raise your eyes a little, would you lower your head, turn a fraction to the right, to the left. Would you mind putting your hair back from your face? Smiling a little, not smiling so much. You have moved, you have changed! Thank you, that is very good, that is much better. Thank you, I am glad you like it, I am sorry you don't like it, I can't help it if you hate it. That will be a pound. No, I cannot discuss its worth, you have seen my charge. No, it does not include a frame. I am sorry that your husband does not like it, that your wife could do better. It is the best portrait you have ever seen? Thank you very much indeed. You do not like the face? No, it is perfectly legal. You cannot call a policeman. There is a litter-bin across the street. You like the face? You think it better than your own? Oh, how could it be better? It is kind of you to say that, very agreeable and kind. You have given me the greatest pleasure. Please stop abusing me, stop threatening me! There are two policemen across the street. Thank you, I am glad you like the eyes. The mouth is too wide? I am sorry I cannot change the mouth. There is someone waiting. Thank you, it is kind of you. *My* face? Oh, how kind of you to say that. I did not know you were looking at it … '

But those who had discovered his makeshift shelter were not greatly concerned with how much or how little he could talk. Their problem was time, and sometimes it was more than a problem. It could be a torment. For a whole life-story might well have to be crushed into the space of a few minutes. And though it was true they managed to make themselves heard above wheels and horns, it was not always easy to get the gist of it. Sometimes the young man had to piece it together from words and odd phrases, and while doing it would try to persuade himself that it mattered very little to him how short or scrappy their account of themselves had to be. The exchange seemed fair enough – a scrappy, half-told episode for a careless half-done sketch.

There were days when few people were around to have their faces drawn, and at these times he tried his hand at anything that came along. The pigeons came, for it was a windy corner, scattered with seed from a derelict patch of ground behind. For a time he had a line in pigeons. He did them as quickly as possible while they were on the ground, then painstakingly from memory when they had flown. His birds did not sell. Even the most unobservant could see that he knew next to nothing about wings or flight, not even the heavy flight of pigeons, and those who looked closely at birds could see that anything approaching the iridescence of the neck was far beyond the scope of cheap crayons. He fared no better with one or two stray cats that came to sit in his corner when the sun was on it. He adjured everything about these cats from their independence to the sheen on the muscles of their thin loins. He caught nothing of this, however, and he sold nothing. For everyone knew cats or had them, and they could see that the crayon cats were miserable creatures, neither sunlit jungle beasts nor fireside pets, but unnaturally stretched on the comfortless limbo of dead white paper. People wondered, seeing he had failed so badly with fur and feathers, what he could possibly make of the vulnerable human face. He was aware of this and after a while stopped this particular line, for he saw it was no good for his trade.

One Friday in early spring, when he was outside, pinning a new sheet of paper to his board, it started to snow. It came very gently and sparsely at first – a few white crystals dissolving on the white paper and lying here and there amongst his crayons – but then more and more swiftly, until pavement and street were almost levelled under a thin coating. The city quickly became silent. Even the heavy lorry wheels rolled secretly and the sharpest heels sank into softness. The young man quickly closed his crayon box, put his drawing-board under his arm and was all set to go, when an elderly man came round the corner and stopped determinedly beside him. There was no doubt what he'd come for. Briskly he tapped on the closed crayon box and in a word or two indicated his intention of taking a seat in the shelter. He didn't wait for yes or no, but quickly parted the curtain and sat himself down under the canvas covering. Nevertheless, the young man had no intention of starting up again, so there was nothing for it but to stay outside, showing – as he busied himself around the place – that if the other had come for shelter, well and good. But faces were over for the day. As soon as possible he must be off. He waited a long time. Once or twice he looked behind him through the curtain then finally, reluctantly, he stepped inside.

The man was no longer on the edge of his chair, but sitting well back, his feet firmly planted, one hand on each knee. With head up and eyes straight before him, he was holding a pose to the manner born. The crayoner sat down with a deep sigh and studied the face in front of him. Then he opened up his box and looked at the blunt ends of pink, blue and white crayon – and he saw that this time, the task was beyond him. This face was made up as entirely of lines as a piece of old bark. The bones of the jaw were angled. There was no softness or roundness about this head. Even the hairs stood up from the crown in sharp bristling stalks, the red and grey mixed. The young man tapped his crayon box sharply as the old man had done. He confessed that he could deal only in softness and bluntness. 'And I have no way of sharpening these,' he said quickly, 'so your face is not possible. If I had a pen or even a pencil perhaps

... but as it is ... ' It was no use. He might as well have talked to a statue. The old man's eyes never flickered in his direction. Stubbornly he continued to hold his pose till the other grabbed up a crayon and started to the job.

He had not been long at it when he realised that his sitter, though he kept his head still as a rock, was going to be moving his lips and his eyes without ceasing. Even more than most, he was determined to talk and there was a lot to tell. Before long it became clear that something more than years had been the cause of lines in his face and the strange springing hair of his head – springing as though endlessly astounded. It was his son. Not that this son of his had given him any trouble in the ordinary sense of the word. No better son had lived from his account. Now *there* was a face, he said, any artist in the land might be proud to draw! And it was not only the face. There had been the character of the young man. There was a good deal of sweetness about his nature, he was kind-hearted. Not that he was a paragon – oh, nothing like that! He could be impatient, intolerant to a degree – hard on others and very hard on himself. He had been a graceful person, said his father, hurrying on, he had danced and he had sung. He had been clever, not in the book-learner's way but in the seaman's way – marvellously clever with his hands. Out of almost nothing he could make anything – model boats, miniature harbours and gardens. He could make chairs, furniture of all kinds. Given the time he could have made a house. The young man, said his father, would have gone far.

Would have gone? The crayoner lifted his head from the paper. For that was the crux of the matter. This boy, who had given his father no trouble at all, had given him the very worst possible trouble in the world. He had got himself drowned with two other sailors like himself far out at sea. Their ages put together, his father said, wouldn't even add up to his own, which was sixty-nine. There were times he could hardly believe he could live so long – to survive three lives so short. His son had been twenty. And where *was* he? Where was he? The crayoner started as he heard such a question addressed to himself.

Yes, where was he, if anywhere? the father asked. He had thought about it for a long time – it was not too much to say he'd thought of it day and night. Not that he was beside himself;

for most of the time nowadays he was quite calm. He was calmly trying to work it out, or simply look at it. He had no idea if that was the way to do it. Probably not. But it was his way, though as yet no answers had come up. Perhaps there were none to come, but that never stopped him from asking: Where is he? He'd imagined him in some odd places.

'Tell me,' said the young man, who was slowly putting the blunt crayons back in their box. He did not want to hear.

To begin with, the father explained, he had simply seen him, naturally enough, in the sea – long separated from his companions – going down with his arms above his head and his legs wide, relaxed after his ordeal, and sometimes softly swinging in the current or twirling, head down, as though peering at something in a crack of rock, or floating on his back, one arm above his head as though reaching out to the other element, or trailing a leg, disentangling a foot amongst weeds – all gentle movements, unhurried, as he saw it. And finally leaving the last glimmer of light and the shoals of fish and going down and down into the darkness. Always, when it got very dark he had lost him, the father said, and he was glad to lose him. He needed to see him whole and bright as he had been. The artist would understand.

'What other places?' said the artist. He understood, but again he did not wish to hear.

The man was silent for a moment. 'No doubt it will sound ridiculous, there is no rhyme or reason in it, but I have sometimes thought of him in the air, or out in the very depths of space. Sometimes he is coasting along like an astronaut, but one with a rather tender skin. He had no time to grow himself a metal surface like the rest of us. His outlines are even less distinct than his sea-farm. He is mixed with all the stuff of the sky, spinning in bright dust and dark. I have never imagined his face, can never guess his expression. That is the hardest thing – to have no idea if or what he is feeling. Has he a voice? In the sea he was silent enough. It is to be hoped he has companions of some kind or another. Oh, I hope to God he is not lonely!'

The crayoner would have much preferred not to hear this particular cry, but that was out of the question. The snow had silenced the street and he was forced to listen. He believed he knew something of loneliness himself, but even so he found nothing whatever to say. It seemed to him that his own experience would sound paltry, hardly worth mentioning beside the thing the father had in mind.

'If you think he is nothing and that he is nowhere – say it, by all means,' said the man. 'Many people have said it with the greatest respect, believe me, and by no means the unkindest people either. Far from being angry I'm thankful for every opinion – all have gone through my head at one time or another. And hearing other views can clear the air. It gives a new line on the thing. You look again. You start again from scratch.' The word seemed to remind him of something. 'Have you finished that drawing?' he said.

'I've had to scrap it,' said the young man. 'I told you I hadn't materials for a proper face.'

'Do what you can,' said the other. 'I don't expect a masterpiece.'

Through the slit in the curtain they could see the snow had stopped falling. Muffled footsteps went past and once or twice a face peered in. Reluctantly the young man pinned a new sheet of paper to his board. The other, who had been sitting absolutely still and silent for a long time, at last said: 'I will never find him, of course. And has he found himself? Maybe he will go through every sort of change, but if he is anywhere at all he will find himself sooner or later. I am happy enough with that idea. It is as good as any other.'

The young man had given up all thought of doing a face. But he was a practised hand at the instant sketch on demand, or if there was no demand he would do anything that came into his head. Occasionally, when the faces became too much for him, he had produced fruit and plants, goldfish in bowls, stormy landscapes, lurid landscapes of purple heather, landscapes of snowy mountains. Flowers were the quickest. He had a peculiar creation of his own – a crossbreed between chrysanthemum, cactus and sunflower, and this he now started on. It had the merit that it could not be criticised by any botanist. Today's version had a spiky head of rough red and brown petals and a staring yellow eye rimmed with hard black spots. The head was supported by a tough, green stalk, ribbed and hairy. If the old man was surprised at the sound of the crayon swishing and jagging over the paper, he showed no sign of it, except that once he smoothed his spiky, startled hair as though this might account for the dramatic change in the artist's rhythm.

The sketch took only a matter of minutes, but the young man had the problem of where to place his flower. He was an expert at bowls and pots and jugs, and if hard-pressed, could even produce some hideous vase from its owner's description. Today he decided on something more ambitious. Behind his flower he sketched in a primitive landscape with a few rocks and a hard blue sky beyond. A primitive landscape was all he was capable of. The thing was quickly done, but it was some time before he could bring himself to hand it over, for he felt the moment was an awkward one. His sitter was not after a striking likeness, but he had come for a face – his own face and no other. Cautiously the young man handed over his drawing. 'I am sorry,' he said. 'It was absolutely not on today. I wouldn't insult you with a worthless face ... another time perhaps when I'm equipped for it. Naturally I want nothing for that. If you want it, keep it. There is no need to take it.'

The other man, dropping his pose for the first time, looked down at the drawing. If he was taken aback, it took him less than a moment to adjust to what he saw. Quickly he scanned the dry-faced flower for some familiar feature, at the same time feeling along the skin of his cheek with one hand. His fingers rasped round his chin and down his throat as he followed the hard-ribbed stalk with his eyes. With an impassive face he studied the crude desert, only glancing aside once to compare its yellow ridges with the folded white snow-space through the curtain. No, he was not angry, the young man saw with relief – neither pleased nor angry. On the other hand, he had no intention of taking away a plant. His face was what he wanted and he would get it. Without fuss then he had to make the change, to feel his blood as sap, his hair as spiked petals, his neck a tough stalk, desert for snow. He seemed to manage this to his satisfaction. What other feeling he might have was harder to guess.

The old man laid the paper down and began to button up his coat. Then again he picked up the drawing and studied it at arm's length, stubbornly taking his time. He was not flattered. Flower or face – it was no masterpiece. He said nothing, but with a rather caustic smile pointed to a bit of stalk which had been smeared under the young man's thumb and to the desert rock behind, pulverised to crumbs by a broken crayon end. Yet in his expression, as he now carefully rolled up the paper, could be seen some confirmation of his belief that every weird change could be expected in the human form and spirit. Indeed, as he tied the string around, he seemed determined on it. He had by no means come to the end himself. It was now well on in the afternoon. The old man nodded goodbye, and as he went out laid a pound note deep inside the jug which the young man kept for ends of crayon, and the assortment of rags which were used when necessary to scrub down crayoned lips and cheeks to a paler pink.

The young man was alone again. First he carefully extracted the pound note from the jug, and for the second time that day packed up his stuff ready to go. He parted the curtain, and saw that the snow had already almost gone from this end of the street. The boots of pedestrians and the warm breath from office basements had melted it. But in the untrampled distance where the old man was walking, it lay thick. He could see him, still bravely, still incredulously lifting his feet from the early wastes and deserts of spring snow.

A WEIGHT PROBLEM

Elspeth Davie

> Elspeth Davie (1918–1995) was a Scottish author.
> Although she wrote novels, she is best known for her short
> stories. Davie won the Katherine Mansfield Prize in 1978.

Very occasionally it happens – when all the baggage has been
safely stowed and the passengers, their eyes already on the sky,
are sitting braced for the revving up – that a plane is pronounced
overweight. Everyone is startled to hear a volunteer being asked
to leave. It happened like this, coming like a bolt from the blue,
late one autumn afternoon. A suave voice came over the intercom
asking for such a person, promising that his fare would be cut by
half if he would come on by the next plane. In the minute following
this request there was no movement to be seen along the lines of
seats. Not a head turned. Hands which had been fixing seatbelts
or fiddling with the overhead knobs were stilled, but there was
no volunteer. The request was repeated more firmly, though still
politely, still promising rewards. And now at last there came a
movement from the rear. All heads swivelled round as a small,
middle-aged man of slight proportions made his way slowly up the
long aisle towards the front of the plane.

It was the first thing his fellow-passengers noticed about him, or
rather it was the only thing, the first and the last – his thinness.
More than a few eyes fixed him, as he went past, with a disbelieving stare.
Could the removal of this lightweight make any difference to the
huge machine? Could their lives depend perhaps on one thin man?
They scanned him hopefully for fat. He had no fat at all. The thin
man may have sensed something of this feeling as he edged past
without meeting the eyes, scarcely touching the seats, as though he
had been searched relentlessly for the very substance of his being and
found wanting. Nor did this passenger have any illusions about the
value of his action. It was not a heroic one. He did not live in an age
of heroes. He had not been asked to jump out of a moving plane nor

to take over the controls from a crew of mad pilots. Indeed, far from gaining respect, he thought it more likely he would be judged as mean-minded, a man willing to give himself endless trouble simply to save a pound or two. It was true his fellow-passengers were glad enough to forget him, for in an aircraft the cause of even one instant's unease is not to be tolerated. When he stepped from the plane he disappeared from their eyes and minds as quickly and surely as though he had stepped over the edge of a cliff.

But the spare passenger had simply stepped down on to the ground of his own home town, and once through the genial formalities at the desk, he could go where he liked for the next two hours. The trouble was he had no desire to go anywhere. He was to be away for seven weeks on a long business trip which would take him first to London and from there to the Continent. He had said his farewells to the family. Now his wife would be peacefully filling up the gap with a visit to a neighbour across the way, his two sons would be round the corner regaling themselves and their friends with extra rounds of beer. His daughter would be preparing to meet her boyfriend and re-doing the cheek where one tear had made serious inroads on the make-up. This was no time to return. The passenger therefore decided to walk about for a while, but unobtrusively, as befitting one who had only half-returned – a kind of ghost coming back to his town to have a last look round before returning to the sky. 'If you break my heart I'll go, but I'll be back again!' a transistor sang for him from some far corner, as he walked out through the waiting-room towards the bus for town.

Even as he approached the city he was still thinking about the plane, following its load of people as they circled farther and farther out into the blue evening. And it seemed to him that he grew lighter as he imagined it, that he grew hollow as if he had unguardedly breathed their thinner air. The bus let him off at a familiar corner where there were a café, a boutique and a flower-shop. He entered the café, went directly to a secluded alcove and almost immediately ran into someone he recognized – a man with whom he had a nodding acquaintance inside the long complex of corridors in his own firm. Over a coffee he told his tale, and the other's eyes bulged.

'I've flown enough myself but I'll admit I've never heard that one!'

'Once in a while it does happen.'

'Why not throw out some baggage instead? Anyway – you're lucky!'

'Lucky? You mean I save half my fare?'

'Not only that. Lucky to be asked to make any gesture at all. Who gets the chance these days? Very few.'

'But it wasn't like that,' said the passenger. 'This was a non-event – the same as stepping off the wrong train.'

'Look,' said the other, 'if someone hadn't got off they wouldn't have gone up. Right now they wouldn't have been up there in that sky at all. I wish I'd been given a chance like that. I'm always waiting but it never comes. The most I've ever done is give up my seat in a bus, and even then you can't be absolutely sure of a smile. Just as likely to be insulted. But you! Now there's a stroke of luck!'

The passenger was silent for a while, looking at the other meditatively over the rim of his cup. 'Don't get me wrong,' he said at last. 'I suppose I think just as well of myself as the next man. On the other hand, I'm unable to see myself nowadays as a person of great weight. I have other things of course. No doubt about it. Not weight. That's simply how I feel.'

The other looked him over quickly as though measuring him in feet, weighing him in stones. He even glanced back at the counter as if to see what could be got there to fatten up the man. But he was no fool. He knew it was not only the physical substance they were discussing. He played for time, however. From the counter he brought back two buttered rolls and two more cups of coffee. And at the same time he added the weight of words. 'But for you,' he repeated softly, 'they wouldn't be in the sky at all!'

The passenger sat and thought about this, once more balancing himself in space against the huge machine – against its tons of steel, against elephantine wheels and whirling blades, against its heavy human load. True enough there was something to be said in his favour. His reluctant presence on solid earth at this very instant was the price of their flight. But it did not answer everything.

The other watched him carefully as he ate his roll – and somewhat anxiously – for he had begun to take an interest in this exceedingly thin man with the weight problem. He waited till the last bite of roll had gone, before asking: 'You feel better now? You look better.'

'As far as the stomach goes – yes.'

'You are still worried about weight?'

The passenger smiled. 'Naturally the middle-aged are expected to worry about *overweight*. What isn't always admitted is their worry about the lack of it. At our stage we're expected, aren't we, to make pronouncements of weight, to have opinions that carry weight, to bring our weight to bear, to throw our weight around and all the other phrases related to what should be? Worst of all, and most ridiculous, we're expected to have gathered up some great load of wisdom …'

'And you?'

'That's the trouble. Less weight. Less with the family, less with the job. My opinions on this and that carry less weight nowadays. My credentials, my references and what have you are exactly the same, of course, but now they weigh less. I very seldom have to weigh my words because they are not listened to anyway.'

'You're weighing them now.'

'Yes, only because you are a sympathetic listener.'

The sympathetic listener looked pleased, but to him it was not enough to listen. He preferred action. Moreover he was afraid that when the thin man began to be really sorry for himself, even listening would be no cure. He suggested a move.

'Where are we going?' said the other as they emerged from the door. 'I've not got much time left.'

'Simply to walk around. Everything's within reach hereabouts. Let's look in here.'

The passenger hesitated on the threshold of a record shop. On window posters and on the sleeves of discs young men were shown singing – gilded youths polished by pink and yellow spotlights, or black-robed, close-cropped with sequined eyelids like frenzied monks, or others again, hairy and sombre as hermits. Song burst from the four walls with ear-splitting fury. 'It is not my scene,' said the thin man. Yet the themes were ancient and universal. Through the raucous, brutal bellow and the rhythmic moan, Love and Freedom were still to the fore.

'Maybe it is not,' said the other in answer, 'but we can go

through from here into the boutique.' They stepped through, past beaded curtains and down some steps into a shop at the back. It was quieter here, though the place still throbbed with drumming. Coats and trousers, scarves and dresses swung gently on their hangers. From ceiling hooks the clustered beads and chains vibrated and a subdued rattling came from the boxes of rings and brooches on the table. There was a smell of spice and incense.

'Have you ever looked ...?' said the sympathiser, putting up his hand towards the ropes of neckchains.

'No, never,' said the passenger, stepping back as a cluster of heavy metal crosses swung before his eyes. 'Besides I am not really what you would call ...'

'No need to be any kind of Christian nowadays to wear these,' said the other. 'You can wear anything you fancy – crosses, amulets, wreaths, witch doctors' charms, ankle bells. These strings of worry beads might be worth looking at. There are some beauties here.'

'Worry beads?' a charming, smiling girl stepped from the counter and began unlooping beads of polished wood, strings of chalk-white shells, beads of yellow glass. Over the traveller's head she slipped a string of small green stones. He held them – pleasant to the touch – smooth, warm and slightly waxy as though some stronger sun in another country had melted their surface. The other two stepped back to admire him. 'Definitely yes,' said the man. 'Those are your stones all right.'

'But what am I supposed ...?'

'Anywhere,' said the girl. 'In your pocket, or just leave them on. Keep them hidden if you like.' Cool, firm hands tucked the beads out of sight inside his waistcoat.

'Would you believe it? – the man has a weight problem,' said his companion.

'Oh, nonsense,' said the girl, glancing at his waistline.

'Yes, he feels that he has not, at his age, made sufficient weighty pronouncements to the world. And now of course he thinks it's too late.'

The passenger could not deny this charge, but he gave his own version and for a few minutes, until the girl was called to another customer, they discussed lightness and weight and the formidable heaviness of the great globe itself. The passenger could not help noticing as he glanced around how light everything here appeared to be – airy fabrics stirring, bird and fish mobiles twirling in a breath of air, swinging bells, ruffled feathers, wings and flowers. The whole pile put together could hardly weigh much. Nothing was meant to last. Was that perhaps its value? The records in the adjoining shop still yelled and moaned of Love and Freedom, but it was of its changing and ephemeral nature that they sang.

'I suppose that was not your kind of place either,' said the younger man, as they moved away towards the windows of the expensive flower-shop next door. There were few ordinary bunches or bouquets on display today. Huge funeral wreaths of dark leaves and waxy yellow flowers were propped up against chrysanthemums bound into hard crosses. Tightly packed balls of dried white flowers were strewn about like plushy graveyard cushions.

'Well then – what now?' said the man again with some irritation. 'Is this your scene?'

'Not yet,' said the passenger, briskly for the first time, and in case there was any suggestion that he was already half-dead, he went decisively in past the wreaths and crosses into the back of the shop where all was earthy, damp and aromatic, with pots of leafy plants on shelves and fresh bunches of roses, iris and carnation standing in tubs of water.

'We are looking for a buttonhole – something bright and perfumed,' said the younger man. 'It's for my friend here and it will have to last him through a journey.'

'I am not going to a wedding!' exclaimed the passenger. But the shop assistants, who had been gravely waiting to assist mourners, clustered round as though it was their last chance at the end of the day to forget the showy displays of death in the front of the shop.

'What's more, he has just stepped out of a plane – well, not a moving one, that's asking a bit much of a human being – but he has removed his own weight so that all the others could go on.' Exclamations of admiration and surprise greeted this announcement, and a few light murmurs of disbelief.

'Naturally he got a cut-price fare out of it. Again it would be asking a bit much if he'd had to do it for nothing,' added the man, as he watched a free red carnation being pinned into the passenger's buttonhole. For a while they fussed about him, wondering how long the flower would last, whether it would survive the heat, the pressure, the wind on the tarmac. And again the passenger wondered why he should ever concern himself with weight or lasting things when the whole shop of flowers would fade and pass into memory. But again – did this give it its value? Tonight he believed he would remember every petal of the place.

Time was almost up and the passenger was ready to board the bus back to the airfield. 'Have you everything you need?' asked the other.

'More than enough.'

'But what about something to eat on the journey – a small bar of chocolate?'

Disregarding the traveller's protests, he stopped at a small newspaper stall where a few boxes of chocolates were laid out. 'Not even a small bar? Is that all you have?' the thin man heard him ask. He came back with a small twist of golden chocolate sovereigns in a net bag.

'But that's ridiculous. I am not a child!'

'They are simply thin chocolates. There is nothing to them.'

'I have never wanted to gain weight of that kind,' said the thin man.

'Of course not. As to the other kind, you will no doubt think of many wise and weighty things when you are up in the air. People often do when they're removed from the earth or even when they're fast asleep. Goodbye now – and good luck!'

The passenger returned to the airfield with not very much time for the next plane. He was greeted by the familiar officials and hustled through the formalities of the next flight. Indeed it seemed they were genuinely pleased to see him – welcoming him back to this scene like some one-line actor who had accidentally added a hint of farce to the show. 'So you managed to put in a couple of hours,' said one. 'The time didn't hang too heavy, I hope?'

'No, no – not in the least.' The passenger went out onto the tarmac which this evening was living up to its tradition of great wings and high wind. As he walked towards the plane he was almost blown off his feet by a gust from the east. Was he always to be reminded of human lightness?

And yet time had hung something upon him after all. It was not only that he was now decorated with beads, with a flower, with counterfeit gold coin, that he carried a little doubtful praise and some misplaced envy. His responsibilities were enlarged. In his own eyes, for better or worse, he had gained weight of a kind. Ahead the great blank eyes of the machine glared impatiently. But the single, late passenger moved steadily, unhurriedly towards the gangway.

THE PRESCRIPTION

Penelope Fitzgerald

Penelope Fitzgerald (1916–2000) was a Man Booker Prize-winning English novelist, poet, essayist and biographer. In 2008, *The Times* included her in a list of the '50 Greatest British writers since 1945' and, in 2012, the *Observer* named her final novel, *The Blue Flower*, as one of 'The 10 best historical novels'. A collection of Fitzgerald's short stories, *The Means of Escape*, and a volume of her non-fiction writings, *A House of Air*, were published posthumously.

After Petros Zarifi's wife died his shop began to make less and less money. His wife had acted as cashier. That was all over now. The shelves emptied gradually as the unpaid wholesalers refused to supply him with goods. In his tiny room at the back of the shop he had, like many Greek storekeepers, an oleograph in vivid colours of his patron saint, with the motto *Embros* – Forward! But he had now lost all ambition except in the matter of his son Alecco.

The shop was not too badly placed, on the very edge of the Phanar, where Zarifi should have been able to sell to both Greeks and Turks. One of his remaining customers, in fact, was an elderly Stamboullu who worked as dispenser to a prosperous doctor in the Beyazit district. Both old Yousuf and Dr Mehmet drank raki, which they regarded as permissible because it had not been invented in the days of the Prophet. One evening when he was refilling the bottles Zarifi asked Yousuf to speak for him to Mehmet Bey.

'Ask him if he will take my son Alecco, who has just turned fourteen, into his employment.'

'Can't his own relatives provide for him?' asked the old man.

'Don't give a father advice on this matter,' said Zarifi. 'What else does he think about when he lies awake at nights?'

Mehmet Bey took the virtue of compassion seriously. Once he had been told that Zarifi was a *good Greek*, who had won a reputation for honesty, and, possibly as a result, had been unfortunate, he sent word that he would see him.

'Your son can clean my boots and run errands. That is all I have to offer. Don't let him have ambitions. There are too many doctors in Stamboul, and, above all, far too many Greeks.'

'Good, well, I understand you, *bey effendi*, you may trust both my son and me.'

It was arranged that Alecco should work and sleep at the doctor's house in Hayreddin Pasha Street. His room was not much larger than a cupboard, but then, neither had it been at home. Loneliness was his trouble, not discomfort. The doctor's wife, Azizié Hanoum, kept to her quarters, and old Yousuf, who was a poor relation of hers, jealously guarded the dispensary, where the drugs must have been arranged on some kind of system since he was able, given time, to make up a prescription when called upon. As to Mehmet Bey himself, his hours were regular. After a sluggish evening visit to the coffee-house to read the newspaper he would return and spend a few hours more than half asleep in the bosom of his family. But Alecco understood very well, or thought he understood, what it was that his father expected him to do.

Polishing the boots of the *hakim bashi* did not take up much of the day. Always obedient, he went about with the doctor as a servant, keeping several paces behind, carrying his bag and his stethoscope. Once a week Mehmet Bey, as a good Moslem, gave his services to the hospital for the poor on the waterfront, and Alecco learned in the wards to recognize the face of leprosy and of death itself. Then, because he was so quick, he began to help a little with the accounts, and from the ledgers he gathered in a few weeks how the practice was run and which were the commonest complaints and how much could be charged for them in each case – always excepting the bills of the very rich, which were presented by Mehmet Bey in person. The doctor, for his part, recognized that this boy was sharp, and did not much like it. A subject race, he reflected, is a penance to the ruler. But he reminded himself that the father was trustworthy and honourable, and in time the son's sharpness might turn into nothing worse than industry, which is harmless.

Every day Alecco asked himself: have I gone one step forward, or one backward? What have I learned that I didn't know yesterday? Books are teachers to those who have none, but the doctor's library reposed behind the wooden shutters of the cupboards fitted into the walls of his consulting-room. His student *Materia Medica* were there, along with herbals in Arabic and the *Gulistan*, or Rose Garden of Medicines. Lately he had acquired a brand-new book, Gray's *Anatomy* in a French translation. Alecco had seen him turning it over heavily, during the late afternoon. But it was put away with the others, and there was no chance to look at it, still less to copy the illustrations.

The dispensary, also, was kept locked and bolted. But that year the month of Ramazan fell in the hot weather, and both the doctor and old Yousuf, being obliged to fast all day until sunset, went out through the hours of darkness to take refreshment, Mehmet Bey at the homes of his friends, Yousuf at the tea-house. Security was less strict, and the house itself, windowless against the street, seemed to relax at the end of its tedious day. During the second week of the fast, Alecco found the door of the dispensary unfastened.

Just before dawn began to lift, Mehmet Bey returned and saw that a single candle lamp was burning in his dispensary. The Greek boy was standing at the bench, copying out prescriptions. He had also taken down a measuring-glass, a pestle and a number of bottles and jars.

Bath-boy, *tellak*, son of a whore, the doctor thought. The hurt pierced deep. His friends had warned him, his wife had told him he was a fool. But in the end he had made a burden for his own back.

Alecco was so deeply absorbed that his keen sense of danger failed him. He did not move until Mehmet Bey towered close behind him. Then he turned, not dropping the pen and ink which he had stolen but gripping them closely to him, and stared up with the leaden eyes of a woken sleepwalker at his master.

'I see that you are studying my prescriptions,' said Mehmet Bey. 'I know from experience that you learn quickly.'

He picked up the empty glass. 'Now: make up a medicine for yourself.'

Sweating and trembling, Alecco shook in a measure of this and a measure of that, always keeping his eyes on his master. He could not have said what he was doing. Mehmet Bey, however, saw a dose of aphrodisiac go into the glass, and then the dried flowers of *agnus castas*, which inhibits sex, opium, lavender, *ecballium elaterium*, the most violent of all purgatives, *datura*, either 14 grams, inducing insanity, or 22½ grams (death) and finally mustard and cinnamon. Silently he pointed to the fuller's earth, which prevents the patient from vomiting. Alecco added a handful.

'Drink!'

The doctor's voice, raised to a pitch of sacred rage, woke up Azizié Hanoum, and standing terrified in her old wrapper at the door of the women's quarters she saw her husband seize the Greek boy by the nose, from which water poured out, and force his head backwards to dislocation point while something black as pitch ran from the measuring-glass down his throat.

In the morning Alecco, who had been crammed into his room unconscious, appeared smiling with the doctor's cleaned boots in his hands. Mehmet Bey made a sign to avert evil.

'You're well? You're alive?'

'My prescription did me a world of good.'

The doctor called his servants and had him turned out of the house. Picking himself up, Alecco walked away with fourteen-year-old jauntiness along the new horse tramway until he was out of sight. Not until he reached the foot of the Galata Bridge did his will-power give way and he collapsed groaning like vermin on a dung-hill.

Preparing slowly for his rounds, Mehmet Bey at first congratulated himself, since if the boy had died he was not quite certain how he would have stood with the law. But the household's peace was destroyed. Old Yousuf was so perturbed by the mess in the dispensary that he collapsed with a slight stroke. He had never been able to read, and now that the drugs were out of order he could find nothing. Azizié Hanoum poured reproaches on her husband and declared that if the little Greek had been better treated he could have been trained to help Yousuf. Zarifi mourned his son, who did not return either to the Phanar or to Hayreddin Pasha Street. In a few months the grocer's shop was bankrupt.

Alecco had been picked up on the waterfront by a Greek ship's cook, coming back on board after a night's absence. He had some confused idea of conciliating the captain, who, he knew, was short of a boy. The *Andromeda* was an irregular trading vessel carrying mail via Malta and Gibraltar, and by the time she reached London Alecco had been seasick to such an extent that he was clear of the poison's last traces. This seemed a kind of providence; he could never have cheated Death without some help. The captain had fancied him from the start, and when the crew were paid off at Albert Docks he gave him five pounds in English money to make a good start in life.

Ten years later Dr Mehmet's career had reached its highest point and was also (he was sixty-five) approaching its end. Having been called, not for the first time, for consultation at the Old Serail, he settled down for a long waiting period before an attendant arrived to escort him to the ante-rooms. He took a seat overlooking the Sea of Marmara, and resigned himself. In contemplation of the lazing water, he allowed his energies to sleep. The ladies here were the old and the pensioned-off, but the appointment was an honour.

Quite without warning, and faintly disagreeable, was the appearance of a secretary: Lelia Hanoum had wished for a second opinion, and he had the honour to present a distinguished young colleague who had hurried here from another appointment. But when a young man walked in wearing a black *stambouline*, the professional's frock-coat, and followed by a servant carrying his bag and stethoscope, Mehmet Bey knew not only who he was, but that he had been expecting him.

'I decline to accept you as a colleague, Alexander Zarifi.'

'I am qualified,' Dr Zarifi replied.

'Your word is not good enough.'

Alecco took out from the upper pocket of his *stamboulim* a card printed in gilt, which showed that he had recently been appointed to attend the Serail. This could not be contradicted, and after putting it away he said:

'I am honoured, then, to join you as a consultant.' He waited for the usual, in fact necessary, reply: 'The honour is mine,' but instead Mehmet Bey said loudly: 'There is no need for us to waste time in each other's company. I know the case history of Lelia Hanoum, you may consult my notes. I have already made the diagnosis. Last year the patient complained of acute pain in the left side and a distention as though a ball or globe was rising from the abdomen to the throat. Palpitations, fits of crying, quantities of wind passed per rectum. A typical case of hysteria, all too common in the Serail, and entirely the result of an ill-balanced regimen. I advised firm treatment, iron pills and a gentian tonic. Recently, however, she has described the initial pain as on the right side. Accordingly I have changed my diagnosis to acute appendicitis, and I propose to operate as soon as permission can be got from the Palace. She is rather old for the operation to be successful, but that is in God's hands.'

'I cannot agree,' Dr Zarifi replied. 'The very fact that the patient is uncertain whether she feels pain on the left or the right side means that we must look beneath her symptoms for an unconscious or subconscious factor. During my training in Vienna I was fortunate enough to work with Dr Josef Breuer, the great specialist in hysteria. It is for the woman herself to lead us to the hidden factor, perhaps under hypnosis. It is my belief that there is no need for medication, still less surgical interference. We must aim at setting her free.'

'Well, now I have your opinion,' said Mehmet Bey. 'If I reject it, it is because I have studied the art of healing, not so much from personal ambition as to answer the simplest of all appeals – *hastayim*, I am ill. I accept that since we last met you have had the advantage of a good training, but your nature will not have changed. You are still Alexander Zarifi. What is more, there are universal laws, which govern all human beings, not excepting men of science. Cast your memory back, and answer me this question: Knowledge is good, but what is the use of knowledge without honesty?'

Dr Alecco looked down at the ground, and withdrew his diagnosis.

HOW DID I GET AWAY WITH KILLING ONE OF THE BIGGEST LAWYERS IN THE STATE? IT WAS EASY.

Alice Walker

> Alice Walker (b. 1944) is an American author, poet, feminist and activist. She is best known for the critically acclaimed novel *The Color Purple*, published in 1982, for which she won the National Book Award and the Pulitzer Prize. Walker's published works include seven novels, four collections of short stories, four children's books and volumes of essays and poetry.

"My mother and father were not married. I never knew him. My mother must have loved him, though; she never talked against him when I was little. It was like he never existed. We lived on Poultry Street. Why it was called Poultry Street I never knew. I guess at one time there must have been a chicken factory somewhere along there. It was right near the center of town. I could walk to the state capitol in less than ten minutes. I could see the top – it was gold – of the capitol building from the front yard. When I was a little girl I used to think it was real gold, shining up there, and then they bought an eagle and put him on top, and when I used to walk up there I couldn't see the top of the building from the ground, it was so high, and I used to reach down and run my hand over the grass. It was like a rug, that grass was, so springy and silky and deep. They had these big old trees, too. Oaks and magnolias; and I thought the magnolia trees were beautiful and one night I climbed up in one of them and got a bloom and took it home. But the air in our house blighted it; it turned brown the minute I took it inside and the petals dropped off.

"Mama worked in private homes. That's how she described her job, to make it sound nicer. 'I work in private homes,' she would say, and that sounded nicer, she thought, than saying 'I'm a maid.'

"Sometimes she made six dollars a day, working in two private homes. Most of the time she didn't make that much. By the time she paid the rent and bought milk and bananas there wasn't anything left.

"She used to leave me alone sometimes because there was no one to keep me – and then there was an old woman up the street who looked after me for a while – and by the time she died she was more like a mother to me than Mama was. Mama was so tired every night when she came home I never hardly got the chance to talk to her. And then sometimes she would go out at night, or bring men home – but they never thought of marrying her. And they sure didn't want to be bothered with me. I guess most of them were like my own father; had children somewhere of their own that they'd left. And then they came to my Mama, who fell for them every time. And I think she may have had a couple of abortions, like some of the women did, who couldn't feed any more mouths. But she tried.

"Anyway, she was a nervous kind of woman. I think she had spells or something because she was so tired. But I didn't understand anything then about exhaustion, worry, lack of a proper diet; I just thought she wanted to work, to be away from the house. I didn't blame her. Where we lived people sometimes just threw pieces of furniture they didn't want over the railing. And there was broken glass and rags everywhere. The place stunk, especially in the summer. And children were always screaming and men were always cussing and women were always yelling about something ... It was nothing for a girl or woman to be raped. I was raped myself, when I was twelve, and my Mama never knew and I never told anybody. For, what could they do? It was just a boy, passing through. Somebody's cousin from the North.

"One time my Mama was doing day's work at a private home and took me with her. It was like being in fairyland. Everything was spotless and new, even before Mama started cleaning. I met the woman in the house and played with her children. I didn't even see the man, but he was in there somewhere, while I was out in the yard with the children. I was fourteen, but I guess I looked like a grown woman. Or maybe I looked fourteen. Anyway, the next day he picked me up when I was coming from school and he said my Mama had asked him to do it. I got in the car with him ... he took me to his law office, a big office in the middle of town, and he started asking me questions about 'how do you all live?' and 'what grade are you in?' and stuff like that. And then he began to touch me, and I pulled away. But he kept touching me and I was scared ... he raped me. But afterward he told me he hadn't forced me, that I felt something for him, and he gave me some money. I was crying, going down the stairs. I wanted to kill him.

"I never told Mama. I thought that would be the end of it. But about two days later, on my way from school, he stopped his car again, and I got in. This time we went to his house; nobody was there. And he made me get into his wife's bed. After we'd been doing this for about three weeks, he told me he loved me. I didn't love him, but he had begun to look a little better to me. Really, I think, because he was so clean. He bathed a lot and never smelled even alive, to tell the truth. Or maybe it was the money he gave me, or the presents he bought. I told Mama I had a job after school baby-sitting. And she was glad that I could buy things I needed for school. But it was all from him.

"This went on for two years. He wouldn't let me get pregnant, he said, and I didn't. I would just lay up there in his wife's bed and work out algebra problems or think about what new thing I was going to buy. But one day, when I got home, Mama was there ahead of me, and she saw me get out of his car. I knew when he was driving off that I was going to get it.

"Mama asked me didn't I know he was a white man? Didn't I know he was a married man with two children? Didn't I have good sense? And do you know what I told her? *I told her he loved me*. Mama was crying and praying at the same time by then. The neighbors heard both of us screaming and crying, because Mama beat me almost to death with the cord from the electric iron. She just hacked it off the iron, still on the ironing board. She beat me till she couldn't raise her arm. And then she had one of her fits, just twitching and sweating and trying to claw herself into the floor. This scared me more than the beating. That night she told me something I hadn't paid much attention to before. She said; 'On top of everything else, that man's daddy goes on the TV every night and says folks like us ain't even human.' It was his daddy who had stood in the schoolhouse door saying it would be over his dead body before any black children would come into a white school.

"But do you think that stopped me? No. I would look at his daddy on TV ranting and raving about how integration was a communist plot, and I would just think of how different his son Bubba was from his daddy! Do you understand what I'm saying. I thought he *loved* me. That *meant* something to me. What did I know about 'equal rights'? What did I care about 'integration'? I was sixteen! I wanted somebody to tell me I was pretty, and he was telling me that all the time. I even thought it was *brave* of him to go with me. History? What did I know about History?

"I began to hate Mama. We argued about Bubba all the time, for months. And I still slipped out to meet him, because Mama had to work. I told him how she beat me, and about how much she despised him – he was really pissed off that any black person could despise him – and about how she had these spells ... Well, the day I became seventeen, the *day* of my seventeenth birthday, I signed papers in his law office, and I had my mother committed to an insane asylum.

"After Mama had been in Carthage Insane Asylum for three months, she managed somehow to get a lawyer. An old slick-headed man who smoked great big black cigars. People laughed at him because he didn't even have a law office, but he was the only lawyer that would touch the case, because Bubba's daddy was such a big deal. And we all gathered in the judge's chambers – because he wasn't about to let this case get out. Can you imagine, if it had? And Mama's old lawyer told the judge how Bubba's daddy had tried to buy him off. And Bubba got up and swore he'd never touched me. And then I got up and said Mama was insane. And do you know what? By that time it was true. Mama *was* insane. She had no mind left at all. They had given her shock treatments or something ... God knows what else they gave her. But she was as vacant as an empty eye socket. She just sat sort of hunched over, and her hair was white.

"And after all this, Bubba wanted us to keep going together. Mama was just an obstacle that he felt he had removed. But I just suddenly – in a way I don't even pretend to understand – woke up. It was like everything up to then had been some kind of dream. And I told him I wanted to get Mama out. But he wouldn't do it; he just kept trying to make me go with him. And sometimes – out of habit, I guess – I did. My body did what it was being paid to do. And Mama died. And I killed Bubba.

"How did I get away with killing one of the biggest lawyers in the state? It was easy. He kept a gun in his desk drawer at the office and one night I took it out and shot him. I shot him while he was wearing his thick winter overcoat, so I wouldn't have to see him bleed. But I don't think I took the time to wipe off my fingerprints, because, to tell the truth, I couldn't stand it another minute in that place. No one came after me, and I read in the paper the next day that he'd been killed by burglars. I guess they thought 'burglars' had stolen all that money Bubba kept in his safe – but I had it. One of the carrots Bubba always dangled before me was that he was going to send me to college: I didn't see why he shouldn't do it.

"The strangest thing was, Bubba's wife came over to the house and asked me if I'd mind looking after the children while she went to Bubba's funeral. I did it, of course, because I was afraid she'd suspect something if I didn't. So on the day he was buried I was in his house, sitting on his wife's bed with his children, and eating fried chicken his wife, Julie, had cooked."

CORRUPTION

Penelope Lively

Penelope Lively (b. 1933) is a critically acclaimed British
author of fiction for both children and adults. She won the
Carnegie Medal for children's fiction in 1973, for *The
Ghost of Thomas Kempe*, and also the Man Booker Prize
for her 1987 novel, *Moon Tiger*. Lively was made Dame
Commander of the Order of the British Empire in the 2012
New Year Honours list.

The judge and his wife, driving to Aldeburgh for the weekend,
carried with them in the back of the car a Wine Society carton filled
with pornographic magazines. The judge, closing the hatchback,
stared for a moment through the window; he reopened the door
and put a copy of *The Times* on top of the pile, extinguishing the
garish covers. He then got into the driving seat and picked up the
road atlas.

"The usual route, dear?"

"The usual route, I think. Unless we spot anything enticing on
the way."

"We have plenty of time to be enticed, if we feel so inclined."

The judge, Richard Braine, was sixty-two; his wife Marjorie, a
magistrate, was two years younger. The weekend ahead was their
annual and cherished early summer break at the Music Festival;
the pornographic magazines were the impounded consignment
of an importer currently under trial and formed the contents of
the judge's weekend briefcase, so to speak. "Chores?" his wife had
said, and he had replied, "Chores, I'm afraid."

At lunch-time, they pulled off the main road into a carefully
selected lane and found a gate-way in which to park the car. They
carried the rug and picnic basket into a nearby field and ate their
lunch under the spacious East Anglian sky in a state of almost
flamboyant contentment. Both had noted how the satisfactions
of life have a tendency to gain intensity with advancing years.

"The world gets more beautiful," Marjorie had once said, "not less so. Fun is even more fun. Music is more musical, if you see what I mean. One hadn't reckoned with that." Now, consuming the thoughtfully constructed sandwiches and the coffee from the thermos, they glowed at one another amid the long thick grass that teemed with buttercup and clover; before them, the landscape retreated into blue distances satisfactorily broken here and there by a line of trees, the tower of a church or a rising contour. From time to time they exchanged remarks of pleasure or anticipation: about the surroundings, the weather, the meal they would eat tonight at the little restaurant along the coast road, tomorrow evening's concert. Richard Braine, who was a man responsive to the moment, took his wife's hand; they sat in the sun, shirt-sleeved, and agreed conspiratorially and without too much guilt that they were quite glad that the eldest married daughter who sometimes accompanied them on this trip had not this year been able to. The daughter was loved, but would just now have been superfluous.

When they arrived at the small hotel it was early evening. The judge carried their suitcase and the Wine Society carton in and set them down by the reception desk. The proprietor, bearing the carton, showed them to their usual room. As she was unpacking, Marjorie said, "I think you should have left that stuff in the car. Chambermaids, you know ..." The judge frowned. "That's a point." He tipped the contents of the box into the emptied suitcase and locked it. "I think I'll have a bath before we go out."

He lay in the steamy cubicle, a sponge resting upon his stomach. Marjorie, stripped to a pair of pants, came in to wash. "The dear old avocado suite again. One day we must have an avocado bathroom suite at home." The judge, contemplating the rise of his belly, nodded; he was making a resolution about reduction of the flesh, a resolution which he sadly knew would be broken. He was a man who enjoyed food. His wife's flesh, in the process now of being briskly soaped and scrubbed, was firmer and less copious, as he was fully prepared to concede. He turned his head to watch her and thought for a while in a vague and melancholy way about bodies, about how we inhabit them and are dragged to the grave by them and are conditioned by them. In the course of his professional life he had frequently had occasion to reflect upon the last point:

it had seemed to him, observing the faces that passed before him in courtrooms, that confronted him from docks and witness boxes, that not many of us are able to rise above physical appearance. The life of an ugly woman is different from that of a beautiful one; you cannot infer character from appearance, but you can suspect a good deal about the circumstances to which it will have given rise. Abandoning this intetesting but sombre theme, he observed his wife's breasts and muscular but not unshapely thighs and the folds of skin upon her neck and remembered the first time he had seen her with no clothes on. She turned to look at him. "If you're jeering at my knickers, they're a pair of Alison's I grabbed out of the laundry basket by mistake." Alison was their youngest, unmarried daughter. "I hadn't really noticed them," said the judge politely. "I was thinking about something quite different." He smiled. "And don't leer," said his wife, flicking him with her flannel. "It's unbecoming in a man of your age." "It's a tribute to your charms, my dear," said the judge. He sat up and began to wash his neck, thinking still about that first time they had both been embarrassed. Embarrassment had been a part of the pleasure, he reflected. How odd, and interesting.

It was still daylight when they drove to the restaurant, a violet summer twilight in which birds sang with jungle stridency. Marjorie, getting out of the car, said, "That veal and mushroom in cream sauce thing for me, I think. A small salad for you, without dressing."

"No way," said the judge.

"I admire your command of contemporary speech." She went ahead into the restaurant, inspecting the room with bright, observant eyes. When they were sitting at the table she whispered, "There's that same woman we met last year. Remember? The classy type who kept putting you right about Britten."

The judge, cautiously, turned his head. "So it is. Keep a low profile."

"Will do, squire," said Marjorie, applying herself to the menu. "Fifteen all?" she added. "Right?"

"Right," said her husband.

Their acquaintance, leaving before them, stopped to exchange greetings. The judge, mildly resenting the interruption to his meal, left the work to Marjorie. The woman, turning to go, said, "So nice to see you again. And have a lovely break from juries and things." She gleamed upon the judge.

He watched her retreating silk-clad back. "Rather a gushing creature. How the hell does she know what I do?"

"Chatting up the hotel people, I don't doubt. It gives you cachet, you note, your job. Me, on the other hand, she considers a drab little woman. I could see her wondering how I came by you."

"Shall we enlighten her? Sheer unbridled lust ..."

"Talking of which," said Marjorie, "Just how unprincipled would it be to finish off with some of that cheese-cake?"

Back at the hotel, they climbed into bed in a state of enjoyable repletion. The judge put on his spectacles and reached out for the suitcase. "You're not going to start going through that stuff *now* ..." said Marjorie. "At least have one whole day off work."

"You're right," he said. "Tomorrow will do. I'll have that Barbara Pym novel instead."

The judge, waking early the next morning, lay thinking about the current trial. He thought, in fact, not about obscenity or pornography but about the profit motive. He did not, he realised, understand the profit motive; he did not understand it in the same way in which he did not understand what induced people to be cruel. He had never coveted the possessions of others or wished himself richer than he was. He held no stocks or shares; Marjorie, once, had been left a small capital sum by an aunt; neither he nor she had ever been able to take the slightest interest in the financial health of her investments. Indeed, both had now forgotten what exactly the money was in. All this, he realised, was the position of a man with a substantial earned income; were he not paid what he was he might well feel otherwise. But he had not, in fact, felt very much otherwise as an impecunious young barrister. And importers of pornography tend, he understood, to be in an upper income bracket. No – the obstacle, the barrier requiring that leap of the imagination, was this extra dimension of need in some men that sought to turn money into yet more money, that required wealth for wealth's sake, the spawning of figures. The judge himself enjoyed growing vegetables; he considered, now, the satisfaction he got from harvesting a good crop of french beans and tried to translate this into a manifestation of the profit motive. The analogy did not quite seem to work.

The profit motive in itself, of course, is innocuous enough. Indeed, without it societies would founder. This was not the point that was bothering the judge; he was interested in those gulfs of inclination that divide person from person. As a young man he had wondered if this restriction makes us incapable of passing judgement on our fellows, but had come to realise at last that it does not. He remembered being involved in an impassioned argument about apartheid with another law student, an Afrikaner; "You cannot make pronouncements on our policies," the man had said, "when you have never been to our country. You cannot understand the situation." Richard Braine had known, with the accuracy of a physical response, that the man was wrong. Not misguided; simply wrong. A murderer is doing wrong, whatever the circumstances that drive him to his crime.

The profit motive is not wrong; the circumstances of its application may well be. The judge – with a certain irritation – found himself recalling the features of the importer of pornography: a nondescript, bespectacled man memorable only for a pair of rather bushy eyebrows and a habit of pulling an ear-lobe when under cross-examination. He pushed the fellow from his mind, determinedly, and got out of bed. Outside the window, strands of neatly corrugated cloud coasted in a milky-blue sky; it looked as though it would be a nice day.

The Braines spent the morning at Minsmere bird sanctuary; in the afternoon they went for a walk. The evening found them, scoured by fresh air and slightly somnolent, listening to Mozart, Bartok and Mendelssohn. The judge, who had never played an instrument and regarded himself as relatively unmusical, nevertheless responded to music with considerable intensity. It aroused him in various ways; in such different ways, indeed, that, being a thorough and methodical man, he often felt bemused, caught up by the onward rush of events before he had time to sort them out. Stop, he wanted to say to the surging orchestra, just let me have a think about that bit ... But already he would have been swept onwards, into other moods, other themes, other passions. Marjorie, who played the piano in an unspectacular but competent way, had often suggested that the problem might be solved at least in part if he learned to read music.

She was no doubt right, he thought, wrestling now with a tortuous passage. When I retire; just the thing for a man reduced to inactivity. The judge did not look forward to retirement. But a few moments of inattention had been fatal – now the music had got away from him entirely, as though he had turned over two pages of a book. Frowning, he concentrated on the conductor.

Standing at the bar in the interval, he found himself beside their acquaintance from the restaurant, also waiting to order a drink. Gallantry or even basic good manners required that he intervene. "Oh," she said. "How terribly sweet of you. A gin and tonic would be gorgeous." With resignation, he led her back to where Marjorie awaited him.

"Your husband was so sweet and insistent – I'm all on my own this evening, my sister had a splitting headache and decided not to come." She was a tall woman in her early fifties, too youthfully packaged in a flounced skirt and high-heeled boots, her manner towards the judge both sycophantic and faintly roguish. "I was reading about you in *The Times* last month, some case about people had up for embezzling, of course I didn't understand most of it, all terribly technical, but I said to Laura, I *know* him, we had such a lovely talk about Britten at the Festival."

"Ah," said the judge, studying his programme: the Tippett next.

"I'm Moira Lukes, by the way – if you're anything like me names just *evaporate*, but of course I remembered yours from seeing it in the paper!" She turned to Marjorie, "Aren't you loving the concert?"; patronage discreetly flowed, the patronage of a woman with a sexual history towards one who probably had none, of a lavishly clad woman towards a dowdy one. The judge's antennae slightly quivered, though he was not himself sure why. Marjorie blandly agreed that the concert was superb. "Excuse me," she said. "I'm going to make a dash to the loo while there's time."

The judge and Moira Lukes, left alone, made private adjustments so each other's company: the judge cleared his throat and commented on the architecture of the concert hall: Moira moved a fraction closer to him and altered the pitch of her voice, probably without being aware that she did either. "You must lead such a fascinating life," she said. "I mean, you must come across such extraordinary people. Dickensian types. I don't think I've ever set eyes on a criminal."

The judge thought again of the importer of pornography. "Most of them are rather mundane, when it comes to the point."

"But you must get to know so much about people." She was looking very directly at him, with large eyes; a handsome woman, the judge conceded, rather a knock-out as a girl, no doubt. He agreed that yes, one did get a few insights into the ways in which people carry on.

"Fascinating," said Moira Lukes again. "I expect you have the most marvellous stories to tell. I envy your wife no end." The large eyes creased humorously at the corners; a practised device, though the judge did not recognise this. "In fact I think she's a lucky woman – I still remember that interesting chat you and I had last year." And she laid on his arm a hand, which was almost instantly removed – come and gone as briefly as though a bird had alighted for a fleeting second. The judge, startled in several ways, tried to recall this chat: something about when *Peter Grimes* was first performed, or was it *The Turn of the Screw*? The interest of it, now, escaped him. He cast a quick glance across the foyer in search of Marjorie, who seemed to be taking an awfully long time. Moira Lukes was talking now about the area of Sussex in which she lived. Do, she was saying, look in and have lunch, both of you, if you're ever in that part of the world. The judge murmured that yes, of course if ever they were ... He noticed the rings on her hand and wondered vaguely what had become of Mr Lukes; somehow one knew that he was no longer around, one way or the other.

"The only time," she said, "I've ever personally had anything to do with the law was over my rather wretched divorce." The judge took a swig of his drink. "And then actually the lawyer was most awfully sweet, in fact he kept my head above water through it all." She sighed, a whiff of a sigh, almost imperceptible; thereby, she implied most delicately, hung a tale. "So I've got rather a soft spot for legal people."

"Good," said the judge heartily. "I'm glad to hear you've been well treated by the profession."

"Oh, *very* well treated."

No sign of Marjorie, still. Actually, the judge was thinking, this Moira Whatshername wasn't perhaps quite so bad after all, behind that rather tiresome manner; appearances, inevitably, deceive. One got the impression, too, of someone who'd maybe had a bit of a rough time. "Well, it's a world that includes all sorts, like most. And it brings you up against life, I suppose, with all that that implies."

The respect with which these banalities were received made him feel a little cheap. In compensation, he told her an anecdote about a case in which he had once been involved; a *crime passionel* involving an apparently wronged husband who had turned out in fact to be the villain of the piece. "A mealy-mouthed fellow, and as plausible as you like, but apparently he'd been systematically persecuting her for years." Moira Lukes nodded sagely. "People absolutely are not what they seem to be."

"Well," said the judge. "Yes and no. On the other hand, plenty of people give themselves away as soon as they open their mouths."

"Oh, goodness," said Moira Lukes. "Now I'll feel I daren't utter a word ever again."

"I had in mind those I come across professionally rather than in private life."

"Ah, then you think I'm safe?"

"Now, whatever could you have to conceal?" said the judge amiably. A bell went. "I wonder where Marjorie's got to. I suppose we'd better start going back in."

Moira Lukes sighed. She turned those large eyes upon him and creased them once again at the corners. "Well, this has been so nice. I'm sure we'll run into each other again over the weekend. But do bear in mind that I'm in the East Sussex phone book. I remember that case I read about was in Brighton – if you're ever judging there again and want a few hours' retreat on your own, do pop over and have a drink." She smiled once more, and walked quickly away into the crowd.

The judge stood for a moment, looking after her. He realised with surprise that he had been on the receiving end of what is generally known as a pass. He realised also that he was finding it difficult to sort out exactly what he felt about this; a rational response and his natural judgement of people (he didn't in fact all that much care for the woman) fought with more reprehensible feelings and a certain complacency (so one wasn't a total old buffer just yet). In this state of internal conflict he made his way back into the concert hall, where he found Marjorie already in her seat.

"What on earth happened to you?"

"Sorry," she said cheerfully. "There was an awful queue in the Ladies and by the time I got out it wasn't worth coming to find you. How did you make out with our friend?"

The judge grunted, and applied himself to the programme. The lights went down, the conductor reappeared, the audience sank into silence ... But the music, somehow, had lost its compulsion; he was aware now of too much that was external – that he could achieve no satisfactory position for his legs, that he had slight indigestion, that the chap in front of him kept moving his head. Beside him, he could see Marjorie's face, rapt. The evening, somehow, had been corrupted.

The next morning was even more seraphic than the one before. "Today," said Marjorie, "we are going to sit on the beach and bask. We may even venture into the sea."

"That sounds a nice idea." The judge had thought during the night of the little episode with that woman and, in the process, a normal balance of mind had returned; he felt irritated – though more with himself than with her – that it had interfered with his enjoyment of the concert. It was with some annoyance, therefore, that he spotted her now across the hotel dining-room, with the sister, lifting her hand in a little finger-waggling wave of greeting.

"What's the matter?" said Marjorie, with marital insight. "Oh ... Her. Well, I'll leave you to hide behind the paper. I'm going upstairs to get sorted out for the beach."

He was half-way through the Home News page when he felt her standing over him. Alone. The sister, evidently, had been disposed of.

"Another heavenly day. Aren't we lucky! All on your own? I saw your wife bustling off ..." She continued to stand, her glance drifting now towards the coffee pot at the judge's elbow.

I am supposed, he thought, to say sit down and join me – have a cup of coffee. And he felt again that quiver of the antennae and knew now the reason. Marjorie does indeed bustle, her walk is rather inelegant, but it is not for you to say so, or to subtly denigrate a person I happen to love. He rattled, slightly, his newspaper. "We're off to the beach shortly."

"Oh, lovely. I daresay we'll go down there later. I wonder ... Goodness, I don't know if I ought to ask you this or not ..." She hesitated, prettily, seized, it seemed, with sudden difference. "Oh, I'll be brave. The thing is, I have this tiresome problem about a flat in London I'm buying, something to do with the leasehold that I simply do not follow, and I just do not have absolute faith in the man who's dealing with it for me – the solicitor, you know – *could* I pick your brains about it at some point?"

The judge, impassive, gazed up at her.

"I don't mean *now* – not in the middle of your holiday weekend. My sister was noticing your address in the hotel register and believe it or not my present flat is only a few minutes away. What would be lovely would be if you could spare an hour or so to look in for a drink on your way home one evening – and your wife too of course, only it might be awfully boring for her if you're going to brief me. Is that the right word? Would it be an imposition? When you're on your own like I am you are so very much at the mercy of ..." – she sighed – "people, the system, I don't know what ... Sometimes I get quite panic-stricken."

I doubt that, thought the judge. He put the newspaper down. "Mrs Lukes ..."

"Oh, Moira ... please."

He cleared his throat. "Conveyancing, as it happens, is not my field. Anything I said might quite possibly be misleading. The only sensible advice I can give is to change your solicitor if you feel lack of confidence in him."

Her eyes flickered; that look of honest appeal dimmed, suddenly. "Oh ... I see. Well, I daresay you're right. I must do that, then. I shouldn't have asked. But of course the invitation stands, whenever you're free."

"How kind," said the judge coolly. He picked up his paper again and looked at her over the top of it; their eyes met in understanding. And he flinched a little at her expression; it was the look of hatred he had seen from time to time, over the years, across a courtroom, on the face in the dock.

"Have a *lovely* day," said Moira Lukes. Composure had

returned; she gleamed, and wrinkled her eyes, and was gone. Well, thought the judge, there's no love lost there, now. But it had to be done, once and for all. He folded the paper and went in search of Marjorie.

She was packing a beach-bag with costumes and towels. The judge, unlocking the suitcase, took out a stack of the pornographic magazines and pushed them into the bottom of the bag. "Oh, lor," said Marjorie, "I'd forgotten about them. Must you?"

"'Fraid so. The case resumes tomorrow. It's the usual business of going through them for degrees of obscenity. There are some books too."

"I'll help you," said Marjorie. "There – greater love hath no woman ..."

The beach was agreeably uncrowded. Family parties were dotted in clumps about the sand; children and dogs skittered in and out of the surf; gulls floated above the water and a party of small wading birds scurried back and forth before the advancing waves like blown leaves. The judge, who enjoyed a bit of unstrenuous bird-watching, sat observing them with affection. The weather, this particularly delectable manifestation of the physical world and the uncomplicated relish of the people and animals around him had induced a state of general benignity. Marjorie, organising the rug and wind-screen, said, "All right?" "All right?" he replied. They smiled at each other, appreciating the understatement.

Marjorie, after a while, resolutely swam. The judge, more craven, followed her to the water's edge and observed. As they walked back up the beach together he saw suddenly that Moira Lukes and her sister were encamped not for off. She glanced at him and then immediately away. Now, at midday, the beach was becoming more occupied, though not disturbingly so. A family had established itself close to the Braines' pitch: young parents with a baby in a pram and a couple of older children now deeply engaged in the initial stages of sandcastle construction. The judge, who had also made a sandcastle or two in his time, felt an absurd urge to lend a hand; the basic design, he could see, was awry and would give trouble before long. The mother, a fresh-faced young woman, came padding across the sand to ask Marjorie for the loan of a tin-opener. They chatted for a moment; the young woman carried the baby on her hip. "That sort of thing," said Marjorie, sitting down again, "can still make me broody, even at my time of life." She too watched the sandcastle-building; presently she rummaged in the picnic basket and withdrew a plastic beaker. "Turrets," she explained to the judge, a little guiltily. "You can never do a good job with a bucket ..." The children received her offering with rewarding glee; the parents gratefully smiled; the sandcastle rose, more stylish.

The judge sighed, and delved in the beach bag. "To work, I suppose," he said. Around them, the life of the beach had settled into a frieze, as though the day were eternal: little sprawled groups of people, the great arc of the horizon against which stood the grey shapes of two far-away ships, like cut-outs, the surface animation of running dogs and children and someone's straw hat, tossed hither and thither by the breeze that had sprung up.

The judge and his wife sat with a pile of magazines each. Marjorie said, "This is a pretty gruesome collection. Can I borrow your hankie, my glasses keep getting salted over."

The judge turned over pages, and occasionally made some notes. Nothing he saw surprised him; from time to time he found himself examining the faces that belonged to the bodies displayed, as though in search of explanations. But they seemed much like any other faces; so presumably were the bodies.

Marjorie said, "Cup of tea? Tell me, why are words capable of so much greater obscenity than pictures?" She was glancing through a book, or something that passed as such.

"That, I imagine, is why people have always gone in for burning them, though usually for quite other reasons."

It was as the judge was reaching out to take the mug of tea from her that the wind came. It came in a great wholesome gust, flinging itself along the beach with a cloud of blown sand and flying plastic bags. It sent newspapers into the air like great flapping birds and spun a spotted football along the water's edge as though it were a top. It lifted rugs and pushed over deck chairs. It snatched the magazines from the judge's lap and from Marjorie's and bore them away across the sand in a helter-skelter whirl of colourful pages, dropping them down only to grab them again and fling them here and there: at the feet of a stout lady snoozing in a deckchair, into the pram of the neighbouring family's baby, onto people's towels and Sunday newspapers.

Marjorie said, "Oh, *lor* ..."

They got up. They began, separately, to tour the beach in pursuit of what the wind had taken. The judge found himself, absurdly, feeling foolish because he had left his jacket on his chair and was plodding along the sand in shirt-sleeves (no tie, either) and tweed trousers. The lady in the deck chair woke and put out a hand to quell the magazine that was wrapping itself around her leg. "Yours?" she said amiably, looking up at the judge, and as she handed him the thing it fell open and for a moment her eyes rested on the central spread, the *pièce de resistance*; her expression changed, rubbed out as it were by amazement, and she looked again at the judge for an instant, and became busy with the knitting on her lap.

Marjorie, stumping methodically along, picked up one magazine and then another, tucking them under her arm. She turned and saw that the children had observed the crisis, abandoned their sandcastle and were scurrying here and there, collecting as though involved in a treasure hunt. The mother, too, had risen and was shaking the sand from a magazine that had come to rest against the wheels of the pram. As Marjorie reached her the little girl ran up with an armful. "Good girl, Sharon," said the mother, and the child – six, perhaps, or seven – virtuously beamed and held out to Marjorie the opened pages of the magazine she held. She looked at it and the mother looked at it and Marjorie looked and the child said, "Are those flowers?". "No, my dear," said Marjorie sadly. "They aren't flowers," and she turned away before she could meet the eyes of the young mother.

The judge collected a couple from a man who handed them over with a wink, and another from a boy who stared at him expressionless, and then he could not find any more. He walked back to their pitch. Marjorie was shoving things into the beach bag. "Shall we go?" she said, and the judge nodded.

It was as they were folding the rug that Moira Lukes came up. She wore neatly creased cotton trousers and walked with a spring. "Yours, apparently," she said; she held the magazine out between a finger and thumb, as though with tongs, and dropped it onto the sand. She looked straight at the judge. "How awfully true," she said, "that people are not what they seem to be." Satisfaction flowed from her; she glanced for an instant, at Marjorie, as though checking that she had heard, and walked away.

The Braines, in silence, completed the assembly of their possessions. Marjorie carried the rug and the picnic basket and the judge bore the beach bag and the wind-screen. They trudged the long expanse of the beach, watched, now, with furtive interest by various eyes.

A REAL DOLL

A. M. Homes

A. M. Homes (b. 1961) is an American writer known for her controversial novels and unusual stories. She released her first collection of short stories, *The Safety of Objects*, in 1990. In 2013 she won the Women's Prize for Fiction with her novel *May We Be Forgiven*.

I'm dating Barbie. Three afternoons a week, while my sister is at dance class, I take Barbie away from Ken. I'm practising for the future.

At first I sat in my sister's room watching Barbie, who lived with Ken, on a doily, on top of the dresser.

I was looking at her but not really looking. I was looking, and all of the sudden realized she was staring at me.

She was sitting next to Ken, his khaki-covered thigh absently rubbing her bare leg. He was rubbing her, but she was staring at me.

"Hi," she said.

"Hello," I said.

"I'm Barbie," she said, and Ken stopped rubbing her leg.

"I know."

"You're Jenny's brother."

I nodded. My head was bobbing up and down like a puppet on a weight.

"I really like your sister. She's sweet," Barbie said. "Such a good little girl. Especially lately, she makes herself so pretty, and she's started doing her nails."

I wondered if Barbie noticed that Miss Wonderful bit her nails and that when she smiled her front teeth were covered with little flecks of purple nail polish. I wondered if she knew Jennifer colored in the chipped chewed spots with purple magic marker, and then sometimes sucked on her fingers so that not only did she have purple flecks of polish on her teeth, but her tongue was the strangest shade of violet.

"So listen," I said. "Would you like to go out for a while? Grab some fresh air, maybe take a spin around the backyard?"

"Sure," she said.

I picked her up by her feet. It sounds unusual but I was too petrified to take her by the waist. I grabbed her by the ankles and carried her off like a Popsicle stick.

As soon as we were out back, sitting on the porch of what I used to call my fort, but which my sister and parents referred to as the playhouse, I started freaking. I was suddenly and incredibly aware that I was out with Barbie. I didn't know what to say.

"So, what kind of a Barbie are you?" I asked.

"Excuse me?"

"Well, from listening to Jennifer I know there's Day to Night Barbie, Magic Moves Barbie, Gift-Giving Barbie, Tropical Barbie, My First Barbie, and more."

"I'm Tropical," she said. I'm Tropical, she said, the same way a person might say I'm Catholic or I'm Jewish. "I came with a one-piece bathing suit, a brush, and a ruffle you can wear so many ways," Barbie squeaked.

She actually squeaked. It turned out that squeaking was Barbie's birth defect. I pretended I didn't hear it.

We were quiet for a minute. A leaf larger than Barbie fell from the maple tree above us and I caught it just before it would have hit her. I half expected her to squeak, "You saved my life. I'm yours, forever." Instead she said, in a perfectly normal voice, "Wow, big leaf."

I looked at her. Barbie's eyes were sparkling blue like the ocean on a good day. I looked and in a moment noticed she had the whole world, the cosmos, drawn in makeup above and below her eyes. An entire galaxy, clouds, stars, a sun, the sea, painted onto her face. Yellow, blue, pink, and a million silver sparkles.

We sat looking at each other, looking and talking and then not talking and looking again. It was a stop-and-start thing with both of us constantly saying the wrong thing, saying anything, and then immediately regretting having said it.

It was obvious Barbie didn't trust me. I asked her if she wanted something to drink.

"Diet Coke," she said. And I wondered why I'd asked.

I went into the house, upstairs into my parents' bathroom, opened the medicine cabinet, and got a couple of Valiums. I immediately swallowed one. I figured if I could be calm and collected, she'd realize I wasn't going to hurt her. I broke another Valium into a million small pieces, dropped some slivers into Barbie's Diet Coke, and swished it around so it'd blend. I figured if we could be calm and collected together, she'd be able to trust me even sooner. I was falling in love in a way that had nothing to do with love.

"So, what's the deal with you and Ken?" I asked later after we'd loosened up, after she'd drunk two Diet Cokes, and I'd made another trip to the medicine cabinet.

She giggled. "Oh, we're just really good friends."

"What's the deal with him really, you can tell me, I mean, is he or isn't he?"

"Ish she or ishn' she," Barbie said, in a slow slurred way, like she was so intoxicated that if they made a Breathalyzer for Valium, she'd melt it.

I regretted having fixed her a third Coke. I mean if she o.d.'ed and died Jennifer would tell my mom and dad for sure.

"Is he a faggot or what?"

Barbie laughed and I almost slapped her. She looked me straight in the eye.

"He lusts after me," she said. "I come home at night and he's standing there, waiting. He doesn't wear underwear, you know. I mean, isn't that strange, Ken doesn't own any underwear. I heard Jennifer tell her friend that they don't even make any for him. Anyway, he's always, there waiting, and I'm like, Ken we're friends, okay, that's it. I mean, have you ever noticed, he has molded plastic hair. His head and his hair are all one piece. I can't go out with a guy like that. Besides, I don't think he'd be up for it if you know what I mean. Ken is not what you'd call well endowed ... All he's got is a little plastic bump, more of a hump, really, and what the hell are you supposed to do with that?"

She was telling me things I didn't think I should hear and all the same, I was leaning into her, like if I moved closer she'd tell me more. I was taking every word and holding it for a minute, holding groups of words in my head like I didn't understand English. She went on and on, but I wasn't listening.

The sun sank behind the playhouse, Barbie shivered, excused

herself, and ran around back to throw up. I asked her if she felt okay. She said she was fine, just a little tired, that maybe she was coming down with the flu or something. I gave her a piece of a piece of gum to chew and took her inside.

On the way back to Jennifer's room I did something Barbie almost didn't forgive me for, I did something which not only shattered the moment, but nearly wrecked the possibility of our having a future together.

In the hallway between the stairs and Jennifer's room, I popped Barbie's head into my mouth, like lion and tamer, God and Godzilla.

I popped her whole head into my mouth, and Barbie's hair separated into single strands like Christmas tinsel and caught in my throat nearly choking me. I could taste layer on layer of makeup, Revlon, Max Factor, and Maybelline. I closed my mouth around Barbie and could feel her breath in mine. I could hear her screams in my throat. Her teeth, white, Pearl Drops, Pepsodent, and the whole Osmond family, bit my tongue and the inside of my cheek like I might accidently bite myself. I closed my mouth around her neck and held her suspended, her feet uselessly kicking the air in front of my face.

Before pulling her out, I pressed my teeth lightly into her neck, leaving marks Barbie described as scars of her assault, but which I imagined as a New Age necklace of love.

"I have never, ever in my life been treated with such utter disregard," she said as soon as I let her out.

She was lying. I knew Jennifer sometimes did things with Barbie. I didn't mention that once I'd seen Barbie hanging from Jennifer's ceiling fan, spinning around in great wide circles, like some imitation Superman.

"I'm sorry if I scared you."

"Scared me!" she squeaked.

She went on squeaking, a cross between the squeal when you let the air out of a balloon and a smoke alarm with weak batteries. While she was squeaking, the phrase *a head in the mouth is worth two in the bush* started running through my head. I knew it had come from somewhere, started as something else, but I couldn't get it right. *A head in the mouth is worth two in the bush*, again and again, like the punch line to some dirty joke.

"Scared me. Scared me. Scared me!" Barbie squeaked louder and louder until finally she had my attention again. "Have you ever been held captive in the dark cavern of someone's body?"

I shook my head. It sounded wonderful.

"Typical," she said. "So incredibly, typically male."

For a moment I was proud.

"Why do you have to do things you know you shouldn't, and worse, you do them with a light in your eye, like you're getting some weird pleasure that only another boy would understand. You're all the same," she said. "You're all Jack Nicholson."

I refused to put her back in Jennifer's room until she forgave me, until she understood that I'd done what I did with only the truest of feeling, no harm intended.

I heard Jennifer's feet clomping up the stairs. I was running out of time.

"You know I'm really interested in you," I said to Barbie.

"Me too," she said, and for a minute I wasn't sure if she meant she was interested in herself or me.

"We should do this again," I said. She nodded.

I leaned down to kiss Barbie. I could have brought her up to my lips, but somehow it felt wrong. I leaned down to kiss her and the first thing I got was her nose in my mouth. I felt like a St. Bernard saying hello.

No matter how graceful I tried to be, I was forever licking her face. It wasn't a question of putting my tongue in her ear or down her throat, it was simply literally trying not to suffocate her. I kissed Barbie with my back to Ken and then turned around and put her on the doily right next to him. I was tempted to drop her down on Ken, to, mash her into him, but I managed to restrain myself.

"That was fun," Barbie said. I heard Jennifer in the hall.

"Later," I said.

Jennifer came into the room and looked at me.

"What?" I said.

"It's my room," she said.

"There was a bee in it. I was killing it for you."

"A bee. I'm allergic to bees. Mom, Mom," she screamed. "There's a bee."

"Mom's not home. I killed it."

"But there might be another one."

"So call me and I'll kill it."

"But if it stings me I might die." I shrugged and walked out. I could feel Barbie watching me leave.

I took a Valium about twenty minutes before I picked her up the next Friday. By the time I went into Jennifer's room, everything was getting easier.

"Hey," I said when I got up to the dresser.

She was there on the doily with Ken, they were back to back, resting against each other, legs stretched out in front of them.

Ken didn't look at me. I didn't care.

"You ready to go?" I asked. Barbie nodded. "I thought you might be thirsty." I handed her the Diet Coke I'd made for her.

I'd figured Barbie could take a little less than an eighth of a Valium without getting totally senile. Basically, I had to give her Valium crumbs since there was no way to cut one that small.

She took the Coke and drank it right in front of Ken. I kept waiting for him to give me one of those I-know-what-you're-up-to-and-I-don't-like-it looks, the kind my father gives me when he walks into my room without knocking and I automatically jump twenty feet in the air.

Ken acted like he didn't even know I was there. I hated him.

"I can't do a lot of walking this afternoon," Barbie said.

I nodded. I figured no big deal since mostly I seemed to be carrying her around anyway.

"My feet are killing me," she said.

I was thinking about Ken.

"Don't you have other shoes?"

My family was very into shoes. No matter what seemed to be wrong my father always suggested it could be cured by wearing a different pair of shoes. He believed that shoes, like tires, should be rotated.

"It's not the shoes," she said. "It's my toes."

"Did you drop something on them?" My Valium wasn't working. I was having trouble making small talk. I needed another one.

"Jennifer's been chewing on them,"

"What?"

"She chews on my toes."

"You let her chew your footies?"

I couldn't make sense out of what she was saying. I was thinking about not being able to talk, needing another or maybe two more Valiums, yellow adult-strength Pez.

"Do you enjoy it?" I asked.

"She literally bites down on them, like I'm flank steak or something," Barbie said. "I wish she'd just bite them off and have it over with. This is taking forever. She's chewing and chewing, more like gnawing at me."

"I'll make her stop. I'll buy her some gum, some tobacco or something, a pencil to chew on."

"Please don't say anything. I wouldn't have told you except …," Barbie said.

"But she's hurting you."

"It's between Jennifer and me."

"Where's it going to stop?" I asked.

"At the arch, I hope. There's a bone there, and once she realizes she's bitten the soft part off, she'll stop."

"How will you walk?"

"I have very long feet."

I sat on the edge of my sister's bed, my head in my hands. My sister was biting Barbie's feet off and Barbie didn't seem to care. She didn't hold it against her and in a way I liked her for that. I liked the fact she understood how we all have little secret habits that seem normal enough to us, but which we know better than to mention out loud. I started imagining things I might be able to get away with.

"Get me out of here," Barbie said. I slipped Barbie's shoes off. Sure enough, someone had been gnawing at her. On her left foot the toes were dangling and on the right, half had been completely taken off. There were tooth marks up to her ankles. "Let's not dwell on this," Barbie said.

I picked Barbie up. Ken fell over backwards and Barbie made me straighten him up before we left. "Just because you know he only has a bump doesn't give you permission to treat him badly," Barbie whispered.

I fixed Ken and carried Barbie down the hall to my room. I held Barbie above me, tilted my head back, and lowered her feet into my mouth. I felt like a young sword swallower practising for my debut. I lowered Barbie's feet and legs into my mouth and then began sucking on them. They smelled like Jennifer and dirt and plastic. I sucked on her stubs and she told me it felt nice.

"You're better than a hot soak," Barbie said. I left her resting on my pillow and went downstairs to get us each a drink.

We were lying on my bed, curled into and out of each other. Barbie was on a pillow next to me and I was on my side facing her. She was talking about men, and as she talked I tried to be everything she said. She was saying she didn't like men who were afraid of themselves. I tried to be brave, to look courageous and secure. I held my head a certain way and it seemed to work. She said she didn't like men who were afraid of femininity, and I got confused.

"Guys always have to prove how boy they really are," Barbie said.

I thought of Jennifer trying to be a girl, wearing dresses, doing her nails, putting makeup on, wearing a bra even though she wouldn't need one for about fifty years.

"You make fun of Ken because he lets himself be everything he is. He doesn't hide anything."

"He doesn't have anything to hide," I said. "He has tan molded plastic hair, and a bump for a dick."

"I never should have told you about the bump."

I lay back on the bed. Barbie rolled over, off the pillow, and rested on my chest. Her body stretched from my nipple to my belly button. Her hands pressed against me, tickling me.

"Barbie," I said.

"Umm Humm."

"How do you feel about me?"

She didn't say anything for a minute. "Don't worry about it," she said, and slipped her hand into my shirt through the space between the buttons.

Her fingers were like the ends of toothpicks performing some subtle ancient torture, a dance of boy death across my chest. Barbie crawled all over me like an insect who'd run into one too many cans of Raid.

Underneath my clothes, under my skin, I was going crazy. First off, I'd been kidnapped by my underwear with no way to manually adjust without attracting unnecessary attention.

With Barbie caught in my shirt I slowly rolled over, like in some space shuttle docking maneuver. I rolled onto my stomach, trapping her under me. As slowly and unobtrusively as possible, I ground myself against the bed, at first hoping it would fix things and then again and again, caught by a pleasure pain principle.

"Is this a water bed?" Barbie asked.

My hand was on her breasts, only it wasn't really my hand, but more like my index finger. I touched Barbie and she made a little gasp, a squeak in reverse. She squeaked backwards, then stopped, and I was stuck there with my hand on her, thinking about how I was forever crossing a line between the haves and the have nots, between good guys and bad, between men and animals, and there was absolutely nothing I could do to stop myself.

Barbie was sitting on my crotch, her legs flipped back behind her in a position that wasn't human.

At a certain point I had to free myself. If my dick was blue, it was only because it had suffocated. I did the honors and Richard popped out like an escape from maximum security.

"I've never seen anything so big," Barbie said. It was the sentence I dreamed of, but given the people Barbie normally hung out with, namely the bump boy himself, it didn't come as a big surprise.

She stood at the base of my dick, her bare feet buried in my pubic hair. I was almost as tall as she was. Okay, not almost as tall, but clearly we could be related. She and Richard even had the same vaguely surprised look on their faces.

She was on me and I couldn't help wanting to get inside her. I turned Barbie over and was on top of her, not caring if I killed her. Her hands pressed so hard into my stomach that it felt like she was performing an appendectomy.

I was on top, trying to get between her legs, almost breaking her in half. But there was nothing there, nothing to fuck except a small thin line that was supposed to be her ass crack.

I rubbed the thin line, the back of her legs and the space between her legs. I turned Barbie's back to me so I could do it without having to look at her face.

Very quickly, I came. I came all over Barbie, all over her and a little bit in her hair. I came on Barbie and it was the most horrifying experience I ever had. It didn't stay on her. It doesn't stick to plastic. I was finished. I was holding a come-covered Barbie in my hand like I didn't know where she came from.

Barbie said, "Don't stop," or maybe I just think she said that because I read it somewhere. I don't know anymore. I couldn't listen to her. I couldn't even look at her. I wiped myself off with a sock, pulled my clothes on, and then took Barbie into the bathroom.

At dinner I noticed Jennifer chewing her cuticles between bites of tuna-noodle casserole. I asked her if she was teething. She coughed and then started choking to death on either a little piece of fingernail, a crushed potato chip from the casserole, or maybe even a little bit of Barbie footie that'd stuck in her teeth. My mother asked her if she was okay.

"I swallowed something sharp," she said between coughs that were clearly influenced by the acting class she'd taken over the summer.

"Do you have a problem?" I asked her.

"Leave your sister alone," my mother said.

"If there are any questions to ask we'll do the asking," my father said.

"Is everything all right?" my mother asked Jennifer. She nodded. "I think you could use some new jeans," my mother said. "You don't seem to have many play clothes anymore."

"Not to change the subject," I said, trying to think of a way to stop Jennifer from eating Barbie alive.

"I don't wear pants," Jennifer said. "Boys wear pants."

"Your grandma wears pants," my father said.

"She's not a girl."

My father chuckled. He actually fucking chuckled. He's the only person I ever met who could actually fucking chuckle.

"Don't tell her that," he said, chuckling.

"It's not funny," I said.

"Grandma's are pull-ons anyway," Jennifer said, "They don't have a fly. You have to have a penis to have a fly."

"Jennifer," my mother said. "That's enough of that."

I decided to buy Barbie a present. I was at that strange point where I would have done anything for her. I took two buses and walked more than a mile to get to Toys R Us.

Barbie row was aisle 14C. I was a wreck. I imagined a million Barbies and having to have them all. I pictured fucking one, discarding it, immediately grabbing a fresh one, doing it, and then throwing it onto a growing pile in the corner of my room. An unending chore. I saw myself becoming a slave to Barbie. I wondered how many Tropical Barbies were made each year. I felt faint.

There were rows and rows of Kens, Barbies, and Skippers. Funtime Barbie, Jewel Secrets Ken, Barbie Rocker with "Hot Rockin' Fun and Real Dancin' Action." I noticed Magic Moves Barbie, and found myself looking at her carefully, flirtatiously, wondering if her legs were spreadable. "Push the switch and she moves," her box said. She winked at me while I was reading.

The only Tropical I saw was a black Tropical Ken. From just looking at him you wouldn't have known he was black. I mean, he wasn't black like anyone would be black. Black Tropical Ken was the color of a raisin, a raisin all spread out and unwrinkled. He had a short afro that looked like a wig had been dropped down and fixed on his head, a protective helmet. I wondered if black Ken was really white Ken sprayed over with a thick coating of ironed raisin plastic.

I spread eight black Kens out in a line across the front of a row. Through the plastic window of his box he told me he was hoping to go to dental school. All eight black Kens talked at once. Luckily, they all said the same thing at the same time. They said he really liked teeth. Black Ken smiled. He had the same white Pearl Drops, Pepsodent, Osmond family teeth that Barbie and white Ken had. I thought the entire Mattel family must take really good care of themselves. I figured they might be the only people left in America who actually brushed after every meal and then again before going to sleep.

I didn't know what to get Barbie. Black Ken said I should go for clothing, maybe a fur coat. I wanted something really special. I imagined a wonderful present that would draw us somehow closer.

There was a tropical pool and patio set, but I decided it might make her homesick. There was a complete winter holiday, with an A-frame house, fireplace, snowmobile, and sled. I imagined her inviting Ken away for a weekend without me. The six o'clock news set was nice, but because of her squeak, Barbie's future as an anchorwoman seemed limited. A workout center, a sofa bed and coffee table, a bubbling spa, a bedroom play set. I settled on the grand piano. It was $13.00. I'd always made it a point to never spend more than ten dollars on anyone. This time I figured, what the hell, you don't buy a grand piano every day.

"Wrap it up, would ya," I said at the checkout desk.

From my bedroom window I could see Jennifer in the backyard, wearing her tutu and leaping all over the place. It was dangerous as hell to sneak in and get Barbie, but I couldn't keep a grand piano in my closet without telling someone.

"You must really like me," Barbie said when she finally had the piano unwrapped.

I nodded. She was wearing a ski suit and skis. It was the end of August and eighty degrees out. Immediately, she sat down and played "Chopsticks."

I looked out at Jennifer. She was running down the length of the deck, jumping onto the railing and then leaping off, posing like one of those red flying horses you see on old Mobil gas signs. I watched her do it once and then the second time, her foot caught on the railing, and she went over the edge the hard way. A minute later she came around the edge of the house, limping, her tutu dented and dirty, pink tights ripped at both knees. I grabbed Barbie from the piano bench and raced her into Jennifer's room.

"I was just getting warmed up," she said. "I can play better than that, really."

I could hear Jennifer crying as she walked up the stairs.

"Jennifer's coming." I said. I put her down on the dresser and realized Ken was missing.

"Where's Ken?" I asked quickly.

"Out with Jennifer," Barbie said.

I met Jennifer at her door. "Are you okay?" I asked. She cried harder. "I saw you fall."

"Why didn't you stop me?" she said.

"From falling?"

She nodded and showed me her knees.

"Once you start to fall no one can stop you." I noticed Ken was tucked into the waistband of her tutu.

"They catch you," Jennifer said.

I started to tell her it was dangerous to go leaping around with a Ken stuck in your waistband, but you don't tell someone who's already crying that they did something bad.

I walked her into the bathroom, and took out the hydrogen peroxide. I was a first aid expert. I was the kind of guy who walked around, waiting for someone to have a heart attack just so I could practice my CPR technique.

"Sit down," I said.

Jennifer sat down on the toilet without putting the lid down. Ken was stabbing her all over the place and instead of pulling him out, she squirmed around trying to get comfortable like she didn't know what else to do. I took him out for her. She watched as though I was performing surgery or something.

"He's mine," she said.

"Take off your tights," I said.

"No," she said.

"They're ruined," I said. "Take them off."

Jennifer took off her ballet slippers and peeled off her tights. She was wearing my old Underoos with superheroes on them, Spiderman and Superman and Batman all poking out from under a dirty dented tutu. I decided not to say anything, but it looked funny as hell to see a flat crotch in boys' underwear. I had the feeling they didn't bother making underwear for Ken because they knew it looked too weird on him.

I poured peroxide onto her bloody knees. Jennifer screamed into my ear. She bent down and examined herself, poking her purple fingers into the torn skin; her tutu bunched up and rubbed against her face, scraping it. I worked on her knees, removing little pebbles and pieces of grass from the area.

She started crying again.

"You're okay," I said. "You're not dying." She didn't care. "Do you want anything?" I asked, trying to be nice.

"Barbie," she said.

It was the first time I'd handled Barbie in public. I picked her up like she was a complete stranger and handed her to Jennifer, who grabbed her by the hair. I started to tell her to ease up, but couldn't. Barbie looked at me and I shrugged. I went downstairs and made Jennifer one of my special Diet Cokes.

"Drink this," I said, handing it to her. She took four giant gulps and immediately I felt guilty about having used a whole Valium.

"Why don't you give a little to your Barbie," I said. "I'm sure she's thirsty too."

Barbie winked at me and I could have killed her, first off for doing it in front of Jennifer, and second because she didn't know what the hell she was winking about.

I went into my room and put the piano away. I figured as long as I kept it in the original box I'd be safe. If anyone found it, I'd say it was a present for Jennifer.

Wednesday Ken and Barbie had their heads switched. I went to get Barbie, and there on top of the dresser were Barbie and Ken, sort of Barbie's head was on Ken's body and Ken's head was on Barbie. At first I thought it was just me.

"Hi," Barbie's head said.

I couldn't respond. She was on Ken's body and I was looking at Ken in a whole new way.

I picked up the Barbie head Ken and immediately Barbie's head rolled off. It rolled across the dresser, across the white doily past Jennifer's collection of miniature ceramic cats, and *boom* it fell to the floor. I saw Barbie's head rolling and about to fall, and then falling, but there was nothing I could do to stop it. I was frozen, paralyzed with Ken's headless body in my left hand.

Barbie's head was on the floor, her hair spread out underneath it like angel wings in the snow, and I expected to see blood, a wide rich pool of blood, or at least a little bit coming out of her ear, her nose, or her mouth. I looked at her head on the floor and saw nothing but Barbie with eyes like the cosmos looking up at me. I thought she was dead.

"Christ, that hurt," she said. "And I already had a headache from these earrings."

There were little red dot/ball earrings jutting out of Barbie's ears.

"They go right through my head, you know. I guess it takes getting used to," Barbie said.

I noticed my mother's pin cushion on the dresser next to the other Barbie/Ken, the Barbie body, Ken head. The pin cushion was filled with hundreds of pins, pins with flat silver ends and pins with red, yellow, and blue dot/ball ends.

"You have pins in your head," I said to the Barbie head on the floor.

"Is that supposed to be a compliment?"

I was starting to hate her. I was being perfectly clear and she didn't understand me.

I looked at Ken. He was in my left hand, my fist wrapped around his waist. I looked at him and realized my thumb was on his bump. My thumb was pressed against Ken's crotch and as soon as I noticed I got an automatic hard-on, the kind you don't know you're getting, it's just there. I started rubbing Ken's bump and watching my thumb like it was a large-screen projection of a porno movie.

"What are you doing?" Barbie's head said. "Get me up. Help me." I was rubbing Ken's bump/hump with my finger inside his bathing suit. I was standing in the middle of my sister's room, with my pants pulled down.

"Aren't you going to help me?" Barbie kept asking. "Aren't you going to help me?"

In the second before I came, I held Ken's head hole in front of me. I held Ken upside down above my dick and came inside of Ken like I never could in Barbie.

I came into Ken's body and as soon as I was done I wanted to do it again. I wanted to fill Ken and put his head back on, like a perfume bottle. I wanted Ken to be the vessel for my secret supply. I came in Ken and then I remembered he wasn't mine. He didn't belong to me. I took him into the bathroom and soaked him in warm water and Ivory liquid. I brushed his insides with Jennifer's toothbrush and left him alone in a cold-water rinse.

"Aren't you going to help me, aren't you?" Barbie kept asking.

I started thinking she'd been brain damaged by the accident. I picked her head up from the floor.

"What took you so long?" she asked.

"I had to take care of Ken."

"Is he okay?"

"He'll be fine. He's soaking in the bathroom." I held Barbie's head in my hand.

"What are you going to do?"

"What do you mean?" I said.

Did my little incident, my moment with Ken, mean that right then and there some decision about my future life as queerbait had to be made?"

"This afternoon. Where are we going? What are we doing? I miss you when I don't see you," Barbie said.

"You see me every day," I said.

"I don't really see you. I sit on top of the dresser and if you pass by, I see you. Take me to your room."

"I have to bring Ken's body back."

I went into the bathroom, rinsed out Ken, blew him dry with my mother's blow dryer, then played with him again. It was a boy thing, we were boys together. I thought sometime I might play ball with him, I might take him out instead of Barbie.

"Everything takes you so long," Barbie said when I got back into the room.

I put Ken back up on the dresser, picked up Barbie's body, knocked Ken's head off, and smashed Barbie's head back down on her own damn neck.

"I don't want to fight with you," Barbie said as I carried her into my room. "We don't have enough time together to fight. Fuck me," she said.

I didn't feel like it. I was thinking about fucking Ken and Ken being a boy. I was thinking about Barbie and Barbie being a girl. I was thinking about Jennifer, switching Barbie and Ken's heads, chewing Barbie's feet off, hanging Barbie from the ceiling fan, and who knows what else.

"Fuck me," Barbie said again.

I ripped Barbie's clothing off. Between Barbie's legs Jennifer had drawn pubic hair in reverse. She'd drawn it upside down so it looked like a fountain spewing up and out in great wide arcs. I spit directly onto Barbie and with my thumb and first finger rubbed the ink lines, erasing them. Barbie moaned.

"Why do you let her do this to you?"

"Jennifer owns me," Barbie moaned.

Jennifer owns me, she said, so easily and with pleasure. I was totally jealous. Jennifer owned Barbie and it made me crazy. Obviously it was one of those relationships that could only exist between women. Jennifer could own her because it didn't matter that Jennifer owned her. Jennifer didn't want Barbie, she had her.

"You're perfect," I said.

"I'm getting fat," Barbie said.

Barbie was crawling all over me, and I wondered if Jennifer knew she was a nymphomaniac. I wondered if Jennifer knew what a nymphomaniac was.

"You don't belong with little girls," I said.

Barbie ignored me.

There were scratches on Barbie's chest and stomach. She didn't say anything about them and so at first I pretended not to notice. As I was touching her, I could feel they were deep, like slices. The edges were rough; my finger caught on them and I couldn't help but wonder.

"Jennifer?" I said, massaging the cuts with my tongue, as though my tongue, like sandpaper, would erase them. Barbie nodded.

In fact, I thought of using sandpaper, but didn't know how I would explain it to Barbie: *you have to lie still and let me rub it really hard with this stuff that's like terrycloth dipped in cement.* I thought she might even like it if I made it into an S&M kind of thing and handcuffed her first.

I ran my tongue back and forth over the slivers, back and forth over the words "copyright 1966 Mattel Inc., Malaysia" tattooed on her back. Tonguing the tattoo drove Barbie crazy. She said it had something to do with scar tissue being extremely sensitive.

Barbie pushed herself hard against me, I could feel her slices rubbing my skin. I was thinking that Jennifer might kill Barbie. Without meaning to she might just go over the line and I wondered if Barbie would know what was happening or if she'd try to stop her.

We fucked, that's what I called it, fucking. In the beginning Barbie said she hated the word, which made me like it even more. She hated it because it was so strong and hard, and she said we weren't fucking, we were making love. I told her she had to be kidding.

"Fuck me," she said that afternoon and I knew the end was coming soon. "Fuck me," she said. I didn't like the sound of the word.

Friday when I went into Jennifer's room, there was something in the air. The place smelled like a science lab, a fire, a failed experiment.

Barbie was wearing, a strapless yellow evening dress. Her hair was wrapped into a high bun, more like a wedding cake than something Betty Crocker would whip up. There seemed to be layers and layers of angel's hair spinning in a circle above her head. She had yellow pins through her ears and gold fuck-me shoes that matched the belt around her waist. For a second I thought of the belt and imagined tying her up, but more than restraining her arms or legs, I thought of wrapping the belt around her face, tying it across her mouth.

I looked at Barbie and saw something dark and thick like a scar rising up and over the edge of her dress. I grabbed her and pulled the front of the dress down.

"Hey, big boy," Barbie said. "Don't I even get a hello?"

Barbie's breasts had been sawed at with a knife. There were a hundred marks from a blade that might have had five rows of teeth like shark jaws. And as if that wasn't enough, she'd been dissolved by fire, blue and yellow flames had been pressed against her and held there until she melted and eventually became the fire that burned herself. All of it had been somehow stirred with the lead of a pencil, the point of a pen, and left to cool. Molten Barbie flesh had been left to harden, black and pink plastic swirled together, in the crater Jennifer had dug out of her breasts.

I examined her in detail like a scientist, a pathologist, a fucking medical examiner. I studied the burns, the gouged-out area, as if by looking closely I'd find something, an explanation, a way out.

A disgusting taste came up into my mouth, like I'd been sucking on batteries. It came up, then sank back down into my stomach, leaving my mouth puckered with the bitter metallic flavor of sour saliva. I coughed and spit onto my shirt sleeve, then rolled the sleeve over to cover the wet spot.

With my index finger I touched the edge of the burn as lightly as I could. The round rim of her scar broke off under my finger. I almost dropped her.

"It's just a reduction," Barbie said. "Jennifer and I are even now."

Barbie was smiling. She had the same expression on her face as when I first saw her and fell in love. She had the same expression she always had and I couldn't stand it. She was smiling, and she was burned. She was smiling, and she was ruined. I pulled her dress back up, above the scarline. I put her down carefully on the doily on top of the dresser and started to walk away.

"Hey," Barbie said, "aren't we going to play?"

YOURS TRULY

A. M. Homes

> A. M. Homes (b. 1961) is an American writer known for
> her controversial novels and unusual stories. She released
> her first collection of short stories, *The Safety of Objects*,
> in 1990. In 2013 she won the Women's Prize for Fiction
> with her novel *May We Be Forgiven*.

I'm hiding in the linen closet writing letters to myself. This is the
place where no one knows I am, where I can think without thinking
about what anyone else would think or at least it's quiet. I don't
want to scare anyone, but things can't go on like this.

Until today I could still go into the living room and talk to my
mother's Saturday morning Fat Club. I could say, "Hi, how are you.
That's a very nice dress. Magenta's such a good color, it hides the
hips. Nice shoes too. I would never have thought of bringing pink
and green together like that." I could pretend to be okay, but that's
part of the problem.

In here, pressed up against the towels, the sheets, the heating
pad, it's clear that everything is not hunky-dory. I've got one of
those Itty Bitty Book Lights and I'm making notes.

Today is Odessa's day. At any minute she might turn the knob
and let the world, disguised as daylight, come flooding in. She
might do that and never know what she's done. She'll open the
door and her eyes will get wide. She'll look at me and say, "Lord."
She'll say, "You could have given me a heart attack." And I'll think,
Yes, I could have, but I'm having one myself and there isn't room
for two in the same place at the same time. She'll look at my face
and I'll have to look at the floor. She won't know that having
someone look directly at me, having someone expect me to look at
her, causes a sharp pain that begins in my eyes, ricochets off my
skull, and in the end makes my entire skeleton shake. She won't
know that I can't look at anything except the towels without being
overcome with emotion. She won't know that at the sight of

another person I weep, I wish to embrace and be embraced, and then to kill. She won't get that I'm dangerous.

Odessa will open the door and see me standing with this tiny light, clipped to the middle shelf, with the pad of paper on top of some extra blankets, with two extra pencils sticking out of the space between the bath sheets and the Turkish towels. She'll see all this and ask, "Are you all right?" I won't be able to answer. I can't tell her why I'm standing in a closet filled with enough towels to take a small town to the beach. I won't say, I'm not all right. God help me, I'm not. I will simply stand here, resting my arm over my notepad like a child taking a test, trying to make it difficult for cheaters to get their work done.

Odessa will do the talking. She'll say, "Well, if you could excuse me, I need clean sheets for the beds." I'll move over a little bit. I'll twist to the left so she can get to the twin and queen sizes. I'm willing to move for Odessa. I can put one foot on top of the other. I'll do anything for her as long as I don't have to put my feet onto the gray carpet in the hall. I can't. I'm not ready. If I put a foot out there too early, everything will be lost.

Odessa sometimes asks me, "Which sheets do you want on your bed?" She knows I'm particular about these things. She knows her color combinations, dots and stripes together, attack me in my sleep. Sometimes I get up in the middle of the night, pull the sheets off the bed, throw them into the hall, and return to sleep. She will ask me what I want and I'll point to the plain white ones, the ones that seem lighter, cleaner than all the others. Odessa reaches for the sheets and in the instant when they're in her hand but still in the closet, I press my face into them. I press my face into the pile of sheets, into Odessa's hands underneath. I won't feel her skin, her fingers, only cool, clean fabric against my cheek. I inhale deeply as if there were a way to draw the sheets into my lungs, to hold the linen inside me. I breathe and take my head away. Odessa will pull her hands out of the closet and ask, "Do you want the door closed?" I nod. I turn away; draw in my breath, and make myself flat. She closes the door.

I'm hiding in the linen closet sending memos to myself. It's getting complicated. Odessa knows I'm here. She knows but she won't tell anybody. She won't go running into the living room and announce, "Jody's locked herself into the linen closet and she won't come out."

Odessa won't go outside and look for my father. She won't find him pulling weeds on the hill behind the house. Odessa won't tell him, "She's in there with paper, pencils, and that little light you gave her for Christmas." She won't say anything. Odessa understands that this is the way things sometimes are. She'll change the sheets on all the beds, serve the Fat Club ladies their cottage cheese and cantaloupe, and then she'll go downstairs into the bathroom and take a few sips from the bottle of Johnnie Walker she keeps there.

I'm hiding in the closet with my life suspended. I'm hiding and I'm scared to death. I want to come clean, to see myself clearly, in detail, like a hallucination, a death-bed vision, a Kodacolor photograph. I need to know if I'm alive or dead.

I'm hiding in the linen closet and I want to introduce myself to myself. I need to like what I see. If I am really as horrible as I feel, I will spontaneously combust, leaving a small heap of ashes that can be picked up with the Dust-buster. I will explode myself in a flash of fire, leaving a letter of most profuse apology.

Through the wall I hear my mother's Fat Club ladies laugh. I hear the rattle of the group and the gentle tinkling of the individual. It's as though I have more than one pair of ears. Each voice enters in a different place, with a different effect.

I hear them and realize they're laughing for me. They're celebrating the fact that I can no longer pretend. There are tears in my eyes. I'm saying thank you and good-bye. I'm writing it down because I can't simply go out there and stand at the edge of the dining room table until my mother looks up from her copy of the *Eat Yourself Slim Diet* and says, "Yes?"

I can't say that I'm leaving because she'll ask, "When will you be back?"

She'll be looking through the book, flipping through the menus, seeing how many ounces she can eat. If I tell the truth, if I say never, she'll look up at me, peering up higher than usual, above the frameless edges of her reading glasses. She'll say, "A comedian. Maybe Johnny Carson will hire you to guest-host. When will you be back?"

If I go without answering, the other ladies will watch me leave. When I get to where they think I can't hear them, when I get to the kitchen door, they'll put a pause in their meeting and talk about their children.

They'll say they were always the best parents they knew how to be. They'll say they gave their children everything and it was never enough. They'll say they hope their children will grow up and have children exactly like themselves. They'll be thinking about how their children hate them and how they hate their children back because they don't understand what it was they did wrong.

"It has nothing to do with you," I'll have to say. "It's me, it's me, all mine. There is no blame."

"Selfish," the mothers will say.

I'm here in the linen closet, doing my spring cleaning. I'm confessing right and left and Odessa knocks on the door. She knocks and then opens the door. She's carrying a plate with a sandwich and a glass of milk. Only Odessa would serve milk and a sandwich. My mother would give me a Tab with a twist of lemon. My father would make something like club soda with a little bit of syrup in it. He would use maple syrup and spend all afternoon telling me he'd invented something new, something better than other sodas because it had no chemicals, less sugar, and no caffeine. Odessa brings me a sandwich and a glass of milk and it looks like a television commercial. The bread is white, the sandwich cut perfectly in half. There are no finger marks on it, no indentations on the white bread where Odessa put her fingers while she was cutting. The glass is full except for an inch at the top. There are no spots in that inch. The milk looks white and thick, with small bubbles near the top. It looks cool and refreshing.

Odessa hands me the plate. I look at her for a moment. She is perfect. I drink the milk and know that I will have a mustache. I look at Odessa and want to say, "I love you." I want to tell her how no one else would bring me a glass of milk. I want to tell her everything, but she starts talking. Odessa says, "Make sure you don't leave that plate in the closet. I don't want your mother finding it and thinking I've lost my mind. I don't want bugs in here. Bring it out and put it in the dishwasher. Don't stay in there all day or you'll lose your color." I nod and she closes the door.

I'm hiding and I'm eating a cream-cheese-and-cucumber sandwich and having my head examined. I'm in the neighborhood of my soul and getting worried. I'm trying not to hate myself so much, trying not to hate my body, my mind, the thoughts I think. I'm hiding in the linen closet having a sex change. I'm in here with a pad of paper writing things I've thought and then unthought. Thoughts that seemed like incest, like they shouldn't be allowed.

I'm trying to find some piece of myself that is truly me, a part that I would be willing to wear like a jewel around my neck. My foot. I love my foot. If I had to send a part of myself to represent myself in some other country, or in some other way, I would amputate my foot and send it wrapped in white tissue on a silk-embroidered cushion. I would send my foot because it is me, more me than I'm willing to let on. There are other parts that are also good – hands, eyes, mouth – but after a few months I might look at them and not see the truth. After a few years I might look at them and think of someone else. But my foot is mine, all mine, the real thing. There is no mistaking it. I look at it; I take off my sock and it screams my name.

I could go on for hours demonstrating how well I know myself, through my foot, but I won't. It's embarrassing. The foot, my foot, that I wish to wear on a ribbon around my neck is an example of grace twisted and trapped. Chunks of bone and flesh conforming to the dictum: form follows function. It's a wonder I'm not a cripple.

I'm hiding in the linen closet, writing a declaration of independence. I'm in the closet, but the worst is over. There is hope, trapped inside my foot; inside my soul there is possibility. I'm looking at myself and slowly I'm falling in love. I've figured out what it takes to live forever. I'm in love and I'm free.

I want to throw the door open and hear an orchestra swell. I want to run out to the Fat Club ladies and tell them, "Life can go on, I'm in love."

I'll stand in the living room, facing the sofa. I'll stand with my arms spread wide, the violins reaching their pitch. I'll be sweating and shaking, unsteady on my feet, my wonderful, loving, lovable feet. At the end of my proclamation my mother will let her glasses fall from her face and dangle from the cord around her neck.

"Miss Dramatic," she'll say. "Why weren't you an actress?"

The fat ladies will look at each other. They'll look at me and think of other declarations of love. They'll look and one will ask, "Who's the lucky man?"

There will be a silence while they wait for a name, preferably the right kind of a name. If I tell them it isn't a man, their silence will grow and they'll expect what they think is the worst. No one except my mother will have nerve enough to say, "A girl then?"

I'll be forced to tell them, It's not like that. One of the ladies, the one the others think isn't so smart, will ask, "What's it like?"

I'll smile, the orchestra will swell, and I'll look at the four ladies sitting on the sofa, the sofa covered with something modern and green, something that vaguely resembles the turf on a putting green.

"It's like falling in love with life itself," I'll say.

My mother will look around the room. She'll look anywhere except at me.

"Are you all right?" she'll ask when I stop to catch my breath. "You look a little flushed." I'll be singing and dancing.

"I'm fine, I'm wonderful, I'm better than before. I'm in love."

I'll sing and on the end note cymbals will crash and the sound will hold in the air for a minute. And then swinging a top hat and cane, I'll dance away. I'll dance down the hall towards the den.

I want to find my father in the den, the family room, watching tennis on television. I want to catch him in the middle of a set and say that I can't wait for a break. I want to tell him, "Life must go on."

He'll say that it's match point. He'll say that he's been trying to tell me that all along.

"But why didn't you tell me what it really means?"

"It seemed pretty obvious."

And then I'll tell him, "I'm in love." There will be a pause. Someone will have the advantage. My feet will go *clickety-clack* over the parquet floor and he'll say, "Yes, you sound very happy. You sound like you're not quite yourself."

"I'm more myself than I've ever been."

I want to find Odessa. "Life will go on," I'll tell her. "I'm in love." I'll take her by the hand and we'll dance in circles around the recreation room. We'll dance until we're dizzy and Odessa will ask me, "Are you all right?"

I'll only be able to mumble "Ummmm hummm," because my grin will have set like cement. I'm hiding in the linen closet writing love letters to myself.

(SHE OWNS) EVERY THING

Anne Enright

> Anne Enright (b. 1962) is an Irish author, born in Dublin. She has published essays, short stories, a work of non-fiction and four novels. Her novel, *The Gathering,* won the 2007 Man Booker Prize.

Cathy was often wrong, she found it more interesting. She was wrong about the taste of bananas. She was wrong about the future of the bob. She was wrong about where her life ended up. She loved corners, surprises, changes of light.

Of all the fates that could have been hers (spinster, murderer, savant, saint), she chose to work behind a handbag counter in Dublin and take her holidays in the sun.

For ten years she lived with the gloves and beside the umbrellas, their colours shy and neatly furled. The handbag counter travelled through navy and brown to a classic black. Yellows, reds, and white were to one side and all varieties of plastic were left out on stands, for the customer to steal.

Cathy couldn't tell you what the handbag counter was like. It was hers. It smelt like a leather dream. It was never quite right. Despite the close and intimate spaces of the gloves and the empty generosity of the bags themselves, the discreet mess that was the handbag counter was just beyond her control.

She sold clutch bags for people to hang on to; folded slivers of animal skin that wouldn't hold a box of cigarettes, or money unless it was paper, or a bunch of keys, 'just a credit card and a condom,' said one young woman to another and Cathy felt the ache of times changing.

She sold the handbag proper, sleek and stiff and surprisingly roomy – the favourite bag, the thoroughbred, with a hard clasp, or a fold-over flap and the smell of her best perfume. She sold sacks to young women, in canvas or in suede, baggy enough to hold a life, a change of underwear, a novel, a deodorant spray.

The women's faces as they made their choice were full of lines going nowhere, tense with the problems of leather, price, vulgarity, colour. Cathy matched blue eyes with a blue trim, a modest mouth with smooth, plum suede. She sold patent to the click of high heels, urged women who had forgotten into neat, swish reticules. Quietly, one customer after another was guided to the inevitable and surprising choice of a bag that was not 'them' but one step beyond who they thought they might be.

Cathy knew what handbags were for. She herself carried everything (which wasn't much) in one pocket, or the other.

She divided her women into two categories: those who could and those who could not.

She had little affection for those who could, they had no need of her, and they were often mistaken. Their secret was not one of class, although that seemed to help, but one of belief, and like all questions of belief, it involved certain mysteries. How, for example, does one *believe* in navy?

There were also the women who could not. A woman for example, who could NOT wear blue. A woman who could wear a print, but NOT beside her face. A woman who could wear beads but NOT earrings. A woman who had a secret life of shoes too exotic for her, or one who could neither pass a perfume counter nor buy a perfume, unless it was for someone else. A woman who comes home with royal jelly every time she tries to buy a blouse.

A woman who cries in the lingerie department.

A woman who laughs while trying on hats.

A woman who buys two coats of a different colour.

The problem became vicious when they brought their daughters shopping. Cathy could smell these couples from Kitchenware.

Cathy married late and it was hard work. She had to find a man. Once she had found one, she discovered that the city was full of them. She had to talk and laugh and be fond. She had to choose.

Did she like big burly men with soft brown eyes? Did she like that blond man with the eyes of pathological blue? What did she think of her own face, its notches and dents?

She went the easy road with a kind teacher from Fairview and a registry office do. She stole him from a coltish young woman with awkward eyes. Cathy would have sold her a tapestry Gladstone bag, one that was 'wrong' but 'worked' all the same.

Sex was a pleasant surprise. It was such a singular activity, it seemed to scatter and gather her at the same time.

Cathy fell in love one day with a loose, rangy woman, who came to her counter and to her smile and seemed to pick her up with the same ease as she did an Argentinian calf-skin shoulder bag in tobacco brown, with woven leather inset panels, pig-skin lining and snap clasp. It was quite a surprise.

The woman, whose eyes were a tired shade of blue, asked Cathy's opinion, and Cathy heard herself say 'DIVE RIGHT IN, HONEY, THE WATER'S JUST FINE!' – a phrase she must have picked up from the television set. The woman did not flinch. She said 'Have you got it in black?'

Brown was the colour of the bag. Cathy was disappointed by this betrayal. The weave would just disappear in black, the staining was everything. Cathy said, 'It's worth it in brown, even if it means new shoes. It really is a beautiful bag.' The woman, however, neither bought the brown nor argued for black. She rubbed the leather with the base of her thumb as she laid the bag down. She looked at Cathy. She despaired. She turned her wide, sporting shoulders, her dry, bleached hair, and her nose with the bump in it, gave a small sigh, and walked out of the shop.

Cathy spent the rest of the day thinking, not of her hands, with their large knuckles, but of her breasts, that were widely spaced and looked two ways, one towards the umbrellas, the other at the scarves. She also wondered whether the woman had a necklace of lines hanging from her hips, whether she had ever been touched by a woman, what she might say, what Cathy might say back. Whether

her foldings and infoldings were the same as her own or as different as daffodil from narcissus. It was a very lyrical afternoon.

Cathy began to slip. She made mistakes. She sold the wrong bags to the wrong women and her patter died. She waited for another woman to pick up the tobacco-brown bag to see what might happen. She sold indiscriminately. She looked at every woman who came her way and she just didn't know anymore.

She could, of course, change her job. She might, for example, work as a hospital maid, in the cardiac ward, which was full of certainties.

Women did not get heart attacks. They would come at visiting time and talk too much or not at all. She could work out who loved simply or in silence. She could spot those who might as well hate. She would look at their bags without judgement, as they placed them on the coverlets, or opened them for tissues. They might even let a tear drip inside.

Cathy emptied out her building-society account and walked up to the hat department with a plastic bag filled with cash. She said, 'Ramona, I want to buy every hat you have.' She did the same at Shoes, although she stipulated size five-and-a-half. She didn't make a fuss when refused. She stuffed the till of her own counter full of notes, called a taxi and hung herself with bags, around her neck and down her arms. All kinds of people looked at her. Then she went to bed for a week, feeling slightly ashamed.

She kept the one fatal bag, the brown calf-skin with a snap clasp. She abused it. She even used it to carry things. She started to sleep around.

WAITING ROOM
(THE FIRST)

Elizabeth Jolley

> Elizabeth Jolley (1923–2007) was a British-born writer
> who settled in Western Australia in the late 1950s. She was
> fifty-three when her first book was published, and went on
> to write fifteen novels, four short story collections and
> three works of non-fiction.

These days I live with the need to have something lined up to do
next. The way in which I live reminds me of a joke; there are two
goldfish swimming round and round in a goldfish bowl and one
fish is telling the other fish that there's no time to chat as it's one of
those 'get things done' days.

I make little lists because I might forget what I am doing,
or more importantly, what I am going to do. Like going to the
doctor's to see if my moles are cancer, like throwing away left-over
food, old clothes, letters and other papers, especially receipts and
bank statements saved over a great many years in case of a possible
taxation audit (random).

It's when I am sitting in waiting rooms that I take stock of the
way things are, of the way I'm living and of the way I used to live. I
compare my life with other people's lives in a rather superficial way.
Not comparisons about money but rather on the quality of roof
beams, joists, floor boards and the sizes and shapes of windows.

I go back in my thoughts quite often. One time I actually try to
remember all the names of the hospitals in the city where I lived for
years in the English Midlands. There was, at that time, the Hospital
for the Diseases of Women, the Sick Children's, the Ear, Nose and
Throat, the Skin Hospital, the Fever, the Cancer, the General, the
Accident (Queens) and the Queen Elizabeth. The QE was Maternity
as well. I manage to stop the litany before going on to the names of
streets, churches, schools and shops, though the names of houses

come to mind – Sans Souci, Barclay, The Hollies, Padua, St Cloud and Prenton. Naturally, the hedges follow, the closely watched hedges, the laurel and the privet, the rhododendrons and the holly, evergreens in a series of repetitive quartets.

Those hedges from another country have given way to the honeysuckle, the hibiscus, the oleander, the plumbago, the white and pink climbing roses, the wistaria and the geraniums. There are too the street lawns, the box trees, the plane trees, the peppermints and the cape lilacs. But perhaps it is the blue metal, the smooth and the rough, which I notice the most when we are walking. The habit of closely watching the hedges is not lost, if anything it is more intense, and intensely, too, the roads. The roads are closely watched; Harold Hammond Goldsworthy Bernard the park Thompson Koeppe Princess Caxton Warwick and Queen and back Queen Warwick Caxton ...

I need a shrink, I say to myself, and go on to say that shrink is not a word I use. The use of it, even if not said aloud, is an indication that I need someone with specialist training.

Really this place! All I seem able to do here is to stare at the other people. We all seem stupid sitting here with a conventional obedience which is expected of us.

The chairs here are all joined together, fixed, making a square space in the middle where children can play. There are some little chairs and a low table for the children. I forget about myself for a bit, when I see a small child staggering about with a big plastic bucket. He has thick dark curls and a pale face and I pity him throwing up so much that he has to take a bucket around.

What's the matter with me, I think then, because 'throwing up' is a phrase I never use; neither do I say 'around' instead of round. I dismiss all this immediately when I see that the child is loading up the bucket with all the toys, the building blocks and farm animals, provided for *all* the children to play with, and is hauling them off to the safe harbour between his squatting mother's possessive spread-out legs.

A man sitting diagonally opposite gives his urine specimen to his wife to hold and she takes it and goes on reading her magazine holding the thing as if she was a specimen-glass holder, as if it is meant that she should just sit there, holding this specimen glass while he sits back stroking his chin and raising his eyebrows in every direction in turn round the waiting room; *see here everybody, meet the wife, my specimen-glass holder.*

The receptionist behind the curved desk has a commanding view of the whole room. When I look at her it is clear to me that she would prefer a dress shop in a not too classy department store. A place in which she could peek round the fitting-room curtains saying with emphasis, 'it's *you* dear' either for a dress, a blouse or a hat. It is probable that the pay is better in the Outpatients' Clinic and the hours less barbaric, especially since the decision not to have the clinic open at all on Fridays. I notice every time, without really meaning to, that she wears mostly red dresses or blouses with low V-neck lines exposing the healthy unworried skin of a woman approaching middle age and a suggestion of a similarly healthy and unworried bosom, more or less out of sight.

Certain days are set aside for walking sticks, crutches and wheelchairs. On these days I remind myself often to count my blessings and to remember that there are people worse off etc. For one thing I am only accompanying a patient and am not a patient myself. Without meaning to, against my will, I notice that some of the patients have a perpetually grieved look and some seem actually to be parading their disability. They exaggerate a grieved way of walking with one shoulder higher than the other, the body turned inwards on itself and the head tilted to one side. They seem to have the special skill of taking up the whole width of any place and then there's no way of getting round them like when you're waiting to go down in the small elevator to the Lab for blood tests. Sometimes people, like these people and unfortunates, will take up all the room in the aisles in the supermarket. Walking on two sticks, lurching first to one side and then the other, they make it impossible for anyone else to pass or even reach round for a tin of dog food, a cereal or some soap powder.

I suppose all this sounds cruel and without sympathy. It is not meant to. I might be on two sticks myself one day. Such thoughts, like everything else at present, are very out of character. Like this morning when there are no oranges to squeeze I am shaken to discover how much the disappearance of a small ritual can disturb me and cause an inability to go on to the next thing – just because one insignificant part of the morning routine is missing.

When I ask Mr George what he had for lunch he does not remember and when I ask was it nice, what he had for lunch, he says that it was very nice and, because it was nice, it is a pity that he does not remember what it was.

It is a pity, he says, to forget something nice.

An occupational therapist, with knitting needles pushed into her hair which is dressed in a firm grey bun, approaches. She has cut, she tells me, some pieces, squares and circles, of foam cushion material. She gives them to me saying that she knows relatives and friends enjoy being involved. She says that making little chintzy covers for these is a nice way of spending the long afternoons. She calls her pieces soft splints for pressure areas. She smiles with real pleasure.

I want to tell her that I don't have long afternoons except in my consulting rooms and I am not able to sew there. I nearly explain that I can't sew, it's a bit like not being able to dance, I mean ballroom dancing, it is always an embarrassment to say, 'I can't dance.' It is the same with sewing.

I can imagine all too easily the sense of futility which would all too quickly obliterate the hopefulness accompanying the giving of these chintz covers to some of my afternoon appointments who do, indeed, need occupation and direction but who have, at the same time, the ability in the face of offered activity to make the activity seem useless and unnecessary. This attribute is of course a symptom of the cause which might not be cured by the covering of soft splints with fragments of a cheerful material.

TELEGONY I: GOING INTO A DARK HOUSE

Jane Gardam

> Jane Gardam (b. 1928) is a British author, who writes for
> both children and adults. Her first novel for adults, *God
> on the Rocks*, was published in 1978 and shortlisted for
> the Man Booker Prize. She has won the Whitbread Award
> twice, for *The Queen of the Tambourines* and *The Hollow
> Land,* and was awarded an OBE in 2009 in recognition of
> her distinguished literary career.

Molly Fielding's mother had been a terrible woman born about the
same time as Tennyson's Maud and as unapproachable.

Nobody knew anything much about her, Molly herself being
now very ancient. Molly had been my grandmother's friend and
my mother's, before she was mine, but with the demise of each
generation she seemed to grow younger and freer – to take
strength. Her hair, her clothes, her house, all were up to the minute.
So were her investments; and her foreign holidays became farther
and farther flung.

I had found the photograph of her mother before my own
mother died. It was a coffee-coloured thing mounted on thick,
fluffy, cream paper, unframed in a drawer, with the photographer's
name in beautiful copperplate across the corner: 'Settimo'.

I could not believe it. Signor Settimo! He had taken my own
photograph when I was a child. I remembered a delicious little
man like a chocolate, with black hair and eyes and Hitler's square
moustache. My Settimo must have been the son – or even grandson
– of course. Molly Fielding's mother must have known the first.
Probably the first Settimo had come over from Italy with the
icecream makers and organ grinders of the *fin de siècle*. It was a
long-established firm when I knew it and a photographer in the
English Midlands with a glamorous, lucky name such as *Settimo*

would be almost home and dry. All he'd need would be flair and a camera and a book of instructions – a match for anyone.

But not for Molly Fielding's mother. Oh, dear me no. There she sits, her strong jaw raised, its tip pointing straight at the lens. Very watchful. She is examining the long hump of Mr Settimo beneath the black cloth behind the tripod. Her eyes – small eyes – are saying, 'Try – but you'll not take me. *I* take.'

Her great face, like his small one, is covered in black cloth. Hers is covered by a fine veil of silk netting, tied tight round the back of her neck by a broad black velvet ribbon. It is stitched at the top round the hat brim – a tight hat, expensive and showy, glittering with jet beads like the head of a snake. Her own head is proudly up, her eyes are very cunning. Oho, how she despises Mr Settimo, the tradesman. She is smiling a most self-satisfied smile. She is armed with a cuirass of necklaces across her beaded front, a palisade of brooches, great gauntlets of rings. She is fair-skinned beneath the veil. She must have been a pretty young girl, and her mouth, above the chin grown fierce, is still small and curly and sexy. No lady. Like somebody's cook but in the way that duchesses can look like somebody's cook. Not born rich, you can see – but now she *is* rich. At this moment, seated before foreign little Mr Settimo, she is rich. I never saw a nastier piece of work than Molly Fielding's mother. I swear it. I don't know how I knew – but I swear it.

'What an awful woman. Who is it?'

My mother said, 'Oh, dear, that's old Molly Fielding's mother. I knew her. She was a character.'

'You *knew* her! She looks before the Punic Wars.'

'She was, just about. God knows. An authentic mid-Victorian. She had Molly very late. She was famous for some sort of reputation but I can't remember what it was. She died about the time Molly married, and that would be all of sixty years ago.'

'What was the husband like?'

'Oh, long gone. Nobody knew him. Molly can't remember him. Maybe there wasn't a husband, but I think I'd have remembered if it was that. I think he was just dispensed with somehow. He was very weak – or silly. But rich.'

'She doesn't look as if she would have needed anyone, ever.'

'Well, she certainly didn't need poor old Molly. Her only child, you know, and she hated her. Molly – such a silent little thing at school. After that she was "at home with mother".'

'Didn't she ever work?'

'Are you mad, child? She had to gather up her mother's shawls and go visiting with her and return the library books.'

'Until she married?'

'Yes. And she'd never have married if her mother could have stopped it. She was always very attractive, Molly. Not beautiful but attractive. She was never let out of her mother's sight – and not let into anyone else's. They lived in hotels, I think, up and down the country. Sometimes in boarding-house places abroad. There had been a big house somewhere but they left it!'

'Were they poor?'

'Rich, dear, rich, just look some time at Molly's rings.'

This conversation was years ago and since then I have often looked at Molly's rings. I looked at them the other day when she came to lunch with me and they still shone wickedly, catching the light of the winter dining room, weighting down her little claws. Molly was a trim, spare, little woman and the claws were smaller now and even sharper-looking than when I'd seen her last, two years ago. Her nails were tiny and beautifully manicured and the prickly old clusters below them looked loose enough at any moment to go sliding off into the chicken supreme.

'Looking at the rings?' she asked. 'You're not getting them, dear. They're for impeccable Alice. My albatrosses. She could have them now if she wanted. I hardly wear them. High days and holidays, like this. I keep them in – no, I'm not going to tell you. You never know. Careless talk … You think they're vulgar, do you?'

'No. I was just – well, remembering them. From way back. They looked smaller then. Your rings were you. Most things look bigger when you're young.'

'I'm smaller,' she said, 'that's all it is. I keep getting them re-made but they can't keep pace with me. I get them done over every year before the insurance runs out. I tell the insurance people the stones rattle. They don't, but you can get them cleaned free if you say that. A jeweller cleans them better than you can yourself. A good jeweller always cleans when he secures. Gin – that's all you can do for yourself, soak them in gin. But it's a waste. You feel you can't drink it afterwards with all the gunge in it.'

The rings shone clear and sharp and there was not a trace of gunge and never had been, for Molly had a code of practice for the maintenance of goods that would have impressed a shipping company; and she had an eye for the free acquisition of necessities and schemes for the painless saving of money that many a government might envy. She also had a talent for the command of luxury. Stories of Molly sharing hotel rooms for which her friends and acquaintants had paid were in my childhood canon. She had slept on the floor of the Hyde Park, for instance, with her daughter's old nanny who had struck it rich with a (now absent) South American lover.

'Nanny had the bed of course – I insisted. Yes, she did fuss about me being on the floor, and we did change over about eleven o'clock, but I'd have been perfectly happy. Who minds sleeping on a floor if it saves two hundred pounds a night? They never notice, you know. I'd been Nanny's dinner guest and we went up to her room after dinner as if to get my coat. No one notices if you don't go home. And it was Harvey Nichols' sale in the morning, just across the road. I felt since I'd saved two hundred pounds I could spend it.'

'But, Molly, you didn't *have* to spend two hundred pounds. You didn't *have* to go into London the night before at all. You only live in Rickmansworth.'

'Oh, but there's nothing in Rickmansworth like the Hyde Park Hotel. Another thing, dear, did you know you can get a jolly good free bath on Paddington Station? There's a very decent bathroom in the Great Western. You just go in there for a coffee and then trot upstairs to the ladies' room and along the corridor and you're in a very nice big bathroom with marble fittings and nice old brass chains to the plugs. Thundering hot water, dear. I take soap and a towel always when I'm in London. In a Harrods bag.'

'You could be arrested.'

'Rubbish. There's not a hint of a sign saying "Private". It says *Bathroom*. Nobody uses it but me because all the rooms are this ghastly thing *En Suite* now. Have you noticed on the motorway – the motels? "24 *En Suites*". I'd never stay in a place like the Great

Western now, of course. It's only for commercial travellers. But the bathroom's useful if you have to change for the evening. It saves that nonsense of belonging to a so-called Club. Deadly places – all full of old women. Victoria Station was very good, too, before the War, and at St Pancras, The Great Northern, you could always stay a night no questions asked if you knew the ropes and wore the right clothes. They used to leave the keys standing in the doors. So unwise.

'And did you know you can spend *such* a pleasant hour or so in the London Library simply by ignoring the Members Only notice? You just walk in looking thoughtful and go upstairs to the Reading Room. It's a pity they've moved the old leather armchairs. They were so comfortable and you could sleep in them before a matinée. I always picked up one of the learned journals from the racks – something like *The John Evelyn Society Quarterly* – so that they'd think I was an old don.'

'They can see you're no don, Molly, with those diamonds.'

'I turn them round, dear. I'm not silly. They used to give you a tray of tea in the London Library once, you know, but all those nice things have stopped since the Conservatives got in. Look – an elastic band. It's the Post Office. I keep these. The postmen drop them all over England – all up the drive of the Final Resting Place. I told the postman they're worth money so now he drops them all through my letter box instead, great showers of them, like tagliatelle.'

We were walking on the common now. Lunch was over. It was a cold day and people were muffled up and pinched of face but Molly looked brisk and scarcely seventy. From the back – her behind neat, her legs and ankles skinny – she might have been forty-five. She wore a beautiful, old, lavender-mixture tweed suit and no glasses and she carried no stick. Trotting around her was a new puppy, a border collie she was training. She walked at a good speed through the spruces, as fast as I did and nearly as fast as the puppy, which she'd let off the lead. Her cheeks were pink, her eyes were bright and several people smiled at her as she went by. One old boy of about sixty gave her the eye and said he agreed about the wastage of elastic bands.

I said we should turn back as it was going to rain and she didn't want to be landed with a cold.

'I never catch cold,' she said. 'It's because I don't use public transport. I like my car. It was quite unnecessary for you to fetch and carry me today, you know. Very nice of you – but I'd have enjoyed crossing London again.'

'Do they let you drive still, Molly?' She had one of the little houses on an estate for the elderly she called the Final Resting Place.

'They can't stop me. Not yet. It's coming up of course – next driving test. Well, yes, they do fuss a bit. I can't remember where I'm going sometimes after I've set off, and the other day I couldn't remember where I'd been.'

'That might be a warning sign, you know, Molly. That it's time to stop.'

'Oh, fish! Wait till I get properly lost, then I'll stop. I've a card in my bag with my telephone number. I haven't forgotten who I am yet.'

'That does happen – '

'Oh, that Alzheimer business. That must be a terrible thing. But it only happens to the old, doesn't it?' She roared with laughter and clipped the dog on the lead.

Molly's dogs have always been wonderfully well behaved and obedient – never smelled or chewed things or wet things or snapped or barked. Rather dispirited animals really. She never appeared to pay much attention to them. Years ago I remembered that she had said it was her mother who had taught her how to handle dogs.

'Come on,' she cried from the traffic island in the middle of the High Street. 'You'll get run over if you hang about. Make a dash.'

At tea – she'd done well at lunch with a couple of sherries and a glass of chablis with the chicken – she settled down to a crumpet and a long and interesting analysis of her investments. As usual I forgot altogether that Molly had been my grandmother's friend. I forgot the great string of years she had known, the winters and winters and winters, the spring after spring, flowing back and back and back to the first mornings of the century. I forgot the huge number of times she had woken to another day.

When I was a girl, Molly would come breezing by to see us in a fast car, usually with a woman friend, never with a man or her husband who had been, like her father, a shadow. (She had married in ten minutes, my grandmother used to say, when her mother was upstairs in bed having measles of all things: absolutely furious, her mother was, too. In fact she died.) When I was a girl, I had always felt that Molly was empowered with an eternal youth, more formidable, much more effective, than my transient youth that seemed longer ago.

'Well, I'm not clever,' she often said. 'I'm a fool, dear. I know my limitations. No education and not a brain in my head. That's the secret. You're all so clever now – and all so good. It does age people. And also of course I'm frightfully mean. I don't eat or drink much unless I'm out.'

But she wasn't mean. When she gave a present, having said she could afford nothing, it tended to be stupendous. Once she gave me a car. And she did leave me one of the rings. But, 'I'm mean,' she said. 'And I'm not intellectual. I always wanted to be a racing driver after motor cars came in. Not allowed to, of course. D'you think I'm embittered?' (She shrieked with laughter.) 'I've struggled through. I've struggled through.'

And struggle it had sometimes looked to be – her freezing house, her empty hearth and fridge, her beautiful but ancient clothes all mended and pressed and hung in linen bags in the wardrobe. She had often sat wrapped in rugs to save coal. She had never had central heating. An ascetic pauper – until you looked at her investments, and they were wonderful. Whenever you saw her reading the financial columns she was smiling.

'And,' she said, 'hand it to me. I'm rational. That's what gets you through in the end, you know – being rational. I've no imagination, thank God. I give to charity but I've the sense not to watch the news. "Thank God" by the way is jargon. I don't believe in God and I don't believe that half the people I know who go to church and carry on at Christmas and go to the *Messiah* and that sort of thing – that they do either. All my Bridge lot, of course they don't believe in God. Religion's always seemed to me to be fairy stories. I go to church now and then, but it's for keeping up friendships and the look of it. And I quite enjoy weddings and funerals, of course.'

She was awesome, Molly. Awful really. But she was so nice.

She was in the midst of one of these 'I'm rational' conversations, the refrain that had threaded all my association with her, and she was eating her crumpet, and I was wondering why she was still insisting on her – well, on her boringness, and why she didn't bore me, why she never annoyed me; and I had decided it was because she never dissembled, that in my life her total truthfulness was unique. The truth Molly told showed her to be good. A good, straight being. Molly the unimaginative was unable to lie.

At which point she suddenly said, 'By the way, my mother's been seen around again.'

I looked at her.

'Around the village. And the FRP. She's looking for me, you know. But she won't find me.'

I said, 'Your *mother*?'

She said, 'Yes. You didn't know her. You were lucky. I hated her. Of course you know I did. You must have heard. She was very cruel to me. Well, she's back. Darling, are you going to take me home to the house of the near-dead? It's getting dark.'

'Yes, of course. Are you ready?'

'I'll just run upstairs.'

This she did and I waited with her coat and gloves and walking shoes and the basket with the dog's belongings and the dog.

'Yes,' she said coming down the stairs, twisting about at her knickers. 'Yes, she's been around for quite a time, a year or so. I don't know where she was before. I've managed to keep out of her way up to now. I hope that she didn't spot me leaving today, she'd have wanted to come, too.'

So, half an hour later I said, 'Molly, do you mean your *mother*?'

'Yes, dear. I'm afraid she was very unkind. I don't often talk about it. I was very frightened of her. D'you know, dear, I don't know when I've *had* such a wonderful day. Oh, how I've enjoyed it. Now if you turn left here and left again we can take the short cut and get straight to the bypass. You see I know exactly where I am. Now don't come in with me – you must get back before the traffic.'

I said, 'Molly – '

She kissed me, hesitated, and then got out. I saw her standing motionless before her mock-Georgian front door looking first at the lock, then at her key.

'Shall I open it?' I called to her.

'No, no. Of course not. Don't treat me as senile. Ninety-four is nothing. It won't be thought anything of soon. When you're ninety-four there'll be hundreds of you, with all this marvellous new medicine that's going on.'

'Goodbye, dear Molly. I'll wait till you're safe inside.'

'It's just that the lights aren't on.' She said, 'If you could just watch me in from the car. Just watch till I light everything up. It's so silly but I don't greatly like going into a dark house.'

I drove to the estate office and spoke to the lady superintendent who said that Molly was indeed still driving, though they were getting worried about it. She said that Molly was utterly sensible, utterly rational and her eyes and mind were very good. In fact she upset the younger ones by doing her stocks and shares and phoning her broker in the public common room.

'No aberrations? Does her mind wander?'

'*Never*,' she said. 'She is our star turn.'

Yet on the way home I decided to ring up her daughter, Alice, and was walking towards the phone the next morning when it began to ring, and it was Alice calling me. There were the statutory empty screams about how long since we'd spoken and then she asked if it were true that Molly had been to lunch with me. I said yes, and that I'd fetched her and taken her back, of course.

'Not "of course" at all, ducky. Do you know she's still driving?'

I went on like the superintendent for a bit: about the beady eye that saw me look at the rings, the high-speed walk, the psychic hold over the dog, the fearlessness on the High Street, the splendid appetite. 'There was just – '

'Ha!'

'Well, she says her *mother* is about. Alice, her mother'd be about a hundred and thirty years old.'

'I know. Oh, heaven, don't I know. Did she say her mother's looking for her around the village?'

'Yes.'

'And making her clean her nails and polish her shoes and – She rings me up and asks me to bring a cake over because her mother's coming to tea. About twice a week.'

'But I've never heard her mention her mother before.'

'The doctors say it's the supply of oxygen to the brain. It's running uneven, like a car with dirty plugs. There are vacuums or something, and it's in the vacuums she really lives. Maybe it's where we all really live.'

'But all the bossy, sensible, happy years?'

'*All* the years. It was all there underneath, always. The fear.'

FAT PEOPLE

Alison Lurie

Alison Lurie (b. 1926) is an American novelist and academic. She won the Pulitzer Prize in 1984 for her novel *Foreign Affairs*. She has published ten novels, one collection of short stories, and a non-fiction work entitled *The Language of Clothes*.

I never ran into any spooks in sheets; no headless horsemen, haunted mansions, nothing like that. But there was something weird once –

It was a while ago, when Scott went to India on that research grant. The first thing that happened was, I began noticing fat people. I saw them snatching the shrimps and stuffed eggs at parties; I saw them strolling along Cayuga Street with the swaying sailor's gait of the obese, and pawing through the queen-size housecoats in J. C. Penney. They were buying tubs of popcorn at the flicks, ahead of me in line at the post office and the bank, and pumping self-serve gas into their pickup trucks when I went to the garage.

I didn't pay much attention at first; I figured that since I was dieting I was more aware of people who should be doing the same. My idea was to lose fifteen pounds while Scott was away – twenty if possible, because of what he'd said just before he left.

We were at the county airport on a cold weepy day in March, waiting for Scott's plane and trying to keep up a conversation, repeating things we'd already said. I'd seen Scott off on trips before; but this time he'd be gone over three months. He was saying he wished I were coming, and promising to wire from Delhi and write twice a week, and telling me he loved me and reminding me again to check the oil on the Honda. I said I would, and was there anything else I should do while he was away?

Then the flight was announced and we grabbed each other. But we were both wearing heavy down jackets, and it didn't feel real. It was like two bundles of clothes embracing, I said, all choked up.

And Scott said, 'Well, there is one thing we could both do while I'm gone, Ellie; we could lose a few pounds.' He was kissing my face and I was trying not to break down and howl.

Then Scott was through the X-ray scanner into the boarding lounge, and then he was crossing the wet tarmac with his carry-on bag, getting smaller and smaller, and climbing the steps. It wasn't till I'd gone back to the main waiting-room and was standing inside the teary steamed-up window watching his plane shrink and blur into fog that I really registered his last remark.

I drove back to Pine Grove Apartments and dragged off my fat coat and looked at myself in the mirror on the back of the closet door. I knew I was a big girl, at the top of the range for my height, but it had never bothered me before. And as far as I knew it hadn't bothered Scott, who was hefty himself. Maybe when he suggested we lose a few pounds he was just kidding. But it was the last thing I'd hear him say for three months. Or possibly forever, I thought, because India was so far away and full of riots and diseases; and maybe in one of the villages he was going to they wouldn't want to change their thousand-year-old agricultural methods, and they would murder Scott with long wavy decorated knives or serve him curry with thousand-year-old undetectable poisons in it.

I knew it was bad luck to think that way, Scott had said so himself. I looked back at the mirror again, turning sideways. Usually I was pleased by what I saw there, but now I noticed that when I didn't breathe in, my tummy stuck out as far as my breasts.

Maybe I had put on some extra pounds that winter, I thought. Well, it should be pretty easy to take them off. It could be a project, something to do while Scott was gone. I wouldn't write him about it, I'd save it for a surprise when he got back. 'Wow, Ellie,' he would say, 'you look great.'

Only it turned out not to be as easy as all that. After two weeks, I weighed exactly the same. One problem was that all our friends kept asking me over and serving meals it would have been a shame to refuse, not to mention rude. And when I didn't have anywhere to go in the evening I started wandering around the apartment and usually ended up wandering into the kitchen and opening the fridge, just for something to do.

It was about then that I began to notice how many fat people there were in town. All sorts and all ages: overweight country-club types easing themselves out of overweight cars; street people shoving rusted grocery carts jammed with bottles and bundles. Fat old men like off-duty Santa Clauses waddling through the shopping mall, fat teenagers with acne, and babies so plump they could hardly get their thumbs into their mouths.

Of course I'd seen types like this before occasionally, but now they seemed to be everywhere. At first I put it down to coincidence, plus having the subject on my mind. It didn't bother me; in a way it was reassuring. When some bulgy high-school senior came for an interview at the college, and tried to fit their rear end onto the chair by my desk, I would think as I smiled nicely and asked the standard questions, Well, at least I don't look like that.

My folks knew I was trying to lose weight, and wanted to help, but they only made it worse. Every time I went over to the house for Sunday dinner Dad would ask first thing if I'd heard from Scott. It got to be over three weeks, and I still had to say 'No, nothing since the telegram,' and remind them that we'd been warned about how bad the mails were.

Then we'd sit down to the table and Mom would pass my plate, and there'd be this measly thin slice of chicken on it, and a bushel of cooked greens, as if I was in some kind of concentration camp for fatties. The salads all started to have sour low-cal dressing, and there was never anything but fruit for dessert: watery melon, or oranges cut up with a few shreds of dry coconut on top, like little undernourished white worms.

All through the meal Mom and Dad wouldn't mention Scott again, so as not to upset me. There was nothing in the dining-room to remind anybody of Scott either, and of course there wasn't any place set for him at the table. It was as if he'd disappeared or maybe had never even existed. By the time dinner was over I'd be so low in my mind I'd have to stop on the way home for a pint of chocolate marshmallow.

I'd hang up my coat and turn on the television and measure out exactly half a cup of ice cream, 105 calories, less than a bagel. I'd put the rest in the freezer and feel virtuous. But when the next commercial came on I'd open the freezer and have a few more spoonfuls. And then the whole process would repeat, like a commercial, until the carton was scraped clean down to the wax.

It got to be four weeks since Scott had left, and I still didn't weigh any less, even when I shifted my feet on the scale to make the needle wobble downwards. I'd never tried to lose weight before; I'd always thought it was ridiculous the way some people went into agonies over diets. I'd even been kind of shocked when one of my married friends made more fuss about taking a second slice of peach pie than she did about taking a lover. Displaced guilt, I used to think.

Now I was as hysterical about food as any of them. I brooded all afternoon over a fudge brownie I hadn't had for lunch; and if I broke down and ordered one I made up excuses for hours afterwards. 'I didn't promise Scott I'd lose weight,' I would tell myself, or 'It's not fair asking someone to give up both food and love at the same time.'

I started to read all the articles on losing weight that I used to skip before, and I took books out of the library. Over the next couple of weeks I tried one crazy diet after another: no-carbohydrate, no-fat, grapefruit and cornflakes, chipped beef and bananas and skimmed milk. Only I couldn't stick with any of them. Things went wrong at night when I started thinking about how I'd written nine letters to Scott and hadn't got one back. I'd lie in bed asking myself where the hell was he, what was he doing now? And pretty soon I'd feel hungry, starving.

Another thing I kept asking myself, especially when I chewed through some dried-out salad or shook Sweet-N-Low into my coffee, was what Scott, assuming he was still alive, was eating over there on the other side of the world. If he wasn't on a diet, what was the point? I would think, watching my hand reach out for the blue-cheese dressing or the half-and-half. He hadn't meant it seriously, I'd tell myself.

But suppose he had meant it? Suppose Scott was becoming slimmer and trimmer every day; what would he think if he knew I hadn't lost a pound in nearly five weeks?

Trying to do it on my own wasn't working. I needed support, and I thought I knew where to find it. There was a young woman in the Admissions Office called Dale. She was only a couple of years older than me, maybe twenty-six, but in two months she'd just about reorganised our files, and she obviously had her life under control. She was a brunette, with a narrow neat little figure and a narrow neat little poodle face; you got the feeling her hair wouldn't dare get itself mussed up, and she'd never weigh one ounce more than she chose to.

I figured that Dale would have ideas about my problem, because she was always talking about interesting new diets. And whenever some really heavy person came in she'd make a yapping noise under her breath and remark later how awful it was for people to let themselves go physically. 'Heaven knows how that hippopotamus is going to fulfil his athletic requirement,' she would say, or 'That girl's mother ought to be in a circus, she hardly looked human.' And I'd think, do I look human to Dale?

So one day when we were alone in the washroom I let on that I was trying to lose some weight. Dale lit up like a fluorescent tube. 'Yes, I think that's a good idea, Ellie,' she said, looking from herself to me, poodle to hippo, in the mirror over the basins. 'And I'd like to help you, okay?'

'Okay, thanks,' I said. I didn't have any idea what I was getting into.

On our way back to the office. Dale explained to me that being overweight was a career handicap. It was a known fact that heavy people didn't get ahead as fast in business. Besides, fat was low-class: the Duchess of Windsor had said you could never be too rich or too thin. When I told her there wasn't much danger of my ever being either one, Dale didn't laugh. She printed her Duchess of Windsor line out in computer-graphic caps, and fastened it on the side of my filing cabinet with two pineapple magnets.

The next thing Dale did was persuade me to see a doctor to make sure I was healthy, the way they tell you to do in the diet books. Then she started organising my life. She got me enrolled in an aerobics class, and set up a schedule for me to jog every day after work, regardless of the weather. Then she invited herself over to my apartment and cleaned out the cupboards and icebox. Bags of pretzels and fritos, butter and cream cheese and cold cuts, a loaf of cinnamon-raisin bread, most of a pound of Jones bacon – Dale packed everything up, and we hauled it down to the local soup-kitchen. I kind of panicked when I saw all that lovely food disappearing, but I was hopeful too.

The next day Dale brought in a calorie-counter and planned my meals for a week in advance. She kept a chart, and every day she'd ask how much I'd weighed that morning and write it down.

Only the scale still stuck at the same number. If there was nothing in the apartment, there was always plenty in the grocery. I'd go in for celery and cottage cheese and Ry-Krisp, but when I was pushing the cart down the last aisle it was as if the packages of cookies on the shelves were crying out to me, especially the chocolate-covered grahams and the Mallomars. I could almost hear them squeaking inside their cellophane wrappers, in these little high sugary voices: 'Ellie, Ellie! Here we are, Ellie!'

When I confessed to falling off my diet, Dale didn't lose her cool. 'Never mind, Ellie, that's all right,' she said. 'I know what we'll do. From now on, don't you go near a supermarket alone. I'll shop with you twice a week on the way home.'

So the next day she did. But as soon as she got a little ahead of me in the bakery section, I began drifting towards a tray of apricot croissants. Dale looked round and shook her poodle curls and said, 'Naughty, naughty,' – which kind of made me feel crazy, because I hadn't done anything naughty yet – and then she grabbed my arm and pulled me along fast.

There'd been several fat people in the A & P that day, the way there always were lately. When we were in line at the checkout with a load of groceries only a rabbit could love, I noticed one of them, a really heavy blonde girl about my own age, leaving the next register. Her cart was full and a couple of plump bakery boxes, a carton of potato chips and a giant bottle of Coke were bulging out of the brown-paper bags. As she came past the fat girl picked up a package of Hershey bars and tore it open, and half-smiled in my direction as if she were saying, 'Come on, Ellie, have one.'

I looked round at Dale, figuring she would make some negative comment, but she didn't. Maybe she hadn't seen the fat girl yet. The funny thing was, when I looked back I didn't see her either; she must have been in a big rush to get home. And she was going to have a really good time when she got there, too, I thought.

Another week dragged by full of carrots and diet soda and

frozen Weight Watchers dinners, and no news from Scott. My diet wasn't making much progress either. I'd take a couple of pounds off, but then I'd go out to dinner or a party and put some back on. Instead of losing I was gaining.

I was still seeing fat people too, more and more of them. I tried to convince myself it was just because they weren't disguised inside winter clothes any longer. The only problem was, the people I was seeing weren't just heavy, they were gross.

The first time I knew for sure that something strange was going on was one day when I was in the shopping plaza downtown, sitting on the edge of a planter full of sticky purple petunias and listening to a band concert instead of eating lunch, which had been Dale's idea, naturally. I was feeling kind of dizzy and sick, and when I touched my head it seemed to vibrate, as if it wasn't attached to my body too well.

Then I happened to glance across the plaza, and through the window of the Home Bakery I saw two middle-aged women, both of them bulging out of flowered blouses and slacks as if they'd been blown up too full. I couldn't make out their faces well because of the way the light shimmered and slid on the shop window; but I could see that one of them was looking straight at me and pointing to a tray of strawberry tarts: big ones with thick ruby glaze and scallops of whipped cream. It was as if she was saying, 'Come and get it, Ellie.'

Without even intending to I stood up and started to push through the crowd. But when I reached the bakery there weren't any fat women, and I hadn't seen them leave either. There'd been a moment when I was blocked by a twin stroller; but it still didn't make sense, unless maybe the fat women hadn't really been there. Suddenly I started feeling sick to my stomach. I didn't want a strawberry tart any more; I just wanted to go somewhere and lie down, only I was due back in the Admissions Office.

When I got there I said to Dale, making my voice casual, 'You know something funny, I keep seeing all these really fat people around lately.'

'There are a lot of them around, Ellie,' Dale said. 'Americans are terribly overweight.'

'But I'm seeing more. I mean, lots more than I ever did before. I mean, do you think that's weird?'

'You're just noticing them more,' Dale said stapling forms together, bang-bang. 'Most people block out unpleasant sights of that sort. They don't see the disgusting rubbish in the streets, or the way the walls are peeling right in this office.' She pointed with her head to a corner above the swing doors, where the cream-coloured paint was swollen into bubbles and flaking away; I hadn't noticed it before. Somehow that made me feel better.

'I guess you could be right,' I said. I knew that Dale was getting impatient with me. She'd stopped keeping my weight chart, and when we went shopping now she read the labels on things aloud in a cross way, as if she suspected I was cheating on my diet and had a package of shortbread or a box of raisins hidden away at home, which was sometimes true.

It was around that time that eating and sex started to get mixed up in my mind. Sometimes at night I still woke up hot and tense and longing for Scott; but more often I got excited about food. I read articles on cooking and restaurants in a greedy lingering way, and had fantasies about veal paprika with sour cream and baby onions, or lemon meringue pie. Once after I'd suddenly gone up to a pushcart and bought a giant hotdog with ketchup and relish I heard myself saying half aloud, 'I just had to have it.' And that reminded me of the way men talked in tough-guy thrillers. 'I had to have her,' they always said, and they would speak of some woman as if she was a rich dessert and call her a dish or a cupcake and describe parts of her as melons or buns. Scott isn't really a macho type, but he's always liked thrillers; he says they relax him on trips. And when he got on the plane that awful day he'd had one with him.

He'd been gone over six weeks by then, and no news since the telegram from Delhi. Either something really terrible had happened to him or he deliberately wasn't writing. Maybe while I was cheating on my diet, Scott was cheating on me, I thought. Maybe he'd found some Indian cupcake to relax him. As soon as I had that idea I tried to shove it out of my head, but it kept oozing back.

Then one sunny afternoon early in June I came home from work and opened the mailbox, and there among the bills and circulars was a postcard from Scott. There wasn't any apology for not writing, just a couple of lines about a beautiful temple he'd visited, and a scrawled 'love and kisses'. On the other side was a picture of a sexy over-decorated Indian woman and a person or god with the head of an elephant, both of them wearing smug smiles.

As I looked at that postcard something kind of exploded inside me. For weeks I'd been telling myself and everyone, 'If only I knew Scott was all right, I'd feel fine.' Now I knew he was all right, but what I felt was a big rush of suspicion and fury.

Pictures from the coffee-table books on India Scott had borrowed from the library crowded into my mind. I saw sleek prune-eyed exotic beauties draped in shiny silk and jewels, looking at me with hard sly expressions; and plump nearly naked blue gods with bedroom eyes; and closeups of temple sculptures in pockmarked stone showing one thousand and one positions for sexual intercourse. The ideas came to me that at that exact moment Scott was making out in one thousand different positions with some woman who had an elephant's head or was completely blue. I knew that was crazy, but still he had to be doing something he didn't want to tell me about and was ashamed of, or he would have written.

I didn't go on upstairs to the apartment. Instead I got back into the car, not knowing where I was going till the Honda parked of its own volition in front of a gourmet shop and cafe that I hadn't been near for weeks. There were five other customers there, which wasn't unusual at that time of day. The unusual thing was, all of them were fat; and not just overweight: humongously huge. All of them looked at me in a friendly way when I came in, as if maybe they knew me and had something to tell me.

For a moment I couldn't move. I just stood there stuck to the indoor-outdoor carpeting and wondered if I was going out of my mind. Five out of five; it wasn't reasonable, but there they were, or anyhow I was seeing them.

The fat people knew about Scott, I thought. They'd known all along. That was what they'd been trying to say to me when they smiled and held up cones or candy bars: 'Come on, honey, why should you deny yourself? You can bet your life Scott isn't.'

A huge guy with a grizzly-bear beard left the counter, giving me a big smile, and I placed my order. A pound of assorted butter cookies, a loaf of cinnamon bread, and a date-walnut coffee ring with white sugar icing. As soon as I got into the car I tore open the box and broke off a piece of the coffee ring, and it was fantastic: the sweet flaky yellow pastry and the sugar-glazed walnuts; a lot better than sex with Scott, I told myself.

For the next four days I pigged out. I finished the cookies and coffee ring that same evening, and on Friday afternoon I sneaked over to the grocery without telling Dale and bought everything I'd dreamt about for weeks: bacon and sausages and sliced Virginia ham, butter and sour cream and baking potatoes, pretzels and barbecue potato chips and frozen french fries. And that was just the beginning.

When I went in to work Monday morning with a box of assorted jam doughnuts I let Dale know I was off my diet for good. Dale tried to shove me back on. It didn't really matter about the weekend binge, she yipped. If I skipped lunch all week and cut way down on dinner and jogged two miles a day I'd be back on track.

'I don't want to be on track,' I told her. 'Eight weeks Scott has been gone, and all I've had from him is one disgusting postcard.'

Dale looked pained and started talking about self-respect and self-image, but I wasn't having any. 'Leave me alone, please,' I said. 'I know what I'm doing.'

Two days and a lot of pork chops and baked potatoes and chicken salad and chocolate almond bark and cherry pie later, I walked into my building, steadied a bag of high-calorie groceries against my hip, and opened the mailbox.

Jesus, I practically dropped the bag. The galvanised-metal slot was crammed with fat white and flimsy blue airmail letters from India. Most of them looked as if they'd been opened and read and crumpled up and walked on, and they were covered with stamps and cancellations.

An hour later, sitting on my sofa surrounded by two months' worth of Scott's letters, I faced facts. He was dieting: his second letter said so, mentioning that he didn't want to look overfed when he walked through a village full of hungry people. All right. I had three weeks, which meant – I went into the bathroom and dragged out the scale from the bottom of the cupboard where I'd shoved it on Friday – which meant, oh God, I'd have to lose over two pounds a week just to get back to where I was when Scott left.

It was an awful three weeks. I had cereal and skimmed milk and fruit for breakfast and lunch, to get through work, but otherwise I didn't eat anything much. Pretty soon I was blurred and headachy most of the time, in spite of all the vitamins and minerals I was scarfing down, and too tired to exercise. And I was still behind schedule on losing weight.

What made it worse was the fat people. I was seeing them again everywhere, only now they didn't look happy or friendly. 'You're making a big mistake, Ellie,' they seemed to be telling me at first. Then they began to get angry and disgusted. 'Sure, he wrote you, stupid,' their expressions said. 'That doesn't prove he's not helping himself to some Indian dish right this minute.'

I quit going out after work; I didn't have the energy. Mostly I just stayed home drinking diet soda and re-reading Scott's letters, kind of to prove to myself that he existed, I guess, because there hadn't been any more. Then I'd watch a little television and go to bed early, hoping to forget about food for a while. But for the first time in my life I was having insomnia, jolting awake in the small hours and lying there starving.

The day Scott was due back, I woke up about four a.m. and couldn't doze off again, even with Valium. For what seemed like hours I thrashed around in bed. Finally I got up and opened a can of diet soda and switched on the TV. Only now, on all the channels that were still broadcasting, everybody was overweight: the third-string newscasters, the punk MTV singers, the comics in an old black-and-white film. On the weather channel I could tell that the girl was hiding thighs like hams under the pleated skirt she kept swishing around as she pointed out the tornado areas. Then the picture changed and a soft plump guy smiled from between chipmunk cheeks and told me that airports were fogged in all over Europe and Scott would never get home.

I turned off the television, dragged on some jeans and a T-shirt, and went out. It was a warm June night full of noises: other tenants' air-conditioners and fans, traffic out on the highway; and planes overhead. There was a hard wind blowing, which made me feel kind of dizzy and slapped about, and it was that uneasy time just before dawn when you start to see shapes but can't make out colours. The sky was a pale sick lemon, but everything else was lumps of blurred grey.

Pine Grove Apartments is surrounded on three sides by an access road, and I'd just turned the corner and was starting towards the dead end. That was when I saw them, way down by the trees. There was a huge sexless person with long stringy hair waving its arms and walking slowly towards me out of the woods, and behind it came more angry fat grey people, and then more and more.

I wanted to run, but I knew somehow that if I turned round the fat people would rush after me the way kids do when you play Giant Steps, and they would catch me and, God, I didn't know what. So I just backed up slowly step by step towards the corner of the building, breathing in shallow gasps.

They kept coming out of the woods in the half-light, more and more, maybe ten or twenty or fifty, I didn't know. I thought I recognised the women from the bakery, and the big guy with the beard – and then I realised I could hear them too, kind of mumbling and wailing. I couldn't take it any more, I turned and raced for home, stumbling over the potholes in the drive.

Well, somehow I made it to the apartment, and slammed the door and double-locked it and put on the chain, and leaned up against the wall panting and gulping. For what seemed like hours I stood there, listening to the sounds of the fat people coming after me, crowding up the stairs, all grey and blubbery, and roaring and sobbing and sliding and thumping against the walls and door.

Then the noises started to change. Gradually they turned into the wind in the concrete stairwell and the air-conditioner downstairs and the six-thirty plane to New York flying over the complex and a dog barking somewhere. It was light out now, nearly seven o'clock. I unbolted my door, keeping the chain on, and eased it open a slow inch. The hall was empty.

I still felt completely exhausted and crazy, but I got myself dressed somehow and choked down some coffee and left for work. On the way I took a detour in the Honda round the corner of the building. At first I was afraid to look, even though I was safe inside the locked car. At the edge of the woods where the mob of fat people had been there was nothing but some big old spirea bushes blowing and tossing about.

That evening Scott came home, ten pounds overweight. A couple of days later, when he was talking about his trip, he said that Indian food was great, especially the sweets, but the women were hard to talk to and not all that good-looking.

'A lot of Indians are heavy too, you know,' he told me.

'Really?' I asked. I wondered if Scott had had some spooky experience like mine, which I still hadn't mentioned: I didn't want him to think I was going to crack up whenever he left town.

'It's a sign of prosperity, actually. You notice them especially in the cities, much more than in this country. I mean, you don't see many fat people around here for instance, do you?'

'No,' I agreed, cutting us both another slice of pineapple upside-down cake. 'Not lately, anyhow.'

G-STRING

Nicola Barker

Nicola Barker (b. 1966) is a British novelist and short story writer. Her novel, *Wide Open*, won the IMPAC Dublin Literary Award in 2000, and another, *Darkmans*, was shortlisted for the Man Booker Prize in 2007.

Ever fallen out with somebody simply because they agreed with you? Well, this is exactly what happened to Gillian and her pudgy but reliable long-term date, Mr Kip.

They lived separately in Canvey Island. Mr Kip ran a small but flourishing insurance business there. Gillian worked for a car-hire firm in Grays Thurrock. She commuted daily.

Mr Kip – he liked to be called that, an affectation, if you will – was an ardent admirer of the great actress Katharine Hepburn. She was skinny and she was elegant and she was sparky and she was intelligent. Everything a girl should be. She was *old* now, too, Gillian couldn't help thinking, but naturally she didn't want to appear a spoilsport so she kept her lips sealed.

Gillian was thirty-four, a nervous size sixteen, had no cheekbones to speak of and hair which she tried to perm. God knows she tried. She was the goddess of frizz. She frizzed but she did not fizz. She was not fizzy like Katharine. At least, that's what Mr Kip told her.

Bloody typical, isn't it? When a man chooses to date a woman, long term, who resembles his purported heroine in no way whatsoever? Is it safe? Is it cruel? Is it downright simple-minded?

Gillian did her weekly shopping in Southend. They had everything you needed there. Of course there was the odd exception: fishing tackle, seaside mementos, insurance, underwear. These items she never failed to purchase in Canvey Island itself, just to support local industry.

A big night out was on the cards. Mr Kip kept telling her how big it would be. A local Rotary Club do, and Gillian was to be Mr Kip's special partner, he was to escort her, in style. He was even taking the cloth off his beloved old Aston Martin for the night to drive them there and back. And he'd never deigned to do that before. Previously he'd only ever taken her places in his H-reg Citroën BX.

Mr Kip told Gillian that she was to buy a new frock for this special occasion. Something, he imagined, like that glorious dress Katharine Hepburn wore during the bar scene in her triumph, *Bringing Up Baby*.

Dutifully, Gillian bought an expensive dress in white chiffon which didn't at all suit her. Jeanie – twenty-one with doe eyes, sunbed-brown and weighing in at ninety pounds – told Gillian that the dress made her look like an egg-box. All lumpy-humpy. It was her underwear, Jeanie informed her – If only! Gillian thought – apparently it was much too visible under the dress's thin fabric. Jeanie and Gillian were conferring in The Lace Bouquet, the lingerie shop on Canvey High Street where Jeanie worked.

'I tell you what,' Jeanie offered, 'all in one lace bodysuit, right? Stretchy stuff. No bra. No knickers. It'll hold you in an' everything.' Jeanie held up the prospective item. Bodysuits, Gillian just *knew*, would not be Mr Kip's idea of sophisticated. She shook her head. She looked down at her breasts. 'I think I'll need proper support,' she said, grimacing.

Jeanie screwed up her eyes and chewed at the tip of her thumb. 'Bra and pants, huh?'

'I think so.'

Although keen not to incur Jeanie's wrath, Gillian picked out the kind of bra she always wore, in bright, new white, and a pair of matching briefs.

Jeanie ignored the bra. It was functional. Fair enough. But the briefs she held aloft and proclaimed, 'Passion killers.'

'They're tangas,' Gillian said, defensively, proud of knowing the modern technical term for the cut-away pant. 'They're brief briefs.'

Jeanie snorted. 'No one wears these things any more, Gillian. There's enough material here to launch a sailboat.'

Jeanie picked up something that resembled an obscenely elongated garter and proffered it to Gillian. Gillian took hold of the scrap.

'What's this?'

'G-string.'

'My God, girls wear these in Dave Lee Roth videos.'

'Who's that?' Jeanie asked, sucking in her cheeks, insouciant.

'They aren't practical,' Gillian said.

Jeanie's eyes narrowed. 'These are truly modern knickers,' she said. 'These are what *everyone* wears now. And I'll tell you for why. No visible pantie line!'

Gillian didn't dare inform her that material was the whole point of a pantie. Wasn't it?

Oh hell, Gillian thought shifting on Mr Kip's Aston Martin's leather seats, 'maybe I should've worn it in for a few days first.' It felt like her G-string was making headway from between her buttocks up into her throat. She felt like a leg of lamb, trussed up with cheese wire. Now she knew how a horse felt when offered a new bit and bridle for the first time.

'Wearing hairspray?' Mr Kip asked, out of the blue.

'What?'

'If you are,' he said, ever careful, 'then don't lean your head back on to the seat. It's real leather and you may leave a stain.'

Gillian bit her lip and stopped wriggling.

'Hope it doesn't rain,' Mr Kip added, keeping his hand on the gearstick in a very male way, 'the wipers aren't quite one hundred per cent.'

Oh, the G-string was a modern thing, but it looked so horrid! Gillian wanted to be a modern girl but when she espied her rear-end engulfing the sliver of string like a piece of dental floss entering the gap between two great white molars, her heart sank down into her strappy sandals. It tormented her. Like the pain of an old bunion, it quite took off her social edge.

When Mr Kip didn't remark favourably on her new dress; when, in fact he drew a comparison between Gillian and the cone-shaped upstanding white napkins on the fancily made-up Rotary tables, she almost didn't try to smile. He drank claret. He smoked a cigar and tipped ash on her. He didn't introduce her to any of his Rotary friends. Normally, Gillian might have grimaced on through. But tonight she was a modern girl in torment and this kind of behaviour quite simply would not do.

Of course she didn't actually *say* anything. Mr Kip finally noticed Gillian's distress during liqueurs.

'What's got into you?'

'Headache,' Gillian grumbled, fighting to keep her hands on her lap.

Two hours later, Mr Kip deigned to drive them home. It was raining. Gillian fastened her seatbelt. Mr Kip switched on the windscreen wipers. They drove in silence. Then all of a sudden, *wheeeu-woing*! One of the wipers flew off the windscreen and into a ditch. Mr Kip stopped the car. He reversed. He clambered out to look for the wiper, but because he wore glasses, drops of rain impaired his vision.

It was a quiet road. What the hell. Mr Kip told Gillian to get out and look for it.

'In my white dress?' Gillian asked, quite taken aback.

Fifteen minutes later, damp, mussed, muddy, Gillian finally located the wiper. Mr Kip fixed it back on, but when he turned the relevant switch on the dash, neither of the wipers moved. He cursed like crazy.

'Well, that's that,' he said, and glared at Gillian like it was her fault completely. They sat and sat. It kept right on raining.

Finally Gillian couldn't stand it a minute longer. 'Give me your tie,' she ordered. Mr Kip grumbled but did as she'd asked. Gillian clambered out of the car and attached the tie to one of the wipers.

'OK,' she said, trailing the rest of the tie in through Mr Kip's window. 'Now we need something else. Are you wearing a belt?'

Mr Kip shook his head.

'Something long and thin,' Gillian said, 'like a rope.'

Mr Kip couldn't think of anything.

'Shut your eyes,' Gillian said. Mr Kip shut his eyes, but after a moment, naturally, he peeped.

And what a sight! Gillian laboriously freeing herself from some panties which looked as bare and sparse and confoundedly stringy as a pirate's eye patch.

'Good gracious!' Mr Kip exclaimed. 'You could at least have worn some French knickers or cami-knickers or something proper. Those are preposterous!'

Gillian turned on him. 'I've really had it with you, Colin,' she snarled, 'with your silly affected, old-fashioned car and clothes and *everything.*'

From her bag Gillian drew out her Swiss Army Knife and applied it with gusto to the plentiful elastic on her G-string. Then she tied one end to the second wiper and pulled the rest around and through her window. 'Right,' she said, 'start up the engine.'

Colin Kip did as he was told. Gillian manipulated the wipers manually; left, right, left, right. All superior and rhythmical and practical and dour-faced.

Mr Kip was very impressed. He couldn't help himself. After several minutes of driving in silence he took his hand off the gearstick and slid it on to Gillian's lap.

'Watch it,' Gillian said harshly. 'Don't you dare provoke me, Colin. I haven't put my Swiss Army Knife away yet.'

She felt the pressure of his hand leave her thigh. She was knickerless. She was victorious. She was a truly modern female.

WESLEY: BLISTERS

Nicola Barker

> Nicola Barker (b. 1966) is a British novelist and short story
> writer. Her novel, *Wide Open*, won the IMPAC Dublin
> Literary Award in 2000, and another, *Darkmans,* was
> shortlisted for the Man Booker Prize in 2007.

Look,' Trevor said, 'you've got to serve from the back, see?'

Wesley dropped the orange he'd just picked up.

'Put it where it was before,' Trevor said sniffily. 'Exactly.'

Wesley adjusted the placement of the orange. There. Just so. It
was neat now. The display looked hunky-dory.

'Let me quickly say something,' Wesley said, as Trevor turned to
go and unload some more boxes from the van.

'What?'

'It's just that if you serve people from the back of the stall they
immediately start thinking that what you're giving them isn't as
good as what's on display.'

Trevor said nothing.

'See what I mean?'

'So what?'

'Well, I'm just saying that if you want to build up customer
confidence then it's a better idea to give them the fruit they can see.'

'It's more work that way,' Trevor said, shoving his hands into
his pockets.

'Well, I don't care about that,' Wesley responded. 'I'm the one
who'll end up having to do most of the serving while you're running
the deliveries and I don't mind.'

Trevor gave Wesley a deep look and then shrugged and walked
off to the van.

Another new job. Selling fruit off a stall on the Roman Road.
Wesley was handsome and intelligent and twenty-three years old
and he'd had a run of bad luck so now he was working the markets.
No references needed. Actually, on the markets a bad temper was

considered something of a bonus. Nobody messed you around. If they did, though, then you had to look out for yourself.

Trevor had red hair and a pierced nose. Wesley looked very strait-laced to him in his clean corduroy trousers and polo-neck jumper, and his hands were soft and he spoke too posh. What Trevor didn't realize however, was that Wesley had been spoilt rotten as a child so was used to getting his own way and could manipulate and wheedle like a champion if the urge took him. Wesley had yet to display to Trevor the full and somewhat questionable force of his personality.

Wesley pulled his weight. That, at least, was something, Trevor decided. After they'd packed up on their first night he invited Wesley to the pub for a drink as a sign of his good faith. Wesley said he wanted something to eat instead. So they went for pie and mash together.

Trevor had some eels and a mug of tea. Wesley ate a couple of meat pies. Wesley liked the old-fashioned tiles and the tables in the pie and mash shop. He remarked on this to Trevor. Trevor grunted.

'My dad was in the navy,' Wesley said, out of the blue.

'Yeah?'

'He taught me how to box.'

'Yeah?'

'Last job I had, I punched my boss in the face. He was up a ladder. I was on a roof. Broke his collar bone.'

'You're kidding!' Trevor was impressed.

'Nope.'

'Fuck.'

'Yeah.'

'What did he do?'

'Tried to prosecute.'

'What!?'

'I buggered off. I live my life,' Wesley said plainly, 'by certain rules. I'll do my whack, but when push comes to shove, I want to be treated decent and to keep my mind free. See?'

Trevor was mystified. He ate his eels, silently.

'I had a brother,' Wesley said, 'and I killed him when I was a kid. An accident and everything. But that's made me think about things in a different way.'

'Yeah?' Trevor was hostile now. 'How did you kill him?'

'Playing.'

'Playing what?'

'None of your fucking business.'

Trevor's eyebrows rose and he returned to his meal.

'I want to do the decent thing,' Wesley said. 'You know? And sometimes that'll get you into all kinds of grief.'

Trevor didn't say anything.

'Watch this.'

Trevor looked up. Wesley had hold of one of the meat pies. He opened his mouth as wide as he could and then pushed the pie in whole. Every last crumb. Trevor snorted. He couldn't help it. Once Wesley had swallowed the pie he asked Jean – the woman who served part-time behind the counter – for a straw. When she gave him one, he drank a whole mug of tea through it up his left nostril.

Trevor roared with laughter. He was definitely impressed.

After a week on the job Wesley started nagging Trevor about the quality of the fruit he was buying from the wholesalers. 'The way I see it, right,' Wesley said, 'if you sell people shit they won't come back. If you sell them quality, they will.'

'Bollocks,' Trevor said, 'this ain't Marks and fucking Spencer's.'

Wesley moaned and wheedled. He told Trevor he'd take a cut in his money if Trevor spent the difference on buying better quality stuff. Eventually Trevor gave in. And he took a cut in his wages too.

After a month, Wesley used his own money to repaint the stall a bright green and bought some lights to hang on it to make it, as he said, 'more of a proposition.'

'Thing is,' Wesley observed, fingering the little string of lights, 'we have to get one of the shops to let us tap into their electricity supply, otherwise we can't use them.'

Trevor didn't really care about the lights but he was grudgingly impressed by the pride Wesley seemed to take in things. He went to the newsagents and the bakery and then finally into the pie and mash shop. Fred, who ran the shop, agreed to let them use his power if they paid him a tenner a week. Wesley said this seemed a reasonable arrangement.

Things were going well. Wesley would spend hours juggling apples for old ladies and did a trick which involved sticking the sharpened end of five or six matches between the gaps in his teeth and then lighting the matches up all at once. He'd burned his lips twice that way and had a permanent blister under the tip of his nose. He'd pick at the blister for something to do until the clear plasma covered his fingers and then he'd say, 'Useful, this, if ever I got lost in a desert. Water on tap.'

After six weeks things had reached a point where Trevor would have done anything Wesley suggested. The stall was flourishing. Business was good. Wesley worked his whack and more so. He kept everyone amused with his tricks and his silly ideas. The customers loved him. He was always clean.

What it was that made Wesley so perfect in Trevor's eyes was the fact that he was a curious combination of immense irresponsibility – he was a mad bastard – and enormous conscientiousness. He wanted to *do* good but this didn't mean he had to *be* good.

One morning, two months after Wesley had started on the stall, Trevor got a flat tyre on his way back from the wholesalers and Wesley was obliged to set up on his own and do a couple of the early deliveries himself into the bargain.

He took Fred at the pie and mash shop his regular bundle of fresh parsley and then asked him for the extension cord so that he could put up his lights on the stall. Fred was busy serving. He indicated with his thumb towards the back of the shop. 'Help yourself, mate. The lead and everything's just behind the door. 'That's where Trevor stashes them each night.'

Fred liked Wesley and he trusted him. Same as Trevor did and all the others. Wesley, if he'd had any sense, should have realized that he was well set up here.

Wesley wandered out to the rear of the shop. He pulled back the door and picked up the extension lead. Then he paused. It was cold. He looked around him.

A big room. Red, polished, concrete floors. Large, silver fridges. And quiet. He could hear the noise from the shop and, further off, the noise from the market. But in here it was still and the stillness and the silence had a special *sound*. Like water.

Wesley closed his eyes. He shuddered. He opened his eyes again, tucked the lead under his arm and beat a hasty retreat.

He was in a world of his own when Trevor finally arrived that morning. On two occasions Trevor said, 'Penny for them,' and then snapped his fingers in front of Wesley's unfocused eyes when he didn't respond.

'I'm thinking of my dad,' Wesley said. 'Don't ask me why.'

'Why?' said Trevor, who was in a fine good-humour considering his tyre hold-up.

'I was just in the pie and mash shop getting the extension lead for the lights. Out the back. And then I was suddenly thinking about my dad. You know, the navy and the sea and all the stuff we used to talk about when I was a kid.'

'Your dad still in the navy?' Trevor asked.

Wesley shook his head. 'Desk job,' he said.

'Probably those bloody eels,' Trevor said, bending down and picking up a crate of Coxes.

'What?'

'Those eels out the back. Making you think of the sea.'

'What?'

'In the fridges. He keeps the eels in there.'

'How's that?' Wesley's voice dipped by half an octave. Trevor didn't notice. He was wondering whether he could interest Wesley in selling flowers every Sunday as a side-interest. A stall was up for grabs on the Mile End Road close to the tube station. Sundays only.

'You're telling me he keeps live eels in those fridges?'

'What?'

'Live eels?' Wesley asked, with emphasis.

'In the fridges, yeah.' Trevor stopped what he was doing, straightened up, warned by the tone of Wesley's voice.

'What, like ...' Wesley said, breathing deeply, 'swimming around in a big tank?'

'Nope.' Trevor scratched his head. 'Uh ... like five or six long metal drawers, horizontal, yeah? And when you pull the drawers open they're all in there. Noses at one end and tails at the other. Big fuckers, though. I mean, five foot each or something.'

A woman came up to the stall and wanted to buy a lemon and two bananas. She asked Wesley for what she needed but Wesley paid her no heed.

'Hang on a second,' he said gruffly, holding up his flat hand, 'just shut up for a minute.'

He turned to Trevor. 'You know anything about eels?' he asked. Trevor knew enough about wild creatures to know that if Wesley had been a dog or a coyote his ears would be prickling, his ruff swelling.

'Not to speak of ...' he said.

'Excuse me,' Wesley said to the customer, 'I'll be back in a minute,' and off he went.

Wesley strolled into the pie and mash shop. Fred was serving. Wesley waited patiently in line until it was his turn to be served.

'What can I get you, Wesley?' Fred asked, all jovial.

Wesley smiled back at him. 'Having a few problems with the lights on the stall,' he said. 'Could I just pop out the back and see if the plug's come loose or something?'

'Surely,' Fred said, thumbing over his shoulder. 'You know the lie of the land out there.'

Wesley went into the back room and up to one of the fridges. He took hold of the top drawer and pulled it open. The drawer contained water, and, just as Trevor had described, was crammed full of large, grey eels, all wriggling, eyes open, noses touching steel, tails touching steel. Skin rubbing skin rubbing skin.

Held in limbo, Wesley thought, in this black, dark space. Wanting to move. Wanting to move. Wanting to move. Nowhere to go. Like prison. Like purgatory.

Wesley closed the drawer. He shuddered. He covered his face with his soft hands. He breathed deeply. He hadn't been all that honest. What he'd said about his dad and everything. True enough, his dad had been in the navy, he'd travelled on ships the world over, to India and Egypt and Hong Kong. Only he never came back from the sea. Never came back home. Sort of lost interest in them all. Only sent a card once, a while after ... a while after ... to say he wouldn't ever be back again.

Wesley knew all about the sea, though. Knew all about fishes and currents and stingrays and everything. His mum had bought him a book about it. For his birthday when he was six. And so he knew about eels and how they all travelled from that one special place in the Sargasso Sea. Near the West Indies. That's where they were spawned and that's where they returned to die.

But first, such a journey! Feeding on plankton, the tiny, little transparent eels, newborn, floated to the surface of that great sea from their deep, warm home in its depths, drifted on the Gulf Stream, travelled over the Atlantic, for three summers, then into European waters, in huge numbers, swam upriver, from salt to freshwater. What a journey. And man couldn't tame them or breed them in captivity or stop them. Couldn't do it.

How did they know? Huh? Where to go? How did they know? But they knew! They knew where to go. Moving on, living, knowing, remembering. Something *in* them. Something inside. Passed down through the generations. An instinct.

Wesley uncovered his face and looked around him. He wanted to find another exit. He walked to the rear of the fridges and discovered a door, bolted. He went over and unbolted it, turned the key that had been left in its lock, came back around the fridges and strolled out into the shop.

'Thanks, mate,' Wesley said as he pushed his way past Fred and sauntered back outside again.

Trevor shook his head. 'No way,' he said. And he meant it.

'You've got to fucking do this for me, Trev,' Wesley said.

'Why?'

'You know how old some of those eels are?'

'No.'

'Some could be twenty years old. They've lived almost as long as you have.'

'They get them from a farm,' Trevor said. 'They aren't as old as all that.'

'They can't breed them in captivity,' Wesley said. 'They come from the Sargasso Sea. That's where they go to breed and to die.'

'The what?'

'Near the West Indies. That's where they go. That's what eels do. They travel thousands of miles to get here and then they grow and then they travel thousands of miles to get back again.'

'Sounds a bit bloody stupid,' Trevor said, 'if you ask me.'

'I'm a travelling man,' Wesley said, 'like my dad was. Don't try and keep me in one place. Don't try and lock me away.'

'They're eels, Wesley,' Trevor said, almost losing patience.

'Imagine how they're feeling,' Wesley said, 'caught in those fridges. Needing to travel. Needing it, needing it. Like an illness, almost. Like a fever. Dreaming of those hot waters, the deep ocean. Feeling cold steel on their noses, barely breathing, crammed together. Nowhere to go. No-fucking-where to go.'

'Forget it,' Trevor said, 'I've got no argument with Fred. Forget it, mate.'

'Take the van, Trevor,' Wesley said calmly. 'Drive it round the back, where they make the deliveries. I already unlocked the door.'

Off Wesley strode again. Trevor jangled the keys in his pocket, swore out loud and then ran after him.

Wesley crept in through the back entrance. He stood still a while. He could hear the chattering of customers in the shop and he could hear the sound of a van pulling into the delivery passage. He went outside, smiling wildly, happy to be fucking up, same as he always was.

'OK, Trev,' he said. 'Open the back doors but keep the tail up so's when I dump them in there they don't escape.'

Trevor looked immensely truculent but he did as Wesley asked.

Wesley went back inside, opened up one of the big, silver drawers, pushed his arms in, down and under all that silky, scaleless eel-flesh. He curled his arms right under, five eels, all wriggling, closed his arms around them and lifted. Water splashed and splattered. He looked over to the doorway leading into the shop, bit his lip, couldn't pause. The eels were whipping and lashing and swerving and writhing. He headed for the exit at top speed.

Trevor stood by the tailgate. When he saw the eels he swore. 'Fuck this man! Fuck this!'

Wesley threw the eels into the back of the van. 'Ten minutes,' he said, 'to get them back to water, otherwise they'll suffocate.'

Trevor watched the eels speeding and curling in the back of his van, swimming, almost, on air. He turned to say something but Wesley was gone. A minute later Wesley re-emerged. More eels. Like snakes. Faces like … faces like cats or otters or something. Little gills. Seal eyes.

As Wesley turned to go back in Trevor caught him by his shirt sleeve. 'I'm not doing this,' he said. 'Things are going well for us here. He's kept eels in this place for years, gets a delivery every week.'

Wesley turned on him. 'Give me the keys.'

'What?'

'Give me the shitting keys and I'll drive them to the canal myself.'

'This is stupid!'

'Don't call me fucking stupid. No one calls me that. Give me the fucking keys.'

Trevor took the keys out of his pocket and dropped them on the floor. He walked off. His eyes were prickling. 'Fuck it!' he shouted, and his voice echoed down the passageway.

Back inside, Wesley pulled open the third drawer, shoved his arms in, took hold of the eels. Water was everywhere now. Thank God it was lunchtime and Fred was busy. He held the fish tight and straightened up. He headed for the back door.

Outside, he met Fred. He was holding the five eels. He looked at Fred.

'What the hell are you doing?' Fred said.

'Why aren't you in the shop?' Wesley asked, stupidly.

'Jean's in,' Fred said, eyeing the eels. 'She's covering.'

'Oh. I didn't know that.'

'What are you doing with my eels?' Fred put out his arms. 'Give them to me.'

'No,' Wesley said. 'You can't own a wild thing.'

As he spoke he took a step back. Fred moved forwards and put himself between Wesley and the tailgate. The eels were itching to get free. Wesley's arms were aching. Fred took a step closer. He was short and square and tough as a boxing hare.

Wesley opened his arms. The eels flew into the air, landed, skidded, flipped, whipped, scissored, dashed. At top speed, they sea-snaked down the passageway, into the market, on to the main road.

'Down the Roman Road,' Wesley yelled. 'Back to the water, back to the frigging sea!'

Fred punched Wesley in the mouth. Jesus, Wesley thought, feels like all my teeth have shifted. He staggered, righted himself, clenched his hands into fists, by way of a diversion, then kicked Fred in the bollocks. Fred buckled.

Wesley skipped past him and sprang into the van. Got the keys in the ignition, started the engine, roared off in a cloud of black exhaust fume.

Beale's Place, Wright's Road, St Stephen's Road. Bollocks to the One Way! Sharp right at the tip of the market. Back on to the Roman Road, screw the traffic, on to the pavement, over the zebra crossing, past the video shop, the church, the intersection, Mile End Park. Sharp left. Over the grass. Tyre tracks. Mud-cut. Foot flat. Brakes.

How long had he taken? He didn't know. He could see the canal, just below. Dirty, dark waters. Dank and littery.

Down with the tailgate! The eels were like flying fish. The air made them pump and shudder. Like spaghetti in a heated pan, boiling and bubbling.

'Get in there!' Wesley yelled at them. 'The Grand Union Canal, the Thames, the Channel, the Ant-bloody-arctic.'

A cluster of eels shuddered down into the grass, rippled on to the concrete path, and then One! Two! Three! Four! Five! Six! Seven! Eight! Into the canal.

One eel split from the others, turned right and darted towards some undergrowth. One stayed in the back of the van, smaller than the others and less agile. Wesley grabbed it by its tail. He swung it in his arms. He ran to the edge of the canal. He threw it. The eel made a whip-cracking motion in the air, shaped itself like a fancy ribbon, just untied from a box of something wrapped and precious. Then splosh! It was under.

Wesley stood by the canal for several minutes. He inspected his hands, he sniffed, he stopped shaking. He started walking. He walked. He walked. He passed by a fisherman. He stopped walking. He looked over his shoulder. 'Which way is it to the sea?' he asked casually. 'From here, I mean?'

The fisherman gave this question some consideration while sucking his tongue and rolling his rod between his two hands.

'I should think,' he said, eventually, 'I should think it's in the exact opposite direction from the one you're travelling.' Then he turned, stared down along the path Wesley had just trodden, and pointed.

EMERALD CITY

Jennifer Egan

Jennifer Egan (b. 1962) is an American writer. She has
published short fiction in the *New Yorker* and *Harper's*,
and her journalism appears frequently in the *New York
Times Magazine*. Egan's novel *A Visit from the Goon
Squad* won the 2011 Pulitzer Prize and the National Book
Critics Circle Award.

Rory knew before he came to New York what sort of life he
would have. He'd read about it in novels by hip young authors
who lived there. He saw the apartment, small but high-ceilinged,
a tall, sooty window with a fire escape twisting past a chemical-
pink sky. Nights in frantic clubs, mornings hunched over coffee in
the East Village, warming his hands on the cup, black pants, black
turtleneck, pointed black boots. He'd intended to snort cocaine,
but by the time he arrived, that was out. He drank instead.

He was a photographer's assistant, loading cameras all day,
holding up light meters, waving Polaroids until they were dry
enough to tear open. As he watched the models move, he sometimes
worried he was still too California. What could you do with sandy
blond hair – cut it off? Short hair was on the wane, at least for men.
So there it hung, golden, straight as paper, reminiscent of beaches
he'd never seen, being as he was from Chicago (in Chicago there
was the lake, but that didn't count). His other option was to gain
or lose some weight, but the starved look had lost its appeal – any
suggestion of illness was to be avoided. Beefy was the way to go;
not fat, just a classic paunch above the belt. But no matter how
much Rory ate, he stayed exactly the same. He took up smoking
instead, although it burned his throat.

Rory stubbed out his cigarette and checked to make sure the
lights were off in the darkroom. He was always the last to leave; his
boss, Vesuvi, would hand him the camera as soon as the last shot
was done and then swan out through the sea of film containers,

plastic cups, and discarded sheets of backdrop paper. Vesuvi was one of those people who always had somewhere to go. He was blessed with a marvelous paunch, which Rory tried not to admire too openly. He didn't want Vesuvi to get the wrong idea.

Rory swept the debris into bags, then he turned out the lights, locked up the studio, and headed down to the street. Twilight was his favorite hour – metal gates sliding down over storefronts, newspapers whirling from the sidewalk into the sky, an air of promise and abandonment. This was the way he'd expected New York to look, and he was thrilled when the city complied.

He took the subway uptown to visit Stacey, a failing model whom he adored against all reason. Stacey – when girls with names like Zane and Anouschka and Brid regularly slipped him their phone numbers during shoots. Stacey refused to change her name. 'If I make it,' she said, 'they'll be happy to call me whatever.' She never acknowledged that she was failing, though it was obvious. Rory longed to bring it up, to talk it over with her, but he was afraid to.

Stacey lay on her bed, shoes still on. A Diet Coke was on the table beside her. She weighed herself each morning, and when she was under 120, she allowed herself a real Coke that day.

'What happened at *Bazaar*?' Rory asked, perching on the edge of the bed. Stacey sat up and smoothed her hair.

'The usual,' she said. 'I'm too commercial.' She shrugged, but Rory could see she was troubled.

'And that was nothing,' Stacey continued. 'On my next go-see the guy kept looking at me and flipping back and forth through my book, and of course I'm thinking, Fantastic, he's going to hire me. So you know what he finally says? I'm not ugly enough. He says, "Beauty today is ugly beauty. Look at those girls, they're monsters – gorgeous, mythical monsters. If a girl isn't ugly, I won't use her." '

She turned to Rory. He saw tears in her eyes and felt helpless. 'What a bastard,' he said.

To his surprise, she began to laugh. She lay back on the bed and let the laughter shake her. 'I mean, here I am,' she said, 'killing myself to stay thin, hot-oiling my hair, getting my nails done, and what does he tell me? I'm not ugly enough!'

'It's crazy,' Rory said, watching Stacey uneasily. 'He's out of his mind.'

She sat up and rubbed her eyes. She looked slaphappy, the way she looked sometimes after a second gin and tonic. Eight months before, after a year's meticulous planning, she had bought her own ticket to New York from Cincinnati. And this was just the beginning; Stacey hoped to ride the wave of her success around the world: Paris, Tokyo, London, Bangkok. The shelves of her tiny apartment were cluttered with maps and travel books, and whenever she met a foreigner – it made no difference from where – she would carefully copy his address into a small leatherbound book, convinced it would not be long before she was everywhere. She was the sort of girl for whom nothing happened by accident, and it pained Rory to watch her struggle when all day in Vesuvi's studio he saw girls whose lives were accident upon accident, from their discovery in whatever shopping mall or hot dog stand to the startling, gaudy error of their faces.

'Rory,' Stacey said. 'Look at me a minute.'

He turned obediently. She was so close he could smell the warm, milky lotion she used on her face. 'Do you ever wish I was uglier?' she asked.

'God no,' Rory said, pulling away to see if she was joking. 'What a question, Stace.'

'Come on. You do this all day long.' She moved close to him again, and Rory found himself looking at the tiny pores on either side of her nose. He tried to think of the studio and the girls there, but when he concentrated on Stacey, they disappeared; and when he thought of the studio, he couldn't see Stacey anymore. It was a world she didn't belong to. As he watched Stacey's tense, expectant face, Rory felt a dreadful power; it would take so little, he thought, to crush her.

'Never mind,' she said when Rory didn't answer. 'I don't want to know.'

She stood and crossed the room, then leaned over and pressed her palms to the floor. She had been a gymnast in high school and was still remarkably limber. This limberness delighted Rory in a way that almost shamed him – in bed she would sit up, legs straight in front of her, then lean over and rest her cheek against her shins. Casually, as if it were nothing! Rory didn't dare tell her how this excited him; if she were aware of it, then it wouldn't be the same.

Stacey stood up, flushed and peaceful again. 'Let's get out of here,' she said.

Her apartment was right off Columbus, a street Rory scorned but one that nevertheless mesmerized him. He and Stacey walked arm in arm, peering into the windows of restaurants as eagerly as diners peered out of them. It was as if they had all been told some friend might pass this way tonight and were keeping their eyes peeled.

'Where should we go?' Stacey asked.

Rory cracked his knuckles one by one. The question made him edgy, as if there were some right answer he should know. Where were the people who mattered? Occasionally Rory would be stricken with a sense that they had been exactly where he was only moments before, but had just left. The worst part was, he didn't know who they were, exactly. The closest he came was in knowing people who seemed to know; his roommate, Charles, a food stylist who specialized in dollops, and of course Vesuvi. Vesuvi was his main source.

They headed downtown, enjoying the last warm days of fall, the pleasant seediness of Seventh Avenue. They passed intersections where patches of old cobblestones were exposed beneath layers of tar, relics of another New York Rory dimly remembered from novels: carriages and top hats, reputations and insults.

'Rory,' Stacey said, 'do you feel more something, now that you've gotten successful?'

Rory turned to her in surprise. 'Who says I'm successful?'

'But you are!'

'I'm no one. I'm Vesuvi's assistant.'

Stacey seemed shocked. 'That's not no one,' she said.

Rory grinned. It was a funny conversation. 'Yeah?' he said. 'Then who is it?'

Stacey pondered this a moment. Suddenly she laughed – the same helpless way she had laughed on the bed, as if the world were funny by accident. Still laughing, she said, 'Vesuvi's assistant.'

At Stacey's suggestion they took a cab to a TriBeCa bistro where Vesuvi often went. It was probably expensive, but Rory had just been paid – what the hell, he'd buy Stacey dinner. Maybe he would even call Charles to see if he was back from LA, where he'd been styling all week for Sara Lee. Rory didn't envy Charles his job, although he made good money; sometimes he was up half the night, using tweezers to paste sesame seeds onto hamburger buns or mixing and coloring the salty dough that looked more like ice cream in pictures than real ice cream did. Rory had been amazed to learn that in breakfast cereal shots it was standard to use Elmer's glue instead of milk. 'It's whiter,' Charles had explained. 'Also it pours more slowly and doesn't soak the flakes.' Rory had found this disturbing in a way he still didn't quite understand.

Inside the restaurant, Rory spotted Vesuvi himself at a large round table in back. Or rather, Vesuvi spotted him, and called out with a heartiness that could only mean he was bored with his present company. With a grand sweep of his arm he beckoned them over.

The waiters pulled up chairs, and Rory and Stacey sat down. Stacey ordered a gin and tonic. Rory could see she was nervous – the girls at the table were faces you saw around a lot: redheaded Daphne, Inge with her guppy-face, others whose names he'd forgotten. What distressed him was seeing Anouschka, a moody girl whose journey from some dour Siberian town to the height of New York fashion seemed to have happened in an afternoon. Once, she had lingered at the studio while Rory cleaned up after work, humming a Fine Young Cannibals song and flipping aimlessly through his copy of *The Great Gatsby*. 'My father is a professor,' she told him. 'He teaches this book.' 'In Russian?' Rory asked incredulously. Anouschka laughed. 'Sure,' she said, curling the word in her accent. 'Why not?'

Outside the studio, Rory and Anouschka had hovered uncertainly in the dusk. Rory was supposed to meet Stacey, but felt awkward saying so to Anouschka. Instead, he blundered forward and hailed a cab, leaving Anouschka standing on the curb, then paid the driver three blocks later and took the subway to Stacey's. He arrived shaking, mystified by his own idiotic behavior.

Anouschka had frightened him ever since; last week, while he was loading Vesuvi's camera, she had casually reported the numerical value of her IQ, then subjected him to a humiliating quiz on the Great Books. 'Have you read much Dostoeysky?' she called up the rickety ladder, where Rory was grappling with a

light. 'The Brothers Karamazov? No? What about War and Peace?'
When Rory called back down that War and Peace was by Tolstoy,
Anouschka colored deeply, stalked back onto the set, and did not
speak to him again, Rory felt terrible; he'd never read a word of
War and Peace. He even considered confessing this to Anouschka
after the shoot as she grumpily gathered her things. But what the
hell, he decided, let her think he was brilliant.

Now Rory looked at Vesuvi sprawled amid the models:
sphinxlike, olive-skinned, his close-cropped beard peppered with
gray, though his wild curly hair showed no sign of it. He was short,
and wore high-heeled boots that Rory found spectacular. Vesuvi
was a man of few words, yet he often gave the impression of being
on the verge of speech. Conversation would proceed around him
tentatively, ready to be swept aside at any moment by whatever
Vesuvi might say. Rory watched him adoringly over his glass of
bourbon, unable to believe he was sitting with Vesuvi after all the
times he had watched him glide away in cabs, feeling as if most of
what mattered in the world were disappearing with him. Yet Rory
wasn't entirely happy: everyone at the table was watching him,
especially Anouschka, and he felt that in return for being included,
he was expected to do something stunning.

He glanced at the next table, where conversation seemed more
lively. It was a group of downtown types, the men like deposed
medieval kings in their bobbed haircuts and gigantic silver
medallions. During his first month in New York, Rory had gone out
with a girl like the ones at that table – Dave, she'd called herself.
She wore nothing but black: bulky sweaters, short loose skirts,
woolen tights, and round-toed combat boots. The thrill of the
relationship for Rory lay mostly in watching Dave undress – there
was something tremendous in the sight of her slender white form
emerging from all of that darkness. Once she finished undressing,
Rory often wished she would put part of the outfit back on, or
better yet, dress completely again and start over.

Vesuvi was eyeing Stacey. 'You look familiar,' he said. 'Did I use
you for something?'

'Once,' she said. 'Four and a half months ago.'

'Right, I remember now. It was that … ' He waved a languid
hand, which meant he had no idea.

'For *Elle*,' Stacey said. 'Bow ties.' It had been her best job, and she was crushed when the pictures the magazine printed had failed to include her head. To use them in her book would look desperate, her agent said, so she kept them pasted to her bathroom mirror. Rory looked at them while he was shaving.

Vesuvi sat back, satisfied. The question of whether or not he had worked with a girl always troubled him, Rory had noticed, as if the world were divided between girls he had shot and girls he hadn't, and not knowing which side a girl was on caused a cosmic instability.

'You worked for *Elle*?' Anouschka asked Stacey.

'Once,' Stacey said.

'So far,' Rory quickly added.

Anouschka glanced at him, and then at Stacey, with the same startled look she'd worn when Rory left her on the curb. He felt guilty all over again.

'You must've worked for them, too,' Stacey said to Anouschka, who nodded absently.

'I heard you got a cover,' someone said.

'Yes,' Anouschka said dully. Then she seemed to take heart, as if hearing this news for the first time. 'Yes!' she said, grinning suddenly. 'I am the cover for December.'

Rory felt Stacey move in her chair. Anouschka lit a cigarette and smoked; exotic, dragonlike, her black hair tumbling past her shoulders. For a moment all of them watched her, and against his will even Rory was moved by a face so familiar from pictures. Never mind what you thought of Anouschka; she was *that woman* – you recognized her. There was an odd pleasure in this, like finding something you'd been looking for.

'When do you leave for Tokyo?' Anouschka asked Inge.

'Next week,' Inge said. 'Have you been?'

'Two years ago,' Anouschka said in her heavy accent. 'It's okay, but when you take the morning airplanes, you see the Japanese men are coughing their lungs into the trash cans. They smoke like crazy,' she concluded, wagging her cigarette between two fingers. Rory listened miserably; poor Stacey was barely surviving in New York and here was Anouschka, who not only had been to Japan but had the luxury of complaining about it. He rattled the ice in his glass and impatiently cleared his throat.

Anouschka glanced at him and turned serious. 'Still,' she said, 'the culture of Japan is quite important.'

'The culture?' Inge said.

'You know, the museums and this sort of thing.'

Vesuvi, who had seemed on the verge of sleep, roused himself and turned to Anouschka. 'You, inside a museum?' he said. 'That I don't see.'

The girl looked startled.

'You must have gone there on location,' he said.

'Not location! I went for fun. How do you know what I do?'

Vesuvi shrugged and sat back in his chair, his lazy eyes filled with amusement. Anouschka blushed to the neck; the pink tinge seemed at odds with her extravagant face. Helplessly she turned to Stacey. 'You have been to Japan?' she asked.

'I wish.'

'But Milano, yes?'

'No,' Stacey said, and Rory noticed with surprise that her drink was almost gone. Normally one cocktail would last Stacey an entire night, her sips were so tiny.

'Paris?'

Stacey shook her head, and Rory noticed a change in Anouschka's face as she sensed her advantage. The others were quiet. Vesuvi sat forward, looking from Anouschka to Stacey with great interest, as if they were posing for him.

'You never worked in Paris? I think everyone has worked in Paris.'

'I've never been to Paris,' Stacey said.

'London? Munich?' Anouschka turned to the other girls, confirming her surprise. Though she didn't glance at Rory, he sensed that all this was meant for him, and felt a strange, guilty collusion with her. He saw Stacey's hand shake as she lifted her glass, and was overcome with sudden and absolute hatred for Anouschka – he had never hated anyone this way. He stared at her, the gush of hair, the braised-looking mouth; she was ugly, as the man had said today. Ugly and beautiful. Confused, Rory looked away.

'So,' Anouschka said, 'what places you have been?'

Stacey didn't answer at first. She looked double-jointed in her chair, heaped like a marionette.

'I've been to New York,' she said.

There was a beat of silence. 'New York,' Anouschka said.

Vesuvi started to laugh. He had a loud, explosive laugh that startled Rory at first. He had never heard it before. 'New York!' Vesuvi cried. 'That's priceless.'

Stacey smiled. She seemed as surprised as everyone else.

Vesuvi rocked forward in his chair, so that his heavy boots pounded the floor. 'I love it,' he said. 'New York. What a perfect comeback.' Anouschka just stared at him.

It began to seem very funny, all of a sudden.

A chuckle passed through the group like a current. Rory found himself laughing without knowing why; it was enough for him that Vesuvi had a reason. His boss gazed at Stacey in the soft-eyed way he looked at models when a shoot was going well. 'It's a hell of a place, New York,' he said. 'No?'

'The best,' Stacey said.

'But she has gone only here!' Anouschka protested. 'How does she know?'

'Oh, she knows,' Rory said. He felt reckless, dizzy with the urge to make Anouschka angry. 'You don't get it, do you?' he said.

'What can I get when there is nothing?' she retorted. But she looked uncertain.

Vesuvi dabbed with a napkin at his heavy-lidded eyes. 'Next time you go to New York,' he told Stacey, 'take me with you.'

This was too much for Anouschka. 'Fuck you!' she cried, jumping to her feet. 'I am in New York. You are in New York. *Here is New York!*'

But laughter had seized the table, and Anouschka's protests only made it worse. She stood helplessly while everyone laughed, Rory hooting all the louder to keep her in her place.

'That's it,' she said. 'Goodbye.'

'Go back to Japan,' Rory cried. He had trouble catching his breath.

Anouschka fixed her eyes on him. Her makeup made them look burned at the rims, and the irises were a bright, clear green. He thought she might do something crazy – he'd heard she once punctured an ex-boyfriend's upper lip by hurling a fork at him. He stopped laughing and gripped the table's edge, poised for sudden movement. To his astonishment, the charred-looking eyes filled with tears. 'I hate you, Rory,' she said.

She yanked her bag from under the table and hoisted it onto her shoulder. Her long hair stuck to her wet cheeks as she struggled to free her jacket from the chair. Rory thought of his high school lunchroom: girls stalking out, mad, clattering trays, their long, skinny legs skittering on high-heeled shoes. He felt a pang of nostalgia. She was just a kid, Anouschka – so much younger than he was.

'Hey,' Vesuvi said, standing and putting his arms around Anouschka. 'Hey, we're just having a joke.'

'Go to hell with your joke.' She turned her face away so that no one could see her crying.

Vesuvi stroked her back. 'Hey now,' he said.

Chastened, the group sat in guilty silence. Stacey and Rory traded a look and stood up. No one protested as they slid their jackets on, but when Rory opened his wallet to pay for their drinks, Vesuvi winced and waved it away. Anouschka still clung to him, her face buried in his neck.

Vesuvi spoke to Stacey in a lowered voice. 'I've got something coming up you'd be perfect for,' he said. 'Who are you with again?'

Stacey told him the name of her agency, barely able to contain her joy. Rory listened unhappily; Vesuvi said this all the time to girls, and forgot the next minute. It was just a pleasant salutation.

They left the restaurant and headed toward the East Village. Rory longed to reach for Stacey's hand, but she seemed far away from him now, lost in her thoughts. Outside a market, a boy was perched on a stool cutting the heads off beans. A barber swept thick tufts of dark hair into one corner of his shop. From an overhead window came music, and Rory craned his neck to catch a glimpse of someone's arm, a lighted cigarette. The famliarity of it all was sweet and painful to him. He searched the dark shopfronts for something, some final thing at the core of everything else, but he found just his own reflection and Stacey's. Their eyes met in the glass, then flicked away. And it struck him that this was New York: a place that glittered from a distance even when you reached it.

*

They climbed the four flights of steps to Rory's apartment. A slit of light shone under the door, which meant Charles was back. They found him standing at the kitchen table, wiping a slab of red meat with a paper towel. He had a blowtorch plugged into the wall, and a dismantled smoke alarm lay at his feet.

'You poor thing,' Stacey said, kissing him on the cheek. 'You never stop working.'

Charles's mouth was like a cat's, small and upturned at the corners. It made him seem happy even when he wasn't. 'Meat is my weak point,' he said. 'I've got a job tomorrow doing steak.'

He was prematurely balding, and Rory admired the look of hardship and triumph this gave him. Lately he'd searched his own hairline for signs of recession, but the blond surfer's mane seemed even more prolific Most cruel of all, it was Charles who'd been born and raised in Santa Cruz.

'Here goes,' Charles said, firing up the blowtorch. They watched as he moved the flame slowly over the meat, back and forth as if he were mowing a lawn. Its surface turned a pale gray. When the entire side was done, he flipped the steak over and lightly cooked its other side.

'Ugh,' said Stacey. 'It's still completely raw.'

'Wait,' Charles said.

He held a long metal spit to the flame until it glowed red. Then he pressed the spit to the meat. There was a hiss, a smell of cooking, and when he lifted the spit, a long black stripe branded the steak. He heated the spit several more times and pressed it to the meat at parallel intervals. Soon it was indistinguishable from a medium-rare steak straight off the grill. Rory felt an irrational surge of appetite, a longing to eat the meat in spite of knowing it was raw and cold.

Stacey opened the refrigerator. Rory always kept a supply of Cokes for her in there; Diet, of course, but also some regulars in case she had earned one that day and not yet rewarded herself. To his surprise, she pulled out a can of regular now.

'What the hell,' she said. 'I mean, really, what difference does it make?'

Rory stared at her. She had never said anything like this before. 'What about Vesuvi?' he asked, regretting it even as he spoke.

'Vesuvi won't hire me. You know it perfectly well.'

She was smiling at him, and Rory felt as if she had peered into the lying depths of his soul. 'Vesuvi doesn't know shit,' he said, but it sounded lame even to himself.

Stacey slid open the window and climbed out onto the fire escape. The sky was a strange, sulfurous yellow – beautiful, yet seemingly disconnected from nature. The shabby tree behind Rory's building was empty of leaves, and made a pattern of cracked glass against the sky. Stacey drank her Coke in tiny, careful sips. Rory stood helplessly inside the window, watching her. He needed to say something to her, he knew that, but he wasn't sure how.

He shook a cigarette from his pack and placed it in his mouth. Charles was working on a second steak. 'By the way,' Charles said, pointing with his chin at a spot near Rory's head, 'I baked us a cake – a real one.'

Rory turned in surprise and lifted a plate from above the refrigerator. It was a tall, elegant cake with giant dollops of whipped cream along its edges. 'Charles,' Rory said, confused, 'haven't you been doing this all week?'

'Yeah,' Charles said, 'but always for strangers. And never to eat.'

He bent over the steak, his blowtorch hissing on the damp meat. He looked embarrassed, as if his preference for real cake were a weakness he rarely confided. Charles's honesty shamed Rory – he said what he felt, not caring how it sounded.

Rory climbed out the window and sat beside Stacey. The bars of the fire escape felt cold through his jeans. Stacey held her Coke in one hand and took Rory's hand in the other. They looked at the yellow sky and held hands tightly, as if something were about to happen.

Rory's heart beat quickly. 'So maybe it doesn't work,' he said. 'The modeling. Maybe that just won't happen.'

He searched her face for some sign of surprise, but there was none. She watched him calmly, and for the first time Rory felt that Stacey was older than he, that her mind contained things he knew nothing of. She stood up and handed her Coke to Rory. Then she grasped the railing of the fire escape and lifted her body into a handstand. Rory held his breath, watching in alarmed amazement as the slender wand of her body swayed against the yellow sky. She had no trouble balancing, and hovered there for what seemed a long time before finally bending at the waist, lowering her feet, and standing straight again.

'If it doesn't work,' she said, 'then I'll see the world some other way.'

She took Rory's face in her hands and kissed him on the mouth – hard, with the fierce, tender urgency of someone about to board a train. Then she turned and looked at the sky. Rory stared at her, oddly frightened to think that she would do it, she would find some way. He pictured Stacey in a distant place, looking back on him, on this world of theirs as if it were a bright, glittering dream she had once believed in.

'Take me with you,' he said.

THE SNOBS

Muriel Spark

Muriel Spark (1918–2006) was a Scottish novelist best known for her novel, *The Prime of Miss Jean Brodie*. In 2008 *The Times* named her in its list of the '50 Greatest British Writers Since 1945'. Spark was twice shortlisted for the Man Booker Prize and was awarded the Golden PEN Award in 1998 by English PEN for her services to literature. She became Dame Commander of the Order of the British Empire in 1993.

Snob: A person who sets too much value on social standing, wishing to be associated with the upper class and their mores, and treating those viewed as inferior with condescension and contempt – *Chambers Dictionary*.

I feel bound to quote the above definition, it so well fits the Ringer-Smith couple whom I knew in the nineteen-fifties and of whom I have since met variations and versions enough to fill me with wonder. Snobs are really amazing. They mainly err in failing to fool the very set of people they are hoping to be accepted by, and above all, to seem to belong to, to be taken for. They may live in a democratic society – it does nothing to help. Nothing.

Of the Ringer-Smith couple, he, Jake, was the more snobbish. She, at least, had a certain natural serenity of behaviour which she herself never questioned. She was in fact rather smug. Her background was of small land-owning farmers and minor civil servants. She, Marion, was stingy, stingy as hell. Jake also had a civil service background and, on the mother's side, a family of fruit export-import affairs which had not left her very well off, the inheritance having been absorbed by the male members of the family. Jake and Marion were a fairly suitable match. He was slightly the shorter of the two. Both were skinny. They had no children. Skeletons in the family cupboard do nothing to daunt the true snob, in fact they provoke a certain arrogance, and this was the case with Jake. A family scandal on a national scale had grown to an international one. A spectacular bank robbery with murder on the part of a brother had resulted in the family name being reduced to a byword in every household. The delinquent Ringer-Smith and his associates had escaped to a safe exile in South America leaving Jake and his ageing mother to face the music of the press and TV reporters. Nobody would have taken it out on them in the normal way if it had not been for the contempt with which they treated police, journalists, interrogators, functionaries of the law and the public in general. They put on airs suggesting that they were untouchably 'good family', and they generally carried on as if they were earls and marquises instead of ordinary middle-class people. No earl, no marquis at present alive would in fact be so haughty unless he were completely out of his mind or perhaps an unfortunate drug addict or losing gambler.

I was staying with some friends at a château near Dijon when the Ringer-Smiths turned up. This was in the nineties. I hardly recognized them. The Ringer-Smiths had not just turned up at the château, they were found by Anne, bewildered, outside the village shop, puzzling over a map, uncertain of their way to anywhere. Warming towards their plight as she always would towards those in trouble, Anne invited these lost English people for a cup of tea at the château where they could work out their route.

Anne and Monty, English themselves, had lived in the château for the last eight years. It was a totally unexpected inheritance from the last member of a distant branch of Monty's family. The house and small fortune that went with it came to him in his early fifties as an enormous surprise. He had been a shoe salesman and a bus driver, among other things. Anne had been a stockbroker's secretary. Their two children, both girls, were married and away. The 'fairy tale' story of their inheritance was in the newspapers for a day, but it wasn't everybody who read the passing news.

Monty was out when Anne brought home the Ringer-Smiths. I was watching the television – some programme which now escapes me for ever due to the shock of seeing those people. Anne, tall, merry, blonded-up and carrying her sixties well, took herself off to the kitchen to put on the kettle. She had made the sitting-room as much like England as possible.

'Who does this place belong to?' Jake inquired of me as soon as Anne was out of the room. Obviously, he had not recognized me in the present context, although I felt Marion's eyes upon me in a penetrating stare of puzzlement, of quasi-remembrance.

'It belongs,' I said, 'to the lady who invited you to tea.'

'Oh!' he said.

'Haven't we met?' Marion was speaking to me.

'Yes, you have.' I made myself known.

'What brings you here?' said Jake outright.

'The same as brings you here. I was invited.'

Anne returned with the tea, served with a silver tea service and pretty china cups. She carried the tray while a young girl who was helping in the house followed with hot water and a plate of biscuits.

'You speak English very well,' Jake said.

'Oh, we are English,' said Anne. 'But we live in France now. My husband inherited the château from his family on his mother's side, the Martineaus.'

'Oh, of course,' said Jake.

The factor came in from the farm and took a cup of tea standing up. He addressed Anne as 'Madame'.

Anne was already regretting her impulse in asking the couple to tea. They said very little but just sat on. She was afraid they would miss the last bus to the station. Looking at me, she said, 'The last bus goes at six, doesn't it?'

I said to Marion, 'You don't want to miss the last bus.'

'Could we see round the château?' said Marion. 'The guidebook says it's fourteenth century.'

'Well, not all of it is.' said Anne. 'But today is a bit difficult. We don't, you know, open the house to the public. We live in it.'

'I'm sure we've met,' said Marion to Anne, as if this took care of their catching the last bus – a point which was not lost on Anne. Kindly though she was I knew she hated to have to ferry people by car to the station and take on other chores she was not prepared for. I could see, already in Anne's mind, the thought: 'I have to get rid of these people or they'll stay for dinner and then all night. They are château-grabbers.'

Anne had often lamented to me about the château-grabbers of her later life. People who didn't want to know her when she was obscure and a bus driver's wife now wanted to know her intimately. Monty didn't care much about this, one way or another. But then the work of organizing meals and entertaining in style fell more on Anne than on Monty, who mostly spent his time helping the factor in the grounds, game-keeping and forest-clearing.

Anne could see that the English couple she had invited in 'for a cup of tea' were clingers, climbers, general nuisances, and she especially cast a look of desperation at me when Marion Ringer-Smith said, 'I'm sure we've met.'

'You think so?' Anne said. She had got up and was leading the way to the back door. 'This is the *Cour des Adieux*,' she said; 'it leads quicker to your bus stop.' Marion stooped and took a cake as if it was her last chance of ever eating a cake again.

I was at this moment coming to the end of a novel I was writing. Anne had offered me the peace and quiet of French château life and the informality of her own life-style which made it an ideal arrangement. She had also undertaken to type out the novel from any handwritten manuscripts on to a word-processor. But now at a quarter to six, I could see the rest of our afternoon's plans slipping away.

I doubted that Marion had indeed seen Anne before. It was by some mental process of transference that she had picked on Anne. The one she had actually met was myself, but she wasn't very much aware of it. After a gap of forty years, she remembered very little of me.

Jake Ringer-Smith asked if he could use the bathroom. Oh, you bore, I thought. Why don't you *go*? There are trees and thick bushes all the way down the drive for you to pee on. But no, he had to be shown the bathroom. It was nearly ten minutes to their bus time. Jake kicked his backpack over to his wife and said, 'Take this, will you?'

'I would really like to see round the château,' Marion said, 'while we're here and since we've come all this way.'

I had come across this situation before. There are people who will hold up a party of tired and worn fellow travellers just because *they* have to see a pulpit. There are people who will arrive an hour late for dinner with the excuse that they *had* to see over some art gallery on the way. Marion was very much one of those. If challenged she would have thought nothing of pointing out that, after all, she had paid a plane fare to arrive at where she was. I remember Marion's shapeless cheesecloth dress and her worn sandals and Jake's baggy, ostentatiously patched, grubby trousers, their avidity to get on intimate terms with the lady of the house, to be invited to supper and, no doubt, to spend the night. I was really sorry for Anne who, I was aware, was sorry for herself and most of all regretting her own impulsive invitation to a cup of tea in her house.

Anne kept a soup kitchen in a building some way from the house, beyond a vegetable garden. She was pledged, I knew, to be there and help whenever possible, at six-thirty every evening. Laboriously, she explained this to the Ringer-Smiths. '… otherwise I'd have been glad to show you the house, not that there's much to see.'

'Soup kitchen!' said Jake. 'May we join it for a bowl of soup? Then perhaps we can stretch out our sleeping-bag for the night under one of your charming archways and see the house tomorrow.'

Does this sound like a nightmare? It was a nightmare. Nothing could throw off these people.

Down at the soup kitchen that evening, dispensing slabs of bread and cheese with bowls of tomato soup, I was not surprised to see the Ringer-Smiths appear.

'We belong to the lower orders,' he said to me with an exaggeratedly selfeffacing grin that meant. 'We do not belong to any lower orders and just see how grand we really are – *we* don't care what we look like or what company we keep. We are Us.'

In fact they looked positively shifty among the genuine skin-and-bone tramps and hairy drop-outs and bulging bag-ladies. I dished out their portions to them without a smile. They had missed the last bus. Somehow, Anne and Monty had to arrange for them to have a bedroom for the night. 'We stayed at the château Leclaire de Martineau at Dijon' I could hear them telling their friends.

Before breakfast I advised Anne and Monty to make themselves scarce. 'Otherwise,' I said, 'you'll never get rid of them. Leave them to me.'

'I'm sure,' said Marion, 'I've met Anne before. But I can't tell where.'

'She has been a cook in many houses,' I said. 'And Monty has been a butler.'

'A cook and a butler?' said Jake.

'Yes, the master and mistress are away from home at present.'

'But she *told me she was the owner*,' Marion said, indicating the dining-room door with her head.

'Oh no, you must be mistaken.'

'But I'm sure she said—'

'Not at all,' I said. 'What a pity you can't see over the château. Such lovely pictures. But the Comtesse will be here at any moment. I don't know how you will explain yourselves. So far as I know you haven't been invited.'

'Oh we have,' said Jake. 'The servants begged us to stay. So typical, posing as the lord and lady of the manor! But it's getting late, we'll miss the bus.'

They were off within four minutes, tramping down the drive with their bulging packs.

Anne and Monty were delighted when I told them how it was done. Anne was sure, judging from a previous experience, that the intruders had planned to stay for a week.

'What else can you do with people like that?' said Anne.

'Put them in a story if you are me,' I said. 'And sell the story.'

'Can they sue?'

'Let them sue,' I said. 'Let them go ahead, stand up, and say Yes, that was Us.'

'An eccentric couple. They took the soap with them,' said Anne.

Monty went off about his business with a smile. So did Anne. And I, too. Or so I thought.

It was eleven-thirty, two hours later that morning, when, looking out of the window of my room as I often do when I am working on a novel, I saw them again under one of the trees bordering a lawn. They were looking up towards the house.

I had no idea where Monty and Anne were at that moment, nor could I think how to locate the factor, Raoul, or his wife, Marie-Louise. This was a disturbance in the rhythm of my morning's work, but I decided to go down and see what was the matter. As soon as they saw me Marion said, 'Oh hallo. We decided it was uncivil of us to leave without seeing the lady of the house and paying our respects.'

'We'll wait till the Comtesse arrives,' Jake stated.

'Well, you're unlucky,' I said. 'I believe there's word come through that she'll be away for a week.'

'That's all right,' said Marion. 'We can spare a week.'

'Only civil ...' said Jake.

I managed to alert Anne before she saw them. They were very cool to her when she did at last appear before them. 'The Comtesse would, I'm sure, be offended if we left without a word of thanks,' said Jake.

'Not at all,' said Anne. 'In fact, you *have to go*.'

'Not so,' said Marion.

Raoul tackled them, joined by Monty. Marion had already reclaimed their bedroom. 'As the beds had to be changed anyway,' she said, 'we may as well stay on. We don't mind eating down at the shed.' By this she meant the soup kitchen. 'We are not above eating with the proletariat,' said Jake.

Raoul and I searched the house, every drawer, for a key to the door of their bedroom. Eventually we found one that fitted and succeeded in locking them out. Monty took their packs and dumped them outside the gates of the château. These operations took place while they were feeding in the soup kitchen. We all five (Marie-Louise had joined us) confronted them and told them what we had done.

What happened to them after that none of us quite knows. We do know that they went to retrieve their bags and found themselves locked out by the factor. Anne received a letter, correctly addressed to her as the Comtesse, from Jake, indignantly complaining about the treatment they had received at the hands of the 'staff'.

'Something,' wrote Jake, 'told me not to accept their invitation. I knew instinctively that they were not one of us. I should have listened to my instincts. People like them are such frightful snobs.'

THIRD FLOOR RISING

Hilary Mantel

Hilary Mantel (b. 1952) is a British writer who has twice been awarded the Man Booker Prize. She won her first Booker for the 2009 novel, *Wolf Hall*, and her second, in 2012, for *Bring Up the Bodies*, making her the first woman to receive the award twice. She has published twelve novels and one collection of short stories, *Learning to Talk*.

The summer of my eighteenth birthday I had my first job. It was to fill the time between leaving school and going away to university in London. The previous summer I'd been old enough to work, but I had to stay at home and mind the children, while my mother pursued her glittering career.

For most of the years until I was sixteen, my mother had devoted herself to the care of a sick child. First it was me, until I went to senior school. Then I got abruptly better, by an act of will on my mother's part. My high fevers ceased, or ceased to be noticed, or if they were noticed they stopped being interesting. My youngest brother, his struggles for breath and his night-time cough, were elected to my old place in the household's economy. In my case I had been to school sporadically, but my brother didn't go at all. He played by himself in the garden under a pewter sky, with the fugitive glitter of snow behind it. He lay on his daybed in the room with the television blaring, and turned the pages of a book. One evening we were watching the news when our whole room lit up with a sick white light, and a bolt of ball lightning ripped the lower limbs from the poplar tree and blew the glass from the window frame, whump, fist of God. The shards were strewed over his crocheted blanket, the dog howled, the rain blew into the wreckage of the room and the neighbours squeaked and gibbered in the streets.

A short time after this my mother answered an advertisement for a saleswoman on the fashion floor at Affleck & Brown, which was a small, cramped, old-fashioned department store in Manchester. She had to walk to the station and then travel by train, then walk again to Oldham Street. This was a wonder to me, because I thought she'd given up going out. To do the job she had to have white blouses and black skirts. She bought some at C & A, and this amazed me too, because in our house we got our clothes by less straightforward methods than purchase: by a process of transmogrification, whereby cardigans were unravelled and reappeared as woollen berets and collars were wrenched off to extend hems and what were armholes for the stout became leg holes for the lean. When I was seven I'd had my winter coats made out of two that had belonged to my godmother. Pockets, lapels, everything was miniaturised: except the buttons, which were the originals, and stood out like banqueting plates, or targets for an arrow on my pigeon chest.

My mother had been to school in an age when most people didn't take exams, and she hadn't much to put on her application form. But she got the job, and soon personal disasters began to overtake the people who had appointed her; with them out of the way, she was promoted first to deputy and then to manageress of her department. She developed an airy meringue of white-blonde hair, very tall shoes – not just high heels but little boosts under the soles – and an airy way of talking and gesturing; and she began to encourage her staff to lie about their ages, which seemed to suggest she was lying about her own. She came home late and quarrelsome, with something unlikely in her crocodile bag. It might be a bag of crinkle-cut chips, which tasted of grease and air, a pack of frozen beefburgers which, under the grill, bubbled up with oily spots the grey-yellow colour of a Manchester smog. In time the chip pan got banned, to save the paintwork and to make a class statement, but by then I was living up the road with my friend Anne Terese, and what the others got for rations was something I preferred not to think about.

When I was seventeen I was as unprepared for life as if I had spent my childhood on a mountainside minding goats. I was given to contemplation of nature, strolling about in the woods and fields. I was given to going to Stockport library and getting seven big books at a time about Latin American revolutions; waiting for an hour in the rain for the bus home, shifting the books at my feet and sometimes picking them up in expectation of a bus and cradling them in my arms, relishing their public dirt-edged pages, and the anticipation of finding inside them urgent notes from small-town obsessives: 'NOT Guatemala!!!!' pencilled in the margin, or rather incised into the page with a stub of graphite and the cedar's ragged edge. In our house, too, we never had a pencil sharpener. If you wanted a point you went to my mother and she held the pencil in her fist and swiped chunks off it with the bread knife.

It wasn't the fault of my education that I was so unworldly, because most of my contemporaries were normal, for their time and place and class. But they seemed to be made of a denser, plusher substance than myself. You could imagine them being women, and having upholstery and airing cupboards. There was air in the spaces between my bones, smoke between my ribs. Pavements hurt my feet. Salt sought out ulcers in my tongue. I was given to prodigious vomiting for no reason. I was cold when I woke up and I thought I would go on being it, always. So later, when I was twenty-four and I was offered a chance to migrate to the tropics, I seized on it because I thought now, now at least I will never be cold again.

My holiday job was secured before the interview; who, at Affleck & Brown, would have turned down the daughter of my ever-popular mother? But it was a formality: the mild personnel officer in his dun-coloured suit, in a back office so brown that I thought I had never seen the colour before, in every variety of tobacco spit and jaundice, every texture of Bakelite and Formica. Here I entered, fresh as 1970 in my little cotton shift, and here I was drawn backwards to the fifties, to the brown world of the National Insurance Card, and the yellowed notice from the Wages Council peeling from the distempered wall. Here I was wished luck and walked out on to the carpet, into the public world. 'Draws your feet, this carpet,' said a voice from between the rails.

It came from a shuddering white face, from wagging jowls, from a slow rolling mass of flesh, fiercely corseted inside a dress of stretched black polyester: corseted into the shape of a bulbous flower vase, and the skin with the murky sheen of carnation water two days old. Reek of armpits, rattling cough; these were my colleagues. life in the stores had destroyed them. They had chronic sniffles from the dust and bladder infections from the dirty lavatories. Their veins bulged through elastic stockings. They lived on £15 per week. They didn't work on commission, so they never sold anything if they could help it. Their rheumy malice drove customers back to the escalators and down into the street.

The personnel officer set me to work in the department next to my mother. I was able to study her in action, wafting across the floor in whatever creation she was wearing that day; she was no longer in subfusc, but picked her garments from her own stock. She had developed a manner that was gracious, not to say condescending, combined with a tip-tilted flirtatiousness that she tried out on the wilting gays who were almost the only men in the store; she was liked by her staff – her girls, as she called them – for her prettiness and high spirits.

They didn't seem, the girls, quite so decrepit as the ones who worked for my department, although I soon found out that they had a variety of intractable personal problems, which were meat and drink to my mother, which were in fact what she had instead of meat and drink, because now it was her role in life to stay a size 10, pretend she was a size 8, and so set an example to womankind. The girls had divorces, bad debts, vitamin deficiencies, premenstrual tension, and children with fits and deformities. Their houses were given to subsidence and collapse, floods and moulds, and it seemed to me that they specialised in obsolescent diseases such as smallpox or conditions such as scrapie that only a few morbid-minded people like me had heard of in those days. The worse off they were, the more disorderly and hopeless their lives, the more my mother doted on them. Even today, thirty years on, many of them keep in touch with her. 'Mrs D rang,' she will say. 'The IRA have bombed her house again and her daughter's been engulfed in a tidal wave, but she asked to be remembered to you.' At Christmas, and on the occasions of her falsified birthdays, these girls would buy my mother coloured glass ornaments, and adjuncts to the good life, like soda siphons. They were inner-city women with flat Manchester voices, but my mother and the other department heads talked in peculiar purse-lipped ways designed not to let their vowels show.

I was not employed by the store itself, but by a 'shop-in-shop' called English Lady. There were women, tending to the elderly, who wanted what it offered: dress-and-coat ensembles that I called wedding uniforms, summer frocks and 'separates' in artificial fabrics and pastel shades, washable and easy-iron. In those days people still went out in April to buy a summer coat of pink showerproof poplin, or a light wool with a shadow check, and they bought blazers, boleros and blouses, and trouser ensembles with long tunic tops under which they wore stockings and suspenders, the bumps of the suspenders showing through the polyester. In winter English Lady specialised in camel coats, which their wearers dutifully renewed every few years, expecting exactly the same style and getting it. There were also – for the winter stock was coming in, long before I left for London – coats called llamas, which were an unhealthy silver-grey, and shaggy, like hair shirts turned out, but hair shirts with pockets. For the autumn also there were bristling tweeds, and lumpen stinking sheepskins which we chained to the rails, because English Lady feared for their safety. Herding them was heavy work; they exhaled with a grunt when they were touched, and jostled for *Lebensraum*, puffing out their bulk and testing their bonds inch by squeaky inch.

Customers were scarce that summer. Once the morning dusting was over and we had done the day's updates on varicose veins, there was a desert of time to be got through: days of stupefying heat, thirst and boredom, with no air, no natural light, only a dim fluorescence above which gave a corpse-tint to the freshest skins. Sometimes as I stood I thought furiously about the French Revolution, which had come to preoccupy me. Sometimes my mother tripped across the carpet, fluttering her fingers at me, smiling upon her workforce.

My own boss was called Daphne. She wore goggle-sized fashion specs with coloured rims, behind which swam void pale eyes. In theory she and my mother were friends, but I soon realised, with a sense of shock, that among her peers my mother was a target for envy, and would have been secretly sabotaged if the other bosses had been bright enough to think how to do it. Daphne worked me relentlessly during those summer weeks, finding for me tasks that no one had done in years: cleaning in the stockrooms that were mice-ridden and thick with dust, boxing up great consignments of wire hangers which leapt from their bundles to claw at my arms like rats breaking out of a pet shop. The north-west was filthy in those days, and the rooms behind the scenes at Affleck & Brown were a dark and secret aspect of the filth. The feet-drawing carpets, the thick polythene in which the clothes came swathed, the neglected warp and weft of those garments that failed to sell and were bastilled in distant stockrooms: all these attracted a nap of sticky fluff which magnetised the particles of the Manchester atmosphere, which coated the hands and streaked the face, so that I must often have looked less like a 'junior sales' than a scab in a pit strike, my eyes travelling suspiciously when I surfaced, my hands contaminated, held away from my body in a gesture designed both to placate and ward off.

Sometimes, behind some packed rail draped in yellowing calico, behind some pile of boxes whose labels were faded to illegibility, I could sense a movement, a kind of shifting of feet, a murmur: 'Mrs Solomons?' I would call. 'Mrs Segal?' No answer: just the whispered exhalation of worsted and mohair: the deep intestinal creak of suede and leather: the faint squeal of unoiled metal wheels. Perhaps it was Daphne, spying on me? But sometimes at five thirty when the fitting rooms had to be cleared, I would come across a closed curtain at the end of a row, and I would turn and walk away without pulling it back, afflicted by sudden shyness or by fear of seeing something that I shouldn't see. It is easy to imagine that hanging fabric is bulked out by flesh, or that stitch and seam rehearse, after hours, a human shape without bones.

My colleagues, breathing over me the faint minted aroma of their indigestion remedies, received me with unbounded kindness. My pallor attracted their tuttutting sanction, and caused them to recommend the red meat that never passed their own lips. Perhaps my remoteness alarmed them, as I stood entranced among the edge-to-edge jackets; and then I would snap back and sell something, which alarmed them too. I liked the challenge of suiting the garments to the women who wanted them, of making a fit, of gratifying harmless desire. I liked tearing off the tickets from the frocks as they were sold, and looping a carrier bag considerately around an arthritic wrist. Sometimes the elderly customers would try to give me tips, which upset me. 'I don't come often now,' said one twisted, gracious old person. 'But when I do come, I always give.'

At the end of each working day my mother and I winced arm in arm to Piccadilly station, up the hill from Market Street, past the hot cafés stewing with grease and the NHS clinic that was always advertising for people to step in and donate blood. (I stepped in as soon as I was eighteen, but they turned me around and stepped me straight back out again.) It seemed to me that my job amounted to standing up for a living, and that no one should have to do it: standing hour after hour, standing when there was no customer in sight, standing in the fuggy heat from nine in the morning till five thirty at night with an hour for lunch in which you sprang out of the building and walked, gulping in the air. You stood long after your feet throbbed and your calves ached, and the ache wasn't gone by next morning when the standing started again. Maybe my mother was better off than me, because she had a tiny shelf of an office to sit in, a chair to perch on. But then she had her shoes, much more pernicious than my small suede sandals; her whole existence was much more high.

Some nights, maybe twice in the week, there were problems with the trains. Once there was an hour's delay. Hunger made us buoyant: talking gaily of the many catastrophes that had beset my mother's girls that day, we nibbled at a green apple she had produced from her bag, turn and turn about. We were not angry or guilty about being late because there was nothing we could do, and our mood was innocent, blithe, until we found ourselves penned up in the hall of our little house with my stepfather snarling. Our giggling stopped: what I have often remarked as brutal is the side of the human hand, tensed, wedge-like, ready to strike like an axe. Something then occurred. I'm not clear what it was. It isn't true that if you're very angry it gives you strength. If you're very angry it gives you a swimming head and limbs weak at the joints, but you do it anyway, a thing you've never done before, you speak the curse, you move, you pin against the wall, you say a certain death formula and what you say you mean; the effect is in proportion to the shock, as if the Meek had got out from the Sermon on the Mount and raked the crossroads with machine-gun fire.

After this, for a while, I left home. My mother and I parted every evening at the end of our road. She was more in sorrow than in anger, but sometimes she was in anger; I realise now that my intervention had interrupted some marital game of hers. When we drew near the end of our day's journey she'd stop chattering about the girls, and she'd move – reluctantly, I often felt – into some remote sniffy territory, putting deliberate distance between us. I would labour on up the hill to where I'd moved in with Anne Terese. She was now alone in the family house. Her parents had parted that summer, and perhaps they hadn't got the hang of it; instead of one going and one staying, both of them had walked out. We didn't compare our families much; we tried on the clothes in the wardrobes, and rearranged the furniture. The house was a peculiar one, prefabricated, contingent but homely, with a stove in the sitting room, and a deep enamel sink, and none of the appliances, like fridges, that people took for granted in the year 1970.

Anne Terese was working for the summer at a factory that made rubber-soled slippers. The work was hard, but every part of her body was hard and efficient too. In the evening, while I sagged feebly on a kitchen chair, she breaded cutlets, and sliced tomato and cucumber on to a glass dish. She made a Polish cake that was heavy with eggs and ripe cherries. At dusk we sat on the porch, in the faint blown scent of old rose. Hope, fine as cobwebs, draped our bare arms and floated across our shoulders, each strand shivering with twilit blue. When the moon rose we moved indoors to our beds, still sleepily murmuring. Anne Terese thought six children would suit her. I thought it would be good if I could stop vomiting.

Sometimes, as I wandered the floor at English Lady, I'd pretend that I was a supervisor at a refugee camp and that the frocks were the inhabitants. When I packed one and threw its ticket into a box I said to myself that I'd resettled it.

Each day began and ended with the count. You took a piece of paper and ruled it into columns for the different types of stock, so that you didn't get the two-pieces mixed up with the dress and jackets, even though they were two pieces also. You had to make categories for the garments that had no name, like the bifurcated items that head office had sent several seasons ago; made of hairy grey-blue tweed, they were some kind of flying suit perhaps, of a kind to be worn by Biggles's nanny. When the sales came around, Daphne would always reduce them, but they remained on the rails, their stiff arms thrust out and their legs wrapped around their necks to keep them from trailing on the carpet.

When you had made your categories you went between the rails and counted, and it was always wrong. You would then patrol the floor looking for English Ladies that had tucked themselves in among the Eastex or Windsmoor. You would haul them back by their necks and thrust them on the rails. But, while it was easy to see why the count should be wrong after the working day, it was less easy to understand why the stock should move around at night. 'Spooks,' I said robustly. I thought they must come down from the third-floor bedding (the sheeted dead) and try on our garments, hissing with spooky excitement, and sliding their phantom limbs into legs and sleeves.

I passed the summer so, in talking to tramps in Piccadilly Gardens; in buying ripe strawberries from the barrows for my lunch; in cooling my forehead against the gunmetal grille of the door of the goods lift. When Daphne castigated me for this failing and that, I would sigh will-do-better, but later I would aim secret kicks at the flying suits, and torture them by wrapping their legs more tightly around their necks and knotting them behind the hanger. To Daphne's face, I was compliance itself. I didn't want my mother to incur even more rancid female hatred, that would snarl invisible about her trim ankles, snag her kitten heels when I was long gone, and marching through London streets.

But then, as September approached, I found that the whole subject of the count was making me restless. Each evening we could only square it with the stock sheets by writing '15 in back' at the end of the dresses and jackets column, and it occurred to me that in all my grovelling and delving I'd never run across these oddments. 'You know,' I said to Daphne, 'where we always write "15 in back"? Where are they?'

'In back,' said Daphne. We were in her office, a scant wedge-shape partitioned off from the sales floor.

'But where?' I said. 'I've never seen them.'

Daphne slotted a cigarette into her mouth. With one hand she flipped a page of a stocklist, in the other hovered a dribbling ballpoint pen. A thin plume of smoke leaked from her lips. 'Don't you smoke yet?' she said 'Aren't you tempted?'

I had wondered, a time or two, why people try to trap you into new vices. Ours was a home that was militantly anti-tobacco. 'I haven't thought about it really ... I don't suppose ... Well, if your parents don't smoke ... I couldn't at home anyway, it would be very bad for my brother.'

Daphne stared at me. A little hoot issued from her, like a hiccup, and then a derisive shout of laughter. 'What! Your mother smokes like a chimney! Every break! Every lunchtime! Haven't you seen her? You must have seen her!'

'No,' I said. 'I have never.' I was the more deceived.

A gobbet of ink dropped from Daphne's pen. 'Have I spoken out of turn?'

'That's all right,' I said.

I told myself I welcomed information, information from any source.

Daphne looked at me glassily. 'Anyway,' she said, 'why should it be bad for your brother?'

I looked at my watch. 'Mrs Segal's lunch,' I smiled. I headed back to the sales floor. I said to myself, it can't matter. Tiny household lies. Pragmatic lies. Amusing, probably: given time. Trivial: like a needle-point snapped under the skin.

But later that afternoon, I sought the 15 in back. I tunnelled my way into lightless holes, where my toes were stubbed by bulging rotten boxes of unknown provenance. The cartons I had made myself, and bound with twine, had never been dispatched by Daphne, but left to squat in collapsing stacks. Now the wire hangers nipped at my calves as they worked their way out. Levering aside the bulky winter stock, thwacking the llamas away from me, I burrowed my way to the farthest corner. Give me that mattock and the wrenching iron.

Nothing. I named every garment I saw, scrabbling inside their shrouds: lifting them by their collars to peep at their labels, or, if I could not lift them, shredding their plastic frills into ruffs around their throats. I saw labels and I saw things that might have been Dress & Jackets but I did not see Dress & Jackets with the label I wanted. The 15 were nowhere to be found. I fought my way back to the air. I never looked back. I scratched it on my pad: zero, nix, nought. Diddly-squat, as the men said. Dress & Jackets, nil. If they had ever been known to exist, they didn't now. I saw how it was; they were to be conjured into being, the 15, to cover a mighty embarrassment, some awesome negligence or theft that had knocked the count to its knees gibbering. They were a fiction, perhaps an antique one; perhaps even older than Daphne. They were an adjustment to reality. They were a tale told by an idiot: to which I had added a phrase or two.

I re-emerged on to the floor. It was three o'clock. One of those dead afternoons, adumbrated, slumberous: not a customer in view. Limp from lack of regard, the stock hung like rags. A long mirror showed a dark smudge across my cheek. My sandals were coated with poisoned grime. I limped to the battered bureau where we kept our duplicate books and spare buttons, and took a duster out of the drawer. I rolled it up and brushed myself down, then moved out on to the floor, between the rails, and dusted between the garments: parting the hangers and polishing the steel spaces between. Somehow the afternoon passed. That night I declined to write '15 in back' at the end of the count; until my colleagues became too upset to bear, and one showed signs of hyperventilating. So in the end I did consent to write the phrase, but I wrote it quite faintly in pencil, with a question mark after it that was fainter still.

When the new school term began, it emerged that there was nothing wrong with my brother any more. He was eleven now, quite fit enough to go to high school. We digested this surprising fact, but no one was quite as glad about it as they should have been. Within months my mother was headhunted, her services sought by mackintosh purveyors and knitwear concessions; she had her pick of jobs, and moved to bigger stores, becoming blonder year by year, rising like a champagne bubble, to command larger numbers of girls and bigger counts and attract even more animosity and spite. At home she pursued her impromptu housekeeping, scouring the bath with powder meant for the washing machine and, when the washing machine broke down, throwing a tablecloth over it and using it as a sort of sideboard while she trained my siblings to go to the launderette.

A few year later Affleck's closed, and the whole district around it went to seed. It was taken over by pornographers, and those kinds of traders who sell plastic laundry baskets, dodgy electric fires and moulded Christmas novelties such as bouncing mince pies and whistling seraphim. The building itself was leased by a high-street clothing store, who traded briefly from its crumbling shell. I was long gone, of course, but I kept friends in the north, and had in my chain of acquaintances a Saturday girl who worked for the new occupiers. They only used the lower floors; from the second floor upwards, the building had been sealed. The fire doors had been closed and locked shut, the escalators had been removed, and the back staircases now ended in blind walls. But the staff were disturbed, said the Saturday girl, by noises from the bricked-in cavity above their heads: by footsteps, and by the sound of a woman screaming.

When I heard this I felt cold and felt sickness in the pit of my stomach, because I knew it was a true ghost story, as true as these things go. It had been no dizzy imp that came down from above and pulled buttons off the frocks, or walked them across the floor and mixed them in with the Jaeger. It was something staler, heavier, grossly sinister and perverse. But I only knew this in retrospect. When I looked back from, say, the age of twenty-three to the age of eighteen, I realised that, in those years, everything had been far worse than it seemed at the time.

THE THING
IN THE FOREST

A. S. Byatt

A. S. Byatt (b. 1936) is a British novelist and poet. In 2008, *The Times* named her on its list of the '50 Greatest British Writers Since 1945'. She won the Man Booker Prize in 1990 for her novel *Possession: A Romance*, and was shortlisted again in 2009 for *The Children's Book*, which won the James Tait Black Memorial Prize. She has published five collections of short stories.

There were once two little girls who saw, or believed they saw, a thing in a forest. The two little girls were evacuees, who had been sent away from the city by train, with a large number of other children. They all had their names attached to their coats with safety-pins, and they carried little bags or satchels, and the regulation gas-mask. They wore knitted scarves and bonnets or caps, and many had knitted gloves attached to long tapes which ran along their sleeves, inside their coats, and over their shoulders and out, so that they could leave their ten woollen fingers dangling like a spare pair of hands, like a scarecrow. They all had bare legs and scuffed shoes and wrinkled socks. Most had wounds on their knees in varying stages of freshness and scabbiness. They were at the age when children fall often and their knees were unprotected. With their suitcases, some of which were almost too big to carry, and their other impedimenta, a doll, a toy car, a comic, they were like a disorderly dwarf regiment, stomping along the platform.

The two little girls had not met before, and made friends on the train. They shared a square of chocolate, and took alternate bites at an apple. One gave the other the inside page of her *Beano*. Their names were Penny and Primrose. Penny was thin and dark and taller, possibly older, than Primrose, who was plump and blonde and curly. Primrose had bitten nails, and a velvet collar to her dressy green coat. Penny had a bloodless transparent paleness, a touch of blue in her fine lips. Neither of them knew where they were going, nor how long the journey might take. They did not even know why they were going since neither of their mothers had quite known how to explain the danger to them. How do you say to your child, I am sending you away, because enemy bombs may fall out of the sky, because the streets of the city may burn like forest fires of brick and timber, but I myself am staying here, in what I believe may be daily danger of burning, burying alive, gas, and ultimately perhaps a grey army rolling in on tanks over the suburbs, or sailing its submarines up our river, all guns blazing? So the mothers (who did not resemble each other at all) behaved alike, and explained nothing, it was easier. Their daughters they knew were little girls, who would not be able to understand or imagine.

The girls discussed on the train whether it was a sort of holiday or a sort of punishment, or a bit of both. Penny had read a book about Boy Scouts, but the children on the train did not appear to be Brownies or Wolf Cubs, only a mongrel battalion of the lost. Both little girls had the idea that these were all perhaps *not very good children*, possibly being sent away for that reason. They were pleased to be able to define each other as 'nice'. They would stick together, they agreed. Try to sit together, and things.

The train crawled sluggishly further and further away from the city and their homes. It was not a clean train – the upholstery of their carriage had the dank smell of unwashed trousers, and the gusts of hot steam rolling backwards past their windows were full of specks of flimsy ash, and sharp grit, and occasional fiery sparks that pricked face and fingers like hot needles if you opened the window. It was very noisy too, whenever it picked up a little speed. The engine gave great bellowing sighs, and the invisible wheels underneath clicked rhythmically and monotonously, tap-tap-tap-CRASH, tap-tap-tap-CRASH. The window-panes were both grimy and misted up. The train stopped frequently, and when it stopped, they used their gloves to wipe rounds, through which they peered out at flooded fields, furrowed hillsides and tiny stations, whose names were carefully blacked out, whose platforms were empty of life.

The children did not know that the namelessness was meant to baffle or delude an invading army. They felt – they did not think it out, but somewhere inside them the idea sprouted – that the erasure was because of them, because they were not meant to know where they were going or, like Hansel and Gretel, to find the way back. They did not speak to each other of this anxiety, but began the kind of conversation children have about things they really disliked, things that upset, or disgusted, or frightened them. Semolina pudding with its grainy texture, mushy peas, fat on roast meat. Listening to the stairs and the window-sashes creaking in the dark or the wind. Having your head held roughly back over the basin to have your hair washed, with cold water running down inside your liberty bodice. Gangs in playgrounds. They felt the pressure of all the other alien children in all the other carriages as a potential gang. They shared another square of chocolate, and licked their fingers, and looked out at a great white goose flapping its wings beside an inky pond.

The sky grew dark grey and in the end the train halted. The children got out, and lined up in a crocodile, and were led to a mud-coloured bus. Penny and Primrose managed to get a seat together, although it was over the wheel, and both of them began to feel sick as the bus bumped along snaking country lanes, under whipping branches, dark leaves on dark wooden arms on a dark sky, with torn strips of thin cloud streaming across a full moon, visible occasionally between them.

They were billeted temporarily in a mansion commandeered from its owner, which was to be arranged to hold a hospital for the long-term disabled, and a secret store of artworks and other valuables. The children were told they were there temporarily, until families were found to take them all into their homes. Penny and Primrose held hands, and said to each other that it would be wizard if they could go to the same family, because at least they would have each other. They didn't say anything to the rather tired-looking ladies who were ordering them about, because with the cunning of little children, they knew that requests were most often counter-productive, adults liked saying no. They imagined possible families into which they might be thrust. They did not discuss what they imagined, as these pictures, like the black station signs, were too frightening, and words might make some horror solid, in some magical way. Penny, who was a reading child, imagined Victorian dark pillars of severity, like Jane Eyre's Mr Brocklehurst, or David Copperfield's Mr Murdstone. Primrose imagined – she didn't know why – a fat woman with a white cap and round red arms who smiled nicely but made the children wear sacking aprons and scrub the steps and the stove. 'It's like we were orphans,' she said to Penny. 'But we're not,' Penny said. 'If we manage to stick together … '

The great house had a double flight of imposing stairs to its front door, and carved griffins and unicorns on its balustrade. There was no lighting, because of the black-out. All the windows were shuttered. No welcoming brightness leaked across door or windowsill. The children trudged up the staircase in their crocodile, hung their coats on numbered makeshift hooks, and were given supper (Irish stew and rice pudding with a dollop of blood-red jam) before going to bed in long makeshift dormitories, where once servants had slept. They had camp-beds (military issue) and grey shoddy blankets. Penny and Primrose got beds together but couldn't get a corner. They queued to brush their teeth in a tiny washroom, and both suffered (again without speaking) suffocating anxiety about what would happen if they wanted to pee in the middle of the night, because the lavatory was one floor down, the lights were all extinguished, and they were a long way from the door. They also suffered from a fear that in the dark the other children would start laughing and rushing and teasing, and turn themselves into a gang. But that did not happen. Everyone was tired and anxious and orphaned. An uneasy silence, a drift of perturbed sleep, came over them all. The only sounds – from all parts of the great dormitory it seemed – were suppressed snuffles and sobs, from faces pressed into thin pillows.

When daylight came, things seemed, as they mostly do, brighter and better. The children were given breakfast in a large vaulted room. They sat at trestle tables, eating porridge made with water and a dab of the red jam, heavy cups of strong tea. Then they were told they could go out and play until lunch-time. Children in those days – wherever they came from – were not closely watched, were

allowed to come and go freely, and those evacuated children were
not herded into any kind of holding-pen, or transit camp. They
were told they should be back for lunch at 12.30, by which time
those in charge hoped to have sorted out their provisional future
lives. It was not known how they would know when it was 12.30,
but it was expected that – despite the fact that few of them had
wrist-watches – they would know how to keep an eye on the time.
It was what they were used to.

Penny and Primrose went out together, in their respectable coats
and laced shoes, on to the terrace. The terrace appeared to them to
be vast, and was indeed extensive. It was covered with a fine layer
of damp gravel, stained here and there bright green, or invaded by
mosses. Beyond it was a stone balustrade, with a staircase leading
down to a lawn, which that morning had a quicksilver sheen on
the lengthening grass. It was flanked by long flowerbeds, full of
overblown annuals and damp clumps of stalks. A gardener would
have noticed the beginnings of neglect, but these were urban little
girls, and they noticed the jungly mass of wet stems, and the wet,
vegetable smell. Across the lawn, which seemed considerably vaster
than the vast terrace, was a sculpted yew hedge, with many twigs
and shoots out of place and ruffled. In the middle of the hedge was
a wicket-gate, and beyond the gate were trees, woodland, a forest,
the little girls said, to themselves.

'Let's go into the forest,' said Penny, as though the sentence was
required of her.

Primrose hesitated. Most of the other children were running up
and down the terrace, scuffing their shoes in the gravel. Some boys
were kicking a ball on the grass. The sun came right out, full from
behind a hazy cloud, and the trees suddenly looked both gleaming
and secret.

'OK,' said Primrose. 'We needn't go far.'

'No. I've never been in a forest.'

'Nor me.'

'We ought to look at it, while we've got the opportunity,' said
Penny.

There was a very small child – one of the smallest – whose name,
she told everyone, was Alys. With ay she told those who could
spell, and those who couldn't, which surely included herself. She

was barely out of nappies. She was quite extraordinarily pretty, pink and white, with large pale blue eyes, and sparse little golden curls all over her head and neck, through which her pink skin could be seen. Nobody seemed to be in charge of her, no elder brother or sister. She had not quite managed to wash the tearstains from her dimpled cheeks.

She had made several attempts to attach herself to Penny and Primrose. They did not want her. They were excited about meeting and liking each other. She said now:

'I'm coming too, into the forest.'

'No, you aren't,' said Primrose.

'You're too little, you must stay here,' said Penny.

'You'll get lost,' said Primrose.

'You won't get lost. I'll come with you,' said the little creature, with an engaging smile, made for loving parents and grandparents.

'We don't want you, you see,' said Primrose.

'It's for your own good,' said Penny.

Alys went on smiling hopefully, the smile becoming more of a mask.

'It will be all right,' said Alys.

'Run,' said Primrose.

They ran; they ran down the steps and across the lawn, and through the gate, into the forest. They didn't look back. They were long-legged little girls, not toddlers. The trees were silent round them, holding out their branches to the sun, breathing noiselessly.

Primrose touched the warm skin of the nearest saplings, taking off her gloves to feel their cracks and knots. She exclaimed over the flaking whiteness and dusty brown of the silver birches, the white leaves of the aspens. Penny looked into the thick of the forest. There was undergrowth – a mat of brambles and bracken. There were no obvious paths. Dark and light came and went, inviting and mysterious, as the wind pushed clouds across the face of the sun.

'We have to be careful not to get lost,' she said. 'In stories, people make marks on tree-trunks, or unroll a thread, or leave a trail of white pebbles – to find their way back.'

'We needn't go out of sight of the gate,' said Primrose. 'We could just explore a little bit.'

They set off, very slowly. They went on tiptoe, making their own narrow passages through the undergrowth, which sometimes came as high as their thin shoulders. They were urban, and unaccustomed to silence. At first the absence of human noise filled them with a kind of awe, as though, while they would not have put it to themselves in this way, they had got to some original place, from which they, or those before them, had come, and which they therefore recognised. Then they began to hear the small sounds that were there. The chatter and repeated lilt and alarm of invisible birds, high up, further in. The hum and buzz of insects. Rustling in dry leaves, rushes of movement in thickets. Slitherings, dry coughs, sharp cracks. They went on, pointing out to each other creepers draped with glistening berries, crimson, black and emerald, little crops of toadstools, some scarlet, some ghostly-pale, some a dead-flesh purple, some like tiny parasols – and some like pieces of meat protruding from tree-trunks. They met blackberries, but didn't pick them, in case in this place they were dangerous or deceptive. They admired from a safe distance the stiff upright fruiting rods of the Lords and Ladies, packed with fat red berries. They stopped to watch spiders spin, swinging from twig to twig, hauling in their silky cables, reinforcing knots and joinings. They sniffed the air, which was full of a warm mushroom smell, and a damp moss smell, and a sap smell, and a distant hint of dead ashes.

Did they hear it first or smell it first? Both sound and scent were at first infinitesimal and dispersed. Both gave the strange impression of moving in – in waves – from the whole perimeter of the forest. Both increased very slowly in volume, and both were mixed, a sound and a smell fabricated of many disparate sounds and smells. A crunching, a crackling, a crushing, a heavy thumping, combined with threshing and thrashing, and added to that a gulping, heaving, boiling, bursting steaming sound, full of bubbles and farts, piffs and explosions, swallowings and wallowings. The smell was worse, and more aggressive, than the sound. It was a liquid smell of putrefaction, the smell of maggoty things at the bottom of untended dustbins, the smell of blocked drains, and unwashed trousers, mixed with the smell of bad eggs, and of rotten carpets and ancient polluted bedding. The new, ordinary forest smells and sounds, of leaves and humus, fur and feathers, so to speak, went out like lights as the atmosphere of the thing preceded it. The two little girls looked at each other, and took each other's hand. Speechlessly and instinctively they crouched, down behind a fallen tree-trunk, and trembled, as the thing came into view.

Its head appeared to form, or become first visible in the distance, between the trees. Its face – which was triangular – appeared like a rubbery or fleshy mask over a shapeless sprouting bulb of a head, like a monstrous turnip. Its colour was the colour of flayed flesh, pitted with wormholes, and its expression was neither wrath nor greed, but pure misery. Its most defined feature was a vast mouth, pulled down and down at the corners, tight with a kind of pain. Its lips were thin, and raised, like welts from whipstrokes. It had blind, opaque white eyes, fringed with fleshy lashes and brows like the feelers of sea-anemones. Its face was close to the ground, and moved towards the children between its forearms which were squat, thick, powerful and akimbo, like a cross between a monstrous washerwoman and a primeval dragon. The flesh on these forearms was glistening and mottled, every colour, from the green of mould to the red-brown of raw liver, to the dirty white of dry rot.

The rest of its very large body appeared to be glued together, like still-wet papier-mâché, or the carapace of stones and straws and twigs worn by caddis-flies underwater. It had a tubular shape, as a turd has a tubular shape, a provisional amalgam. It was made of rank meat, and decaying vegetation, but it also trailed veils and prostheses of manmade materials, bits of wire-netting, foul dishcloths, wire-wool full of pan-scrubbings, rusty nuts and bolts. It had feeble stubs and stumps of very slender legs, growing out of it at all angles, wavering and rippling like the suckered feet of a caterpillar or the squirming fringe of a centipede. On and on it came, bending and crushing whatever lay in its path, including bushes, though not substantial trees, which it wound between, awkwardly. The little girls observed, with horrified fascination, that when it met a sharp stone, or a narrow tree-trunk, it allowed itself to be sliced through, flowed sluggishly round in two or three smaller worms, convulsed and reunited. Its progress was achingly slow, very smelly, and apparently very painful, for it moaned and whined amongst its other burblings and belchings. They thought it could not see, or certainly could not see clearly. It and its stench passed within a few feet of their tree-trunk, humping along, leaving behind it a trail of bloody slime and dead foliage, sucked to dry skeletons.

Its end was flat and blunt, almost transparent, like some earthworms.

When it had gone, Penny and Primrose, kneeling on the moss and dead leaves, put their arms about each other, and hugged each other, shaking with dry sobs. Then they stood up, still silent, and stared together, hand in hand, at the trail of obliteration and destruction, which wound out of the forest and into it again. They went back, hand in hand, without looking behind them, afraid that the wicket-gate, the lawn, the stone steps, the balustrade, the terrace and the great house would be transmogrified, or simply not there. But the boys were still playing football on the lawn, a group of girls were skipping and singing shrilly on the gravel. They let go each other's hand, and went back in.

They did not speak to each other again.

The next day they were separated and placed with strange families. Their time in these families – Primrose was in a dairy farm, Penny was in a parsonage – did not in fact last very long, though then the time seemed slow-motion and endless. These alien families seemed like dream worlds into which they had strayed, not knowing the physical or social rules which constructed those worlds. Afterwards, if they remembered the evacuation it was as dreams are remembered, with mnemonics designed to claw back what fleets on waking. So Primrose remembered the sound of milk spurting in the pail, and Penny remembered the empty corsets of the vicar's wife, hanging bony on the line. They remembered dandelion clocks, but you can remember those from anywhere, any time. They remembered the thing they had seen in the forest, on the contrary, in the way you remember those very few dreams – almost all nightmares – which have the quality of life itself, not of fantasm, or shifting provisional scene-set. (Though what are dreams if not life itself?) They remembered too solid flesh, too precise a stink, a rattle and a soughing which thrilled the nerves and the cartilage of their growing ears. In the memory, as in such a dream, they felt, I cannot get out, this is a real thing in a real place.

They returned from evacuation, like many evacuees, so early that they then lived through wartime in the city, bombardment, blitz, unearthly light and roaring, changed landscapes, holes in their world where the newly dead had been. Both lost their fathers. Primrose's father was in the Army, and was killed, very late in the war, on a crowded troop-carrier sunk in the Far East. Penny's father, a much older man, was in the Auxiliary Fire Service, and died in a sheet of flame in the East India Docks on the Thames, pumping evaporating water from a puny coil of hose. They found it hard, after the war, to remember these different men. The claspers of memory could not grip the drowned and the burned. Primrose saw an inane grin under a khaki cap, because her mother had a snapshot. Penny thought she remembered her father, already grey-headed, brushing ash off his boots and trouser-cuffs as he put on his tin hat to go out. She thought she remembered a quaver of fear in his tired face, and the muscles composing themselves into resolution. It was not much, what either of them remembered.

After the war, their fates were still similar and dissimilar. Penny's widowed mother embraced grief, closed her face and her curtains, moved stiffly, like an automat, and read poetry. Primrose's mother married one of the many admirers, visitors, dancing partners she had had before the ship went down, gave birth to another five children, and developed varicose veins and a smoker's cough. She dyed her blonde hair with peroxide when it faded. Both Primrose and Penny were only children who now, because of the war, lived in amputated or unreal families. Penny developed crushes on poetical teachers and in due course – she was clever – went to university, where she chose to study developmental psychology. Primrose had little education. She was always being kept off school to look after the others. She too dyed her blonde curls with peroxide when they turned mousy and faded. She got fat as Penny got thin. Neither of them married. Penny became a child psychologist, working with the abused, the displaced, the disturbed. Primrose did this and that. She was a barmaid. She worked in a shop. She went to help at various church crêches and Salvation Army reunions, and discovered she had a talent for story-telling. She became Aunty Primrose, with her own repertoire. She was employed to tell tales to kindergartens and entertain at children's parties. She was much in demand at Hallowe'en, and had her own circle of bright yellow plastic chairs in a local shopping mall, where she kept an eye on the children of burdened women, keeping them safe, offering them just a *frisson* of fear and terror that made them wriggle with pleasure.

The house aged differently. During this period of time – whilst the little girls became women – it was handed over to the Nation, which turned it into a living museum, still inhabited by the flesh and blood descendants of those who had built it, demolished it, flung out a wing, closed off a corridor. Guided tours took place in it, at regulated times. During these tours, the ballroom and intimate drawing-rooms were fenced off with crimson twisted ropes on little brass one-eyed pedestals. The bored and the curious peered in at four-poster beds and pink silk *fauteuils*, at silver-framed photographs of wartime Royalty, and crackling crazing Renaissance and Enlightenment portraits of long-dead queens and solemn or sweetly musing ancestors. In the room where the evacuees had eaten their rationed meals, the history of the house was displayed, on posters, in glass cases, with helpful notices, and opened copies of old diaries and records. There were reproductions of the famous paintings which had lain here in hiding during the war. There was a plaque to the dead of the house: a gardener, an undergardener, a chauffeur and a second son. There were photographs of military hospital beds, and of nurses pushing wheelchairs in the grounds. There was no mention of the evacuees whose presence appeared to have been too brief to have left any trace.

The two women met in this room on an autumn day in 1984. They had come with a group, walking in a chattering crocodile behind a guide, and had lingered amongst the imagery and records, rather than going on to eavesdrop on the absent ladies and gentlemen whose tidy clutter lay on coffee tables and escritoires. They prowled around the room, each alone with herself in opposite directions, without acknowledging each other's presence. Both their mothers had died that spring, within a week of each other, though this coincidence was unknown to them. It had made both of them think of taking a holiday, and both had chosen that part of the world. Penny was wearing a charcoal trouser suit and a black velvet hat. Primrose wore a floral knit long jacket over a shell-pink cashmere sweater, over a rustling long skirt with an elastic waist, in a mustard-coloured tapestry print. Her hips and bosom were bulky. They coincided because both of them, at the same moment, half saw an image in a medieval-looking illustrated book. Primrose thought it was a very old book. Penny assumed it was nineteenth-century mock-medieval. It showed a knight, on foot, in a forest, lifting has sword to slay something. The knight shone on the rounded slope of the page, in the light, which caught the gilding on his helmet and sword-belt. It was not possible to see what was being slain. This was because, both in the tangled vegetation of the image, and in the way the book was displayed in the case, the enemy, or victim, was in shadows.

Neither of them could read the ancient (or pseudo-ancient) black letter of the text beside the illustration. There was a typed explanation, or description, under the book, done with a faded ribbon and uneven pressure of the keys. They had to lean forward to read it, and to see what was worming its way into, or out of, the deep spine of the book, and that was how they came to see each other's face, close up, in the glass which was both transparent and reflective. Their transparent reflected faces lost detail – cracked lipstick, pouches, fine lines of wrinkles – and looked both younger and greyer, less substantial. And that is how they came to recognise each other, as they might not have done, plump face to bony face. They breathed each other's names, Penny, Primrose, and their breath misted the glass, obscuring the knight and his opponent. I could have died, I could have wet my knickers, said Penny and Primrose afterwards to each other, and both experienced this still moment as pure, dangerous shock. But they stayed there, bent heads together, legs trembling, knees knocking, and read the caption, which was about the Loathly Worm, which, tradition held, had infested the countryside and had been killed more than once by scions of that house, Sir Lionel, Sir Boris, Sir Guillem. The Worm, the typewriter had tapped out, was an English Worm, not a European dragon, and like most such worms, was wingless. In some sightings it was reported as having vestigial legs, hands or feet. In others it was limbless. It had, in monstrous form, the capacity of common or garden worms to sprout new heads or trunks if it was divided, so that two worms, or more, replaced one. This was why it had been killed so often, yet reappeared. It had been reported travelling with a slithering pack of young ones, but these may have been only revitalised segments. The typed paper was held down with drawing-pins and appeared to continue somewhere else, on some not visible page, not presented for viewing.

Being English, the recourse they thought of was tea. There was a tea-room near the great house, in a converted stable at the back. There they stood silently side by side, clutching floral plastic trays spread with briar roses, and purchased scones, superior raspberry jam in tiny jam jars, little plastic tubs of clotted cream. 'You couldn't get cream or real jam in the war,' said Primrose in an undertone as they found a corner table. She said wartime rationing had made her permanently greedy, and thin Penny agreed, it had, clotted cream was still a treat.

They watched each other warily, offering bland snippets of autobiography in politely hushed voices. Primrose thought Penny looked gaunt, and Penny thought Primrose looked raddled. They established the skein of coincidences – dead fathers, unmarried status, child-caring professions, recently dead mothers. Circling like beaters, they approached the covert thing in the forest. They discussed the great house, politely. Primrose admired the quality of the carpets. Penny said it was nice to see the old pictures back on the wall. Primrose said, funny really, that there was all that history, but no sign that they, the children, that was, had ever been there. Penny said no, the story of the family was there, and the wounded soldiers, but not them, they were perhaps too insignificant. Too little, said Primrose, nodding agreement, not quite sure what she meant by too little. Funny, said Penny, that they should meet each other next to that book, with that picture. Creepy, said Primrose in a light, light cobweb voice, not looking at Penny. We saw that thing. When we went in the forest.

Yes we did, said Penny. We saw it.

Did you ever wonder, asked Primrose, if we *really* saw it?

Never for a moment, said Penny. That is, I don't know what it was, but I've always been quite sure we saw it.

Does it change – do you remember all of it?

It was a horrible thing, and yes, I remember all of it, there isn't a bit of it I can manage to forget. Though I forget all sorts of things, said Penny, in a thin voice, a vanishing voice.

And have you ever told anyone of it, spoken of it, asked Primrose more urgently, leaning forward, holding on to the table edge.

No, said Penny. She had not. She said, who would believe it, believe them?

That's what I thought, said Primrose. I didn't speak. But it stuck in my mind like a tapeworm in your gut. I think it did me no good.

It did me no good either, said Penny. No good at all. I've thought about it, she said to the ageing woman opposite, whose face quivered under her dyed goldilocks. I think, I think there are things that are real – more real than we are – but mostly we don't cross their paths, or they don't cross ours. Maybe at very bad times we get into their world, or notice what they are doing in ours.

Primrose nodded energetically. She looked as though sharing was solace, and Penny, to whom it was not solace, grimaced with pain.

'Sometimes I think that thing finished me off,' said Penny to Primrose, a child's voice rising in a woman's gullet, arousing a little girl's scared smile which wasn't a smile on Primrose's face. Primrose said:

'It did finish *her* off, that little one, didn't it? She got into its path, didn't she? And when it had gone by – she wasn't anywhere,' said Primrose. 'That was how it was?'

'Nobody ever asked where she was, or looked for her,' said Penny.

'I wondered if we'd made her up,' said Primrose. 'But I didn't, we didn't.'

'Her name was Alys.'

'With a y.'

There had been a mess, a disgusting mess, they remembered, but no particular sign of anything that might have been, or been part of, or belonged to, a persistent little girl called Alys.

Primrose shrugged voluptuously, let out a gale of a sigh, and rearranged her flesh in her clothes.

'Well, we know we're not mad, anyway,' she said. 'We've got into a mystery, but we didn't make it up. It wasn't a delusion. So it was good we met, because now we needn't be afraid we're mad, need we, we can get on with things, so to speak?'

They arranged to have dinner together the following evening. They were staying in different bed and breakfasts and neither of them thought of exchanging addresses. They agreed on a restaurant in the market square of the local town – *Seraphina's Hot Pot* – and a time, seven-thirty. They did not even discuss spending the next day together. Primrose went on a local bus tour. Penny asked for sandwiches, and took a long solitary walk. The weather was grey, spitting fine rain. Both arrived at their lodgings with headaches, and both made tea with the teabags and kettle provided in their rooms. They sat on their beds. Penny's bed had a quilt with blowsy cabbage roses. Primrose's had a black-and-white checked gingham duvet. They turned on their televisions, watched the same game show, listened to the inordinate jolly laughter. Penny washed herself rather fiercely in her tiny bathroom: Primrose slowly changed her underwear, and put on fresh tights. Between bathroom and wardrobe Penny saw the air in the room fill with a kind of grey smoke. Rummaging in a suitcase for a clean blouse, Primrose felt giddy, as though the carpet was swirling. What would they say to each other, they asked themselves, and sat down, heavy and winded, on the edges of their single beds. Why? Primrose's mind said, scurrying, and Why? Penny asked herself starkly. Primrose put down her blouse and turned up the television. Penny managed to walk as far as the window. She had a view with a romantic bit of moorland, rising to a height that cut off the sky. Evening had caught her: the earth was black: the house-lights trickled feebly into gloom.

Seven-thirty came and went, and neither woman moved. Both, indistinctly, imagined the other waiting at a table, watching a door open and shut. Neither moved. What could they have said, they asked themselves, but only perfunctorily. They were used to not asking too much, they had had practice.

*

The next day they both thought very hard, but indirectly, about the wood. It was a spring day, a good day for woods, and yesterday's rain-clouds had been succeeded by clear sunlight, with a light movement of air and a very faint warmth. Penny thought about the wood, put on her walking-shoes, and set off obliquely in the opposite direction. Primrose was not given to ratiocination. She sat over her breakfast, which was English and ample, bacon and mushrooms, toast and honey, and let her feelings about the wood run over her skin, pricking and twitching. The wood, the real, and imagined wood – both before and after she had entered it with Penny – had always been simultaneously a source of attraction and a source of discomfort, shading into terror. The light in woods was more golden and more darkly shadowed than any light on city terraces, including the glare of bombardment. The gold and the shadows were intertwined, a promise of liveliness. What they had seen had been shapeless and stinking, but the wood persisted.

So without speaking to herself a sentence in her head – 'I shall go there' – Primrose decided by settling her stomach, setting her knees, and slightly clenching her fists, that she would go there. And she went straight there, full of warm food, arriving as the morning brightened with the first bus-load of tourists, and giving them the slip, to take the path they had once taken, across the lawn and through the wicket-gate.

The wood was much the same, but denser and more inviting in its new greenness. Primrose's body decided to set off in a rather different direction from the one the little girls had taken. New bracken was uncoiling with snaky force. Yesterday's rain still glittered on limp new hazel leaves and threads of gossamer. Small feathered throats above her, and in the depths beyond, whistled and trilled with enchanting territorial aggression and male self-assertion, which were to Primrose simply the chorus. She heard a cackle and saw a flash of the loveliest flesh-pink, in feathers, and a blue gleam. She was not good at identifying birds. She could do 'a robin' – one hopped from branch to branch – 'a black bird' which shone like jet, and 'a tit' which did acrobatics, soft, blue and yellow, a tiny scrap of fierce life. She went steadily on, always distracted by shines and gleams in her eye-corner. She found a mossy bank, on which she found posies of primroses, which she recognised and took vaguely, in the warmth of her heart labouring in her chest, as a good sign, a personal sign. She picked a few, stroked their pale petals, buried her nose in them, smelled the thin, clear honey-smell of them, spring honey without the buzz of summer. She was better at flowers than birds, because there had been *Flower Fairies* in the school bookshelves when she was little, with the flowers painted accurately, wood-sorrel and stitchwort, pimpernel and honeysuckle, flowers she had never seen, accompanied by truly pretty human creatures, all children, from babies to girls and boys, clothed in the blues and golds, russets and purples of the flowers and fruits, walking, dancing, delicate material imaginings of the essential lives of plants. And now as she wandered on, she saw and recognised them, windflower and bryony, self-heal and dead-nettle, and had – despite where she was – a lovely lapping sense of invisible – *just* invisible life swarming in the leaves and along the twigs, despite where she was, despite what she had not forgotten having seen there. She closed her eyes a fraction. The sunlight flickered and flickered. She saw glitter and spangling everywhere. She saw drifts of intense blue, further in, and between the tree-trunks, with the light running over them.

She stopped. She did not like the sound of her own toiling breath. She was not very fit. She saw, then, a whisking in the bracken, a twirl of fur, thin and flaming, quivering on a tree-trunk. She saw a squirrel, a red squirrel, watching her from a bough. She had to sit down, as she remembered her mother. She sat on a hummock of grass, rather heavily. She remembered them all, Nutkin and Moldywarp, Brock and Sleepy Dormouse, Natty Newt and Ferdy Frog. Her mother didn't tell stories and didn't open gates into imaginary worlds. But she had been good with her fingers. Every Christmas during the war, when toys, and indeed materials, were not to be had, Primrose had woken to find in her stocking a new stuffed creature, made from fur fabric with button eyes and horny claws, Or, in the case of the amphibians, made from scraps of satin and taffeta. There had been an artistry to them. The stuffed squirrel was the essence of squirrel, the fox was watchful, the newt was slithery. They did not wear anthropomorphic jackets or caps, which made it easier to invest them with imaginary natures. She believed in Father Christmas, and the discovery that her mother had made the toys, the vanishing of magic, had been a breath-taking blow. She could not be grateful for the skill and the imagination, so uncharacteristic of her flirtatious mother. The creatures continued to accumulate. A spider, a Bambi. She told herself stories at night about a girl-woman, an enchantress in a fairy wood, loved and protected by an army of wise and gentle animals. She slept banked in by stuffed creatures, as the house in the blitz was banked in by inadequate sandbags.

Primrose registered the red squirrel as disappointing – stringier and more rat-like than its plump grey city cousins. But she knew it was rare and special, and when it took off from branch to branch, flicking its extended tail like a sail, gripping with its tiny hands, she set out to follow it as though it was a messenger. It would take her to the centre, she thought, she ought to get to the centre. It could easily have leaped out of sight, she thought, but it didn't. It lingered and sniffed and stared nervily, waiting for her. She pushed through brambles into denser greener shadows. Juices stained her skirts and skin. She began to tell herself a story about staunch Primrose, not giving up, making her way to 'the centre'. She had to have a reason for coming there, it was to do with getting to the centre. Her childhood stories had all been in the third person. 'She was not afraid.' 'She faced up to the wild beasts. They cowered.' She laddered her tights and muddied her shoes and breathed heavier. The squirrel stopped to clean its face. She crushed bluebells and saw the sinister hoods of arum lilies.

She had no idea where she was, or how far she had come, but she decided that the clearing where she found herself was the centre. The squirrel had stopped, and was running up and down a single tree. There was a sort of mossy mound which could almost have had a throne-like aspect, if you were being imaginative. So she sat on it. 'She came to the centre and sat on the mossy chair.'

Now what?

She had not forgotten what they had seen, the blank miserable face, the powerful claws, the raggle-taggle train of accumulated decay. She had come neither to look for it nor to confront it, but she had come because it was there. She had known all her life that she, Primrose, had *really* been in a magic forest. She knew that the forest was the source of terror. She had never frightened the litl'uns she entertained at parties, in schools, in crèches, with tales of lost children in forests. She frightened them with slimy things that came up the plughole, or swarmed out of the U-bend in the lavatory, or tapped on windows at night, and were despatched by bravery and magic. There were waiting hobgoblins in urban dumps beyond the street-lights. But the woods in her tales were sources of glamour, of rich colours and unseen hidden life, flower fairies and more magical beings. They were places where you used words like spangles and sequins for real dewdrops on real dock leaves. Primrose knew that glamour and the thing they had seen came from the same place, that brilliance and the ashen stink had the same source. She made them safe for the litl'uns by restricting them to pantomime flats and sweet illustrations. She didn't look at what she knew, better not, but *she did know she knew*, she recognised confusedly.

Now what?

She sat on the moss, and a voice in her head said, 'I want to go home.' And she heard herself give a bitter, entirely grown-up little laugh, for what was home? What did she know about home?

Where she lived was above a Chinese takeaway. She had a dangerous cupboard-corner she cooked in, a bed, a clothes-rail, an armchair deformed by generations of bottoms. She thought of this place in faded browns and beiges, seen through drifting coils of Chinese cooking-steam, scented with stewing pork and a bubbling chicken broth. Home was not real, as all the sturdy twigs and roots in the wood were real, it had neither primrose-honey nor spangles and sequins. The stuffed animals, or some of them, were piled on the bed and the carpet, their fur rubbed, their pristine stare gone from their scratched eyes. She thought about what one thought was *real*, sitting there on the moss-throne at the centre. When Mum had come in, snivelling, to say Dad was dead, she herself had been preoccupied with whether pudding would be tapioca or semolina, whether there would be jam, and subsequently, how ugly Mum's dripping nose looked, how she looked as though she was *putting it on*. She remembered the semolina and the rather nasty blackberry jam, the taste and the texture, to this day, so was that real, was that home? She had later invented a picture of a cloudy aquamarine sea under a gold sun in which a huge fountain of white curling water rose from a foundering ship. It was very beautiful but not real. She could not remember Dad. She could remember the Thing in the Forest, and she could remember Alys. The fact that the mossy hump had lovely colours – crimson and emerald, she said, maiden-hairs, she named something at random – didn't mean she didn't remember the Thing. She remembered what Penny had said about 'things that are more real than we are'. She had met one. Here at the centre, the spout of water was more real than the semolina, because she was where such things reign. The word she found was 'reign'. She had understood something, and did not know what she had understood. She wanted badly to go home, and she wanted never to move. The light was lovely in the leaves. The squirrel flirted its tail and suddenly set off again, springing into the branches. The woman lumbered to her feet and licked the bramble-scratches on the back of her hands.

Penny had set off in what she supposed to be the opposite direction. She walked very steadily, keeping to hedgerows and field-edge paths, climbing the occasional stile. For the first part of the walk she kept her eyes on the ground, and her ears on her own trudging, as it disturbed stubble and pebbles. She slurred her feet over vetch and stitchwort, looking back over the crushed trail. She remembered the Thing. She remembered it clearly and daily. Why was she in this part of the world at all, if not to settle with it? But she walked away, noticing and not noticing that her path was deflected by fieldforms and the lie of the land into a snaking sickle-shape. As the day wore on, she settled into her stride and lifted her eyes, admiring the new corn in the furrows, a distant skylark. When she saw the wood on the horizon she knew it was the wood, although she was seeing it from an unfamiliar aspect, from where it appeared to be perched on a conical hillock, ridged as though it had been grasped and squeezed by coils of strength. The trees were tufted and tempting. It was almost dusk when she came there. The shadows were thickening, the dark places in the tumbled undergrowth were darkening. She mounted the slope, and went in over a suddenly discovered stile.

Once inside, she moved cautiously, as though she was hunted or hunting. She stood stock-still, and snuffed the air for the remembered rottenness: she listened to the sounds of the trees and the creatures, trying to sift out a distant threshing and sliding. She smelled rottenness, but it was normal rottenness, leaves and stems mulching back into earth. She heard sounds. Not birdsong, for it was too late in the day, but the odd raucous warning croak, a crackle of something, a tremulous shiver of something else. She heard her own heartbeat in the thickening brown air.

She had wagered on freedom and walked away, and walking away had brought her here, as she had known it would. It was no use looking for familiar tree-trunks or tussocks. They had had a lifetime, her lifetime, to alter out of recognition.

She began to think she discerned dark tunnels in the undergrowth, where something might have rolled and slid. Mashed seedlings, broken twigs and fronds, none of it very recent. There were things caught in the thorns, flimsy colourless shreds of damp wool or fur. She peered down the tunnels and noted where the scrapings hung, thickest. She forced herself to go into the dark, stooping, occasionally crawling on hands and knees. The silence was heavy. She found things she remembered, threadworms of knitting wool, unravelled dishcloth cotton, clinging newsprint. She found odd sausage-shaped tubes of membrane, containing fragments of hair and bone and other inanimate stuffs. They were like monstrous owl-pellets, or the gut-shaped hair-balls vomited by cats. Penny went forwards, putting aside lashing briars and tough stems with careful fingers. It had been here, but how long ago? When she stopped, and sniffed the air, and listened, there was nothing but the drowsy wood.

Quite suddenly she came out at a place she remembered. The clearing was larger, the tree-trunks were thicker, but the fallen one behind which they had hidden still lay there. The place was almost the ghost of a camp. The trees round about were hung with threadbare pennants and streamers, like the scorched, hacked, threadbare banners in the chapel of the great house, with their brown stains of earth or blood. It had been here, it had never gone away.

Penny moved slowly and dreamily round, watching herself as you watch yourself in a dream, looking for things. She found a mock tortoiseshell hairslide, and a shoe-button with a metal shank. She found a bird-skeleton, quite fresh, bashed flat, with a few feathers glued to it. She found ambivalent shards and several teeth, of varying sizes and shapes. She found – spread around, half-hidden by roots, stained green but glinting white – a collection of small bones, finger-bones, tiny toes, a rib, and finally what might be a brain-pan and brow. She thought of putting them in her knapsack, and then thought she could not, and heaped them at the foot of a holly. She was not an anatomist. Some at least of the tiny bones might have been badger or fox.

She sat down on the earth, with her back against the fallen trunk. She thought that she should perhaps find something to dig a hole, to bury the little bones, but she didn't move. She thought, now I am watching myself as you do in a safe dream, but then, when I saw it, it was one of those appalling dreams, where you are inside, where you cannot get out. Except that it wasn't a dream.

It was the encounter with the Thing that had led her to deal professionally in dreams. Something which resembled unreality had walked – had rolled, had wound itself, had *lumbered* into reality, and she had seen it. She had been the reading child, but after the sight of the thing, she had not been able to inhabit the customary and charming unreality of books. She had become good at studying what could not be seen. She took an interest in the dead, who inhabited real history. She was drawn to the invisible forces which moved in molecules and caused them to coagulate or dissipate. She had become a psychotherapist 'to be useful'. That was not quite accurate or sufficient as an explanation. The corner of the blanket that covered the unthinkable had been turned back enough for her to catch sight of it. She was in its world. It was not by accident that she had come to specialise in severely autistic children, children who twittered, or banged, or stared, who sat damp and absent on Penny's official lap and told her no dreams, discussed no projects. The world they knew was a real world. Often Penny thought it was *the* real world, from which even their desperate parents were at least partly shielded. Somebody had to occupy themselves with the hopeless. Penny felt she could. Most people couldn't. She could.

All the leaves of the forest began slowly to quaver and then to clatter. Far away there was the sound of something heavy, and sluggish, stirring. Penny sat very still and expectant. She heard the old blind rumble, she sniffed the old stink. It came from no direction; it was on both sides; it was all around; as though the Thing encompassed the wood, or as though it travelled in multiple fragments, as it was described in the old text. It was dark now. What was visible had no distinct colour, only shades of ink and elephant.

Now, thought Penny, and just as suddenly as it had begun, the turmoil ceased. It was as though the Thing had turned away; she could feel the tremble of the wood recede and become still. Quite suddenly, over the tree-tops, a huge disc of white-gold mounted and hung, deepening shadows, silvering edges. Penny remembered her father, standing in the cold light of the full moon, and saying wryly that the bombers would likely come tonight, there was a brilliant, cloudless full moon. He had vanished in an oven of red-yellow roaring, Penny had guessed, or been told, or imagined. Her mother had sent her away before allowing the fireman to speak, who had come with the news. She had been a creep-mouse on stairs and in cubby-holes, trying to overhear what was being imparted, to be given a fragment of reality with which to attach herself to the truth of her mother's pain. Her mother didn't, or couldn't, want her company. She caught odd phrases of talk – 'nothing really to identify', 'absolutely no doubt'. He had been a tired gentle man with ash in his trouser turn-ups. There had been a funeral. Penny remembered thinking there was nothing, or next to nothing, in the coffin his fellow-firemen shouldered, it went up so lightly, it was so easy to set down on the crematorium slab.

They had been living behind the black-out anyway, but her mother went on living behind drawn curtains long after the war was over.

She remembered someone inviting her to tea, to cheer her up. There had been indoor fireworks, saved from before the war. Chinese, set off in saucers. There had been a small conical Vesuvius, with a blue touch-paper and a pink and grey dragon painted on. It had done nothing but sputter until they had almost stopped looking, and then it spewed a coil of fantastically light ash, that rose and rose, becoming five or six times as large as the original, and then abruptly was still. Like a grey bun, or a very old turd. She began to cry. It was ungrateful of her. An effort had been made, to which she had not responded.

The moon had released the wood, it seemed. Penny stood up and brushed leaf mould off her clothes. She had been ready for it and it had not come. She did not know if she had wanted to defy it, or to see that it was as she had darkly remembered it; she felt obscurely disappointed to be released from the wood. But she accepted her release and found her way back to the fields and her village along liquid trails of moonlight.

The two women took the same train back to the city, but did not encounter each other until they got out. The passengers scurried and shuffled towards the exit, mostly heads down. Both women remembered how they had set out in the wartime dark, with their twig-legs and gas-masks. Both raised their heads as they neared the barrier, not in hope of being met, for they would not be, but automatically, to calculate where to go, and what to do. They saw each other's face in the cavernous gloom, two pale, recognisable rounds, far enough apart for speech, and even greetings, to be awkward. In the dimness they were reduced to similarity – dark eyeholes, set mouth. For a moment or two, they stood and simply stared. On that first occasion the station vault had been full of curling steam, and the air gritty with ash. Now, the blunt-nosed sleek diesel they had left was blue and gold under a layer of grime. They saw each other through that black imagined veil which grief, or pain, or despair hang over the visible world. They saw each other's face and thought of the unforgettable misery of the face they had seen in the forest. Each thought that the other was the witness, who made the Thing certainly real, who prevented her from slipping into the comfort of believing she had imagined it, or made it up. So they stared at each other, blankly and desperately, without acknowledgement, then picked up their baggage, and turned away into the crowd.

Penny found that the black veil had somehow become part of her vision. She thought constantly about faces, her father's, her mother's – neither of which would hold their form in her mind's eye. Primrose's face, the hopeful little girl, the woman staring up at her from the glass case, staring at her conspiratorially over the clotted cream. The blonde infant Alys, an ingratiating sweet smile. The half-human face of the Thing. She tried, as though everything depended on it, to remember that face completely, and suffered over the detail of the dreadful droop of its mouth, the exact inanity of its blind squinneying. Present faces were blank discs, shadowed moons. Her patients came and went, children lost, or busy, or trapped behind their masks of vagueness or anxiety or over-excitement. She was increasingly unable to distinguish one from another. The face of the Thing hung in her brain, jealously soliciting her attention, distracting her from dailiness. She had gone back to its place, and had not seen it. She needed to see it. Why she needed it, was because it was more real than she was. It would have been better not even to have glimpsed it, but their paths had crossed. It had trampled on her life, had sucked out her marrow, without noticing who or what she was. She would go and face it. What else was there, she asked herself, and answered herself, nothing.

So she made her way back, sitting alone in the train as the fields streaked past, drowsing through a century-long night under the cabbage-rose quilt in the B&B. This time she went in the old way, from the house, through the garden-gate; she found the old trail quickly, her sharp eye picked up the trace of its detritus, and soon enough she was back in the clearing, where her cairn of tiny bones by the tree-trunk was undisturbed. She gave a little sigh, dropped to her knees, and then sat with her back to the rotting wood and silently called the Thing. Almost immediately she sensed its perturbation, saw the trouble in the branches, heard the lumbering, smelt its ancient smell. It was a greyish, unremarkable day. She closed her eyes briefly as the noise and movement grew stronger. When it came, she would look it in the face, she would see what it was. She clasped her hands loosely in her lap. Her nerves relaxed. Her blood slowed. She was ready.

Primrose was in the shopping mall, putting out her circle of rainbow-coloured plastic chairs. She creaked as she bent over them. It was pouring with rain outside, but the mall was enclosed like a crystal palace in a casing of glass. The floor under the rainbow chairs was gleaming dappled marble. They were in front of a dimpling fountain, with lights shining up through the greenish water, making golden rings round the polished pebbles and wishing-coins that lay there. The little children collected round her: their mothers kissed them goodbye, told them to be good and quiet and listen to the nice lady. They had little transparent plastic cups of shining orange juice, and each had a biscuit in silver foil. They were all colours – black skin, brown skin, pink skin, freckled skin, pink jacket, yellow jacket, purple hood, scarlet hood. Some grinned and some whimpered, some wriggled, some were still. Primrose sat on the edge of the fountain. She had decided what to do. She smiled her best, most comfortable smile, and adjusted her golden locks. Listen to me, she told them, and I'll tell you something amazing, a story that's never been told before.

There were once two little girls who saw, believed they saw, a thing in a forest ...

GOOD PEOPLE

Maggie Gee

Maggie Gee (b. 1948) is a British novelist who has written eleven novels and a collection of short stories. She was the first female Chair of the Royal Society of Literature, and is now one of the Vice-Presidents of the organisation. Her 2003 novel, *The White Family*, was shortlisted for the Orange Prize. She was awarded an OBE in 2012.

Justine wondered, what is the good of these people?

Ten minutes to take-off. They were running late. To Justine, the plane smelled slightly of burning. (She had asked the stewards several times for an aspirin, but they were busy fussing with the old and the young, pillows for two ancient tortoises with sticks, colouring books for two fractious children, one of whom didn't seem quite normal. It wasn't pleasant; she looked away.)

The man came down the gangway at the edge of her vision, hauling his flight-bag, short jacket, lean hips. She sent a silent text message, *sit by me*. It was a nine-hour flight home. She had missed her husband badly while writing her piece on 'Unseen Kampala'.

As the stranger grew nearer, scanning the seat numbers, his image snapped into sharp focus. Hair very black for the colour of his skin. Dark as his sunglasses. Skin taut. Jaw clenched.

He took the window seat beside her. The smile he gave her was formal, wary. 'Excuse me, ma'am.' He took off his glasses. Sharp against the African sun in the window, the line of his cheek was a clear white cliff. His forehead was remarkably clear and unlined. Older than she thought, perhaps.

'We are waiting for a final check on a successfully replaced component in one of the turbines,' the captain crackled on the PA system. 'I hope we can still make our scheduled arrival time in London. Some high winds today but they should be behind us.'

The smell of burning seemed stronger, but she ignored it.

'How long have you been in Uganda?' she asked.

'Long enough,' the man answered. 'What a country.'

'I liked it,' she said. 'I loved the people.' Now he had come, her headache was going, though the snot-covered child was still wailing in the arms of one of the blandly smiling stewards.

'Oh there are good people,' he agreed. 'I was lucky enough to work with some very good people.'

'This year was my first time in Africa,' she offered. His teeth were very white and even.

Half an hour later they were still on the tarmac. The captain had announced the engineer's arrival. The two stewards were bent over a Ugandan mother with big twin babies who were crying lustily. No one had remembered to bring her aspirin. Reassuring music on a faintly snagged tape puffed cloudlets of travel, escape, romance, into the warm air above their heads.

The economy seats seemed very close together. She was inches away from the stranger's lean thighs. She wondered, craning round for a second at the tens of human beings, belted in, pacified, but buzzing very faintly with desire and frustration, what would happen if suddenly they all released themselves, curled into pairs and made love to each other? She found herself remembering the fault in the turbine. No one could leave now. The great doors were fastened.

The man had been talking; Justine only half listened. There was something slightly odd about the skin under his ears. Money had been stolen from his hotel room, one of the hundred-dollar bills in his jacket.

'Of course, they're poor,' she interrupted. 'It must be hard to see so many rich foreigners.' She saw his mouth twitch with impatience.

'Way I see it, there's right and wrong. If we blur that line, we all get confused. And the Bible can help us with –'

'What do you do?' she interrupted again. The plane was quivering, gathering itself. The strange child pealed with eerie laughter. She heard a steward say 'Good boy' as he hurried past to his position for take-off.

'Pardon me? I'm a freelance evangelist.'

Suddenly the engine note screamed to a climax and they were

roaring full-tilt down the runway. The nose rose steeply into blue heaven.

'A freelance evangelist? Oh, I see.'

Perhaps stung by her tone of voice, he began telling her what he had been doing. 'I was working with Mrs Museveni's people. You know, the president's wife? They're good people, around Janet.' The project had been AIDS education.

Justine rushed to show she could relate to this. 'It's so impressive, how Uganda is handling it. AIDS posters all over the place. Were you encouraging them to use protection?'

'Well, first of all, let's get the basics straight. See, I believe the Bible is the Word of God. And the Bible tells us to be pure until marriage –'

'I respect what you're saying,' she said, untruthfully, and raised her voice slightly, putting him right. 'But the reality is, young people have bodies, and their bodies push them in a certain direction.'

'And their souls, ma'am? Shouldn't we be saving their souls?'

The molten lake. The dark flames of hell. She drew a deep breath and prepared to refute him, but the captain came on, sounding cheerful and English. A little light turbulence: fasten your seat-belts.

They sat in silence, turned away from each other. The seat-belt sign went off again. Then the lunch trolley pulled them in the same direction. She wanted the wine, but she didn't want him judging her. 'Just water, please,' the evangelist said. The stewardess had a kind, tired face. The plane juddered and she lurched sideways. 'Are you okay ma'am?' the evangelist asked. A steward came and helped his colleague straighten her trolley, where a dozen little bottles had toppled over, and patted her uniformed arm, consoling. The seat-belt indicator flicked back to life.

Angrily, Justine snatched the red wine, giving the small bottle a rather silly flourish. *I don't have to be a good girl any more.* Once she'd taken a deep drink, she was ready to confront him. 'Did you say Janet Museveni? The president's wife? They say the government is deeply corrupt. Wasn't it a problem working with them?'

His expression of annoyance came slowly, with effort, as if it was pulling against bands of tight tissue, as if his whole head was muscle-bound. 'What I can tell you is that these are good people. All the people round Janet are saved.'

Justine sat there watching him drink his water and read his book: *The Fire this Time*. The sun had moved, and fell directly on him. With a little shiver of triumph and horror, she began to understand his face again, the lean, craggy jaw, the smoothed pale skin. His hair and eyebrows were carefully dyed. His features had all been shifted slightly, spring-cleaned, tightened, purified. She remembered, with a jolt, watching Ugandan TV. A snowy-haired, arthritic, spruce evangelist, a tiny moon-man who must have been near eighty, had solicited gifts of $70, more than the average Ugandan annual income. He had no lines; his eyes were badly skewed.

They're all the same, she thought. Liars. Inhuman. They will not grow old, like the rest of us.

At that moment, the plane fell out of the air.

People were screaming, and a trolley crashed past them, and something hard hit her on the shoulder. Everything was changed, in violent motion. The world left them, they began again –

their arms came together, and they clutched each other's hands, clutched and held, and the plane fell further –

flesh and bone, they gripped each other she was praying to everything and nothing to save her, to some God of love who cared if she fell, to anyone who loved her, to the universe, the great blue unsteadiness outside their thin shell, but it was her neighbour's hand that held her, and she held him –

then the plane stopped falling.

In the relative silence, someone was moaning. A child, or a woman, began to cry. A stewardess lay half under a trolley. The lockers had spewed forth some of their bags. But the engines were still working. There was no fire. Remarkably few people seemed to be hurt. Her neck felt bad, but she could look around. The plane moved confidently through bumpy air.

Now the captain came on to reassure them, sounding out of breath, but more English than ever. Sorry he had not seen that coming. Fortunately able to pull her up again. 'I gather there's some cleaning up to be done, but I hope you will enjoy the rest of the flight.' There was scattered clapping; one man shouted 'Well done.' Then the volume of talk became deafening. Two stewards, glistening with perspiration, something wild about their pupils, came down the aisle, checking who was hurt, calming people down, handing out bandages and consolation.

Justine and her neighbour remembered they were touching, and smiled at each other, washed clean by terror, and gingerly let each other go.

'Thank the Lord,' he said, but his voice was different, his pressed blue shirt black with sweat.

Garrulous with relief she began to tell a story. All round the plane, people turned to each other, talked about what was important to them, the things they had felt in the dying moments which had suddenly, sweetly lifted back into living.

'What you said about the thief who took your hundred-dollar bill. Nothing like that ever happened to me. But one day I got on the wrong *matatu*, and it dropped me off in a rough part of Kampala ... I was being jostled in a crowd of people, and suddenly an old woman pressed up close to me and shouted, in English, "She's with me! She's with me!" and put her arm around me, and said "That youth want to take your bag" and pointed to a thin boy running away. Then she walked with me to some better streets. She did all that to help a stranger. I said "God bless you" from the bottom of my heart. When she left me she asked "Are you saved?" And you know, I'm not religious the way you are,' (she smiled, tried to catch his eye) 'but I told her "Yes," because she *had* saved me.'

The evangelist shifted, his face a reproof. 'But ma'am, excuse me, you are not saved.'

'It was a white lie,' Justine cried, indignant.

'It was false witness,' he insisted.

Her voice rose shrilly in self-defence. 'But when the plane was falling, weren't we both praying? What about love? That woman showed me love.'

Then, angered by the haloes of ice in his eyes, neat in their tight new wallets of skin, she reached out and took his hand again, reached out and locked his fingers in hers, palping him to warmth as he resisted, and he pulled away restrainedly, because she was a woman, but she held him, mercilessly, making him love her, and after a bit she saw he was weeping, but Justine held on, sure she was right, converting him, forcing him to see she was a good person.

(And hidden by their uniforms, unquestioning, the faithful stewards worked on in the background, quietly doing whatever was needed.)

THE CHILD

Ali Smith

Ali Smith (b. 1962) is a Scottish writer whose work has
appeared in the *Guardian*, the *Scotsman* and the *Times
Literary Supplement*. In 2007 she was elected a Fellow of
the Royal Society of Literature. She has published five
novels and four collections of short stories.

I went to Waitrose as usual in my lunchbreak to get the weekly
stuff. I left my trolley by the vegetables and went to find bouquet
garni for the soup. But when I came back to the vegetables again I
couldn't find my trolley. It seemed to have been moved. In its place
was someone else's shopping trolley, with a child sitting in the little
child seat, its fat little legs through the leg-places.

Then I glanced into the trolley in which the child was sitting and
saw in there the few things I'd already picked up: the three bags
of oranges, the apricots, the organic apples, the folded copy of the
Guardian and the tub of Kalamata olives. They were definitely my
things. It was definitely my trolley.

The child in it was blond and curly-haired, very fair-skinned
and flushed, big-cheeked like a cupid or a chub-fingered angel on a
Christmas card or a child out of an old-fashioned English children's
book, the kind of book where they wear sunhats to stop themselves
getting sunstroke all the postwar summer. This child was wearing a
little blue tracksuit with a hood and blue shoes and was quite clean,
though a little crusty round the nose. Its lips were very pink and
perfectly bow-shaped; its eyes were blue and clear and blank. It was
an almost embarrassingly beautiful child.

Hello, I said. Where's your mother?

The child looked at me blankly.

I stood next to the potatoes and waited for a while. There were
people shopping all round. One of them had clearly placed this
child in my trolley and when he or she came to push the trolley
away I could explain these were my things and we could swap

trolleys or whatever and laugh about it and I could get on with my shopping as usual.

I stood for five minutes or so. After five minutes I wheeled the child in the trolley to the Customer Services desk.

I think someone somewhere may be looking for this, I said to the woman behind the desk, who was busy on a computer.

Looking for what, Madam? she said.

I presume you've had someone losing their mind over losing him, I said. I think it's a him. Blue for a boy, etc.

The Customer Services woman was called Marilyn Monroe. It said so on her name-badge.

Quite a name, I said pointing to the badge.

I'm sorry? she said.

Your name, I said. You know. Monroe, Marilyn.

Yes, she said. That's my name.

She looked at me like I was saying something dangerously foreign-sounding to her.

How exactly can I help you? she said in a singsong voice.

Well, as I say, this child, I said.

What a lovely boy! she said. He's very like his mum.

Well, I wouldn't know, I said. He's not mine.

Oh, she said. She looked offended. But he's so like you. Aren't you? Aren't you, darling? Aren't you, sweetheart?

She waved the curly red wire attached to her keyring at the child, who watched it swing inches away from its face, nonplussed. I couldn't imagine what she meant. The child looked nothing like me at all.

No, I said. I went round the corner to get something and when I got back to my trolley he was there, in it.

Oh, she said. She looked very surprised. We've had no reports of a missing child, she said.

She pressed some buttons on an intercom thing.

Hello? she said. It's Marilyn on Customers. Good, thanks, how are you? Anything up there on a missing child? No? Nothing on a child? Missing, or lost? Lady here claims she found one.

She put the intercom down. No, Madam, I'm afraid nobody's reported any child that's lost or missing, she said.

A small crowd had gathered behind us. He's adorable, one woman said. Is he your first?

He's not mine, I said.

How old is he? another said.

I don't know, I said.

You don't? she said. She looked shocked.

Aw, he's lovely, an old man, who seemed rather too poor a person to be shopping in Waitrose, said. He got a fifty-pence piece out of his pocket, held it up to me and said: Here you are. A piece of silver for good luck.

He tucked it into the child's shoe.

I wouldn't do that, Marilyn Monroe said. He'll get it out of there and swallow it and choke on it.

He'll never get it out of there, the old man said. Will you? You're a lovely boy. He's a lovely boy, he is. What's your name? What's his name? I bet you're like your dad. Is he like his dad, is he?

I've no idea, I said.

No idea! the old man said. Such a lovely boy! What a thing for his mum to say!

No, I said. Really. He's nothing to do with me, he's not mine. I just found him in my trolley when I came back with the—

At this point the child sitting in the trolley looked at me, raised its little fat arms in the air and said, straight at me: Mammuttm.

Everybody round me in the little circle of baby admirers looked at me. Some of them looked knowing and sly. One or two nodded at each other.

The child did it again. It reached its arms up, almost as if to pull itself up out of the trolley seat and lunge straight at me through the air.

Mummmaam, it said.

The woman called Marilyn Monroe picked up her intercom again and spoke into it. Meanwhile the child had started to cry. It screamed and bawled. It shouted its word for mother at me over and over again and shook the trolley with its shouting.

Give him your car keys, a lady said. They love to play with car keys.

Bewildered, I gave the child my keys. It threw them to the ground and screamed all the more.

Lift him out, a woman in a Chanel suit said. He just wants a little cuddle.

It's not my child, I explained again. I've never seen it before in my life.

Here, she said.

She pulled the child out of the wire basket of the trolley seat, holding it at arm's length so her little suit wouldn't get smeared. It screamed even more as its legs came out of the wire seat; its face got redder and redder and the whole shop resounded with the screaming. (I was embarrassed. I felt peculiarly responsible. I'm so sorry, I said to the people round me.) The Chanel woman shoved the child hard into my arms. Immediately it put its arms around me and quietened to fretful cooing.

Jesus Christ, I said because I had never felt so powerful in all my life.

The crowd round us made knowing noises. See? a woman said. I nodded. There, the old man said. That'll always do it. You don't need to be scared, love. Such a pretty child, a passing woman said. The first three years are a nightmare, another said, wheeling her trolley past me towards the fine wines. Yes, Marilyn Monroe was saying into the intercom. Claiming it wasn't. Hers. But I think it's all right now. Isn't it Madam? All right now? Madam?

Yes, I said through a mouthful of the child's blond hair.

Go on home, love, the old man said. Give him his supper and he'll be right as rain.

Teething, a woman ten years younger than me said. She shook her head; she was a veteran. It can drive you crazy, she said, but it's not forever. Don't worry. Go home now and have a nice cup of herb tea and it'll all settle down, he'll be asleep as soon as you know it.

Yes, I said. Thanks very much. What a day.

A couple of women gave me encouraging smiles; one patted me on the arm. The old man patted me on the back, squeezed the child's foot inside its shoe. Fifty pence, he said. That used to be ten shillings. Long before your time, little soldier. Used to buy a week's worth of food, ten shillings did. In the old days, eh? Ah well, some things change and some others never do. Eh? Eh, Mum?

Yes. Ha ha. Don't I know it, I said shaking my head.

*

I carried the child out into the car park. It weighed a ton.

I thought about leaving it right there in the car park behind the recycling bins, where it couldn't do too much damage to itself and someone would easily find it before it starved or anything. But I knew that if I did this the people in the store would remember me and track me down after all the fuss we'd just had. So I laid it on the back seat of the car, buckled it in with one of the seatbelts and the blanket off the back window, and got in the front. I started the engine.

I would drive it out of town to one of the villages, I decided, and leave it there, on a doorstep or outside a shop or something, when no one was looking, where someone else would report it found and its real parents or whoever had lost it would be able to claim it back. I would have to leave it somewhere without being seen, though, so no one would think I was abandoning it.

Or I could simply take it straight to the police. But then I would be further implicated. Maybe the police would think I had stolen the child, especially now that I had left the supermarket openly carrying it as if it were mine after all.

I looked at my watch. I was already late for work.

I cruised out past the garden centre and towards the motorway and decided I'd turn left at the first signpost and deposit it in the first quiet, safe, vaguely-peopled place I found then race back into town. I stayed in the inside lane and watched for village signs.

You're a really rubbish driver, a voice said from the back of the car. I could do better than that, and I can't even drive. Are you for instance representative of all women drivers or is it just you among all women who's so rubbish at driving?

It was the child speaking. But it spoke with so surprisingly charming a little voice that it made me want to laugh, a voice as young and clear as a series of ringing bells arranged into a pretty melody. It said the complicated words, representative and for instance, with an innocence that sounded ancient, centuries old, and at the same time as if it had only just discovered their meaning and was trying out their usage and I was privileged to be present when it did.

I slewed the car over to the side of the motorway, switched the engine off and leaned over the front seat into the back. The child still lay there helpless, rolled up in the tartan blanket, held in place by the seatbelt. It didn't look old enough to be able to speak. It looked barely a year old.

It's terrible. Asylum-seekers and foreigners come here and take all our jobs and all our benefits, it said preternaturally, sweetly. They should all be sent back to where they come from.

There was a slight endearing lisp on the *s* sounds in the words asylum and seekers and foreigners and jobs and benefits and sent.

What? I said.

Can't you hear? Cloth in your ears? it said. The real terrorists are people who aren't properly English. They will sneak into football stadiums and blow up innocent Christian people supporting innocent English teams.

The little words slipped out of its ruby-red mouth. I could just see the glint of its little coming teeth.

It said: The pound is our rightful heritage. We deserve our heritage. Women shouldn't work if they're going to have babies. Women shouldn't work at all. It's not the natural order of things. And as for gay weddings. Don't make me laugh.

Then it laughed, blondly, beautifully, as if only for me. Its big blue eyes were open and looking straight up at me as if I were the most delightful thing it had ever seen.

I was enchanted. I laughed back.

From nowhere a black cloud crossed the sun over its face, it screwed up its eyes and kicked its legs, waved its one free arm around outside the blanket, its hand clenched in a tiny fist, and began to bawl and wail.

It's hungry, I thought and my hand went down to my shirt and before I knew what I was doing I was unbuttoning it, getting myself out, and planning how to ensure the child's later enrolment in one of the area's better secondary schools.

I turned the car around and headed for home. I had decided to keep the beautiful child. I would feed it. I would love it. The neighbours would be amazed that I had hidden a pregnancy from them so well, and everyone would agree that the child was the most beautiful child ever to grace our street. My father would dandle the child on his knee. About time too, he'd say. I thought you were never going to make me a grandfather. Now I can die happy.

The beautiful child's melodious voice, in its pure RP pronunciation, the pronunciation of a child who's already been to an excellent public school and learned how exactly to speak, broke in on my dream.

Why do women wear white on their wedding day? it asked from the back of the car.

What do you mean? I said.

Why do women wear white on their wedding day? it said again.

Because white signifies purity, I said. Because it signifies—

To match the stove and the fridge when they get home, the child interrupted. An Englishman, an Irishman, a Chinaman and a Jew are all in an aeroplane flying over the Atlantic.

What? I said.

What's the difference between a pussy and a cunt? the child said in its innocent pealing voice.

Language! please! I said.

I bought my mother-in-law a chair, but she refused to plug it in, the child said. I wouldn't say my mother-in-law is fat, but we had to stop buying her Malcolm X t-shirts because helicopters kept trying to land on her.

I hadn't heard a fat mother-in-law joke for more than twenty years. I laughed. I couldn't not.

Why did they send premenstrual women into the desert to fight the Iraqis? Because they can retain water for four days. What do you call an Iraqi with a paper bag over his head?

Right, I said. That's it. That's as far as I go.

I braked the car and stopped dead on the inside lane. Cars squealed and roared past us with their drivers leaning on their horns. I switched on the hazard lights. The child sighed.

You're so politically correct, it said behind me charmingly. And you're a terrible driver. How do you make a woman blind? Put a windscreen in front of her.

Ha ha, I said. That's an old one.

I took the B roads and drove to the middle of a dense wood. I opened the back door of the car and bundled the beautiful blond child out. I locked the car. I carried the child for half a mile or so until I found a sheltered spot, where I left it in the tartan blanket under the trees.

I've been here before, you know, the child told me. S'not my first time.

Goodbye, I said. I hope wild animals find you and raise you well. I drove home.

But all that night I couldn't stop thinking about the helpless child in the woods, in the cold, with nothing to eat and nobody knowing it was there. I got up at four a.m. and wandered round in my bedroom. Sick with worry, I drove back out to the wood road, stopped the car in exactly the same place and walked the half-mile back into the trees.

There was the child, still there, still wrapped in the tartan travel rug.

You took your time, it said. I'm fine, thanks for asking. I knew you'd be back. You can't resist me.

I put it in the back seat of the car again.

Here we go again. Where to now? the child said.

Guess, I said.

Can we go somewhere with broadband or wifi so I can look at some porn? the beautiful child said beautifully.

I drove to the next city and pulled into the first supermarket car park I passed. It was 6.45 a.m. and it was open.

Ooh, the child said. My first 24-hour Tesco's. I've had an Asda and a Sainsbury's and a Waitrose but I've not been to a Tesco's before.

I pulled the brim of my hat down over my eyes to evade being identifiable on the CCTV and carried the tartan bundle in through the out doors when two other people were leaving. The supermarket was very quiet but there was a reasonable number of people shopping. I found a trolley, half-full of good things, French butter, Italian olive oil, a folded new copy of the Guardian, left standing in the biscuits aisle, and emptied the child into it out of the blanket, slipped its pretty little legs in through the gaps in the child-seat.

There you go, I said. Good luck. All the best. I hope you get what you need.

I know what you need all right, the child whispered after me, but quietly, in case anybody should hear. Psst, it hissed. What do you call a woman with two brain cells? Pregnant! Why were shopping trolleys invented? To teach women to walk on their hind legs!

Then it laughed its charming peal of a pure childish laugh and I slipped away out of the aisle and out of the doors past the shopgirls cutting open the plastic binding on the morning's new tabloids and arranging them on the newspaper shelves, and out of the supermarket, back to my car, and out of the car park, while all over England the bells rang out in the morning churches and the British birdsong welcomed the new day, God in his heaven, and all being right with the world.

STORY OF MY LIFE

A. L. Kennedy

A. L. Kennedy (b. 1965) is a Scottish writer, known for her characteristically dark tone, which blends realism and fantasy. She has written six novels and six short story collections as well as non-fiction and screenplays. She won the Costa Book of the Year award in 2007 for her novel *Day*.

In this story, I'm like you.

Roughly and on average, I am the same: the same as you.

The same is good. The same is that for which we're meant. It's comforting and gently ties us, makes us unified and neat and it tells us the most pleasant kinds of story, the ones that say how beautifully we fit, the ones that summon up their own attention, make us look.

I understand this.

I understand a lot – very often – almost, all the time – most especially the stories. They are an exercise of will: within them whatever I think, I can wish it to be. They are the worlds that obey me, kinder and finer worlds: in many of them, for example, I'd have no teeth.

Because I believe I'd do better with a beak. So why not have one? That shouldn't be impossible. I feel a beak could make me happy, quite extraordinarily content: sporting something dapper and useful in that line – handy for cracking walnuts, nipping fingers, tweezing seeds. Not that I've ever fancied eating seeds, but one can't predict the path of appetite.

And beaks come in different sizes: that's a plus, along with the range of designs. The toucan would be good for parties, shouting, grievous bodily harm. Ibis: mainly funerals and plumbing. Sparrow: best for online dating and eating crisps. The options, while not infinite, are extensive. In a reasonable world my personality would give rise to my true beak, would nurture it, my proper fit – parrot, hummingbird, bullfinch, albatross – and through it I'd express myself, be jauntily apparent fulfilled, really start going somewhere with my whole appearance – somewhere free from teeth – somewhere other than the dentist.

Story of my life – maybe – going to the dentist.

Because my teeth, they've always been ambitious, problematic, expansive. I never have had enough room for all of them and so out they've come: milk teeth, adult teeth, wisdom teeth: handfuls of them over the years, practically a whole piano's worth. Of course, when I was a kid they still gave you gas for extractions – general, potentially fatal, anaesthetic gas administered, in my case, by an elderly man with unhygienically hairy ears who would bend in at me, eerily grinning, and exclaim – every single time – 'Good Lord, dearie, they're some size, those teeth,' while he flourished that black rubber mask and then cupped me under it, trapped my mouth in one hard, chilly pounce: 'Breathe deeply, dearie. Count backwards from ten.'

I'd shut my eyes and picture his tufted, werewolf earlobes and count until I'd reached as far as seven or so before I'd see these angles of tilting grey that folded in towards a centre point, bolted and sleeked at the backs of my eyes and then rolled me down and away to the dark.

Now, as it happens, I'm not good with chemicals. No choice here – I am made the way I'm made. Sensitive.

In the chair they'd give me nitrous oxide and it put me out nicely enough. I'd swim deep through a cartoony, bendy blank while the dentist did his work – the tugging, the twists – then I'd float straight back up and just bob at the surface like a tiny shore-leave sailor: changeable and land-sick and absolutely smashed.

My first experience of the freedom within incapacity.

That swoop and rock and thunder of delight. It's always best to meet your pleasures before you can tell what they mean.

As I came round some nurse would be attending with her kidney dish and towels: a bit broody perhaps, protective – the motherly type but not a mother and therefore idealistic, if not ridiculous, about kids. She would, shall we say, not entirely expect the violence of my post-operative dismay: my tiny swinging fists and my confusion, my not unjustifiable sense of loss.

I have no idea what I shouted on these occasions – a small person turning expansive, losing it, throwing it, swarming clear out into beautiful rage. I'll pretend, while I tell you the story, that I know.

I'll say I produced – at great speed and with feeling – 'You get away from me! I'll have you! I'll set the Clangers on you. And Bagpuss! Taking my teeth out ... no one ever takes *me* out – except to the dentist – to take out more teeth. I need my teeth for the Tooth Fairy – I'm only five, for Chrissake – that's my one source of income, right there. How else can I save up to run away from here? I could go on the stage – be a sideshow – my manager would want me absolutely as I am – *the Shark Tooth Girl: the more you pull, the more she grows: ivory from head to toes.* I'd be laughing. With all of my teeth, I'd be laughing.'

This is untrue, but diagnostic – it helps to make me plain.

Because I wouldn't ever want to hide from you.

The surprise of my own blood, that's true – thick and live and oddly tasty – I never did get used to that, my inside being outside – on my face, my hands. Even today, if I take a tumble, suffer a lapse, my blood can halt and then amaze me. It's almost hypnotic – seeing myself run. And persons of my type, we run so easily: birds' hearts thumping in us and broad veins full of shocks.

Back from the surgery, next came the hangover – naturally, naturally, naturally – but as I was a child it would be kind, more a mild type of fog than a headache. Beyond it I'd be given soldiers with boiled eggs, gentle food for an affronted mouth and a sudden hunger – oh, such a lively hunger – and a quiet mother comfort to meet it with a little spoon. Then a bath and an early night pelting with lurid dreams of thieves and tunnels and running for my life, right through my life and out the other side and into nowhere: the coppery taste of absence, liquid heat.

Once I was older, I decided I had no more time to waste – people to do and things to be – and avoiding the dental issue became attractive. I brushed regularly, kept my head down, ate everything wholemeal for added wear, but it did no good: my teeth are forceful. They insist.

So when I'm twenty-four, twenty-five, I'm back in the surgery – new dentist – and the first of my wisdom teeth is leaving. Local anaesthetic this time, much more practical and safe, and I haven't enjoyed the injections, but I'm hoping they'll do the trick – mostly my eye's gone a little blurry, but that's nothing to fret about – and here comes the dentist – big man, meaty forearms, substantial grip – and it's plain that he'll check now, tap about to see if I'm numb and therefore happy – except he doesn't. He does not.

And I should pause here briefly, because it lets the story breathe and even possibly give a wink. I step back to let you step forward and see what's next. This way you'll stay with us. With me.

Which is the point.

You staying with me is the point.

And, no, the dentist doesn't check, he is incurious and generally impatient, goes at it fiercely with the pliers and no preamble and here comes a clatter, a turning yank, and then tooth – I am looking at my tooth without me, grinning redly in the light – and I am puzzled because of this feeling, this building feeling which I cannot quite identify – it is large, huge, and therefore moving rather slowly, takes a full *count backwards from tennineeight* to arrive and then I know, then I am wholly, supernaturally aware, I am certain in my soul that I'm in pain. This is hitherto unguessed-at pain – pain of the sort I have tried to anticipate and forestall with insulating activities and assistance. Numb is best – I always aim for numb, for numb of any type – but pain has found me anyway. Worse than imagination, here it is.

To be fair, the dentist was upset – looking down at me and saying, 'Oh, dear,' a number of times before offering a seat in his office and an explanation involving wrongly positioned nerves – it was technically my fault for having provided them. His secretary gave me a comforting and yet excruciating cup of tea.

I walked home – it wasn't far – dizzy and racing with adrenalin. They put it in the anaesthetic, presumably to give it extra zip. Which is to say that you go to the dentist – somebody worrying – and he then injects you with terror – pure fear – you feel it rush your arms, cup its lips hard over that bird inside your chest.

And it is possibly, conceivably, odd that this is so familiar, so really exactly the simple jolt of many mornings and you draw near to your house and wonder, as usual, if so much anxiety should not have a basis in fact. Perhaps a leak under your floorboards has caused rot, perhaps you're ill – genuinely threatened by what, as soon as they knew you weren't suing, your dentist and his secretary called *a head injury* – this making you feel very noble for not complaining, but nevertheless, in many ways it sounds dire. And if you really want to fret, then perhaps you shouldn't lend that guy your money – your guy, your money, but shouldn't they still be apart? You like them both but they should surely be apart? And what if he isn't exclusively your guy, you've had that unease, felt that whisper, about him before – and it's screaming today. And what if your life is, in some degree, wrong or maladjusted when hauling a live tooth raw from the bone leaves you and your state no worse than an average night, a convivial night, a pace or two along your path of joy.

Sensitivity you see? It causes thoughts.

When I reached the flat, I let myself in and sat on the sofa, hands holding each other to dampen their shake and keep out the sense of having gone astray: twenty-five and no real profession, no prudent strategy not much of a relationship.

And too many teeth.

But you try to keep cheery, don't you? And you have time. At twenty-five you've bags of it.

Thirty-five, that's a touch more unnerving – wake up with thirty-five and you'll find that it nags, expects things you don't have: kitchen extensions and dinner parties, DIY, the ability to send out Christmas cards signed *With love from both of us. With love from all of us.*

Instead I'm house-sitting for friends.

And this section of the story is here, for you to like and to let your liking spread to me. Frailty and failure, they're charismatic, they have a kind of nakedness that charms.

So.

Minding the house is company for me.

Well, it *isn't* company – the owners are obviously away, hence my minding – and they've left their cats. And this is domesticity without effort: Brazilian cleaning lady, leather cushions, large numbers of superfluous and troubling ornaments.

This isn't like me owning cats, me living alone with cats, me growing six-inch fingernails and giggling through the letter box when the pizza-delivery man comes, peering out at him and smelling of cats – that's not how it is.

There are these other people who are not me and they are the ones who have the cats and I am treating their animals politely but with an emotional distance, no dependency and no indications of despair. There should be no suggestion that these friends are sorry for me, that the husband is more sorry than the wife and that they have argued about my trustworthiness in their absence and their possessions and have doubted the supervisory skills of a Portuguese-speaking obsessive-compulsive who polishes their every surface twice a week: tables, glasses, apples, doorknobs, the skin between the end of the air and the beginning of my wine. I will not tell you they left behind them a plethora of mildly hysterical notes, or that their act of charity has been overshadowed by a sense of filth, oncoming sadness.

It is only important to mention that I was, on this particular house-sitting evening, chipper and at ease. I had fed both of the creatures and I was going out – out on a date – a variation on a theme of what could be a date. We had reached a transitional stage, the gentleman and I – which is to say, I had reached it and wondered if he had too – and I have to make the best of what I may get, so I was dressed presentably and poised to be charming and, had it not been for the stitches in my mouth, I would have been perfectly on form.

More dentistry – surgical dentistry but with mouthwash and antibiotics and painkillers – big ones.

I like them big.

So I'm all right.

I'm stylish.

And I slip into the restaurant – once I've found it – with what I consider to be grace and it's an agreeable establishment. Italian. So I can have pasta – which is soft.

And here's my date – my approaching a date – and he's looking terrific.

He's looking great. Like a new man.

Truly amazing.

He's looking practically as if he's someone else.

Yes.

Yes, he is.

He is someone else.

I am waving at someone else. The man I am meeting is sitting behind him and to the left and not waving. No one, to be accurate, *is* waving apart from me and I would love to stop waving, but have been distracted by the expression on my almost-date's face.

He is experiencing emotions which will not help me.

But I can still save the evening. I'm a fighter. I calmly and quietly explain the particular story which is presently myself: the drugs I am currently taking – prescribed drugs – the residual levels of discomfort, the trouble I have enunciating – and perhaps he might like to tell me about *his* week and I can listen.

People like it when you listen.

They have stories, too.

But he doesn't give me anything to hear.

And so I talk about my roots – *that* story – a little bit angry, because he should have been better than he is, should have been a comfort. My roots are 23 millimetres long, which is not unimpressive, is almost an inch. I tell him about my root canals. I summarise the activities involved in an apesectomy – the gum slicing, tissue peeling, the jaw drilling, the noise.

This is not romantic, because I no longer wish to be, not any more. I am watching a space just above his head and to the right where another part of my future is closing, folding into nowhere, tasting coppery and hot.

Could be worse, though: could be forty-five, when everything tilts and greys and comes to point behind your eyes and you have not run away, you have waited for the world to come towards you, given it chance after chance. And, besides this, you find it difficult to name what else you have done, or who is yours. After so many years you are aware of certain alterations, additions, the ones that would make you like everyone else, that would join you, tie you gently, allow you to fit.

But they don't make a story – they're only a list.

More dental adventure, that'll keep us right – another practice, another extraction, another tale to tell and that remaining wisdom tooth: it's shy, it lacks direction, the time has come to cut it out.

Cheery dentist, in this instance, talkative, 'This is an extremely straightforward operation. It is, of course, *oral surgery* but you'll

be fully anaesthetised.' Which is frankly the least I would hope
– and dialogue, that's always a boon – a voice beyond my own,
someone in whom I can believe.

He puts his needle in, 'There we are ...' and the numbness goes
up to my eye. Again. Faulty wiring. So my mouth is now more
painful than it was and I'm also half blind. 'Well, I'll just deal with
that, then – there you go.'

Oh, that's better, that is good. Thass gread.

And this is my speaking voice, my out-loud voice, the one for
everyone but you. *So it's in italics* – that way you'll know.

*Thass bedder. Thass suffithiently aneasssetithed. You may
protheed.*

When we're in private – like now – and I say this, to no one but
you, then italics are unnecessary.

We can be normal and alone.

'No, I think you need more than that.'

And this is where the dentist gives me more anaesthetic and
I notice his hands smell a little like cornflakes – his gloves, they
have this cornflaky scent – which is a detail that makes him seem
credible and not simply a nightmare.

'Perhaps a touch more there.'

Whad? No, no thass a bid mush.

'And some more.'

Shurly nod?

'And more than that. Splendid.'

I can'd feed by arms.

'Of course, the effects of the anaesthetic will usually pass after
three or four hours. But working so close to a nerve, as we will, in
very unusual patients the numbness will pass in three or four ...'

It would be tiresome to pause here.

So we won't.

'... months and in some extraordinary cases, you will be like
that ...

'... for the rest of your life.'

Unf?

'Here we go then.'

It's not that I don't appreciate the chance to feel nothing at all
– but this isn't that – this is horror combined with paralysis – only

very minutely exaggerated paralysis. I can't see to hit him, I can't fight him off and he's digging and drilling, drilling and digging and the extraction takes forty-five minutes.

Honestly.

That's how long it takes – no exaggeration.

There's blood in his hair.

It's mine.

Finally, I'm released, it's over, the stitches have been stitched, and I ran out of the surgery.

Well, I pay the bill and I run out of the surgery.

Well, I pay the bill and ask them to call me a cab and I run out of the surgery.

Well, I can't really run, but I leave the surgery as best I can and I wait for the cab in what happens to be a colourful urban area, one where relaxed gentlemen stroll the boulevards of an afternoon and possibly sing. Perhaps there may be vomit on a lapel here and there. Perhaps there may be vomit and no lapel. And I'm standing – just about – and I can hear a relaxed gentleman coming along behind me.

He says something approaching, 'Hhaaaaa.' Which is not much of a story but is true and I know what he means because I can speak alcoholic. I have learned.

He reaches me and he says what might be expected – 'Scuse me cunyou spare twenny pence furra cuppa tea?' And I turn to him with my bleeding mouth and my lazy eye and my dodgy arm and my swollen tongue and I say, 'I don no. Havin a biddofa bad day mysel.'

So he gave me twenty pence.

And a slightly used sweet.

And a kiss.

It's best, if you can, to close up every story with a kiss. If you can.

Story of my life – maybe – going to the dentist.

The story that kept you here with me and that was true. In its essentials it was never anything other than true.

True as going to sleep tonight with the idea of blood beneath my tongue and meeting the old dreams of robbery and tunnels, the ones where I run straight through and beyond myself and on.

And sometimes I wake up sore and wanting to set out nice fingers of bread and runny egg and avoiding the issue is always attractive, but I am tired of speaking languages that no one understands and I have only these words and no others and this makes my stories weak, impossible – impossible as the Christmas cards – *with love from all of us* – the night hugs and pyjamas, the tantrums and the lost shoes and the hoarding of eccentric objects: figurines, sea glass, washers: which are the kind of details that should not be discussed. They are impossible as hiding the so many ways that my insides leak out, show in my hands, my face.

Impossible as telling you a story of a new arrival – a small person, turning expansive – someone growing and beautiful, but not perfect, the story of their first trip to the dentist, their first real fear I'd want to drive away. My duty would be to ensure that we would conquer, because every pain is survivable, although it may leave us different, more densely ourselves. The child and I, we would be unafraid and we'd have stories and every one of them would start with

In this story you are not like me.

All of my life I'll take care we are never the same.

THE MAN ACROSS THE RIVER

Polly Samson

Polly Samson (b. 1962) is a British author, journalist and songwriter. As well as contributing stories to many anthologies, Samson has published two collections of short stories, *Lying in Bed*, and *Perfect Lives,* and a novel, *Out of the Picture.* She has also co-written lyrics with her husband David Gilmour for his band Pink Floyd.

'Fear grips me from behind, with a knife to my throat. Fear wears a dark cloak. He mourns, the loss of his wife. He's on drugs ...'

My mother laughs a little cruelly as she reads from the stapled sugar-paper book. It's a childhood dirge, yes, one of mine that she's just found in an old biscuit tin.

'They were always so full of terror.' She chuckles, turning the page with an air of confusion, and I try to raise my eyebrows at Simon in a *See what I have to put up with?* sort of a way without her noticing.

She has taken to wearing kaftans of Demis Roussos proportions of late and her hair hangs down her back in a single long grey plait: a bell-pull that secretly I long to tug. I silently thank Simon for ignoring Tim, his twin brother, when he advised him to take a long hard look at the mother before considering the daughter as a wife.

She reaches into the Peak Freans tin and unfolds another effort, clears her throat, ready to mock. It's about a dead jackdaw.

'What do you think of Mummy's poem?' she asks when the jackdaw is duly buried, possibly still alive, in the cruel black earth of my childhood imagination, but Angus and Ivan are more interested in picking the combination lock on her sweets and treasures box than listening to any poem.

'Do you know Mummy won a prize?'

'I had my name in the newspaper,' I tell the boys, who look at me blankly.

'It was for the poem that you wrote about cruise missiles,' my mother remembers. Simon snorts loudly into his mug of tea and she gives him that teacher's look of hers, only these days it rarely works as a corrective, it's just funny.

'Do you think the boys want to watch Cee-bee-bees?' she asks, clapping her hands together, and I almost grind my teeth as the boys jump down, crying: 'Cee-bee-bees! Cee-bee-bees!'

'It's really quite educational.' She leads them off, plait swinging, and as usual I wonder if she's playing an elaborate game.

'It's ridiculous,' I moan to Simon. 'I was never allowed to watch television.' Now she seems to revel in turning my children into couch potatoes. She even bought a DVD of an American television show purporting to be child-friendly science that, when they all watched it, turned out to be nothing but overgrown boys demonstrating massive ejaculations using the explosive properties of Mentos and Diet Cola. Bombs and sweets and America, all at the flick of a switch. What fun. And she buys them sweeties, or even *candy*, to cram into their mouths while they watch this stuff, though she draws the line at Haribo, which she tells them are made from boiled-down bones and will give them cancer. Then she has to explain to them about cancer.

'What sort of child writes poems about cruise missiles?' Simon asks, picking it out of the tin and holding it up. There's an illustration of a wire fence with a rabbit hanging from it, done in felt-tips, and I'm surprised to see how my writing used to slope backwards as though my letters were all trying to jam on the brakes.

Simon goes to her pantry for a loaf of bread so that we can all have toast. White sliced bread, I notice.

'Funnily enough,' I say, 'I can remember writing it.'

It had been fine and dusty that day, the ground hard beneath my flip-flops, the grass just beginning to get scorched, bright sun I could feel against my skin. I was pleased with my tan, I liked the tickle of the grass on my bare brown arms and legs and I had a small white dog at my heels, a rather bouncy and optimistic terrier that my mother had taken pity on.

Up at the cottage she was busy plotting the next revolution with her friend Suzanne. Their uniform was pretty standard dangly earrings and CND T-shirts, their brigade the militant wing of Primary School Teachers for Peace, against Coca-Cola, fur coats, fighting, whatever.

Suzanne had been my class teacher, as well as being my mother's first lieutenant and partner in placards, and was still in the habit of demanding that I write poetry. In those days I couldn't ask her to pass the salt without her thinking I should write about passing salt, though it was usually current affairs that my self-appointed muse felt should inspire me: starving Africans, homelessness, the sort of things that eleven-year-old girls are keen not to think about too much.

'You should write a poem about the cruise missiles,' she said to me that sunny afternoon. 'It would be interesting to have a child's-eye view of the danger.'

She and my mother had already scared me witless with stories of nuclear attack: it was all coming to Britain, they said, while gloomily sipping their rosehip tea. 'Bloody Americans again.'

Suzanne and my mother were considering going to Greenham Common for the holidays. 'We have to do our bit to stop them storing their missiles here,' they said. 'Sitting ducks we'll be. We have to go for the sake of our children,' and they looked at me cramming my mouth with peanut butter from a spoon and nodded.

I had seen Greenham Common on the news: the high fences and the righteous feral women, in the mud, arms linked, singing protest songs and shouting: 'Whose side are you on?' at the dead-eyed troops.

'I don't think I could live with myself another moment if I didn't do my bit to keep the missiles out.' My mother was emphatic and I didn't think I could live for another moment full stop if I had to stay and listen to another word. I slipped from my chair and headed for the door.

'It might be fun to live in a bender, take the kids,' Suzanne was saying and I thought how much more fun it would be if they all dropped dead. Suzanne's own children were much younger than me. One of each, with permanently encrusted nostrils. They looked like trolls with their fuzzy hair and the girl, whose name was Coriander, had a habit of following me around.

I knew from a home-educated girl with a lisp at Woodcraft Folk that a bender was an unglamorous tent made out of bent-over saplings and tarpaulin. She had already been to Greenham Common and the news from the front wasn't good: lavatories that were holes in the ground, 'everyone stinks like wet dogs'. I wondered why I couldn't just spend the summer on a beach somewhere with my dad.

I rolled up my vest in the way that my mother hated me to do and trudged along for a bit on the dirt track past the hazel woods, whipping the heads from weeds and long grass with a swishy branch I'd pulled from a sapling. The white terrier was doing its best to lighten me up, springing back and forth, bringing me the black corpse of a tennis ball that it'd found in the long grass.

Cruise was such a wind-in-the-hair carefree word, I thought, whipping the dry grass, sending little darts of grass-seed flying. Cruise. I choose. To amuse. There were rusty-brown butterflies at every footfall and birds singing, an endless sky that matched the faded denim of my cutoffs. I threw the ball and the dog jumped for it. I swung my arms, enjoying their length and slenderness and the near-burn of the sun on my shoulders.

Heading towards the river I decided that cruise missiles were probably bad in the way that sweets were bad for the teeth, and television, particularly American television, was bad for the soul.

I knew these fields well from walking with my mother. The farmer would be topping the grass for hay soon so I should try not to make tracks and opted for the well-trodden path along the riverbank. Until all this stuff about Greenham Common had arisen the long summer had stretched before me as blissfully as empty golden sands. I was dying for school to end. There were girls in the third form with spiteful nails. In the loos there were girls who waited for you to thump you, to write your name on the wall, to surround you and bruise you or nuke you with their words. Sign here if you hate so and so.

Cruise. The last thing I needed was another thing to be afraid of. The terrier ran for the ball and startled a duck who shot from the reeds, desperately calling to her ducklings who fell in two by two behind her, leaving chevrons in their wake.

Cruise, cruising by. The river was at its widest, practically a pool and smooth as glass. In the winter it flooded completely and the footpath was submerged in knee-deep water meadow, it even had a current running through it then. In the spring the drowned grass was flattened and feathered, littered with plastic bottles. But in the summer the grass was tall and unswayed with buttercups, and lily pads bloomed on the black river that ran through it, easing itself along the sloping bank from which some people swam, though not me because I never liked the ooze of mud between my toes.

I stopped for a moment on the bank and watched the river slip by, its glossy surface shirred by the breeze and stippled with small circles from darting insects. A pair of damselflies were disco dancers, dressed in blue sequins. The water lily buds looked fit to burst their corsets in the heat.

The bank on the opposite side of the river was in shadow and heavily wooded so I didn't see him at first. A couple of times as I wandered along the sunny side I thought I saw a flash of white in the woods and I later realised that this must have been the white of his T-shirt.

I could only look once. First, I saw his dogs snuffling around and then the man emerged between the trees. The dogs were large, not a breed I recognised, with muscular hind limbs and hacksawed tails. The man was powerfully built too, his white T-shirt looked stretched across his chest and he was holding a stick. His hair stuck up from his head, an army sort of style, so blond it was almost yellow. He didn't look like the sort of person that you normally encountered on a footpath and I was immediately glad that we had a river between us. It was the stick in his hand that spooked me most: it wasn't long and thin like a walking stick, nor was it the sort of rough stick that you might throw for a dog. His stick was squat and thick at the end like a baseball bat and he was holding it in front of his chest like he meant business.

I found myself walking a bit faster and calling to the little terrier, though I wasn't quite sure which way to head. Jumping beans had started in my stomach. I kept walking faster still and wondered if I was crazy to have this reaction to a man out walking his dogs. The spit in my mouth turned to paste as I tried to work out how far I was from the bridge that separated his side of the river from mine. I rounded the bend and the bleached carcass of the lightning oak came into view. The oak, I knew, wasn't far beyond the bridge; if I could see the bleached oak then the iron bridge that crossed the river was maybe five minutes away at a fast pace. I'd frightened myself enough by then to turn heel and started heading back in the direction I'd come, trying not to run at first. When I did run I felt foolish, almost cursing myself, my disbelieving legs disobeying me all the way.

They seemed to have taken on a life of their own: it was as though at each step my ankles and knees had become spongy, cartilage rather than bone. I tripped on a rut, my ankle twisted, and it was as I clambered back up on to my knees that I knew for sure that the man had indeed turned around and was keeping up because I could see his dogs reflected in the river.

I pounded along, not even aware of the pain in my ankle; I saw the dogs running, heard the crack of branches from across the water. Though we had left the lightning oak bridge far behind I knew there was another bridge, a stone one, just ahead. I was going to have to veer off the path and cut across the fields to get back to the cottage quickly; it would only be trespassing a little bit. It seems mad now that my degree of trespass should even have entered my mind. I might have done better to think about the barbed wire fences and hedges I would have to fight my way through. As I started to run up the field I heard a splash and turned to look back at the river. The two dogs were crouched over the bank, barking. The man's head appeared, breaking the surface like a seal; the sunlight hit the rivulets running off his shoulders as his arms parted the river around him in a muscular vee. He was shouting to me but I couldn't hear what as my heart hammered in my ears. It just sounded like, 'Oi oi oi.'

Fear gripped me. I ripped my thigh on the barbed wire of the first fence. I raced on, barely aware of the blood running down the inside of my leg and having to rid myself of my flip-flops which were getting tangled between the toes with grass, as if trying to run wasn't hard enough anyway. I fell over twice, expecting to see the man looming over me as I scrambled to my feet. I could hear his dogs bark and as I hurtled past the hazel copse I almost imagined I could see the shadow of his club, their breath at my heels.

I didn't go back to the river all summer long. It was restful to be in the company of the women and the girls at the camp, gathering firewood on the Common, singing songs, becoming gently smoked by the fire. I became skilled at fence rattling and chanting: 'Take the toys from the boys!' I wore tie-dye and rainbow braids in my hair. I enjoyed the singing but grew to hate the underwater sounds of the ululating at the fence.

We ate loads of apples and cheese instead of meals and I pretended not to mind when someone shouted 'Lesbians!' out of the car window while my mother and I were walking up the hot tarmac to find a standpipe.

When we packed up our stuff at the end of the summer I tied my floppy stuffed rabbit to the perimeter fence. The part of the fence where we camped was festooned with other people's toys and bras and babies' booties and bits and pieces that were supposed to remind everyone of peace. Suzanne's children tied their teddy bears to it. My mother handed me a shoelace and I fixed the small silky-eared rabbit to a higher part of the fence where it immediately hung its head like any other tatty thing. It seemed a pity then because I had slept with my nose pressed to its silky ears for every night I could remember.

I never told my mother about the man across the river because I couldn't be sure about what I had seen. It only happened a couple of weeks before we left for Greenham Common and my shame had grown by the day. I was first to switch on the local news every night and I scoured the county gazette. After a while I doubted myself more and more and the face of a drowning man started to surface in my dreams and I would wake with the sheets wound around my legs like weeds. When we moved later that year, though I had loved the cottage and my bedroom in the eaves, I was relieved that I would never have to go anywhere near the river again.

Simon puts the cruise missiles poem down. 'You poor little thing,' he says, ruffling my hair, and I nearly cry. From the other room we can hear the blare of Cee-bee-bees and Angus's throaty laugh. 'Daddy,' he calls.

I refold the poem and fix the lid back on the tin.

'Your mother wants to know if we're bringing the kids to the climate change demo on Sunday.' Simon's her messenger, returning to the kitchen with an article she's clipped from the *Guardian*. 'She said she thought we ought to.'

'Did you tell her that last week Angus had nightmares every night about the sun exploding?' I say.

Unlike my mother, I don't want Angus and Ivan to have to worry about cancer or have images of people jumping from burning tower blocks scorched into their retinas. I don't want the terror to live in the marrow of my children's growing bones.

Simon shrugs. 'It's climate change,' he says. 'It's all about them—'

I interrupt. 'They don't like crowds,' I say, and gesturing with my thumb towards the noise of canned laughter: 'And I'm not like her.'

Simon shushes me.

'Remember when Angus was a baby and we took him to the Iraq War demonstration in Hyde Park?' My mother has come back into the kitchen though she'd kicked her shoes off in the other room and I didn't hear her approach. 'You and Simon didn't dress properly,' she says.

'What?' I say.

'You were both freezing.' She says it as though somehow even in protesting we were deficient and I wonder if she overheard me telling Simon that I was different from her, telling him as though being different from her was something to boast about.

Remembering the demonstration makes me shiver. As it happens my clothing had been perfectly adequate against the clear cold day, as was Simon's: thick padded jackets, pashminas and hats. My mother worried that people taking photographs were from M15. 'Look at that man,' she kept saying when we'd finally come to a standstill with the crowds in the park. 'Dressed in tawny colours, big camera. He's not part of the protest. He's here to keep a record of the people.'

'Don't be so paranoid,' I said, laughing.

'Look, he's systematically moving along the lines. He doesn't look right.'

There were two million people in Hyde Park that day and not a single arrest. Having Angus in his pushchair made me feel historic, like Demeter charged with a flaming torch. It was his future we were all shouting about, my fists were aloft with the rest of them. Ken Livingstone called for peace, and I looked at Angus sleeping, wrapped safe and warm in his cocoon, just his palely beautiful face appearing from the folds like a Russian doll.

My mother was carrying a banner that said NOT IN MY NAME, and wearing a colourful Peruvian knitted hat with little woollen plaits that made her look like a rather incongruous schoolgirl. She met a woman in the crowd and they embraced. 'Yes, here we are again,' she said, shaking her woolly plaits. 'Nothing changes.'

It was during a lull in the speeches that she told me what she'd read in that morning's newspaper. Something grisly about a missing girl and a man who drove a butcher's van.

'Remember the one?' she asked. I shook my head. 'It was a green van. When we lived at Riversdale,' she prompted, raising her arm in a fist as high as her shoulder would allow her. 'Impeach Bush, Impeach Blair!'

'I thought you were vegetarians,' Simon said, blowing into his hands and putting them back into his pockets.

'We were vegetarians,' said my mother, as wistfully as a woman remembering her miniskirt days, 'but it didn't stop him calling. No matter how often I told him we didn't eat meat, he still called in the van every Friday.

'Impeach Bush, Impeach Blair! It *stank* of meat,' she said.

'Sometimes, I think, he hunted deer with his dogs, and butchered them himself. Oh, what a horrible thought. It's been in all the newspapers, you know.'

Something small but monstrous was hatching in my memory.

'That's what the smell was,' she said, 'the venison. In the end I had to ring up the butcher and complain but I think he still came even after that.'

I thought I could picture the green van parked outside our cottage, the blond man hulked at the wheel. The thing that was hatching grew tentacles that slithered down the back of my neck.

'It's horrible to think of myself talking to him now,' she continued.

There was something glinting in my mother's eyes that made me think of a cat bringing a mouse to the door. 'It must have been around the same time that he did it,' she said, shuddering. 'Around the time he used to park outside our place. They only caught him because of his DNA on a completely separate charge.'

Just then Angus started to whimper. My breast tingled, filling with milk. It was as though it was a separate entity, beating to a different tune, with a different conductor from the other parts of my body. A man from the United Nations had just taken to the podium and a cheer went up from the crowd. The rest of me was running with ice but my only thought was that I would have to find a bench to sit down and produce warm milk to comfort my crying son.

AHEAD OF THE PACK

Helen Simpson

> Helen Simpson (b. 1959) is a British novelist and short
> story writer. She worked at *Vogue* for five years before
> becoming a writer full-time. Her first collection, *Four Bare
> Legs in a Bed and Other Stories*, won The Sunday Times
> Young Writer of the Year award, and her second, *Hey Yeah
> Right Get A Life*, won the Hawthornden Prize. In 1993 she
> was selected as one of *Granta*'s top twenty novelists under
> the age of forty.

Thank you for making the time to see me. I do appreciate how busy
you are; so, I'll talk fast! I'd like you to think of this presentation
as a hundred metre dash.

Yes, you're right, it can be difficult to find finance for a new
idea. But not in this case. I'm far more concerned about someone
stealing this idea than turning it down, to be honest; which is why
I want to tie up a joint venture agreement as soon as possible. By
the end of the week, preferably.

So. A little bit about where I'm coming from first. My original
background was in TEFL, then in PR for various NGOs – I've
had something of a portfolio career – but in the last decade I have
concentrated on developing my motivational skills in the areas of
personal training and weight loss. I'm a zeitgeisty sort of person
and I've found I have this unerring instinct for homing in on what
the next big thing will be. You could say I was like a canary in a
mineshaft – but more positive, I hope!

The next big thing? Carbon dioxide is the next big thing! Yes, I
am talking global warming, but please don't glaze over quite yet.
Yes, I do know how boring it is, how much of a downer it can be
but bear with me for the next seven minutes and I promise you'll
be glad you did so.

I know, I know, there are still some people who say it isn't really
happening, but they're like my weight-loss clients who say, 'It's

glandular' or 'I've got big bones'. What they're really saying is, they're not ready to change. Whereas the client who *is* ready to change is very often the one who's had a nasty scare. My prize slimmer is a man who'd been living high for years and then a routine scan revealed completely furred-up carotid arteries. He had a great sense of humour, he used to wear a T-shirt with 'I Ate All the Pies' on it, but underneath his heart was breaking. Literally. At twenty stone he was threatened with the very real prospect of a triple bypass, not to mention a double knee replacement, early-onset diabetes and gout.

Now, another client in a similar situation might have chosen to ignore the warning; opted to dig his grave with his own teeth, basically. I've seen that happen, I've been to the funeral. Fair enough, their choice. This man, though – a well-known local entrepreneur as it happens (no, I'm sorry, client confidentiality, I'm sure you'll understand) – this man directed his considerable drive towards losing seven stone over ten months, and as a matter of fact he finished in the first thirty-five thousand in this year's London Marathon.

And my point is? My point is: either we can carry on stuffing our faces and piling it on; or we can decide to lose weight. We've suddenly acquired this huge communal spare tyre of greenhouse gases; our bingeing has made the planet morbidly obese and breathless. Food, fuel; same difference. See where I'm coming from? And that was my eureka moment, when I realised that what's needed is a global slimming club.

I thought of calling it *Team Hundred*, because we in the motivational world have a belief that it takes a hundred days to change a habit; plus, there are only a hundred months left in which to save the world, apparently. Then I tried *Enough's Enough*, but *that* was too strict, and possibly a teensy bit judgemental. Finally I came up with *Ahead of the Pack*, which I think you'll agree sounds both positive and urgent plus it has the necessary lean competitive edge. Perfect!

It's simply a matter of time before it's compulsory for everyone, but those who've managed to adapt by choice, in advance, will be at a huge advantage. Ahead of the Pack! I mean, think of the difference between someone who's achieved gradual weight loss by adjusting their portion size and refusing second helpings, and someone else who's wolfed down everything but the kitchen sink for years and years and then wonders why he needs gastric banding. I know which one I'd rather be.

Yes, you're right, that is exactly what I'm proposing – to set up as a personal Carbon Coach! In fact, I think you'll find that very soon it'll he mandatory for every company to employ an in-house Emissions Expert, so you might well find me useful here too in the not-too-distant future, if we're counting our chickens. The thing is, I have this programme tailor-made and ready to rock. I've already test-driven it for free on several of my clients, and it's been fantastic.

First off I take their measurements, calculate the size of their carbon footprint – very like the BMI test, obviously, as carbon dioxide is measured in kilos too – and work out how far outside the healthy range they've strayed. We talk about why shortcuts don't work. Carbon capture and control pants, for example, squash the bad stuff out of sight rather than make it disappear. And, somehow, magic solutions like fat-busting drugs and air-scrubbers always seem to bring a nasty rash of side-effects with them.

Anyway, we visit the fridge next, discuss the long-distance Braeburn apples and the Antipodean leg of lamb, calculate their atmospheric calorie content. My clients generally pride themselves on their healthy eating habits and they're amazed when I tell them that a flight from New Zealand is the equivalent of scoffing down two whole chocolate fudge cakes and an entire wheel of Brie. We move on, room by room, talking weight loss as we go, how to organise loft insulation, where to find a local organic-box scheme; I give advice on fitting a Hippo in the loo, and practical help with editing photo albums.

Photo albums? Oh yes. Very important.

In ten years' time we'll be casting around for scapegoats. Children will be accusing parents, and wise parents will have disappeared all visual evidence of Dad's gap year in South America and Mum on Ayers Rock and the whole gang over in Florida waiting in line to shake Mickey's hand. Junk your fatso habits now, I advise them, get ahead of the pack, or you'll find yourself exposed – as hypocritical as a Victorian adjusting his antimacassars while the sweep's boy chokes to death up the chimney. Nobody will be able to plead ignorance, either. We can all see what's happening, on a daily basis, on television.

And if they have a second home I advise them to sell it immediately – sooner, if the second home is abroad. Of course! Instant coronary time! Talk about a hot potato.

Really? Oh. Oh.

I hear what you're saying. You think I'm going directly against my target client base with that advice. Yes. Well, maybe I do need to do some tweaking, some fine-tuning.

Basically though, and I'm aware that I've had my ten minutes, and I'd like to take this opportunity to thank you for your time – basically, is it your feeling that you're prepared to invest in *Ahead of the Pack?*

You'll get back to me on that one. I see. I see.

So, you happen to have a house near Perpignan, do you? Yes, it certainly is your hard-earned money. A bit of a wreck but if you can get there for twentynine pounds, why shouldn't you? No reason, no reason. O reason not the need, as Shakespeare says! As long as you know of course it means that, globally speaking, in terms of your planetary profile, you've got an absolutely vast arse.

TO BRIXTON BEACH

Stella Duffy

Stella Duffy (b. 1963) is a writer and performer, born in London and raised in New Zealand. She has written thirteen novels, ten plays and fifty short stories. Duffy has twice been longlisted for the Orange Prize, for her novels, *State of Happiness* and *The Room of Lost Things*. She is a member of the comedy improvisation company, Spontaneous Combustion.

There are images in the water. The pool holds them, has held them, since it was built in the thirties and before. And before that too, when there were ponds here, in the park, ponds the locals used to bathe in. Men at first, then men and women, separate bathing times, of course. A pond before the pool, a house with gardens before the park, perhaps a common before that, a field, a forest. We can go back for ever. And on, and on.

6 a.m. The first swimmers arrive, absurd to the gym-goers, the yoga-bunnies, those impatient, imperfect bodies readying for the cold, clear, cool.

When Charlie was a boy he and his brother Sid used to run all the way up from Kennington to swim, skipping out in the middle of the night, long hot summer nights, too sweaty in their little room, no mother there to watch over them anyway, sneaking off on their mate Bill's bike, to where the air was fresher, the trees greener, the sky and stars deeper, wider. And the pond so clean, green. Charlie hadn't been to the sea or to the mountains then, but the air in Brockwell Park felt cool enough.

8 a.m., the pre-office rush, pushing at the entrance desk, swimmers to the right, gym-ers to the left, one half to fast breath, hot body, pumping music, the other to cold, cool, clear.

Mid-morning and the local kids begin to arrive. Jayneen lives in the Barrier Block, in summer she and her friend Elise and Elise's cousin Monique go to the lido every day. They walk along streets named for poets, poets Monique has read too, poets she knows, smart girl, smart mouth an all, they walk in tiny shorts and tinier tops and they know what they do, and they laugh as they do it, as those boys slow down on the foolish too-small bikes they ride, slow down and look them up, look them lower, look them over. They three are all young woman skin and flesh showing and body ripe. And they know it, love it. The girls walk along and make their way to the lido that is Brixton Beach and they don't bother getting changed, they are not here to swim, Elise spent five hours last weekend getting her hair made fine in rows, tight and fine, she doesn't want to risk chlorine on that, they come to the lido to sit and soak up the sun and the admiring glances. Jayneen looks around, smoothing soft cocoa butter on her skin, as she does twice a day, every day, as she knows to do, and sucks her teeth at the skinny white girl over there by the café, all freckles and burned red, burned dry, silly sitting in the sun. Jayneen's skin is smooth and soft, she's taught Monique too, white girls need to oil their skin too. Maybe white girls need black mothers to teach them how to take care of themselves.

Charlie is in the water. He is already always in the water. Strong powerful strokes pulling him through. He slips past the young men who are running and cartwheeling into the pool, trying to get the girls' attention, trying not to get the lifeguard's attention, paying no attention to the long low deco lines. The young men look only at the curving lines on young women's bodies. Charlie finds himself thinking of young women and turns his attention back to water, to swimming hard and remembering how to breathe in water. He swims fast and strong up to the shallow end, avoids the squealing, screeching little ones, babes in arms, and turns back, to power on down, alone.

Lunchtime, the place is full. Midday office escapees, retired schoolteachers and half of Brixton market, rolled up Railton Road to get to the green, the water, the blue. One end of the café's outdoor tables over-taken with towels and baby bottles and children's soft toys, floating girls and boys in the water with the yummy mummies, wet mummies, hold me mummy, hold me.

Two babies hanging on to each arm. Helen can't believe it. This is not what she'd planned when she booked that first maternity

leave, four years ago. Can it really be so long? She looks at her
left hand where Sophia and her play-date Cassandra jump up and
down, pumping her arm for dear life (dear god, who calls their
daughter Cassandra? Foretelling the doom of the south London
middle classes), while in her right arm she rocks the little rubber
ring that Gideon and Katsuki hang on to. Helen shakes her head.
Back in the day. Back in the office, loving those days in the office,
she wondered what it would feel like, to be one of them, the
East Dulwich mummies clogging cafés and footpaths with their
designer buggies. She looks up as a shadow crosses her, it is Imogen,
Cassandra's mother. Imogen is pointing to the table, surrounded
by buggies. Their friends wave, lunch has arrived, Helen passes
the children out one by one and immediately they start whirling,
wanting this, wanting that, she can feel the looks, the disapproval
from the swimmers who have come here for quiet and peace. Helen
has become that mother. The one with the designer buggy. And she
hates the lookers for making her feel it, and hates that she feels
it. And she wouldn't give up her babies for anything. And they
do need a buggy, and a big one at that, they're twins. (At least
she didn't call them Castor and Pollux;) Helen can't win and she
knows it. Sits down to her veggie burger. Orders a glass of wine
anyway. After all.

Charlie swims, back and forth, back and forth. He lurches into
the next lane to avoid the young men dive-bombing to impress the
girls and irritate the life guards, makes his perfect turns between
two young women squealing at the cold water. He swerves around
slower swimmers, through groups of chattering children, he does
not stop. Charlie is held in the water, only in the water.

3 p.m., a mid-afternoon lull. Margaret and Esther sit against
the far wall, in direct sunlight, they have been here for five hours,
moving to follow the sun. From inside the yoga studio they can
hear the slow in and out breaths, the sounds of bodies pulled and
pushed into perfection. At seventy-six and eighty-one Margaret
and Esther do not worry about perfection, though Margaret still
has good legs and Esther is proud of her full head of perfectly white
hair. Margaret looks down at her body, the sagging and whole
right breast, the missing left. She had the mastectomy fifteen years
ago, they spoke to her about reconstruction, but she wasn't much

interested, nor in the prosthesis. Margaret likes her body as it is, scars, white hair, wrinkles, lived. She and Esther have been coming to the pool every summer, three times a week for fifty years, bar that bad patch when the council closed it in the 80s. They swim twenty lengths together, heads above the water, a slow breaststroke side by side because Esther likes to chat and keep her lovely hair dry. Then Esther gets out and Margaret swims another twenty herself, head down this time, breathing out in the water, screaming out in the water sometimes, back then, when it was harder, screaming in the water because it was the only time Esther couldn't hear her cry. It's better now, she is alive and delighted to be here, glad to be sharing another summer with the love of her life. Esther passes her a slice of ginger cake, buttered, and they sit back to watch the water. Two old ladies, holding age-spotted hands.

Charlie swims on.

5.30 p.m., just before the after-office rush. In the changing rooms, Ameena takes a deep breath as she unwraps her swimming costume from her towel. She sent away for it a week ago, when she knew she could no longer deny herself the water. It arrived yesterday. It is a beautiful, deep blue. It makes her think of water even to touch it, the texture is soft, silky. She has been hot for days, wants to give herself over to the water, to the pool. She slowly takes off her own clothes and replaces them as she does with the deep blue costume. When she has dressed in the two main pieces – swim pants and tunic – she goes to the mirror to pull on the hood, fully covering her hair. Three little girls stand and stare unashamedly. She smiles at them and takes the bravery of their stare for herself, holds her covered head high, walks through the now-quiet changing room, eyes glancing her way, conversations lowered, walks out to the pool in her deep blue burkini. Ameena loved swimming at school, has been denying herself the water since she decided to dress in full hijab. She does not want to deny herself any more. The burkini is her choice, the water her desire. She can have both, and will brave the stares to do so. In the water, Ameena looks like any other woman in a wetsuit, swims better than most, and gives herself over to the repetitive mantra that are her arms and legs, heart and lungs, working in unison. It is almost prayer and she is grateful.

Charlie swims two, three, four lengths in time with Ameena, and then their rhythm changes, one is out of sync with the other, they are separate again.

8 p.m., the café is almost full, the pool almost empty, a last few swimmers, defying the imploring calls of the lifeguards. Time to close up, time to get out. Diners clink wine glasses and look through fairy lights past the lightly stirring water to the gym, people on treadmills, on step machines, in ballet and spinning classes. Martin and Ayo order another beer each and shake their heads. They chose food and beer tonight. And will probably do so again tomorrow evening, they are well matched, well met.

It is quiet and dark night. Charlie swims on, unnoticed. Eventually the café is closed, the gym lights turned off, the cleaners have been and gone, the pool and the park are silent but for the foxes telling the night, tolling the hours with their screams. And a cat, watching.

Charlie climbs from the water now, his body his own again, reassembled from the wishing and the tears and the could be, might be, would be, from hope breathed out into water, from the grins of young men and the laughter of old women and the helpless, rolling giggles of toddlers on soft towels. Remade through summer laughter spilling over the poolside. He dresses. White shirt, long pants, baggy trousers falling over his toes, a waistcoat, tie just-spotted, just-knotted below the turned-up collar, then the too-tight jacket, his big shoes. Without the cane and the moustache and the bowler hat he was just another man, moving at his own pace, quietly through the water. With them, he is himself again. The Little Tramp walking away, back to Kennington, retracing the path he and Sid ran through summer nights to the welcome ponds of Brockwell Park.

Behind him the water holds the memory of a man moving through it in cool midnight, a celluloid pool which he flickers to life, and is gone.

EXTENDED COPYRIGHT

Margaret Atwood: 'Betty' from *Dancing Girls* by Margaret Atwood, published by Jonathan Cape. Reprinted by permission of The Random House Group Limited.

Nicola Barker: 'G-String' and 'Wesley: Blisters' from *The Three Button Trick* by Nicola Barker © Nicola Barker, 1996. Reproduced by permission of the author c/o Rogers, Coleridge & White Ltd., 20 Powis Mews, London W11 1JN.

A. S. Byatt: 'The Thing in the Forest' by A. S. Byatt © A. S. Byatt, 2003. Reproduced by permission of the author c/o Rogers, Coleridge & White Ltd., 20 Powis Mews, London W11 1JN.

Elspeth Davie: 'Change of Face' and 'A Weight Problem' taken from *The Night of the Funny Hats* by Elspeth Davie, published by Penguin © 1980. Reproduced by permission of Sheil Land Associates, Ltd.

Anita Desai: 'Sale' by Anita Desai © Anita Desai, 1978. Reproduced by permission of the author c/o Rogers, Coleridge & White Ltd., 20 Powis Mews, London W11 1JN.

Stella Duffy: 'To Brixton Beach' by Stella Duffy © Stella Duffy. Reprinted with permission from the author.

Jennifer Egan: 'Emerald City' by Jennifer Egan © Jennifer Egan. Reproduced by permission of Constable & Robinson.

Anne Enright: '(She Owns) Every Thing' taken from *The Portable Virgin* by Anne Enright. Published by Secker & Warburg. Reprinted by permission of The Random House Group Limited.

Penelope Fitzgerald: 'The Axe' and 'The Prescription' by Penelope Fitzgerald © Penelope Fitzgerald. Reproduced by permission of the author c/o Rogers, Coleridge & White Ltd., 20 Powis Mews, London W11 1JN.

Jane Gardam: 'Telegony I: Going into a Dark House' from *Going Into A Dark House* by Jane Gardam. Reprinted with permission from Abacus.

Maggie Gee: 'Good People' © Maggie Gee, 2006, *The Blue,* Telegram.

Ellen Gilchrist: 'Precious Pieces' is reprinted by permission of Don Congdon Associates, Inc. Copyright © 1981 by Ellen Gilchrist.

A. M. Homes: 'A Real Doll' and 'Yours Truly' from *The Safety of Objects* by A. M. Homes. First published in Great Britain by Granta Books, 2004. Acknowledgement is made to the following periodical these stories originally appeared in: *Christopher Street*.

Elizabeth Jolley: 'Waiting Room (The First)' by Elizabeth Jolley, taken from *The Georges' Wife*. Reprinted with permission from Jenny Darling Associates on behalf of the Estate of Elizabeth Jolley.

A. L. Kennedy: 'Story of My Life' from *What Becomes* by A. L. Kennedy. Reprinted with permission from House of Anansi Press, Toronto and Antony Harwood Limited.

Doris Lessing: 'Through the Tunnel' by Doris Lessing. Reprinted by permission of HarperCollins Publishers Ltd. © 1955, Doris Lessing.

Penelope Lively: 'Corruption' from *Corruption* by Penelope Lively, 1984, William Heinemann, Ltd. 'A World of Her Own' from *Nothing Missing but the Samovar* by Penelope Lively, 1978, William Heinemann, Ltd.

Alison Lurie: 'Fat People' from *Women and Ghosts* by Alison Lurie. Reprinted with permission from A P Watt at United Agents on behalf of Alison Lurie.

Hilary Mantel: 'Third Floor Rising' by Hilary Mantel. Reprinted by permission of HarperCollins Publishers Ltd. © 2003, Hilary Mantel.

Alice Munro: 'Mischief' from *Who Do You Think You Are?*, published by Chatto & Windus. Reprinted by permission of The Random House Group Limited.

Dorothy Parker: 'The Waltz' by Dorothy Parker. Reprinted by permission of Gerald Duckworth & Co. Ltd.

Polly Samson: 'The Man Across the River' from *Perfect Lives* by Polly Samson. Published by Virago Press. Reproduced by permission of Little, Brown Book Group.

Helen Simpson: 'Ahead of the Pack' taken from *In-Flight Entertainment* by Helen Simpson. Published by Jonathan Cape. Reprinted by permission of the Random House Group Limited.

Ali Smith: 'The Child' taken from *The First Person and Other Stories* by Ali Smith (Hamish Hamilton 2008, Penguin Books 2009). Copyright © Ali Smith, 2008. Reproduced by permission of Penguin Books, Ltd.

Muriel Spark: 'The Snobs' taken from *The Complete Short Stories* by Muriel Spark. Reprinted with permission from Canongate.

Alice Walker: 'How Did I Get Away With Killing One of the Biggest Lawyers in the State? It Was Easy.' from *The Complete Stories* by Alice Walker. Reprinted with permission from Orion.